ALSO BY COLM TÓIBÍN

THE
MAGICIAN

- A Novel -

COLM TÓIBÍN

SCRIBNER

New York   London   Toronto   Sydney   New Delhi

Scribner
An Imprint of Simon & Schuster, Inc.
1230 Avenue of the Americas
New York, NY 10020

Copyright © 2021 by The Heather Blazing Ltd.

First Scribner hardcover edition September 2021

SCRIBNER and design are registered trademarks of The Gale Group, Inc., used under license by Simon & Schuster, Inc., the publisher of this work.

For information about special discounts for bulk purchases, please contact Simon & Schuster Special Sales at 1-866-506-1949 or business@simonandschuster.com.

The Simon & Schuster Speakers Bureau can bring authors to your live event. For more information or to book an event, contact the Simon & Schuster Speakers Bureau at 1-866-248-3049 or visit our website at www.simonspeakers.com.

Manufactured in the United States of America

1   3   5   7   9   10   8   6   4   2

Library of Congress Cataloging-in-Publication Data
Names: Tóibín, Colm, 1955– author.
Title: The magician : a novel / Colm Tóibín.
Description: New York : Scribner, [2021]
Identifiers: LCCN 2021004476 (print) | LCCN 2021004477 (ebook) | ISBN 9781476785080 (hardcover) | ISBN 9781476785097 (paperback) | ISBN 9781476785103 (ebook)
Classification: LCC PR6070.O455 M34 2021 (print) | LCC PR6070.O455 (ebook) | DDC 823/.914—dc23
LC record available at https://lccn.loc.gov/2021004476
LC ebook record available at https://lccn.loc.gov/2021004477

ISBN 978-1-4767-8508-0
ISBN 978-1-4767-8510-3 (ebook)

For Nan Graham

THE
MAGICIAN

Chapter 1
Lübeck, 1891

His mother waited upstairs while the servants took coats and scarves and hats from the guests. Until everyone had been ushered into the drawing room, Julia Mann remained in her bedroom. Thomas and his older brother Heinrich and their sisters Lula and Carla watched from the first landing. Soon, they knew, their mother would appear. Heinrich had to warn Carla to be quiet or they would be told to go to bed and they would miss the moment. Their baby brother Viktor was sleeping in an upper room.

With her hair pinned back severely and tied in a colored bow, Julia stepped out from her bedroom. Her dress was white, and her black shoes, ordered specially from Majorca, were simple like a dancer's shoes.

She joined the company with an air of reluctance, giving the impression that she had, just now, been alone with herself in a place more interesting than festive Lübeck.

On coming into the drawing room, having glanced around her, Julia would find among the guests one person, usually a man, someone unlikely such as Herr Kellinghusen, who was neither young nor old, or Franz Cadovius, his squint inherited from his mother, or Judge August Leverkühn, with his thin lips and clipped mustache, and this man would become the focus of her attention.

Her allure came from the atmosphere of foreignness and fragility that she exuded with such charm.

Yet there was kindness in her flashing eyes as she asked her guest about work and family and plans for the summer, and, speaking of the summer, she would wish to know about the relative comfort of various hotels in Travemünde, and then she would ask about grand hotels in places as distant as Trouville or Collioure or some resort on the Adriatic.

And soon she would pose an unsettling question. She would ask what her interlocutor thought about some normal and respectable woman within their group of associates. The suggestion was that this woman's private life was a matter of some controversy and speculation among the burghers of the town. Young Frau Stavenhitter, or Frau Mackenthun, or old Fraulein Distelmann. Or someone even more obscure and retiring. And when her bewildered guest would point out that he had nothing other than good to say of the woman, in fact had nothing beyond the very ordinary to transmit, Thomas's mother would express the view that the object of their discussion was, in her considered opinion, a marvelous person, simply delicious, and Lübeck was lucky to have such a woman among its citizens. She would say this as if it were a revelation, something that must stay quite confidential for the moment, something, indeed, that even her husband, the senator, had not yet been told.

The following day, news would spread about their mother's deportment and whom she had singled out for comment, until Heinrich and Thomas would hear about it from their school friends, as if it were a very modern play, fresh from Hamburg, that had been performed.

In the evenings, if the senator were at a meeting, or in the time when Thomas and Heinrich, having done their violin practice and eaten their supper, were in their nightclothes, their mother would tell them about the country of her birth, Brazil, a place so vast, she said, that no one knew how many people were there or what they were like or what languages they spoke, a country many,

many times the size of Germany, where there was no winter, and never any frost or real cold, and where one river, the Amazon, was more than ten times longer than the Rhine and ten times as wide, with many smaller rivers flowing into it that reached back deep into the forest, with trees higher than trees anywhere else in the world, with people whom no one had ever seen or would see, since they knew the forest as no one else did, and they could hide if an intruder or an outsider came.

"Tell us about the stars," Heinrich would say.

"Our house in Paraty was on the water," Julia would reply. "It was almost part of the water, like a boat. And when night came and we could see the stars, they were bright and low in the sky. Here in the north the stars are high and distant. In Brazil, they are visible like the sun during the day. They are small suns themselves, glittering and close to us, especially those of us who lived near water. My mother said you could sometimes read a book in the upstairs rooms at night because the light from the stars against the water was so clear. And you could not sleep unless you fastened the shutters to keep the brightness out. When I was a girl, the same age as your sisters, I really believed that all the world was like that. The shock on my first night in Lübeck was that I could not see the stars. They were covered over by clouds."

"Tell us about the ship."

"You must go to sleep."

"Tell us the story of all the sugar."

"Tommy, you know the story of the sugar."

"But just a small part again?"

"Well, all the marzipan that is made in Lübeck uses sugar that comes from Brazil. Just as Lübeck is famous for marzipan, Brazil is famous for sugar. So when the good people of Lübeck and their children eat their marzipan on Christmas Eve, little do they know that they are eating a part of Brazil. They are eating sugar that came across the sea just for them."

"Why don't we make our own sugar?"

"You must ask your father that."

Years later, Thomas wondered if his father's decision to marry Julia da Silva-Bruhns, whose mother was reputed to have had in her veins blood from South American Indians, rather than a stolid daughter of one of the local shipping magnates or old trading and banking families, was not the beginning of the decline of the Manns, evidence that a hunger for the richly strange had entered the spirit of the family, which had, up to then, possessed an appetite only for what was upright and certain to yield a steady return.

In Lübeck, Julia was remembered as a small girl arriving with her sister and her three brothers after their mother had died. They were taken care of by an uncle, and they did not, when they appeared first in the city, have a word of German. They were watched suspiciously by figures such as old Frau Overbeck, known for her staunch adherence to the practices of the Reformed Church.

"I saw those children blessing themselves one day as they passed the Marienkirche," she said. "It may be necessary to trade with Brazil, but I know no precedent for a Lübeck burgher marrying a Brazilian, none at all."

Julia, only seventeen at the time of her marriage, gave birth to five children who carried themselves with all the dignity required of the children of the senator, but with an added pride and self-consciousness, and something close to display, which Lübeck had not seen before and which Frau Overbeck and her circle hoped would not become fashionable.

Due to this decision to marry unusually, the senator, eleven years older than his wife, was viewed with a certain awe, as though he had invested in Italian paintings or rare majolica, acquired to satisfy a taste that, up to then, the senator and his antecedents had kept in check.

Before leaving for church on Sunday, the Mann children had to be carefully examined by their father while their mother delayed them by remaining upstairs in her dressing room, trying on hats or changing her shoes. Heinrich and Thomas had to show a good example by maintaining an expression of gravity, while Lula and Carla tried to stand still.

By the time Viktor was born, Julia was less attentive to the strictures that her husband laid down. She liked the girls to have colorful bows and stockings, and she did not object to the boys having longer hair and greater latitude in their comportment.

Julia dressed elegantly for church, often wearing only one color—a gray, for example, or a dark blue, with matching stockings and shoes and the only sign of relief a red or yellow band on her hat. Her husband was known for the precision of the cuts made by his tailor in Hamburg and for his impeccable appearance. The senator changed his shirt every day, sometimes twice a day, and had an extensive wardrobe. His mustache was trimmed in the French manner. In his fastidiousness, he represented the family firm in all its solidity, a century of civic excellence, but in the luxury of his wardrobe he offered his own view that being a Mann in Lübeck meant more than money or trade, it suggested not only sobriety but a considered sense of style.

To his horror, on the short journey between the Manns' house on Beckergrube and the Marienkirche, Julia often greeted people, gleefully and freely calling out their names, something that had never been done before on a Sunday in the history of Lübeck, further convincing Frau Overbeck and her spinster daughter that Frau Mann was, in her heart at least, still a Catholic.

"She is showy and silly, and that is the mark of a Catholic," Frau Overbeck said. "And that band on her hat is pure frivolity."

In the Marienkirche itself as the wider family assembled, it was noted how pale Julia was, and how oddly alluring her pallor was against her heavy chestnut hair and mysterious eyes, which rested on the preacher in an expression of half-veiled mockery, a mockery that was alien to the seriousness with which her husband's family and their friends treated religious observance.

Thomas realized that his father disliked hearing about his wife's childhood in Brazil, especially if the girls were present. His father, however, loved when Thomas asked him to talk about old Lübeck and to explain how the family firm had grown from modest beginnings in Rostock. His father appeared to derive satisfaction when Thomas, calling at his office on his way home from school, sat and listened about ships and warehouses and banking partners and insurance schemes, and then later remembered what he had been told.

Even distant cousins came to believe that while Heinrich was dreamy and rebellious like his mother and was to be found reading books, young Thomas, alert and grave in his demeanor, was the one who would take the family firm into the next century.

As the girls grew older, all the children would gather in their mother's dressing room if their father had left for his club or for some meeting, and Julia would resume her stories about Brazil, telling of the whiteness of the clothes the people wore there, the amount of washing that was done so that everyone looked special and beautiful, the men as well as the women, the black people as well as the white.

"It was not like Lübeck," she said. "No one saw any need to be solemn. There were no Frau Overbecks pursing their lips. No families like the Esskuchens in perpetual mourning. In Paraty, if you saw three people, then one was talking and the other two were laughing. And they were all in white."

"Were they laughing at a joke?" Heinrich asked.

"Just laughing. That is what they did."

"But laughing at what?"

"Darling, I don't know. But that is what they did. Sometimes at night I can hear that laughter still. It comes in on the wind."

"Can we go to Brazil?" Lula asked.

"I don't think your father wants you to go to Brazil," Julia said.

"But when we are older?" Heinrich asked.

"We can never tell what will happen when we are older," she said. "Perhaps you will be able to go anywhere then. Anywhere!"

"I would like to stay in Lübeck," Thomas said.

"Your father will be happy to hear that," Julia replied.

Thomas lived in a world of his dreams more than his brother Heinrich did, or his mother, or his sisters. Even his discussions with his father about warehouses were further aspects of a fantasy world that often included himself as a Greek god, or as a figure in a story from a nursery rhyme, or the woman in the oil painting that his father had placed on the stairwell, the expression on her face ardent, anxious, expectant. He was not sure sometimes that he was not, in reality, older than Heinrich and stronger, or that he did not go out each day with his father as an equal to the office, or that he was not Matilde, his mother's maid in charge of the dressing room, who took care that his mother's shoes were kept in pairs and that her bottles of perfume were never empty and that her secret things remained in the correct drawers away from his prying eyes.

When he heard them say that he was the one who would shine in the world of business, when he impressed visitors by knowing about consignments due to arrive, and the names of ships and faraway ports, he almost shuddered at the thought that if these people knew who he really was, they would take a different view of him. If they could actually see into his mind and know how much at night and even in the day he allowed himself to become the woman in the painting on the stairwell with all her fervid desires, or someone who moved across the landscape with a sword or with a song, then they would shake their heads in wonder at how cleverly he had fooled them, how cunningly he had won his father's approval, what an imposter and confidence man he was, and how little he could be trusted.

Heinrich, of course, knew who he was, and was aware enough of his younger brother's dream life to realize not only that it exceeded his own in scope and scale, but that, as he warned him, the more Thomas extended his ability to dissimulate, the greater the danger of being found out. Heinrich, unlike his brother, made himself clear to the household. His fascination, as he grew into his teens, with Heine and Goethe, with Bourget and Maupassant, was as transparent as his indifference to ships and warehouses. He saw these latter things as dull, and no amount of admonishment could prevent him from emphasizing to his father that he wanted nothing whatsoever to do with the family business.

"I saw you over lunch doing an imitation of a little business-man," he said to Thomas. "Everyone was fooled except me. When are you going to let them know that you are only pretending?"

"I am not pretending."

"You don't mean a word of it."

Heinrich had developed a way of disassociating himself so completely from the family's main concerns that his father learned to leave him alone, concentrating instead on correcting small failures in the manners or bearing of his second son and his two daughters. Julia tried to interest Heinrich in music, but he did not want to go on playing the piano or the violin.

Heinrich would, Thomas thought, have become totally detached from the family had it not been for his intense devotion to his sister Carla. There were ten years between the two, so that Heinrich's response to his sister was more fatherly than brotherly. From the time she was a baby, Heinrich carried Carla about the house. And then, as she got older, he taught her card games and played a gentle version of hide-and-seek in which only they were involved.

His affection for Carla allowed others to admire the softness in him, the consideration. Even though he had friends and manly activities to attend to, Heinrich would react to Carla's demands with tenderness. If Lula became jealous of the attention paid to her sister, Heinrich would include her too, but she often grew bored as her sister and her older brother appeared to have a private way of communicating with and amusing each other.

"Heinrich is very kind," a cousin said. "If only he were practical as well, then the family's future would be secure."

"There is always Tommy," Aunt Elisabeth said, turning to Thomas. "Tommy is going to take the firm into the twentieth century. Is that not your plan?"

Thomas would smile as best he could, having noted the faint irony in her tone.

Even though it was believed that his recalcitrance came from her side of the family, Heinrich, as he grew older, began to be bored by his mother's stories, nor did he seem to have inherited her fragility of spirit, her engagement with the rare, the exquisite. Strangely, for all his talk about poems and art and travel, Heinrich, in his air of frankness and determination, was, despite himself, becoming a pure, genuine Mann. Indeed, when he was seen walking through Lübeck, his aunt Elisabeth loved to remark how much he resembled his grandfather Johann Siegmund Mann, how he had the heavy gait that she associated with old Lübeck, and also the ponderous tone of his father's line. It was such a pity that he lacked any enthusiasm for trade.

It was clear to Thomas that the business would, in time, be left to him to manage rather than to his older brother, that the house that had been his grandparents' would eventually be his domain. He could fill it with books, he thought. He saw how he would reconfigure the upstairs rooms and move the offices to some other building. He would order books from Hamburg, as his father ordered his clothes, and from farther afield, perhaps even from France if he could learn to read French, or from London when his English was more fluent. He would live in Lübeck as no one had ever done, with a business that he would have consolidated, enough for it to be merely a way to fund his other concerns. He would like a French wife, he thought. She would add luster to their lives.

He imagined his mother coming to visit the house on Mengstrasse, when he and his wife would have decorated it, and admiring what they had done, the new piano they had bought, the paintings from Paris, the French furniture.

As Heinrich grew taller, he came to let Thomas know more emphatically that his younger brother's efforts to behave like a Mann were still a pose, a pose whose falsity was increasingly apparent when Thomas began to read more poetry, when he could no longer keep his enthusiasm for culture a secret, and when he would fitfully allow his mother to accompany him on the Bechstein in the drawing room as he played the violin.

Time passed and Thomas's efforts to pretend that he was interested in ships and trade gradually crumbled. While Heinrich had grown defiantly unequivocal in his ambitions, Thomas was nervous and evasive, but still he could not disguise how he had changed.

"Why don't you stop by your father's office anymore?" his mother asked. "He has mentioned it several times."

"I will go there tomorrow," Thomas said.

On the way home from school, however, he thought of the ease he would feel in his own house, finding a place away from everyone, reading his book or just dreaming. He decided that he would go to his father's office later in the week.

Thomas had a memory of a day in that house in Lübeck with his mother at the piano and himself at the violin, when Heinrich appeared in the doorway without warning and stood watching them. As Thomas continued playing, he was alert to Heinrich's presence. They had shared a room for some years, but did not do so anymore.

Heinrich, four years older than he, fairer in complexion, had become a handsome man. That was what Thomas noticed.

Heinrich, who was eighteen then, clearly saw that he was being studied by his younger brother. For one or two seconds, he must also have spotted that the gaze included an element of uneasy desire. The music, Thomas remembered, was slow and undemanding to play, one of Schubert's early pieces for piano and violin, or perhaps even a transcription of a song. His mother's attention was on the sheet music so that she did not take in the way in which her two sons looked at each other. Thomas was not sure that she even knew Heinrich was there. Slowly, as he blushed in embarrassment at what his brother had seen in him, Thomas looked away.

When his brother had gone, Thomas desperately tried to play the violin in time with his mother as though nothing had occurred. Finally, however, they had to stop; he was making too many mistakes for them to carry on.

Nothing like this ever happened again. Heinrich had needed to let him know that he saw into his spirit. That was all. But the memory remained: the room, the light from the long window, his mother at the piano, his own solitude as he stood close to her trying to play, and the music, the soft sounds they made. And then the sudden eye contact. And the return to normality, or something that might have resembled normality were an outsider to have come into the room.

Heinrich was happy to leave school and take up employment in a bookshop in Dresden. In his absence Thomas grew even dreamier. He simply could not apply himself to study or to listen much to teachers. In the background, like some thundering noise, was the ominous idea that he would turn out, once the time came for him to behave like a grown-up, to be no use to anyone.

Instead, he would embody decline. Decline would be in the

very sound of the notes he played when he practiced the violin, in the very words when he read a book.

He knew that he was being observed, not just in the family circle, but at school, at church. He loved listening to his mother playing the piano and following her when she went to her boudoir. But he also liked being pointed out on the street, respected as an upright son of the senator. He had soaked up his father's self-importance, but he also had elements of his mother's artistic nature, her whimsicality.

Some in Lübeck took the view that the brothers were, in fact, not merely examples of a decline in their own household but presentiments of a new weakness in the world itself, especially in a northern Germany that had once been proud of its manliness.

Much then depended on their younger brother, Viktor, born when Heinrich was nineteen and Thomas almost fifteen.

"Since the first two boys have grown so attached to poetry," Aunt Elisabeth said, "we can only hope that this new one prefers ledgers and account books."

In the summer, once the family arrived at Travemünde for their four weeks' holiday by the sea, all thought of school and teachers, grammar and ratios and the dreaded gymnastics was banished.

In the beachside hotel, a Swiss-style lodge, Thomas, who was fifteen, woke in a tidy little room with old-fashioned furniture to the sound of the gardener raking the gravel under the bright white sky of a summer morning on the Baltic.

With his mother and Ida Buchwald, her female companion, he had breakfast on the balcony of the dining room or under the tall chestnut tree outside. Beyond them was the short grass, giving way to the taller shore vegetation and then the sandy beach.

His father seemed to take pleasure in the hotel's minor shortcomings. He believed the tablecloths to be too hastily laundered and the tissue-paper napkins to be vulgar; the strange bread and the metal eggcups were not to be tolerated. And then, having listened to him complain, Julia would calmly shrug.

"Everything will be perfect when we go home."

When Lula asked her mother why their father seldom came to the beach with them, she smiled.

"He enjoys being in the hotel, and he doesn't want to come to the beach. So why should we make him?"

Thomas and his siblings would go with his mother and Ida to the beach and curl up on the chairs put in place by the hotel staff. The hum of conversation between the two women would stop only when anyone new appeared and they would both sit up to see who it was. And then, curiosity satisfied, they would start up again in a kind of languid whisper. And soon, at their urging, in his bathing suit, Thomas would approach the waves, edging himself in, afraid first of the cold, jumping as each gentle wave came, and then letting the water embrace him.

In the interminable late afternoons, there were hours by the bandstand, or times when Ida read to him under the trees behind the hotel before they would go to sit at the end of the rampart in the twilight and wave a handkerchief at the ships going by. And then it would be time for supper, and later he would often go to his mother's room to watch her prepare for her descent to the dining room on the hotel's glassed-in veranda to have dinner with her husband, surrounded by families not only from Hamburg but from England and even Russia, as he himself got ready for sleep.

On the days when it rained, when the west wind blew the sea back, he would spend time at the upright piano in the lobby. It had been battered by all the waltz music played on it, and he could not get the same rich tones and undertones that the grand piano at home yielded, but it had a funny, muted, gurgling tone of its own that he knew he would miss once the holiday was over.

His father, that last summer, returned to Lübeck after a few days, under the pretext that he had urgent work to do. But when he appeared again, he did not join them for breakfast and, no matter how fine the day was, remained reading in the drawing room with a rug around him as though he were an invalid. Since he did not accompany them on any of their outings, they carried on as if he were still away.

It was only when Thomas went looking for his mother one evening, finally finding her in his father's room, that he was forced to notice his father, who was lying in bed staring at the ceiling with his mouth open.

"Poor dear," his mother said, "work has tired him out so much. This holiday will do him good."

The next day, his mother and Ida followed their normal routine, without any mention that they had left the senator in bed in his room. When Thomas asked his mother if his father was sick, she reminded him that the senator had had a minor bladder operation some months earlier.

"He is still recovering," his mother said. "Soon he will be running into the water."

What was strange, Thomas thought, was how little he could remember of his father ever swimming or lying on the beach during earlier summer holidays. Instead, he recalled him reading the newspaper in a deck chair on the veranda, his supply of Russian cigarettes on the table beside him, or waiting outside his mother's room as Julia drifted dreamily inside in the time before dinner.

One day as they walked back from the beach, his mother asked him to visit his father in his room, perhaps even read to him should his father ask. When Thomas demurred, letting her know that he wanted to hear the band play, she insisted, saying that his father was expecting him.

In the room, his father was sitting up in bed, with a crisp white sheet around his neck, while the hotel barber shaved him. He nodded to Thomas and indicated that he should sit on the chair nearest the window. Thomas found a book that was open with its pages facing downwards and began to flick through it. It was the sort of book that Heinrich might read, he thought. He hoped his father did not want him to read from this.

He became absorbed in the slow, intricate way the barber was shaving his father, following broad sweeps of the open razor with tiny movements. When the barber had done one half of the face, he stood back to examine his work and then set about cutting away tiny hairs near the nose and on the upper lips with a small scissors. His father stared straight ahead.

Then the barber got to work again, taking off the rest of the lather. When he had finished, he produced a bottle of cologne and, as his father winced, he applied it liberally and then clapped his hands in satisfaction.

"This will put the barbers of Lübeck to shame," he said, taking off the white sheet and folding it. "And people will flock to Travemünde for the best shave."

Thomas's father lay on the bed. His striped pajamas were perfectly ironed. Thomas saw that his father's toenails were cut with care, except for the little toe on the left foot where the nail seemed to have curled around the toe. He wished he had scissors so that he could try to cut it properly. And then he realized what an absurd idea this was. His father would hardly let him cut his toenails.

He was still holding the book. If he did not put it aside quickly, his father might see it and call on him to read from it, or he might ask him something about it.

His father soon closed his eyes and appeared to be asleep, but presently he opened them again and gazed blankly at the wall opposite. Thomas wondered if this would be an opportune moment to ask his father about ships, which ones were due in port and which were due to depart. And maybe, if his father became loquacious, inquire about fluctuations in the price of grain. Or mention Prussia so that his father could complain about the unpleasant manners and uncouth eating habits of Prussian officials, even men who claimed to come from good families.

He glanced at his father again and saw that he was fast asleep. Within a short time, he was snoring. Thomas thought that he might now put the book on the bedside table. He stood up and went closer to the bed. The shaving had made his father's face look pale as well as smooth.

He wasn't sure how long he was expected to stay. He wished someone from the hotel would come with fresh water or fresh towels, but he supposed all of that was already in place. He did not expect his mother to come. He knew that she had sent him to the room so that she could relax in the hotel gardens or go back to the beach with Ida and his sisters or with Viktor and the maid. If he set foot outside this room, he believed, his mother would surely hear about it.

He walked around, touching the newly laundered sheets, but, worried that he might disturb his father, he stepped away.

When his father let out a cry, the sound was so strange that he believed for an instant that someone else was in the room. But then his father began to shout out words and it was a familiar voice that Thomas heard, even though the words made no sense. His father was sitting up in bed, holding his stomach. After some effort, he managed to stand out on the floor only to fall back weakly onto the bed.

Thomas's first response was to move away from him in fright, but as his father lay back moaning with his eyes closed, his hands still holding his stomach, Thomas approached him and asked if he should go and look for his mother.

"Nothing," his father said.

"What? Should I not get my mother?"

"Nothing," his father repeated. He opened his eyes and looked at Thomas, his expression a kind of grimace.

"You know nothing," his father said.

Thomas darted from the room. On the stairs, having found that he had descended one floor too many, he ran up to the lobby and found the concierge, who called the manager. As he was explaining to both what had happened, his mother and Ida appeared.

He followed all of them to the room, only to find that his father was peacefully asleep on the bed.

His mother sighed and quietly apologized for the fuss. Thomas knew that it would be futile to try to explain to her what he had witnessed.

His father continued to weaken when they returned to Lübeck, but he lived until October.

He heard his aunt Elisabeth complain that as the senator lay on his deathbed he interrupted the sacred words of the clergyman with a brisk "Amen."

"He was never good at listening," she said, "but I would have thought that he would listen to the clergyman."

In the last days of their father's life, Heinrich seemed to know how to be with his mother, but Thomas could not think what to say to her. When she hugged him, she pulled him too close; he believed that he offended her by his strenuous efforts to release himself.

When he heard Aunt Elisabeth whispering to a cousin about his father's will, he moved nonchalantly away and then sneaked in close, enough to hear her say that Julia could not be given too much responsibility.

"And the boys!" she said. "Those two boys! The family is over now. I suppose people will laugh at me in the street, the very people who would always bow."

As she continued, the cousin noticed Thomas listening and nudged her.

"Thomas, go and make sure your sisters are properly dressed,"

Aunt Elisabeth said. "I saw Carla wearing the most unsuitable shoes."

At the funeral, Julia Mann smiled wanly at those who offered her sympathy but did not encourage them to say anything more to her. She retreated into her own world, keeping her daughters close, allowing her sons to represent the family, should that be necessary, by speaking to those who came to console them.

"Can you keep these people away from me?" she asked. "If they ask if there is anything they can do, could you implore them not to look at me in that sorrowful way?"

Thomas had never seen her as so elaborately foreign and mysterious.

A day after the funeral, with her five children in the drawing room, Julia observed that her sister-in-law Elisabeth, with the help of Heinrich, was moving the sofa and one of the armchairs.

"Elisabeth, don't touch the furniture," she said. "Heinrich, put the sofa back where it was."

"Julia, I think the sofa needs to be against the wall. There are too many tables around it where it is. You always have too much furniture. My mother always said—"

"Don't touch the furniture!" Julia interrupted.

Elisabeth moved proudly towards the fireplace and stood there dramatically, like a woman in a play who has been wounded.

When Thomas observed Heinrich getting ready to accompany his mother to the court where the will was to be read, he wondered why he had not been included. His mother was so preoccupied, however, that he decided not to complain.

"I have always hated being on display here. How barbaric that they will read the will in public! All Lübeck will know our business. And, Heinrich, if you could keep your aunt Elisabeth from trying to link my arm as we leave the court, that would be very kind of you. And if they wish to burn me in the public square after the reading, tell them I will be free at three o'clock."

Thomas wondered who would run the business now. He imagined that his father would have named some prominent men to oversee one or two of the clerks who would look after things until the family decided what to do. At the funeral, he had felt that he was being watched and pointed out as the second son upon whose shoulders a weight of responsibility would now land. He went into his mother's room and looked at himself in the full-length mirror. If he stood sternly, he could easily see himself arriving at his office in the morning, giving instructions to his subordinates. But when he heard the voice of one of his sisters calling him from downstairs, he stepped away from the mirror and felt instantly diminished.

He listened from the top of the stairs when Heinrich and his mother came back.

"He remade that will, to let the world know what he thought of us," Julia said. "And there they all were, the good people of Lübeck. Since they can't burn witches anymore, they take the widows out and humiliate them."

Thomas came down to the hall; he saw that Heinrich was pale. When he caught his brother's eye, he realized that something bad and unexpected had happened.

"Take Tommy into the drawing room and close the door," Julia said, "and tell him what has befallen us. I would play the piano now except that our neighbors would gossip about me. I will go to my room instead. I don't want the details of this will ever mentioned again in my presence. If your aunt Elisabeth has the nerve to call, tell her I am suddenly stricken with grief."

Having shut the door behind them, Heinrich and Thomas started to read the copy of the will that Heinrich had taken from the court.

It was dated, Thomas saw, three months earlier. It began by assigning a guardian to direct the future of the Mann children. Below that, the senator made clear his low opinion of them all.

"As far as possible," he had written, "one should oppose my eldest son's literary inclinations. In my opinion, he lacks the requisite education and knowledge. The basis for his inclination is fantasy and lack of discipline and his inattention to other people, possibly resulting from thoughtlessness."

Heinrich read it out twice, laughing loudly.

"And listen to this," he went on. "This is about you: 'My second son has a good disposition and will adjust to a practical occupation. I can expect that he will be a support for his mother.' So it will be you and your mother. And you will adjust! And who ever thought you had a good disposition? That is another of your disguises."

Heinrich read to him his father's warning against Lula's passionate nature and his suggestion that Carla would be, next to Thomas, a calming element within the family. Of the baby Viktor, the senator wrote: "Often children who are born late develop particularly well. The child has good eyes."

"It gets worse. Listen to this!"

He read aloud in an imitation of a pompous voice.

"'Towards all the children, my wife should be firm, and keep them all dependent on her. If she should become dubious, she should read *King Lear*.'"

"I knew my father was petty-minded," Heinrich said, "but I did not know that he was vindictive."

In a stern and official voice, Heinrich then told his brother the provisions of their father's will. The senator had left instructions that the family firm was to be sold forthwith, and the houses also. Julia was to inherit everything, but two of the most officious men in the public life of Lübeck, men whom she had always viewed as unworthy of her full attention, were designated to make financial decisions for her. Two guardians were also appointed to supervise the upbringing of the children. And the will stipulated that Julia was to report to the thin-lipped Judge August Leverkühn four times a year on how the children were progressing.

When Elisabeth came to visit the next time, she was not invited to sit down.

"Did you know about my husband's will?" Julia asked her.

"I was not consulted," Elisabeth replied.

"That was not the question. Did you know about it?"

"Julia, not in front of the children!"

"There is something I have always wanted to say," Julia said, "and I can say it now that I am free. And I will say it in front of the children. I have never liked you. And it's a pity your mother is no longer alive, because I would say the same to her."

Heinrich made to stop her but Julia brushed him aside.

"The senator made that will to humiliate me."

"You could hardly have run the business yourself," Elisabeth said.

"I could have decided. My sons and I could have decided."

For the citizens of Lübeck, for those whom Julia had teased or spoken of lightly at parties in her husband's house, men such as Herr Kellinghusen or Herr Cadovius, women such as young Frau Stavenhitter or Frau Mackenthun, or for women who watched her carefully and deplored what they saw, such as Frau Overbeck and her daughter, Julia's decision, made public soon after the reading of the will, to move to Munich with her three youngest children and set up home there, leaving Thomas behind to complete his final year at school while boarding in the house of Dr. Timpe, and encouraging Heinrich to travel to improve his chances in the literary world, could not have been more perverse.

If the widow of Senator Mann had decided to move to Lüne-
burg or Hamburg, the good people of Lübeck might have seen
this as a mere aspect of her unreliability, but in those years,
Thomas knew, for these Hanseatic burghers, Munich represented
the south, and they disliked the south and did not trust it. The city
was Catholic; it was bohemian. It had no solid virtues. None of
them had ever been there for longer than was necessary.

Lübeck's attention was on his mother, especially when Aunt
Elisabeth told people in confidence how rude Julia had been to
her and how she had sullied the memory of her mother.

For a while, in their world, the talk was of nothing except the
lack of placidity displayed by the senator's widow and her unwise
plans. It struck no one, not even Heinrich, how wounded Thomas
was that the family firm had not been left to him, even if it were
to be supervised by others until he came of age.

Thomas lived with the shock of the knowledge that he was destined to have taken away from him what he had believed, in some
of his dreams, would be his. He knew that running the family business was merely one of the many ways he had imagined his future,
but he felt anger at his father for the presumption in his decision.
He disliked the idea that his father had seen through his illusions
without realizing how real they often appeared to him. He wished
he had had the opportunity to give his father evidence enough to
have left a more generous will.

Instead, his father had cut the family adrift. Since the senator could not live, he had set about vitiating the lives of others.
Thomas felt a persistent and gnawing sorrow that all the effort of
the Manns in Lübeck would come to nothing now. The time of
his family was over.

No matter where they went in the world, the Manns of Lübeck
would never be known as they had been known when the senator
was alive. This did not seem to bother Heinrich or his sisters, or
indeed his mother; they had other, more practical concerns. He

knew that his aunt Elisabeth felt that the status of the family had been fatally undermined, but he could hardly discuss this with her. Instead, he was alone with these thoughts. The family would now be uprooted from Lübeck. No matter where he went, he would never be important again.

Chapter 2
Lübeck, 1892

The orchestra was playing the Prelude to *Lohengrin*. As Thomas listened, the string section seemed to be holding back, offering hints of what the melody might eventually become. Then the sound began to rise and fall naturally until a single plaintive note on the violin lifted and lingered; the playing then became louder and more luscious, more intense.

The sound almost comforted him, but then as it increased in volume, grew more piercing, and the dark undertone of the cellos came in, forcing the violins and violas to rise further above them, what the orchestra gave him was only a sense of his own smallness.

And then all the instruments, the conductor with his arms spread out wide to encourage them, began to play; once the drums had been beaten and the cymbals had clashed, he noticed the gradual slowing down, the move towards conclusion.

When the audience applauded, he did not join them. He sat and watched the stage and the lights and the musicians, as they prepared for the Beethoven symphony that would end the evening. When the concert was over, he did not want to go out into the night. He wanted to remain enfolded by the music. He wondered if there were other people among this crowd who shared how he felt, but he did not think so.

This was Lübeck, after all, and people were not given to such emotions. Those around him, he thought, would easily be able to forget, or brush off, the memory of the music they had heard.

It struck him, as he remained in his seat, that this might have mattered to his father in the last days of his life, when he knew death was coming, this idea of a soaring, shifting sound, over-whelming, suggesting a power beyond earthly power, opening a door to some other realm where the spirit would survive and prevail, where there might be rest once death itself in its sheer indignity had been endured.

He thought of his father's dead body laid out like a spectacle, dressed in his formal clothes like a parody of a sleeping public man, ready for inspection. The senator lay there, cold, contained, the mouth downturned and closed tight, the face changing as the light changed, the hands drained of all color. He remembered people watching his mother turning away from the coffin with her hand over her face, their looks of disapproval.

Thomas walked to the house where his mother, who wished him to concentrate more formally on his studies, had found him lodgings with Dr. Timpe, one of his schoolmasters. Tomorrow, once more, he would face the drudgery of the Katharineum; he would write out equations and study the rules of grammar and learn poetry by rote. Throughout the day he would pretend, as the others did, that all this was somehow natural, preordained. It was easier to let his mind wander over how much he dreaded the classroom than to think about his own bedroom, the one where he had slept before his mother and Lula and Carla and Viktor had moved to Munich, that was now lost to him. He was conscious that if he thought about how warm and comfortable he had been there he would become too sad. He would have to try to force his mind to linger on something else.

He would think about girls. He knew that his fellow students' efforts to look diligent were often a way of concealing their constant thinking about girls. When they made jokes and stray remarks, however, these were usually suffused with shyness or embarrassment or self-conscious bravado. But sometimes as he watched them jostling one another on the street, or walking in twos or threes laughing coarsely, he saw the hidden energies.

Despite the boredom of the lessons, a sense of heady expectation filled the air as the afternoon wore on and the chance of them all moving together into the open air grew closer. And even though his fellow students might meet no one special on the way home, they were excited, he understood, by the possibility that they could encounter a young woman on the street or a girl could become visible through a window.

As, after the concert, he neared his own destination, he thought about the upstairs rooms of these houses where, even now as he walked along, a girl might be getting ready for bed, shedding some of her outer garments, lifting her arms high to take off a blouse, or bending to remove what she was wearing below.

He looked up and saw a flickering light in an uncurtained window; he wondered what scene might be enacted in the room. He tried to imagine a couple coming into that space, the man closing the door; he pondered on the image of the girl undressing, her white underclothes and her soft flesh. But when it came to contemplating then how it might feel if he himself were the man, he held back, his thoughts retreated. He found himself unwilling to pursue what had been so graphic just a moment before.

He supposed that his schoolmates, as they imagined such a scene, must also become less than certain about what would, in any case, live only in their most private dreams.

He would wait until he was in his small bedroom at the back of the top floor of Dr. Timpe's house before he would entertain his own dreams. Sometimes, before he turned off the lamp, he began a poem or added a stanza to one that he had been working on. As he sought suitable metaphors for the complex workings of love, he did not think of girls in shadowy rooms; he did not conjure up the intimacy between couples.

There was a boy in his class with whom he had a different sort of intimacy. This boy's name was Armin Martens. Like Thomas, he was sixteen, although he looked younger. His father, who was a mill owner, had known Thomas's father, even though the Martens family was less prominent than the Manns had been.

When Armin noticed Thomas's interest in him, he did not appear surprised. He started to take walks with Thomas, making sure that they were not joined by any of their classmates. Thomas was both disturbed and impressed by Armin's ability to talk to him about the soul, about the real nature of love, about the enduring importance of poetry and music, and with the same facility discuss girls or gymnastics with other classmates.

Armin could be completely at ease with anyone, Thomas saw, his smile warm and open, his aura filled with sweetness and innocence.

When Thomas wrote a poem about wanting to rest his head on his lover's breast, or walk with his lover in the deepening twilight to a place of beauty where they would be fully alone, when he spoke of the urge he felt to intertwine with the soul of his loved one, the figure he imagined, the object of his desire, was Armin Martens.

He wondered if Armin would show him some sign, or would, on one of their walks, allow the conversation to move away from poems and music to focus on their feelings for each other.

In time, he realized that he set more store by these walks than Armin did. On waking, he knew that he should temper his behavior accordingly, permit Armin to become distant from him if that was what his friend desired. As he ruminated sadly on how little he could really expect from Armin, the possibility of rejection caused a surge in his blood, something sharply painful and then almost satisfying.

Such thoughts came as fleetingly as a change in the light or a sudden coldness in the air. He could not easily manage them or entertain them. And as the day went on in all its dullness and ordinariness, they faded from his mind. In his desk, he kept his own poems and some love poems by the great German masters that he had copied out on single pages. During lessons, if the teacher were at the blackboard, he would take one of these sheets out and surreptitiously read a poem, glancing often at Armin Martens, who sat one row ahead of him across the narrow passageway.

He wondered how Armin would react if he were to show him these poems as a way of explaining how he felt.

Sometimes they walked together in silence, Thomas relishing their closeness. If they met anyone they knew, Armin had a firm but friendly way of establishing that they did not want company on their stroll.

Most days, especially at the beginning of their walk, Thomas allowed Armin to lead the conversation. He noted that his companion never spoke badly of their fellow students or their teachers. His view of the world was tolerant and relaxed. A mention of the name of their mathematics teacher Herr Immerthal, for example, a man for whom Thomas felt a profound loathing, merely caused Armin to smile.

When Thomas wanted to discuss poetry and music, his friend often had more mundane concerns such as the riding lessons that he took, or some game in which he had been involved. Once Thomas managed to shift to loftier themes, however, Armin's way of approaching the subject did not change, it had the same lightness and lack of intensity.

It was his naturalness, his evenness, his acceptance of the world, his lack of nervousness, self-consciousness or pretense, that made Thomas want to have him as his special friend.

Thomas noticed as the year went on that Armin was beginning to change, becoming taller and broader in the shoulders, starting to shave. His friend, he thought, was half-boy, half-man. This made Thomas feel more tenderly towards him. Late at night, certain that the time had come to declare what his feelings were, he was determined that he would show him his new love poem, a poem that did not disguise the fact that the loved one was Armin himself.

In the first stanza of his poem, Thomas wrote of how his loved one spoke eloquently of music. And in the next stanza he described how his loved one spoke of poetry. In the final stanza he wrote that the object of his affection combined the beauty of both music and poetry in his voice and in his eyes.

One day in winter, as they walked, they held their caps and bent their heads before the strong, damp wind that rattled and groaned in the leafless trees. Although Thomas had the new poem in his jacket pocket, he knew that despite his previous determination it would be impossible to share it with his friend. Armin was talking about the pleasure to be had, once he was home, sliding down the banisters of the stairs. He sounded like a child. Thomas thought it might be better were he to burn the poem.

On other days, especially if there had been a concert in Lübeck, or if Thomas had pointed him towards one of Goethe's love poems, Armin's response could be more serious and thoughtful. When Thomas tried to describe how he had felt as the *Lohengrin* Prelude was played, Armin studied him with curiosity, nodding his head, letting him know that he was in full sympathy with the emotions Thomas described. As they walked on, Thomas was content that they were both contemplating the power of music. He was with the companion he had dreamed about.

He wrote a poem about the lover and the loved one walking in silence, each thinking the same thoughts, with only the noise of the wind keeping them separate, only the bareness of the trees reminding them that nothing lasts, nothing except their love. In the last stanza, the poet called on his lover to live with him forever, thus resisting time, moving together into eternity.

Thomas was aware that Armin was often taunted by their classmates about their friendship. He was viewed as lacking the finer masculine qualities, being too conceited and too interested in poetry, too proud of his family's former importance in Lübeck. He knew that Armin just laughed this off and saw no reason why he should not keep Thomas as a close companion. It was obvious that Armin felt a real affection for him. Surely then it would not surprise him were Thomas to show him the poems, or let him know his feelings in some other way?

One day at school, when the teacher's back was turned, Armin looked around and smiled at him. His hair was freshly washed, his skin clear and luminous; his eyes were bright. Thomas could see how beautiful he was becoming. It occurred to him that Armin was possibly as alert to him now as he was to Armin. He did not smile at anyone else in the same way.

They had planned a walk the following day. The wind was mild and the sun appeared intermittently as they strolled down towards the docks. Armin was in high good humor, talking excitedly about a trip to Hamburg he and his father were making.

They moved along, avoiding horses and carts and men loading wood, then paused to watch as several logs fell from a small cart, forcing the driver to stop and ask those around to help him reload the cart. The more the driver appealed to his fellow dockworkers, the more playful was the abuse they directed at him, using dialect that amused both Thomas and Armin.

"I wish I knew how to talk like they do," Armin said.

When one man began to help the driver, more logs rolled from the cart. Armin became more and more engaged by the scene. He laughed, putting his arm around Thomas's shoulder and then around his waist. As the men set about rearranging the logs but managed instead to displace some more, causing hoots of derision, Armin hugged Thomas.

"This is what I love about Lübeck," he said. "In Hamburg everything is more orderly and modern and governed by rules. I would like never to leave Lübeck."

It struck Thomas as they watched the two men piling the logs more securely that he should respond in some way to Armin's embraces. He wondered if he might turn and hug him, but he did not think he could make it seem natural.

They walked towards a cluster of old warehouses, veering into a side street where there was no traffic, no sign of life. Armin said they could get to the waterfront by this route and inspect what ships had come into port.

"I have something to show you," Thomas said.

He took the two poems from his jacket pocket and handed them to Armin, who began quietly to read them, concentrating hard, as though some words or lines presented him with difficulty.

"Who wrote this?" he asked when he had finished reading the poem that compared the loved one to music and to poetry.

"I did," Thomas said.

Armin busied himself with the second poem; he did not look up.

"Did you write this one as well?" he asked.

Thomas nodded.

"Does anyone else know?"

"No. I wrote them only for you to see."

Armin did not respond.

"I wrote them *to* you," Thomas said, almost whispering. He thought to reach out and touch Armin on the arm or the shoulder, but he held back.

Armin's face reddened. He looked at the ground. Thomas worried for a moment that Armin might believe that his intentions were compromising, that he might soon suggest, for example, they slip into an empty warehouse together. He needed to let him know there was nothing further from his mind. What he sought from Armin should come not in some quick consummation, but in soft words, or a look, or a gesture. He wished for nothing more.

He found, as he kept his eyes on Armin, that he was close to tears. Armin checked the other side of both sheets of paper to see if there was anything more written on them. He perused the two poems again.

"I don't think I am like music or like poetry," he said. "I am like myself. And some people say that I am like my father. And as regards living forever with a poet, I don't know. I think I will live in my father's house until the time comes for me to buy my own residence. Let's go down and look at the ships."

As he handed the poems to Thomas, he punched him gently and mockingly in the chest.

"Make sure no one finds those poems. My friends have already made up their minds about you, but it would ruin my reputation."

"The poems mean nothing to you?"

"I prefer ships to poems, and girls to ships, and so should you."

Armin strode ahead. When he looked behind and saw that Thomas still had the sheets of paper in his hand, he laughed.

"Put that stuff away or someone will find it and throw us in the water."

In his last year at the Katharineum, Armin Martens changed as Thomas himself did. He lost all his friendliness and boyishness. He became serious. Soon he would begin working at his father's mill. He would have his own office. He already carried with him a sense of his future importance. Unaware of the dullness of his destiny, he would, Thomas saw, integrate himself naturally into the business life of Lübeck.

On the top floor of Dr. Timpe's house, his son Willri, a year older than Thomas, had the front room. Although they knew each other from school, Willri made clear to Thomas as soon as he moved into his new quarters that he had no interest in becoming his friend. It surprised Thomas that Dr. Timpe was almost proud of Willri's lack of interest in books and learning.

"He likes the open air and machines," the professor said, "and maybe the world would be a better place if we all shared his preferences. Maybe books have had their day."

No one protested when Willri stood up from the table before the meal had ended and left the room. He had grown taller than his own father and heavier too. This appeared to amuse Dr. Timpe.

"Soon he will be ordering me around. So what is the point of me giving him orders? He has his own mind made up about everything. He is a complete adult."

He looked at Thomas, suggesting that perhaps Thomas, who took time over his meals, could learn something from his son.

At night, since the wall was thin, he was aware of Willri in the next room. He imagined him preparing for bed and lying warm beneath the blankets. He smiled at the thought that he would not write poems about Willri; no one ever would. But perhaps he had written enough poems for the moment. Nonetheless, the thought of Willri in the next room stayed with him and often excited him.

One night, Willri knocked on his door and asked him to come into his room to help him with a Latin translation. As Thomas studied the text, sitting on the edge of the bed, he was surprised that Willri had begun to undress. Embarrassed, he was about to propose that they look at the Latin in the morning when he saw that Willri, with his back to him, would soon be naked. It took him a while to realize that Willri had no interest at all in the Latin. He had invited him into his room for other reasons.

Soon an encounter in that front bedroom became part of their ritual. Tiptoeing on the creaky floorboards, Thomas would open the door of Willri's room without knocking. The lamp would still be burning. Willri would be lying fully clothed on the single bed.

One evening, having made his way home from a visit to his aunt Elisabeth, Thomas, as usual, ascended the stairs without making a sound, taking the steps lightly one by one. On the upper landing, he saw that Willri's lamp was still on. In his own room, he removed his overcoat and sat down on the edge of the bed. Sometimes, it was more exciting if he waited for Willri to come and look for him.

He listened. In the silence that reigned, he knew that the smallest sound up here would be heard on the floors below where the rest of the Timpe family was sleeping.

Willri tried to appear casual when he came into Thomas's room and stepped towards the window and opened a chink in the curtains. He made it seem as if looking out into the emptiness of the night was his sole reason for being here. And when he turned, the expression on his face displayed a slow ease and contentment. He reached towards Thomas and for a second touched his face. Then he smiled and stood looking at Thomas, who gazed at him in return.

When Willri indicated, Thomas, having taken off his shoes, followed his companion to his room at the front. Willri closed the door behind them and pointed to the bed, putting a finger to his lips. Thomas went across the room, lying down on the bed, his hands behind his head. With his back to him, Willri started to undress.

This was the ritual they conducted on nights when the others were sleeping. Willri began by removing his jacket, hanging it on the back of the single chair in the room. He acted like someone who was alone. He unfastened his trousers and took them off, placing them on the chair. From the bed, Thomas examined his strong, hairless legs. He knew that once Willri had shed his underwear, he would then bend to take off his socks. This would be the moment he would try to remember later when he returned to his room. He propped himself up on his elbows so that he could see more clearly. Once Willri had tucked the socks into his shoes, he stood up straight again and opened the buttons on his shirt.

Soon he was completely naked. He lifted his arms and put his hands behind his head, mirroring Thomas's pose on the bed. For some time, he did not change his position or make a sound. Thomas studied his body carefully, but knew that he should not move from the bed or attempt to embrace Willri.

One night, when Willri had faced him, displaying an erection, Thomas loosened his own clothes and approached him. For the first time, he touched Willri, who encouraged him to come closer. Thomas was just as shocked as Willri when he found that, without warning, he had climaxed and begun to utter short and urgent cries. Instantly, Willri whispered to him that he must leave now, go to his room and put out the lamp. And get into bed without any delay.

Stealing into the corridor, Thomas could hear a door opening downstairs and Willri's father shouting: "Are the two of you not in bed? What is going on up there?" Then he heard footsteps on the stairs.

Thomas knew that if Dr. Timpe entered his room and touched the lamp he would know from the heat that it had just been extinguished. And if he pulled back the blankets, he would see that Thomas was fully clothed. And if he stood close enough, he would be able to guess from the smell what Thomas and his son had been doing.

Thomas heard him opening Willri's door and asking his son what the noise was about. He did not hear Willri's reply. Soon, he knew, Dr. Timpe would come to check his room. He turned his face towards the wall and remained still, attempting to mimic the breathing of someone who was fast asleep.

When he heard Dr. Timpe opening his door, he made his breath even and soft, presuming that he would be carefully watched for any sign that he was really awake. Dr. Timpe must know that it was Thomas's voice that had woken him, that it was Thomas who had been making the sounds that were out of control.

Even when he heard the door closing, he did not move, afraid that Dr. Timpe had shut it only as a way of enticing him to do so. He could be still in the room.

He waited for some time, listening for the smallest sound, before getting out of bed and, slowly in the dark, removing his clothes and putting on his night attire.

In the morning, he wondered what Willri's father would have to say about the cries he had heard the night before. At breakfast, however, Dr. Timpe appeared distracted and silent, preoccupied by something in the newspaper. He barely looked up as Thomas joined the family at the table.

In school, now that his father was dead and the firm no longer existed, now that he lodged in a sort of boardinghouse, no one seemed to notice him.

The power and prestige that he had taken as a natural inheritance had all gone. Until his father's death, he had been a sort of prince, enjoying the solid comfort of the family house and basking in his mother's colorful presence.

Before his father's death, Thomas's indolence at school and his inattentiveness were subjects of hushed discussion between teachers, becoming scandalous at the end of term when reports were sent out. Some teachers did everything they could to detach him from his idleness; others singled him out for special scolding. All of them added copiously to the strain of each day.

Now the strain was different. It came from being a lost cause, someone not worth bothering with. Teachers had ceased to care if he understood a formula or was reduced to looking furtively at his neighbor's copybook. No one asked him to recite a poem by heart, even though privately he had begun to take pleasure from the work of Eichendorff and Goethe and Herder.

What happened between him and Willri Timpe was not part of any soulful connection. In the future, he knew, what they did in that upper room would matter little to Willri. Their intermittent intimacy was not only furtive and unmentionable but shrouded with an attitude of indifference that they showed to each other during the daylight hours. After meals in the house, or on Sundays when they had free time, Willri and he still did not seek each other out.

It was almost impossible not to sneer openly at his teachers, even those whom he had previously tolerated. To Herr Immerthal, the mathematics teacher, he took pride in being insolent and mocking. The class reveled in his smart remarks and enjoyed watching the teacher being humiliated. When Herr Immerthal complained about Thomas to the principal, the principal wrote to his mother, who, in turn, wrote to Thomas saying that if his father were alive, he would take a very dim view of his refusal to conform and apply himself to his studies. Since his father had named two guardians—Herr Krafft Tesdorpf and Consul Hermann Wilhelm Fehling—to monitor his development, she would be forced to contact them were she to receive any more complaints.

Thomas discovered that there were students in the class who were starting to take an interest in poetry. Most of them had been so quiet and timid in earlier years that he had barely noticed them. None of them came from the significant families in Lübeck.

Now, as they approached the end of their schooling, these boys were filled with enthusiasm for essays and stories and poems. The fact that they loved Schubert and Brahms more than Wagner did not disappoint him; it meant that he could keep Wagner for himself. All of them wanted to contribute to a literary magazine they might publish, see their poems in print. Without any effort, Thomas, as editor, became almost a mentor to them. Even though they were mostly his age, they looked up to him. His knowledge of the work of the German poets mattered more to them than his dire performance in the classroom. And despite the fact that he found a few of them handsome, he knew not to write poems dedicated to them.

While many of his schoolmates had no ambition to move beyond Lübeck, it was obvious to Thomas that, once he himself finished school, he would leave. With the firm sold, there was no place for him there. He often walked around the city and down to the docks, or he stopped by Café Niederegger and bought some marzipan with its Brazilian sugar, knowing that he would inevitably relinquish these streets and cafés, they would live only in his memory. When he felt the harsh wind from the Baltic, he knew that this would soon be something that belonged to the past.

Although his mother and his sisters wrote to him, he felt that what they omitted from their letters was more significant than what they included. Their tone was too formal. This gave Thomas permission to reply to each of them in the same tone, telling them nothing important, especially nothing about how badly he was doing in school. His mother, he knew, received reports; he noted, however, that she had given up mentioning them.

The first hint of what his mother and his guardians had in mind for him came from his aunt Elisabeth. In his visits to her she spoke too much about the family's erstwhile greatness and then took him through all the slights that had been offered to her in the recent past by shopkeepers, milliners, drapers and the wives of men who had been socially beneath her all of her life.

"And now this," she said, nodding her head sadly. "Now this."

"What?" he asked.

"They are trying to find you a job as a clerk. A clerk! One of my brother's sons!"

"I don't think that is true."

"Well, you are useless at school. They have given up on you. People love stopping me and telling me that. There is no point in your staying in the classroom much longer. So a clerk it will be. Do you have any better ideas?"

"No one has mentioned it to me."

"I suppose they are waiting until it is all arranged."

When Thomas sent Heinrich poems, his brother replied to express his admiration for some of them. Thomas wished he had commented more specifically on lines or images. But it was a passage at the end of the letter that made him sit up: "I hear you will soon be quitting Lübeck, exchanging the school desk for an office desk. As long as there is earth, water and air, there will be fire. And that can only be good news for you."

He wrote back, asking Heinrich what he meant, but he did not answer.

One day, he found one of his guardians, Consul Fehling, waiting for him sternly in a small sitting room at Dr. Timpe's when he returned from school. Since the consul did not greet him or shake his hand, Thomas wondered in horror if he had somehow found out about the nocturnal activities on the top floor.

"Your mother has been in touch and it is all arranged. I think your father would be pleased. Some of your teachers, I hear, will not miss you."

"What is arranged?"

"In a few weeks, you will start work at Spinell's Fire Insurance in Munich. It is a position that many young men would envy."

"Why has no one told me?"

"I am telling you now. And there is no need for you to return to the classroom. Instead, you can make sure that Dr. Timpe has nothing to complain about as you vacate your room. You should also visit your aunt before you leave for Munich."

The consul arranged his journey to Munich. Since he had heard nothing from his mother about a job as a clerk in fire insurance, he was sure that he could convince her that such a job would not suit him. Among the letters he had received from the family, there had been one from Lula that had interested him. In the middle of what was mostly anodyne material, she had declared casually that Heinrich was receiving a decent monthly allowance from their mother.

Thomas knew that the sale of the company after his father's death had brought in a great deal of money, but he thought that the capital was tied up in investments and that his mother could merely use the interest. He had never realized that any of the money would be due to Heinrich or to him or to his sisters.

But Heinrich was now living between Munich and various Italian locations. His first book had appeared, whose publication, Lula told him, was funded by their mother; he was publishing stories in magazines. Since his mother had agreed to support him, according to Lula, Heinrich was devoting all his time to his literary career and had developed, she wrote, a languid air since spending time in Italy.

Thomas wished that, in his correspondence with his mother, he had written more about his school magazine and the poems he had published. He should have emphasized to her how dedicated he was to his literary career and how seriously his work was taken by his friends. Then he would have paved the way for asking her for a monthly stipend so that he could live like Heinrich.

He put everything he had written and the few pieces he had published in a neat pile. As soon as he got to Munich, he would hand them to his mother. While Heinrich wrote only stories, he would show her that he was a true poet, in the tradition of Goethe and Heine. He hoped that she would be impressed.

When he arrived in Munich, he expected that his mother, once the others had gone to bed, would explain to him what the job in fire insurance was and why he had been removed from school. On the first night, however, she spoke of everything except the reason for his arrival.

He was taken aback by her appearance. She still wore black, but her clothes were in a mode that belonged to a much younger woman. Her hairstyle, with its fringe at the front and an intricate system of combs and clips, was youthful too. She painted her face and wore a lipstick that she proudly told him had been imported from Paris. When he went into her bedroom, he saw that one whole tabletop was packed with cosmetics. She and Lula, who had grown into a beautiful young woman, discussed fashion as equals and, to Thomas's amazement, talked about eligible men who might call in the evening as potential suitors for one or the other of them.

On the second night, when Thomas hoped to have a serious discussion with her, she and Lula spoke about some party they had not attended where some new fashion in dress length was on display.

"I don't think it will catch on," his mother said.

"But it has caught on," Lula said. "We are the ones who have been left behind."

"We will rectify that."

"But how?"

"By following fashion. I have never done that before but I will do it now if you feel I should. In Lübeck, I set the fashion."

Thomas decided that he would go out for a walk. The spring evenings in Munich were warm. He was glad that Heinrich was still in Italy, thus leaving him free to explore the city on his own. The streets were full of strollers; there were even people sitting outside cafés. He found a place where he could sit and distract himself by looking at people as they paraded by.

As the days passed, he found that he did not miss Lübeck. Even in high summer, there had always been an edge of coldness in the wind there. People looked away if you glanced at them. It was the custom there to be home by six in the evening and remain indoors no matter what the season. People lived as if winter were always approaching. They appeared happiest when on their way to a long, dreary church service made even more tedious by the heaving, interminable sound of Buxtehude's works for organ. He felt disdain for the cold Protestantism of the north and the blinkered interest in trade in Lübeck. In Munich, priests were as common on the streets as policemen and could be seen strolling around as though they had no precise destination. It was a relaxed, entertaining place, he thought, and he made plans to settle in the city on his own terms once he had spoken to his mother.

Even though he had stayed in his mother's apartment before, he was still surprised at seeing the furniture from Lübeck, even pieces from his grandmother's house, in the new, more confined space. His mother's grand piano filled almost half the living room. He found the presence of tables and chairs, paintings and candelabra that had been familiar in Lübeck both disturbing and faintly comic, as none of them seemed to fit in with the rest of the decor.

Despite the fact that she still emphasized her own foreignness and originality, treating the apartment as though it were the refuge of some famously ruined heiress, his mother was defeated. She believed, as she often let her children know, that the social success she desired in Munich had eluded her. There were parties and dinners every night to which she was not invited.

The sparkle had left her, Thomas thought, to be replaced by melancholy and a readiness to take offense. Whereas in the old days in Lübeck she had found the society around her both lightly amusing and engrossing, she now became prone to resentments. She was indignant when the postman did not arrive on time, or when a messenger delivered a package in the afternoon rather than the morning, or when one of her friends did not see fit to include her in their party at the opera, or, ominously for Thomas, when one of her children did not behave as she wished.

As Thomas walked around Schwabing, where his mother's apartment was, he discovered a world that he had not taken in before. Young men, who looked like artists or writers, walked confidently in the streets, talking loudly. He wondered if this were new, or why he had not seen it on previous visits. In the cafés that had recently opened, groups were involved in deep conversation. Although they were only a few years older than he was, they suggested a different world. He noticed the odd combinations: if their clothes were worn carelessly, their haircuts could be old-fashioned. They radiated an old-world politeness as they greeted one another or when one of them was departing. But they also had a way of laughing with abandon, displaying teeth that had been shamelessly stained with tobacco. They appeared amused and then suddenly earnest. They often lounged back lazily, and then leaned forward, pointing a finger into the smoke-filled air to underline a point.

He tried to listen to their conversation. Some of them, he learned, were journalists, others were critics or worked in the university. On the street, he saw groups of two or three carrying portfolios. They must be artists, he thought, on their way to a class or a studio or a gallery. They moved and spoke as though not only the city but the future itself would soon be fully theirs.

After supper in that first week, he walked until he was tired, returning silently to the apartment, hoping not to wake the others. Once he made the decision each night to go home, he felt a great desolation. Sitting on his own in cafés, he was shut out from the world that was so alluring to him. He wondered if Heinrich knew any of these people. Were they to see his poems, he thought, they would not want him in their company. They looked and sounded so ironic and cosmopolitan, he was sure they would find simple love poetry worthy only of their mockery. He would have nothing to add to their conversation. He would appear too callow, too innocent, merely a schoolboy. But this did not stop him wanting desperately to be a part of these gatherings.

At meals in his mother's apartment, the talk focused on clothes and gentlemen. If his father were alive, he was sure that what was said at the table would be more edifying and the contributions of his sisters would be carefully monitored and controlled.

One evening, when the talk about a new set of visitors seemed to be reaching an intense pitch, he could take no more.

"I hope not to have to see any of these gentlemen. They sound like bank clerks."

His sisters were not amused by this observation. His mother stared straight ahead.

One night, when he went up to his room, he found a letter with headed notepaper from Spinell's on the bed informing him that he would be expected at their Munich office on Monday morning, when his duties would be outlined for him. His mother must have left it there. Since the date in question was just five days away, he determined that he would have to speak to her, he could not let any more time go by.

The next afternoon, when his sisters had gone shopping and one of the servants had taken Viktor to the park, he heard his mother playing Chopin. Having collected the pile of papers that contained all the poems he had written and some prose pieces, he came into the room where she was and sat quietly and listened.

When she had finished, she stood up wearily.

"I wish we had a bigger apartment, or a nice house," she said. "It is all so cramped here."

"I like Munich," Thomas said.

She turned back to the piano as if she had not heard him. As she was looking through sheet music, he came towards her with his poems.

"I wrote these," he said, "and a few were published. I want to dedicate my life to being a writer."

His mother flicked through the sheets of paper.

"I have seen most of these," she said.

"I don't think you have."

"Heinrich sent them to me."

"Heinrich? He never told me that."

"Perhaps that is just as well."

"What do you mean?"

"He did not think very highly of them."

"He wrote to me saying that he admired some of them."

"That was very sweet of him. But he wrote a very different letter to me. I have it somewhere."

"He gave me great encouragement."

"Did he?"

"Can I see what he wrote?"

"I don't think that would be advisable, but you have a job now. And you start on Monday."

"I am a writer and I don't want to work in an office."

"I can read you out a sample of Heinrich's views if that might help to put your feet on the ground."

She moved away from the piano and left the room. When she returned, she had a bundle of letters in her hand. She sat on the sofa as she tried to find the ones she was looking for.

"Here! I have both letters here. In this one, he describes you as 'an adolescent, loving soul, led astray by loose feeling.' And in this second letter, he refers to your verses as 'effeminate, sentimental poeticizing.' But I myself liked some of the poems, so perhaps this is too harsh. And he may have liked some of them too. When I read what he wrote, I really did see that some decision would have to be made about your future."

"I have no interest in Heinrich's views," Thomas said. "He is not a critic of poetry."

"Yes, but his views do point the way for us."

Thomas looked down at the carpet.

"And so we contacted Herr Spinell," she went on, "who was an old friend of your father's when he ran a very successful fire insurance company in Lübeck. Now he runs a similar one that is much respected in Munich. It's a large business and there is every chance for someone diligent to rise through the ranks there. We did not tell Herr Spinell about your record at school. He sees you as solid, as your father's son."

"Heinrich has an allowance," Thomas said. "You paid for the publishing of his first book."

"Heinrich has applied himself to writing. He has won much admiration."

"I will apply myself to writing too."

"I wish to discourage your urge to write. I know from the school reports that you have no talent at applying yourself to anything. Perhaps I should not have shared your brother's opinion on your poetry with you, but I need to bring you down to earth. This job in fire insurance will steady you. Now I realize that we must go the tailor's and get you measured for some suitable clothes, clothes that will impress Herr Spinell. We should have done that as soon as you arrived."

"I don't want to work in fire insurance."

"I'm afraid that your guardians, who still have control, have made a firm decision. It is all my fault. You see, I was too lax. I did not know what to do when I saw the school reports so I did nothing. But then the guardians saw them and it was all taken out of my hands. I would have resisted them were it not for the poems."

His mother crossed the small room and sat again at the piano. He looked at her elegant neck, her narrow shoulders, her slim waist. She was only forty-three. Before this, she had always been gentle with him, too distracted by other things to notice him too much or be irritated by him. Just now, she had sounded officious, using a tone that she herself often deplored in others. She was trying to mimic his guardians or his father. It would not take much to bring her back to herself, but he did not know at that moment how he might do that. And he could not believe that Heinrich, in whom he had confided his ambitions to be a poet, had betrayed him, had written so savagely and cynically about his poems.

As his mother returned to her Chopin, putting more and more energy into her playing, he was glad that he could not see her face. And he was even happier that his mother could not see his as he began to steel himself against her and against his brother.

Chapter 3
Munich, 1893

At Spinell's, when he started, he dreaded each day. The work they gave him was deadening. They wanted all the accounts in one ledger to be transferred to another ledger so they would have a second copy that could be held in the head office.

They left him alone, trusting him to do this work, having let him know where he could find fresh nibs for his pen, ink and blotting paper. As he worked at the high desk, some of the older men in the office greeted him when they passed. The sight of a young man from a good family learning his trade in the fire insurance business seemed to please them. One of them, Herr Huhnemann, was the friendliest.

"Soon you will be promoted," he said, "I can see that. You look like a most competent young man. We are lucky to have you."

No one ever checked how much progress he was making. He kept the two ledgers open, making sure that he appeared to be concentrating on the work. He did some transcribing, but less and less each day. If he had written poems, he might have drawn attention to himself by knitting his brows too much or singing out the rhythms under his breath, so he wrote a story. He worked calmly, the dream life he tried to summon up pleased him, and soon put him in a good humor that lasted through the evening so that his mother began to believe that he was benefiting from the discipline of office work and that he might have a serious future in fire insurance.

Breaking the rules, defying both his employers and his guardians, gave him satisfaction. He no longer dreaded going to work.
But there were nights when he could not bear it at the table, when
the apartment was stuffy and the hours ahead were hard to face.

He knew that his mother disapproved of him walking the streets
of Munich and sampling the cafés on his own. If he were drinking
too much, or spending time with unsuitable people, it might have
made more sense.

"But who do you see on these walks?" she asked him.

"No one. Everyone."

"Heinrich always stays with us when he is here."

"He is the perfect son."

"But why do you stay out for hours?"

He smiled.

"For no reason."

Thomas felt timid and withdrawn, unable to present himself
to his mother with the confidence and panache of Heinrich. At
night, it came to him that he would be found out at Spinell's soon
unless he set himself to work with speed on the transcription of
the ledger. But he continued to write, relishing the idea that he
had plenty of paper and other supplies and, if he needed, he had
all day to rewrite a scene. When the story was accepted by a magazine, he enjoyed not telling anyone. He hoped that when his story
appeared in print no one might notice.

Herr Huhnemann had a way of looking at him intently and
then glancing away as if he had been caught breaking a rule. His
steel-gray hair stood on his head like little spikes. His face was long
and thin, his eyes a deep blue. Thomas found him unsettling, but
realized that holding the man's gaze, and then forcing Herr Huhnemann to look down, also gave him a strange sense of power. As
time went by, he knew that these small encounters, the mere meeting of eyes, were an important part of Herr Huhnemann's day.

One morning, soon after work began, Herr Huhnemann approached his desk.

"Everybody will be wondering how your great work is going," he said in a low and confidential voice. "I know that the head office will be making inquiries before long so I took a look myself. And you, you little scamp, have been idling. Not only idling but worse. I found many pages in your writing underneath the main ledger. Whatever it was, it was not what the company asked you to do. If you had just been slow, then we would understand."

He rubbed his hands together and moved closer to Thomas.

"Perhaps it was a mistake," he continued, "perhaps the work has been copied into some other ledger that is not on the desk. Could that be the case? What does young Herr Mann have to say for himself?"

"What do you intend to do?" Thomas asked him.

Herr Huhnemann smiled.

For a moment, Thomas thought that the man was contemplating some way of helping him, of making his indolence into a conspiracy in which they both could pleasurably share. Then he saw his colleague's face darken and his jaw set.

"I intend to report you, my boy," Herr Huhnemann whispered. "What do you have to say to that?"

Thomas put his hands behind his head and smiled.

"Why don't you do it now?"

On arriving home, Thomas found Heinrich's suitcase in the hall and Heinrich himself in the living room with his mother.

"I have been sent home from work," he said when his mother asked him why he was not at Spinell's.

"Are you ill?"

"No, I was found out. Instead of doing my work, I have been writing stories. This is a letter I have received from Albert Langen, the editor of the magazine *Simplicissimus*, accepting my most recent story. I care more about his opinion than I do about the entire future of fire insurance."

Heinrich indicated that he wished to see the letter.

"Albert Langen is a most respected figure," he said when he read it. "Most young writers, and many older ones, would give a great deal to receive such a letter. But that doesn't give you permission to walk out of work."

"Have you become my guardian?" Thomas asked.

"Clearly, you need one," his mother said. "Who gave you permission to come home from work?"

"I am not going back there," Thomas said. "I am determined to write more stories and a novel. If Heinrich is going to Italy, I want to go with him."

"What will your guardians think of this?"

"My time under their control will soon end."

"And what will you do for money?"

Thomas put his hands behind his head, as he had done with Herr Huhnemann, and smiled at his mother.

"I will appeal to you."

It took a week of sulking and cajoling and insisting that Heinrich be on his side.

"How will I explain it to the guardians?" his mother asked. "Someone from Spinell's might already have told them."

"Tell them I have consumption," Thomas said.

"Don't reply to the guardians," Heinrich added.

"Neither of you seems to understand that if I do not report to them, they can have my allowance cut off."

"Illness, then," Heinrich said. "Illness. Needs Italian air."

She shook her head.

"I don't take illness lightly," she said. "I think you should go back and apologize and learn to do your work."

"I won't go back," Thomas said.

He knew that his mother had, in fact, already concluded that he would not return to Spinell's. With Heinrich, he tried to work out how best to encourage her to give him an allowance. In the end, since his appeal to his mother had not succeeded, he appealed to his two sisters.

"It's bad for the family to have me in such a menial job."

"What will you do instead?" Lula asked.

"I'll write books, like Heinrich."

"No one I know reads books," Lula said.

"If you help me, I'll help you when you have a problem with Mother."

"Will you help me too?" Carla asked.

"I'll help both of you."

They told their mother that having two brothers who were writers would assist them socially in Munich. They would be invited to more places and noticed more.

Julia finally told him that she thought it best if he went to Italy. She had written a formal letter to the guardians to let them know that this was being done for health reasons, on the best advice. She sounded stern and in control.

"My only worry is that Italy is a place where people, I am told, walk in the streets at night. We have had enough of that. To this day, I can't imagine what you do in the streets. I am going to make Heinrich promise to make sure you are in your bed early."

As they made plans to travel south, Heinrich told him how much he had pleaded Thomas's cause with their mother. He said that he had told her that he admired Thomas's poetry. Thomas simply thanked him.

He liked the idea of traveling with someone whom he could not trust completely. It would encourage him, even more than usual, to share no secrets. They could discuss literature and even politics, perhaps music too, but, still alert to how much power Heinrich and their mother had over him, Thomas would remain wary of letting his brother find out anything that could be used against him in the future. He did not wish to return to fire insurance.

They went first to Naples, avoiding any Germans they saw, and then they traveled, using the mail coach, to Palestrina in the Sabine Hills east of Rome, situated above a valley, the roads lined with mulberry bushes, olive groves and vine garlands, the tilled fields divided into small holdings by stone walls. They settled in Casa Bernadini, where Heinrich had stayed before. It was a solid sober edifice on a sloping side street.

With a bedroom each, they shared a shaded, stone-floored living room, furnished with wicker chairs and horsehair sofas, where they had two desks installed so that they could work, like two hermits or two dutiful clerks, with their backs to each other.

The landlady, known to all as Nella, held court on the floor above, the large kitchen her headquarters. She informed the brothers that they had been preceded by a Russian aristocrat who had been visited by wandering spirits.

"I am glad," she said, "that he took the spirits with him. Palestrina has its own spirits and we do not need visiting ones."

While in Naples, Thomas had barely slept. His room was too hot, but also the sensations, as he strolled in the city during the day, were too strong. When, one morning, a young man followed him and his brother, he was aware how overdressed they were and formal, how much they stood out. The young man hissed at them in English first, but then, drawing closer, changed to German. He offered them girls. As the brothers ignored him and sought to get away from him, he came nearer still, held Thomas by the arm and whispered that he had girls, but not only girls. The tone was confidential and insinuating. The phrase "but not only girls" was clearly one he had used before.

When they had forced a way past him in the busy street, Heinrich nudged Thomas.

"It's better after dark and also better to be alone. He's just playing with us. Nothing ever happens during the day."

Heinrich sounded casual, worldly, but Thomas was unsure that it was not mere bravado. He looked at the run-down buildings in the narrow streets and asked himself if there were rooms, shadowy, guarded spaces, in some of those houses where transactions might take place. As Thomas studied faces, including the faces of young men, many of them fresh and exquisitely alive with beauty, he wondered if they, or young men like them, made themselves available when night fell.

He saw himself going out alone, quietly passing Heinrich's door. He pictured these streets at night, the waste, the fetid smell, the stray dogs, the sounds of voices from windows and doorways, perhaps figures standing at corners, watchful. He imagined how he might intimate to one of these men what it was he wanted.

"You look like a man with something on his mind," Heinrich said as they walked into a large square with a church on one side.

"The smells are all new to me," Thomas replied. "I was thinking of words I could use to describe them."

The atmosphere they had encountered in Naples filled Thomas's waking time and entered his dreams. Even as he worked on new stories in Palestrina, even as he could hear Heinrich's pen scratching against the paper when he wrote at the other desk, what might have happened in Naples on one of those nights gave him energy. He imagined being led into a room with a yellowish glare from a lamp, some broken furniture, a faded rug on the floor. And then a solemn young man in a suit and tie opened the door and closed it quietly behind him, his hair shiny black, his eyes dark, the expression on his face purposeful. Without speaking, without paying Thomas the slightest attention, the young man began to undress.

Trying to put away these thoughts, making a deal with himself that when he finished an episode in the story he could let his mind wander back to that moment in the room, he started to write again, realizing that the flushed vitality he felt was making its way into the very scene he was composing. When Heinrich's pen went silent, he found that he needed to go on writing so that the silence in the room would not be complete. Having finished the scene, he stood up noiselessly from his chair and, as he crossed the room, he saw Heinrich stealthily stuff some sheets of paper under a note-book.

Later, when Heinrich went out for a walk, Thomas lifted the notebook to find four or five pages beneath covered in drawings of naked women with enormous breasts. In some of the drawings he had included arms and legs, even hands and feet. In a few, the woman was holding a cigarette or a drink. But in all of them the breasts were large and bare, complete with carefully executed nipples.

How strange, he thought, that both of them, as they worked each day on their fiction, had something else on their minds, something that depended for its impact on the strength of their imaginations. He wondered if his father, as he made deals, as he visited the bank and sought to find partners for investments, had really been thinking all the time about more private matters that quickened his breath.

Often, when Heinrich was out walking, Thomas felt an urge to join him, but he knew that his brother's need for solitude was even greater than his own, or his brother's sense was more developed of how peculiar they would look, two young bachelor brothers out walking together.

Their landlady had two such brothers herself, both edging towards infirmity, who lived together. They came some evenings and sat in the kitchen, or appeared on Sundays after mass. Thomas was aware how odd they seemed, even in familiar surroundings. They were neither married nor single. They bore each other a sort of mild dislike. One of them had been a lawyer and there was some mystery over his retirement from that profession. It was often referred to by his brother, who was immediately ordered to be silent by his sister, the landlady. One brother was superstitious but the other brother, the lawyer, disapproved. When the superstitious one slyly informed Thomas and Heinrich that a man was obliged to place his right hand on his testicles on seeing a priest, the lawyer insisted that there was no such obligation.

"In fact," he said, "there is an obligation not to do any such thing. As there is an obligation to be rational. That is why we have minds."

Thomas wondered if he and Heinrich were a paler version of this pair. Once they relaxed into middle age, he thought, the similarities would become more apparent. They remained together now, he presumed, because it was easier to ask their mother for more money if the request came from both of them, combined with anecdotes about their travels and serious references to their work.

Only once in that Italian sojourn did the Mann brothers have an argument. It began when Heinrich expressed an opinion that Thomas had never heard before: he insisted that the unification of Germany had been a mistake and had served only to further Prussian dominance.

"They seized control," he said, "and all in the name of progress."

For Thomas, German unification, which took place the very year of Heinrich's birth and four years before he himself was born, was settled business. No one could dispute its value. It had evolved gradually as a project and then it made official something that was already clear. Germany was one nation. Germans spoke one language.

"You think Bavaria and Lübeck are part of the same nation?" Heinrich asked.

"Yes, I do."

"Germany, if I can use the word, contained two elements that were direct opposites. One was all emotion, about the language, the people, the folktales, the forest, the primeval past. It was all ridiculous. But the other was about money and control and power. It used the language of dreams to mask pure greed and naked ambition. Prussian greed. Prussian naked ambition. It will end badly."

"Will the unification of Italy end badly too?"

"No, just Germany. Prussia gained its hegemony by winning wars. It is controlled by the military. The Italian army is a joke. Try making a joke about the Prussian army."

"Germany is a great modern nation."

"You are talking nonsense. You often talk nonsense. You believe what you hear. You are a young poet who longs for lost love. But you are from a country that is interested in expansion, dominance. You must learn to think. You will never be a novelist unless you learn to think. Tolstoy could think. So could Balzac. It is a misfortune that you cannot think."

Thomas stood up and left the room. Over the days that followed he tried to formulate an argument that would show that Heinrich was wrong. It struck him that Heinrich might have been trying out an argument and that he had not really meant what he had said. Perhaps he had been arguing for the sake of it. He had never heard him say anything like that before.

Palazzo Barberini, overlooking the town, was a vast barracks. Without telling Heinrich, Thomas slipped away to visit the Nile mosaic from the second century B.C. that the guidebook referred to. There was a woman at the door who expressed surprise when Thomas materialized; she informed him in a melancholy tone what time the building would be closing. She directed him to the mosaic, which was guarded by a desultory-looking young man in threadbare livery.

What fascinated Thomas was the sheer dullness of the color of the mosaic, which must have faded with time, how much gray and watery blue now prevailed, how the color of slate and mud had come to dominate.

The washed light over the Nile made him think of the docks at Lübeck, the clouds blown back by the wind, his father telling him that he could, if he wished, run from one bollard to the next, but he must avoid tripping on ropes and must not go too close to the water.

His father was with one of his clerks; they were talking about ships and cargo and schedules. Drops of rain came, causing the two men to inspect the sky and put out their hands to see if it really did mean to pour down on them.

Something came to him then. He saw the novel he had been thinking about in its entirety. For this book, he would re-create himself as an only child and make his mother a delicate, musical German heiress. He would make Aunt Elisabeth a mercurial heroine. The hero would not be a person, but the family firm itself. And the atmosphere of mercantile confidence in Lübeck would be the background, but the firm would be doomed, as the only son of the family would be doomed.

Just as the artist of the mosaic had imagined a liquid world washed by cloud and by light from water, he would remake Lübeck. He would enter his father's spirit, and the spirits of his mother, his grandmother, his aunt. He would see all of them and chart the decline of their fortunes.

When they arrived back in Munich, Thomas began to map out the novel *Buddenbrooks*. Even though he saw Heinrich regularly, he told him little about the project, allowing him instead to see the stories he had been working on, which would soon be published in a book. But when he tried to concentrate solely on his work, he found Munich itself too distracting. He was taking too many walks, reading too many newspapers and literary journals and staying up too late. He needed to be in a place where the novel could take up all of his life and where there would be no temptation, at this early stage, to share its contents with anyone else.

He went to Rome, where he started to write the book in earnest. Knowing no one in the city gave him freedom. There must have been a place where young literary men gathered, but he did not try to find it. He moved the table in his small room to the window. He made a rule that if he wrote for half an hour, he could then lie on the narrow bed for ten minutes. He started work each day as soon as he woke.

The Lübeck he remembered came in disparate images, almost fragments. It was like something that had shattered and his memory held only shards. When he embarked on each scene he created a world that connected and was complete. It made him feel that he could rescue what had ended. The lives of the Manns in Lübeck would soon be forgotten, but if he could make this book succeed, a book that was growing longer than anything he had planned, the lives of the Buddenbrook family would matter in the future.

By the time he returned to Munich, he had completed the early chapters of the book.

Since Heinrich and Thomas had been published, they could, if they chose, join their colleagues in any of the literary cafés in Munich. As they moved from one café to another, they were recognized and sought out. Gradually, Thomas found himself sitting at the very tables in the very company that only a year earlier he had watched from afar.

Soon he found a part-time job on a magazine that allowed him to rent a small flat of his own. As often as he could, he worked late into the night on his book. On one of those evenings when he was almost twenty-three, when the novel was almost halfway done, he joined a group at a table that included two young men whom he did not know. He was interested in them because they were brothers who did not appear uneasy in each other's presence. They spoke to each other warmly as though they were friends or colleagues. They were Paul Ehrenberg and his brother Carl, both musicians, Carl studying at Cologne and Paul, who also studied painting, at Munich.

Thomas was amused at how naturally they both moved in and out of a sort of folksy way of speaking. Everything about them was whimsical. They had been brought up in Dresden, and they spoke to each other in imitation of some ancient burgher of that city, or some farmer from the surrounding countryside who had come into the city with pigs and a cartload of produce for the market. He tried to imagine himself and Heinrich imitating the people of Lübeck, but he did not think it was something that would amuse Heinrich.

As he got to know Paul, he made the mistake of introducing him to his family, to find that Paul harbored amorous thoughts about his sister Lula, and that his mother wished Paul to be a regular caller.

Sometimes the conversation between Thomas and Paul could be frank, as they agreed that male sexuality was complex and could take many turns. It was tacitly acknowledged that they shared certain feelings. So when they spoke of avoiding loose women or women of the street and expressed an interest instead in high-class ladies, Thomas understood that, since high-class ladies were not easily obtainable, this was a code for something else.

They began to meet alone in the cafés less frequented by their literary and artistic friends and to find a table at the back of the establishment rather than sit in the glare of the front window. They did not feel compelled to speak. They could each look into the distance, live with unspoken thoughts, and then catch each other's eye and let the gaze linger.

Paul was the only one whom Thomas told about the novel. It started as a joke when he let Paul know just how many pages he had completed, with no end in sight.

"No one will read it," he said. "No one will publish it."

"Why don't you shorten it?" Paul asked.

"It needs every scene. It is the story of decline. In order to make the decline matter I have to show the family at their most confident."

He had to try not to be too earnest about the book, content to play the part of the self-indulgent writer in attic quarters producing a book with a mixture of wild ambition and supreme lack of caution. He understood that Paul knew he was serious, but Paul also found his efforts to return to a discussion of his work-in-progress tedious.

One evening, it was clear that Paul did not know how to react to revelations about his novel.

"I killed myself in the novel today," Thomas said. "It began last night. I will read it over and make some changes, but it is done. I found the details in a medical textbook."

"Will everyone know it is you?"

"Yes. I am the boy Hanno and he has died of typhoid."

"Why did you kill him?"

"The family cannot go on. He is the last of the family."

"There is no one left?"

"Just his mother."

Paul became silent and seemed uncomfortable. Thomas realized that he would soon tire of the subject.

"I had come to love him," he went on, "his delicacy, his way of playing music, his solitude, his suffering. All these elements of him I knew, because they were elements of me. I felt a strange control over him and I wanted not to let him live, as though I had found a way of overseeing my own death, directing it sentence by sentence, living it as if it were something sensual."

"Sensual?"

"That is what I felt when I wrote it."

• • •

Since Paul knew how much these meetings meant to Thomas as he came to the end of his novel, he started to tease him by changing plans at short notice or by dropping a note around to Thomas's apartment to cancel a tryst. Paul was the one with the power. Sometimes he pulled Thomas close to him, and then, without warning, he let the rope slacken.

On the day Thomas got news that the novel would be published in two volumes, he needed to find Paul to tell him. He tried his home address first and left a note there, and then at Paul's studio. He went to the various cafés, but it was too early. Finally, after supper, he located Paul. He was surrounded by fellow artists. When Thomas, having sat down with them, tried to talk to him, Paul did not respond, but joined in the laughter at the expense of some professor who lectured on light and shade.

"For shade, you must mix the gray and the brown and then add some blue," Paul said, doing an imitation of an old man. "But the mix must be the right mix. The wrong mix will get the wrong shade."

As the conversation went on, Thomas turned to Paul, who was two places away from him.

"My novel has been accepted," he said.

Paul smiled remotely and then turned to the young man on the other side of him. For the next hour, Thomas sought to get his full attention, but Paul did further imitations of people or made jokes about colleagues. He even did his imitation of a farmer selling a field to another farmer. He would not catch Thomas's eye. When Thomas finally decided to leave, he imagined that Paul might follow him. But he found himself alone in the street, and walked back on his own to his apartment.

When his novel came out, it was clear to some what he had achieved. But word came from Lübeck that it was an insult to the city. His aunt Elisabeth expressed her dislike of the book in a curt note to his mother.

"I am recognized in the street, and not as myself, but that terrible woman in the book. And this was all done without anyone's permission. It would kill my mother if she were still alive. He is a little pup, that son of yours."

Thomas heard nothing from Heinrich, who was living in Berlin, and even wondered if a letter from him might have gone astray. His mother showed *Buddenbrooks* to all her visitors, insisting that she loved the portrait her son had painted of her.

"I am so musical in the book. Now, I *am* musical, of course, but in the book, I am much more talented and dedicated than I really am. I will have to practice my scales to get to be as good as Gerda. But I think I am more intelligent than she is, or so I have been told."

In the cafés, some of the writers and painters suggested that the last thing Munich needed was another two-volume novel about a declining family. Complaining to Paul, who professed to admire the novel, Thomas insisted that he would be more celebrated had he written a short book of confused poems about the dark side of his soul.

His sisters wanted to know why they had been excluded.

"People will think we didn't exist," Carla said.

"And I hope no one associates us with that ghastly little Hanno," Lula added. "Mother says that he is exactly like you when you were that age."

Thomas understood that while the book was based on the Manns in Lübeck, there was some source for it that was outside of himself, beyond his control. It was like something in magic, something that would not come again so easily. The praise he received also made him realize how much the success of the book masked his failure in other areas.

He remained secretive. Indeed, he had never confessed to Paul what he actually wanted from him. But, as his time in Munich went on, he grew increasingly sure that what was between them would have to change. Were Paul to visit him, it would just take an hour, maybe two, on one of those winter evenings for everything to be transformed.

One evening, in a fit of impatience, losing all the guarded-ness that usually protected him, he wrote to Paul, saying that he longed for someone who would say yes to him. Sending the letter made him feel elated, but that did not last long. When they met the next time, Paul did not refer to the letter. Instead, he smiled at him, touched his hand, talked to him about painting and music. At the end of the evening he put his arms around him and held him close, whispering some words of endearment as though they were already lovers. Thomas wondered if he were not being mocked.

In the light of morning, he could ask himself what he wanted from Paul. Did he want a night of love, each of them yielding to the other? He recoiled from the thought of sleeping with another man, waking in his arms, feeling their legs touch.

Instead, he wanted Paul to appear in lamplight in his study. He wanted to touch his hands, his lips; he wanted to help him undress.

More than anything, he wished to live intensely in the vora-cious moments before this, in the sure knowledge that it would happen.

Thomas awaited a visit to Munich from Heinrich. At first, he was determined not to ask his mother if she had heard from his elder brother about the book. When his resolve failed him, he immedi-ately regretted it.

"I have had several letters from Heinrich," his mother said, "and he seems very busy. He did not mention the book at all. He will visit soon, and then we will hear all about his opinion of it."

Thomas presumed that Heinrich, as the family had supper together after his arrival, was waiting to discuss the novel with him once the others had gone to bed. Later, in the living room as Heinrich and Carla talked, he was tempted to raise the matter, but because of the intimate way they spoke, it was impossible for him to intervene. Eventually, Thomas left, feeling relieved to be on the street, away from his family.

He became resigned to the idea that Heinrich was not going to make any comment on *Buddenbrooks*. One Sunday morning, however, when he called, he found that Heinrich was alone in the apartment, the others having gone to church. After discussing the habits of a number of magazine editors for a while, they fell silent. Heinrich began to flick through a magazine.

"It struck me that you never received my book," Thomas said.

"I read it, and will read it again. Perhaps we can discuss it when I have read it the second time?"

"Or perhaps not?"

"It changes everything about the family, how people will see our mother and father. How they see you. People will feel they know us everywhere we go."

"Would you like one of your books to do that?"

"I think novels should not deal so obsessively with private life."

"*Madame Bovary*?"

"I see that as a book about changing mores, a changing society."

"And my book?"

"It may be about that. Yes, it may. But readers will feel more that they are peering in through a window."

"That might be the perfect description of what a novel is."

"In that case, you have written a masterpiece. I should not be surprised that you are already so famous."

• • •

The novel went into a second edition, so Thomas had more money to spend. As Carla grew more interested in becoming an actress, Thomas often bought tickets for plays and the opera. One evening, as they sat in the front seats of a box at the opera, she drew his attention to a family that was arriving, with much fuss and animation, in a box across from them.

"They are the children from that painting," she said. "Look at them!"

Thomas did not know what she meant.

"They were dressed as Pierrots," she said, "in that magazine, and you cut it out and pinned it to the wall of your bedroom in Lübeck. They are the Pringsheims. No one can get an invitation to their house. You have to be Gustav Mahler to be invited."

He remembered a painting of several children, including one sole girl, reproduced in a magazine his mother had brought home. He remembered their black hair, the girl's large, expressive eyes, and the placid beauty of her brothers. More than anything he remembered the glamour of these young people, and a sort of youthful arrogance and insouciance in the way they gazed out from the picture. No one in Lübeck, except his mother, had ever looked like that.

Since his mother had often made clear her longing, when their father was still alive, to visit Munich and enjoy its easy bohemian mores, he had pinned this picture to the wall as a way of offering her solidarity. These were the sort of people with whom he wanted to associate when he was older; but more than that, these were the sort of people he wanted to be.

He studied the Pringsheim family as they made themselves comfortable in the box. The sister and her brother sat at the front, their parents behind. That, in itself, was unusual. The impression the girl gave was dignified, withdrawn, almost sad. When her brother whispered to her, she did not respond. Her haircut was noticeably short. She had grown up since the portrait was painted, but she still had something childlike about her. When her brother whispered to her again, laughing this time, she shook her head as if to let him know that she did not find him amusing. When she turned to look at her parents, she seemed self-contained, preoccupied. As the lights went down, Thomas looked forward to the first interval, when he could observe her again.

"They are fabulously rich," Carla said. "The father is a professor but they have other money."

"Are they Jewish?" Thomas asked.

"I don't know," she said. "But they must be. Their house is like a museum. Not that I have ever been invited there."

In the months that followed, if any Wagner were playing, the Pringsheims were in the audience; they were also to be seen at concerts of modern or experimental music. Thomas did not worry about staring at the daughter. Since he thought he would never actually meet her, her reaction to him hardly mattered.

As more people read his book, it occurred to him that he himself was being observed at concerts and plays, in cafés and in the street. Also, the Pringsheim girl, when she was at a concert, let him know that she knew he was watching her. Her gaze in response to his was open and fearless. Her brother, he saw, had noticed him too.

One evening as he sat with some literary young men at the table nearest the window in a café, he found himself conversing with a poet whom he did not know well. The fellow appeared frail and shy. He hesitated before he spoke and had to squint to read the menu in the café.

"There are friends of mine who talk all the time about you," he said.

"They have read my book?" Thomas asked.

"They like how you watch them at concerts. They call you Hanno, after the boy in your novel who dies."

Thomas realized that the poet was speaking of the girl, the Pringsheim girl, and her brother.

"What is her name?"

"Katia."

"And her brother's?"

"Klaus. He is her twin. They have three older brothers."

"What does the twin do?"

"Music. He has a great talent. He has studied with Mahler. But so does Katia have a great talent."

"For music?"

"She studies science. Her father is a mathematician. And a fanatical Wagnerian. She is very cultivated."

"Could I meet them?"

"She and her brother admire your book. And they think you are too much alone."

"Why do they think that?"

"Because they watch you as much as you watch them. Maybe more. You are one of their subjects."

"Should I be proud?"

"I would be."

"Are you one of their subjects too?"

"No. I am merely a poet. My aunt goes to their house on Arcisstrasse. It is very splendid. That is how I know them. Because of my aunt who is a painter. They collect her work."

"Do you think I could meet them?"

"Perhaps they could invite you to one of their evenings at home. They don't go to cafés."

"When?"

"Soon. They will have an evening soon."

When Thomas called on his mother, he often found gentlemen who would previously have been deemed unsuitable making themselves comfortable in the small living room. Heinrich had expressed concern for the reputation of his sisters and Thomas

shared his unease. They thus had the disintegration of standards in their mother's apartment as a topic to discuss, a topic
that allowed them both to present themselves as wise men of the
world, worried about appearances, as though their father's ghost
had wandered into the space between them to encourage them to
pay homage to the gods of respectability.

Among the gentlemen who called at his mother's was a banker
called Josef Löhr. Thomas, when he was introduced to him, presumed that he had come to court his mother, who was becoming
more vague and ethereal. Some of her teeth, Thomas saw, were
loosening. If she wanted to become Frau Löhr she had better be
quick about it.

He was surprised when it became clear that Löhr was coming to the apartment to seek the hand not of the mother but of
his sister Lula, who was almost twenty years his junior. Lula had
nothing at all in common with the banker, who was banal and
unashamedly bourgeois. Löhr was the sort of man, Paul Ehrenberg said, who, if money were to pour from heaven, would advise
those around him to think carefully before spending it. Lula, on
the other hand, liked spending money; she enjoyed outings and
laughter. Thomas wondered what she and Löhr might ever talk
about during the long nights of marriage.

Paul disapproved of the engagement when it was announced
because he liked to have all of them, even the mother, in thrall
to him. He enjoyed playing with them. But Heinrich, who had
returned to Berlin, was even more disapproving. He wrote to
their mother urging her that she forbid the match and insisting
that she close her apartment to all gentlemen, since she could not
be trusted to chaperone her daughters with any form of diligence.
He did not care how well placed this banker was, he went on.
Löhr would not do for Lula. He would bore her to death if he
did not smother her with his demands. The thought of his sister
organizing the household of Josef Löhr made him ill, he wrote.

His mother handed the letter to Thomas.

"He must think that suitable men grow on trees," she said.

"I think he loves his sisters."

"That may be so, it's just a pity he can't marry one of them—or indeed both of them."

As Thomas gave his mother the letter back, he noticed how defeated she looked. It was not merely that she was wearing too much makeup and the color of her hair was unnatural. It was in her voice and in her eyes. The old sparkle had gone from her, now completely extinguished by the news of her daughter's engagement.

There were, he guessed, more than a hundred people at the Pringsheims' supper, the first one he attended, with tables spread over several of the reception rooms. Most of these rooms had carved ceilings and inlaid paintings and murals. No surface was undecorated. He arrived, accompanied by the nervous young poet and the poet's aunt, the painter, who wore many glittering jewels around her neck and in her hair.

"The Pringsheim boys, especially Klaus and Peter, are a lesson to the youth of Munich," the aunt said. "They are refined and civilized. They have already achieved such a great deal."

Thomas wanted to ask her what precisely they had achieved, but as soon as they had handed over their coats, she moved away from them, leaving the two young men to linger in the shadows, watching the scene.

A few times he caught Katia Pringsheim's eye and, while she seemed amused at his presence, she did not acknowledge him directly. Once supper was over, he asked his friend to introduce him to Katia and Klaus, who were standing in the doorway having an intense conversation. He could see Katia smiling as she interrupted her brother, putting her finger to his lips to stop him speaking. Although they must have been conscious that Thomas and the poet were approaching, they did not turn. The poet reached out and touched Klaus's shoulder.

As Klaus looked at him, Thomas saw how beautiful he was. He almost understood why Klaus did not frequent the cafés. He would have been singled out and stared at. His politeness, the understatement in his tone, the neatness of his dress, would have stood apart from the abrasiveness and the shabbiness then in vogue.

Thomas, aware that Katia was watching him as he took in her brother, directed his full attention to her. Her eyes were the same deep dark color as her brother's, her skin was even softer; her gaze was unembarrassed.

"Your book is much admired in this house," Klaus said. "In fact, we all fell out because one of us hid the second volume."

Katia stretched lazily. He could see the boyish strength in her body.

"I will not mention the culprit," Klaus went on.

"My brother is tedious," Katia said.

"We call you Hanno," Klaus said.

"Some of us do," Katia said.

"We all do, even my mother, who hasn't finished the book yet."

"She has finished it."

"As of two p.m. today, she had not finished it."

"I told her the end," Katia said.

"My sister spoils things for people. She told me the end of *Die Walküre*."

"My father had already told us and I was worried that he'd find out you hadn't been listening."

"Our brother Heinz told us the end of the Bible," Klaus said. "And it ruined everything."

"That was, in fact, Peter," Katia said. "He is horrible. Our father had to ban him from gatherings."

"My sister spends her life listening to our father," Klaus said. "She actually studies with him."

Thomas looked from one to the other. Their conversation, he sensed, was their underhand way of laughing at him, or at least excluding him and his companion. He knew that, on arriving home, he would remember every word they had said. When he had cut out the portrait of the young Pringsheims from that magazine, this was what he had imagined—a world filled with elegant people and rich interiors, with conversations going on that were both clever and oddly inconsequential. He did not mind that the décor was perhaps too rich, and that some of the people were too effusive. He minded nothing as long as these two young people continued to allow him to listen to them and watch them.

"Oh no!" Katia exclaimed. "My mother is being held in a vise-like grip by that woman whose husband plays the viola."

"Why was she invited?" Klaus asked.

"Because you or my father or Mahler or someone admires how her husband plays the viola."

"My father knows nothing about the viola."

"My grandmother thinks there should be a ban on any woman marrying," Katia said. "Imagine how different these rooms would be if people had only listened to her."

"My grandmother is Hedwig Dohm," Klaus said to Thomas as though he were confiding in him. "She is very advanced."

As they left the house, the young poet told Thomas that he had asked his aunt if the Pringsheims were Jewish.

"What did she say?" Thomas asked.

"They used to be. On both sides. But not anymore. They are Protestants now, even though they seem very Jewish. Jewish in a grand way."

"They converted?"

"My aunt said that they assimilated."

• • •

One evening, when Thomas had reached the entrance to his building, having stayed late with Paul and his brother in a café, someone came up behind him while he was fumbling to put his key in the lock. When he turned, he saw a tall, thin, middle-aged man with glasses. It took him a moment to recognize Herr Huhnemann from Spinell's.

"I need to speak with you," Herr Huhnemann said in a hushed, hoarse voice.

Thomas thought he was in some trouble, that he had been attacked or perhaps robbed. He wondered how he knew where he lived. The street was deserted. He felt that he had no choice but to invite Herr Huhnemann into the building. When he got to his apartment door, however, he had second thoughts.

"Do you really need to see me tonight?" he asked.

"Yes," Herr Huhnemann said.

In the apartment, he invited his guest to remove his coat. Once it was established that he had no injuries, Thomas thought, Herr Huhnemann could go. He might need money for a cab.

"It took me a while to get your address," Herr Huhnemann said as they sat opposite each other in the small living room. "But I found a friend of yours in a café and I told him it was urgent."

Thomas looked at him, bewildered. The hair was still gray and spiky. But there was something else apparent now that he had never seen before, a sort of delicacy in the features that became more noticeable when his guest was silent.

"I want to ask your forgiveness," Herr Huhnemann said.

Thomas was about to say that he was grateful for being found out at Spinell's, but Huhnemann stopped him.

"Since I had a key to the building, I could gain access to the office when it was empty. I must confess to you that I would go there at night just to touch the seat where you sat. I would do more. I would put my whole face down on that seat. And all I wanted during the day was some response from you."

It struck Thomas that it might have been Paul Ehrenberg who had given this man his address.

"No matter what I did, no matter how many times I passed, no matter how many times I spoke to you, you saw me as merely another clerk in the office. And then, when I observed that you had not been copying the ledger, I took my revenge on you. I must ask your forgiveness. I cannot sleep unless I have your forgiveness."

"You have my forgiveness," Thomas said.

"Is that all?"

When Huhnemann stood up, Thomas presumed that he was preparing to leave. He stood too. Huhnemann moved slowly towards him and kissed him. At first, it was just his lips against Thomas's, but then he slid his tongue into Thomas's mouth as he put his hands inside Thomas's shirt and then, with more deliberation, let his hands edge lower. His breath was sweet. He waited for a response before he did anything else.

What happened between them seemed natural, as though no other set of actions was possible. Herr Huhnemann, clearly, had more experience than Thomas. Thus, he could guide him and encourage him. Naked, he was tender and vulnerable, almost soft. Compared to his severity during the day, this was strange. He came to climax with astonishing gasps like a man suddenly possessed by some demon.

It was only when Huhnemann had left that Thomas began to believe that he had not actually wanted what had occurred. Huhnemann had managed to lure him into it. It had been gradual and enacted with skill. Once he had dressed himself, he felt the deep revulsion he should have felt as soon as Huhnemann had made his intentions plain.

He got his coat. The street was still empty. Huhnemann had

disappeared into the night. Whatever happened in the future, Thomas determined, that man would never gain access to his apartment again. If he ever presented himself at his doorway, Thomas would let him know that what had occurred between them would not ever be repeated.

He found a café that was quiet and stayed open late and he sat at a table towards the back. He ordered a coffee. What disturbed him most was his own reaction. He had wanted to be kissed and touched, even by Huhnemann, whom he had viewed before only as a bustling middle-aged man whose attention irritated him, a busybody who caused him to be found out at work.

How was it that he had felt even a sliver of desire for him? Would he, as he grew older, wait at night in the hope that Huhnemann or someone like him would approach his building on the chance that there was a light on in his living room? Would he have to watch as his visitor hastily dressed himself, unwilling even to catch his eye?

Or would he meet other versions of Paul, who would tease him and fill his dreams? Would he be known in Munich, or in whatever city he moved to, as a man who could be discreetly visited at night?

He stood up to pay, sure what he was going to do. The certainty remained with him as he walked home and was even more present when he woke in the morning. He would ask Katia Pringsheim to marry him. If she refused, he would ask her again. Once the dream of marrying her came into his mind, he felt a new sort of contentment.

Over the next while the battle lines were carefully drawn on the question of whether Katia should accept his offer of marriage. Her grandmother was vehemently opposed to the idea, while her mother greatly favored the match. Katia's father thought that, if she were marrying anyone, he should be a professor rather than a writer.

Thomas's mother, in turn, thought Katia was spoiled by her rich family. She wished that Thomas would ally himself with someone sweeter, less inclined to show off. Heinrich, who was now in Italy, wrote to Thomas mainly on literary matters while his sisters expressed themselves happy to have Katia as a sister-in-law.

As he sat with the twins Katia and Klaus, Thomas realized the extent of the chasm between them and him. They had never known loss. They had never been uprooted from anywhere. It was presumed from childhood that they were talented; they were encouraged to follow wherever their talents led. Had one of the family wanted to be a clown, then they would have proudly been given a false nose and sent to the circus. But they did not wish to be clowns. They were musicians and scientists. Each one of them excelled at something. And each one of them would inherit a fortune. While Katia's father could behave like a distracted mathematician, he managed the vast amount of money and the valuable property and shares he had inherited from his father. He made clear to Thomas a number of times that his only daughter was, in his opinion, the most intelligent of his children. She could, if she were ready to make sacrifices, become a distinguished scientist.

The Pringsheims took for granted a knowledge of literature and music and painting. A few times when Thomas found himself talking at some length about a writer or a book, he noticed Katia and Klaus surreptitiously glancing at each other. It must have seemed, he thought, as if he were trying to display his learning. That was something that the Pringsheims never did. They had no time for earnestness.

When, in a letter, he first proposed marriage to Katia, she replied to say that she was perfectly happy as she was. She enjoyed her studies, she wrote, as well as the company of her family and her time spent cycling and playing tennis. She was only twenty-one, she emphasized, eight years younger than he was. She had no desire for a husband or for a role as manager in the domestic sphere.

Every time he saw her, he felt exposed. She often said little, leaving him and her brother to talk. Klaus refused to be serious. From the beginning, also, Klaus understood the effect he could have on Thomas, how he could draw Thomas's eyes from his sister to himself. The game Klaus played with Thomas appeared to amuse Katia.

Her handwriting was almost childish, her epistolary style pithy and simple. Thomas realized that the only way he could get her attention was by writing her long and complex letters, the sort of letters that he might write to Heinrich. Since he could not prevail if he attempted to be sophisticated or effortlessly stylish like her brothers, then he would not try. Instead, he would take her seriously as no one else ever had by writing to her with considerable gravity. One risk was that his letters would bore her. But the other possibility was that Katia, coming from a family that, despite all their wit and irony, viewed artists with respect, would see him as a novelist in command of his own thoughts, rather than a nervous, overenthusiastic son of a Lübeck merchant.

One evening, as he sat in a café, he saw Paul Ehrenberg enter. They had not been in touch for some time.

"I hear that you have found a princess and are seeking to awaken her," he said.

Thomas smiled.

"Marriage is not for you," Paul said. "You should know that."

Thomas indicated that Paul should keep his voice down.

"Everyone at this table knows that marriage is not for you. Anyone who follows your eyes can see where they land."

"How is your work?" Thomas asked.

Paul shrugged, ignoring his question.

"She is young, your princess. And rich."

Thomas did not respond.

Paul waited for a week before he appeared without warning at the door of Thomas's apartment. It had been raining and his clothes were wet. Thomas found him a towel for his hair and a hanger for his overcoat. He thought that Paul had perhaps come to talk about Julia, who had announced her intention of leaving Munich to live in rural Bavaria.

"I hope you will advise her not to contemplate such a move," Thomas said.

"I have already told her that I don't know what she might do in rural Bavaria. Most people would do anything not to live there."

"She thinks my younger brother will do better in a rural school."

Thomas wondered how long they could go on talking like this. He went to the two windows and pulled down the blinds.

"What were you about to say?" Paul asked.

"Nothing."

"I don't think you should marry," Paul said.

"I will surprise you, then," Thomas replied.

Chapter 4
Munich, 1905

Once the engagement was announced, the Pringsheims gave a dinner for Julia Mann, her daughter Lula and her son-in-law, Josef Löhr. It was the first formal dinner that Thomas had attended in their house. On entering the main drawing room, Löhr exclaimed: "I would say that all of this cost a pretty penny." Katia turned to smile at Thomas as if to suggest that there was no remedy for his brother-in-law's banality. He wished that Carla were not on tour with a play; her abilities as an actress might be some use in this company.

They were received with warmth and openness by Katia's parents. With great ceremony, the mother oversaw the serving of drinks while Katia's father directed his remarks on the day's news to Löhr, who replied suitably. When they were called to the dining room, Thomas's mother had wandered into one of the farthest reception rooms, where he found her examining the fabric on a set of chairs. He encouraged her to follow him to the dining room. While the food was served, she remained silent, attempting, Thomas thought, to play the part of a demure, refined widow.

A glass vase holding an orchid stood close to each setting on the table. The glassware and tableware were old, Thomas thought, but he could not be sure how old. The candelabra looked modern. All around them on the walls hung modern pictures. If this were Lübeck, Thomas saw, his mother would be familiar with this house, invited regularly. She would be able to talk freely to Katia's father about his neighbors and his colleagues. She would speak to him with teasing familiarity about his decorative skills and his taste in art. She would find that she had friends in common with his wife.

Here at the Pringsheims', however, Julia Mann was out of her depth. Alfred Pringsheim was not a merchant. He did not own shops or warehouses or export anything. He was merely a professor of mathematics who had inherited money from his father, who had invested in coal and railways. While he could look after his money, he enjoyed declaring that he knew nothing whatsoever about making it. And he was not even sure he knew how to spend it, he would add. He had built the house because he needed shelter and bought the paintings because he and his wife admired them.

"Where do you do your banking, might I ask?" Löhr responded.

"Oh, I always say that I myself look after my family," Alfred said, "and the Bethmanns look after me."

"That makes sense," Löhr replied. "Bethmann's. A good old firm. Jewish."

"That has nothing to do with it," Alfred said. "I would bank with Bavarian Catholics if I thought they knew anything about money."

"Well, if you were ever changing bankers, I could introduce you to the very best people. I mean, investment bankers who have their ear to the ground and know which way the wind is blowing."

Katia looked at Thomas, her gaze filled with irony.

"The man who thinks too much about money is himself poor," Alfred said. "That is my motto."

He sipped his wine, nodded his head and sipped his wine again.

"I wonder if there will come a time when there won't be banks at all, when there won't even be money," he said.

Löhr looked at him sharply.

"In the meantime," Pringsheim added, "every morning I feel a little thrill when I wake to find that my bedcover is made of silk. Strange for a man who doesn't care about money!"

Thomas noticed that his mother was looking around the room, taking in the paintings and pieces of sculpture and then moving her attention to the carved ceiling, craning her neck to see the elaborate designs between the beams.

While Hedwig Pringsheim, Katia's mother, made sure that everyone had enough to eat and drink, a few times signaling to her husband that he should let others speak, she herself did not contribute to the conversation at all. Her silence seemed like an artful way of asserting herself.

The evening was more relaxed because Klaus Pringsheim was in Vienna. Katia did not have anyone with whom to share her amusement. Instead, her brother Heinz, a student of physics, immensely proper, sat at the table like a young man destined for a military career. When his face was in repose, he appeared to Thomas even more beautiful than Klaus, the skin of his face smoother, his hair shinier, his lips fuller.

As Thomas heard Katia trying to make conversation with his sister, explaining the family's love for the music of Wagner and, in recent years, Mahler, he felt even more deeply the difference between his own family and the family into which he was marrying.

"And we love hardly anyone in between," Katia said. "My mother is almost more particular than my father."

"She likes Mahler too?" Lula asked.

"Gustav Mahler is an old friend of hers," Katia said and smiled innocently. "He always says that Vienna would be perfect if only my mother could come and live there. He admires her hugely. But she can't live in Vienna because my father's work is here."

"But did your father not mind him saying that?"

"Luckily, my father never listens to anyone. He listens to music. Maybe that is enough. So he doesn't know what Mahler says. He thinks about mathematics most of the time. There are theorems named for him."

Thomas could see that Lula did not know what a theorem was.

"It must be wonderful living in this beautiful house," Lula said.

"Tommy says that your family owned a beautiful house in Lübeck," Katia replied.

"But not like this!"

"I think there are better houses in Munich," Katia said. "But we have this, so what can we do?"

"Enjoy it, I suppose," Lula said.

"Well, I'm getting married to your brother, so I won't be enjoying it for much longer."

A few times in the weeks before the wedding, Thomas managed to kiss Katia, but her twin brother hovered too much for him to be comfortable, and Katia had a way of suggesting to him that he should exercise discretion while making clear also that she found the restrictions imposed on her almost a joke.

When Klaus entered the room, having briefly left them alone together, he would smile insinuatingly. Often, he would go straight to his sister and tickle her, making her squirm and giggle. Thomas wished Klaus would devote more time to his music and perhaps allow his brother Peter to take his place and represent the family with more decorum.

Because Katia spent a deal of time in her room preparing herself for outings, Klaus sat with Thomas, discussing art and music in a lazy, relaxed way, or questioning him about his life.

"I have never been to Lübeck," he said one day while Katia was upstairs. "And no one I know has ever been to Hamburg, let alone Lübeck. Munich must be strange for you. I feel free here. Freer than in Berlin or Frankfurt or indeed Vienna. In Munich, for example, if you wanted to kiss a boy, no one would mind. Can you imagine the fuss such a thing would create in Lübeck?"

Thomas smiled faintly, pretending that he had barely taken in what Klaus had said. If Klaus persisted, he thought, he would find a new subject and make sure that they did not return to this one.

"Of course, it would all depend on whether the boy actually wanted to be kissed or not," Klaus said. "I think most boys do."

"Does Mahler make much money?" Thomas asked.

He knew that the subject of Mahler would be too enticing for Klaus.

"He lives quite comfortably," Klaus said. "But he worries about everything. That is his nature. In the middle of a huge symphony, he worries about the few notes he has written for some poor little piccolo player who is hiding at the back."

"And Mahler's wife?"

"She bewitched him. She loved his fame. She behaves as though he is the only man in the world. She is beautiful. She enchants me."

"Who enchants you?" Katia said as she came into the room.

"You do, my twin, my double, my delight. Only you."

Katia made her hands into claws to scratch his face. She let out a loud animal sound.

"Who wrote the rule that twins cannot marry each other?" Klaus asked. He made the question sound serious.

Thomas, as he examined the twins, one of whom he was to marry, realized that he would never be completely included in the little world they created.

Neither he nor Katia complained when Alfred Pringsheim set about furnishing their apartment without consulting them. On the third floor of a building on Franz-Joseph-Strasse, it had seven rooms and two water closets and a view over the park of the Prince

Leopold Palace. Alfred installed a telephone for them and a baby grand piano.

It did not occur to Thomas that Alfred would decide also on the decoration for his study. Since he had thought of this as a private domain, he was surprised to find that a desk had been chosen for him and bookcases made, designed by Alfred himself. He thanked his father-in-law profusely, pleased at the thought that Alfred did not detect his determination not to be beholden to the Pringsheims ever again, nor sit at their table more than was entirely necessary.

His mother was aghast that the wedding was not to be held in a church.

"What are they?" she asked. "If they are Jewish, why don't they come out and say so?"

"Katia's mother's family became Protestants."

"And her father?"

"He has no religion."

"He does not have much respect for marriage either, I believe. Your brother-in-law says that he has actually entertained his mistress, an actress, in his own drawing room. I trust we will be spared her at the wedding."

The meal after the civil ceremony was, Thomas thought, such a desultory affair that it would have been much improved by the presence of an actress. Katia's family could not conceal their sorrow at losing their daughter. Klaus paid too much attention to Julia, Thomas thought, giving her an opportunity to air her resentments and her memories of grand events in Lübeck, glancing regularly at Katia to register his amusement at her new mother-in-law. Only Viktor, Thomas's younger brother, now fourteen, seemed to enjoy the day.

Katia and Thomas went by train to Zürich. The Pringsheims had reserved them the finest quarters in the Hotel Baur au Lac. In the dining room, having dressed for dinner, Thomas was aware what a picture they made, the famous writer not yet thirty and his young bride from a rich family, one of the few women ever to go to university in Munich, her tone self-assured and sardonic, her clothes understated and expensive.

Throughout the meal, he imagined Katia naked, her white skin, her full lips, her small breasts, her strong legs. As she spoke, her voice low, he saw that she could easily be a boy.

That night, he was excited as soon as Katia came close to him. He could not believe that he was allowed to touch her, that he could put his hand wherever he liked on her body. She kissed him with her tongue, opening her mouth wide. She was fearless. But, when he heard her breathing with greater intensity and he realized what she wanted from him, he became hesitant, almost afraid. But he continued to explore her, nudged her to turn on her side so that he could lie facing her, her nipples touching his chest, his hands on her buttocks, his tongue in her mouth.

He was intrigued by Katia's way of speaking, her response to the books she read and the music she heard and the galleries they visited. In conversation, she had a way of finding the very center of an argument and following a logic that she established from the beginning. Opinions did not interest her. Rather, she was concerned with the shape of a discussion and on what basis conclusions were drawn.

She applied her mind to small matters, such as whether there should be art books on the low table in the main sitting room in the apartment, or if an extra lamp were needed, setting out reasons for and against. In the same spirit, she examined his contracts and his bank accounts, and got to know about his finances. She began to manage his affairs in a way that appeared effortless.

She was unlike his sisters and his mother in every possible way. He wished that Heinrich would return from Italy and could know her, since Heinrich was the only one with whom he could share his fascination by what seemed to him to be her Jewishness. A few times, when he tried to encourage her to talk about her heritage, she made it clear that she did not want to discuss it.

"Even in the wildest arguments we have had in our family, we never talked about that," she said. "You see, it does not interest us. My parents love music and books and paintings and witty, intelligent company, as do my brothers, as do I. You can hardly put this down to a religion that we do not even practice. Such a thought is absurd."

When they were a few months married, they went to Berlin to stay with Katia's aunt Else Rosenberg and her husband. Thomas loved the grandeur of their house in Tiergarten and was flattered at how well the Rosenbergs knew *Buddenbrooks*. What surprised him was how nonchalantly and casually they spoke about their Jewishness, and how relaxed Katia was when this matter was alluded to. The Rosenbergs did not go to the synagogue, he discovered, and did not even recognize High Holy Days, but they referred to themselves, often jokingly and self-deprecatingly, as Jewish. It appeared to amuse them.

Like the Pringsheims, the Rosenbergs loved Wagner. One evening as they sat in the large drawing room after dinner, Katia's uncle found the sheet music for piano for some of *Die Walküre*. When Else asked him if he would locate the scene between Brünnhilde and Siegmund and Sieglinde, he searched and found it, then studied it for a while, but said it was too difficult to play. Instead, he began to sing Brünnhilde's lines in a light tenor voice and then, deepening his voice, he sang Siegmund's lines as Siegmund asked Brünnhilde if his twin sister, the woman whom he loved, could come to Valhalla with them.

He faltered a few times, but he knew the words by heart.

Eventually, he stopped and put down the sheet music.

"Is there anything more beautiful than that?" he asked. "I do it a grave disservice."

"Theirs is a great love," his wife said. "It always brings tears to my eyes."

For a second, Thomas thought of his parents, imagined them hearing the story of the twins, the brother and sister, who realize that they are desperately in love. Since he knew that Julia and the senator had attended performances of these operas, he wondered about his father's response to the image of a brother and sister being in love with each other.

The Rosenbergs and Katia were discussing various singers who had taken on these Wagner roles. As Thomas listened, he felt like someone who had come to visit a cosmopolitan household from somewhere deep in the German provinces. He could not identify any of the singers of whom they spoke.

His eye was caught by the tapestry on the walls, the faded colors. At first, he could not make it out, but soon he detected the outline of Narcissus staring into the water, savoring his own reflection. As the conversation went on around him, he imagined what could be done in a story with twins who had to separate because one of them was to marry. It would be like Narcissus being separated from his own reflection.

He could call them Siegmund and Sieglinde, but have them live in the contemporary world. When he and Katia went back to Munich, Thomas began to see the story more clearly and immediately understood the dangers. He wanted to set his story in the Rosenbergs' house, or in a wealthy household in Berlin like theirs, but the family sitting around the table would be Katia's family. The interloper, the man who had come to take Sieglinde in marriage, would be a version of himself. His character would not be a writer, rather some sort of government official, a dull man out of place in the glamorous company of Sieglinde's family.

He called the story *The Blood of the Walsungs*. It excited him that he wrote most of it while Katia was in the next room. Sometimes, if he needed to concentrate, he closed the door of his study, but often he kept the door open. He enjoyed hearing Katia move around the apartment as he created a fictional version of her, a girl who always held hands with her twin brother. They were, he wrote, very like each other, with the same slightly drooping nose, the same full lips, the same prominent cheekbones and black, bright eyes.

His own double was to be called Beckerath. He was short, with a pointed beard and a yellow complexion. His manners were punctilious. He began every sentence by drawing his breath in quickly through his mouth, a detail he took from Josef Löhr.

Frau Aarenhold, the mother of the twins, he wrote, was small, prematurely aged. She spoke in dialect. Her husband had made his money in coal. It was clear in the story that while Beckerath, the man who had come to marry the daughter, was a Protestant, the Aarenholds were Jewish.

The lunch at the center of the story showed Beckerath being made more and more uncomfortable by the family. When Siegmund, the son, scoffed at an acquaintance who did not know the difference between dress clothes and a dinner jacket, Beckerath realized, to his mortification, that he did not know this either.

Soon, as the conversation turned to art, Beckerath felt even less assured.

As they were sprinkling sugar on their slices of pineapple, Siegmund announced that he and his sister wished to ask Beckerath's permission to go to a production of *Die Walküre* that very evening. When Beckerath assented, he added that he too would be free to attend, only to be told that no, the twins wished to be alone one more time before the wedding.

In the story, after the opera, knowing the house was empty, Siegmund returned to his room certain that his sister would follow him. When she entered his bedroom, he told her that because she was just like him, her experiences with the man she was to marry would be his too. She kissed him on his closed eyelids; he kissed her on her throat. They kissed each other's hands. They forgot themselves in caresses, passing into a tumult of passion.

Thomas composed the last pages of the story at speed, knowing that if he stopped to think, he would become worried about Katia and her family. He had not told Katia what he was writing, and when the last sentence was completed he left the piece aside, without looking at it for some days. Aware that the Pringsheims did not like being categorized, he knew they would disapprove of the open way in which the family was described as Jewish.

Eventually, having made some corrections, he showed it to Katia and was surprised at her calm response.

"I enjoyed it. I do love how you write about music."

"But the topic?"

"It served Wagner well. Who can complain if you use it?"

She smiled. Surely, he thought, she must have noticed the connections between the Aarenhold family and her own! But she seemed not to see anything strange in the story.

A few days later she told him that she had informed her mother and Klaus that he had written a new story and they had asked for him to come to the house and read it to them after supper.

He wondered if this were Katia's way of warning him, or if she were hoping that, faced with the prospect of having to read it to her mother and brother, he might put the story aside. But since he planned to send it to a magazine, it would be better to read it to them first.

As he perused the pages in the sitting room in the house on Arcisstrasse, Klaus and Katia, who had been out of the room, joined him and found chairs close to each other while their mother sat apart.

He cleared his throat, took a sip of water, and began. Klaus, he felt, despite his talk about kissing boys, was an innocent soul. He would be less innocent, Thomas thought with some satisfaction, when the reading was over. However, he foresaw the mother run-

ning out of the room shrieking in disgust, calling for her husband
or her maid or her mother.

Since all three listeners were familiar with *Die Walküre*, they
made sounds of satisfaction when the names of the twins were
mentioned and further sounds of approval when it became clear
that the twins were to attend the actual opera.

The fire crackled, servants came in and out of the room and
Thomas worked on his enunciation during the sections that might
cause least offense. Despite his previous determination, however,
he was not brave enough when he came to the parts most likely to
disturb them. He left out a few passages and went quickly through
the scene where the twins blissfully coupled at the end, dropping
a few phrases here and there. By the time he was finished, he
believed that they had missed the point of the story.

"It is wonderful and was beautifully delivered," Katia's mother
said.

"Have you been teaching him about opera?" Klaus asked his
sister.

He soon sent the text of *The Blood of the Walsungs* to the magazine *Neue Rundschau*, which quickly agreed that the story would
be included in its January issue. He then forgot about it as Katia's
time to deliver their first child approached.

No one had prepared him for the long night of agony that Katia
went through while giving birth. When the child came, he felt
relief, but also knew that Katia had been marked in some way.
This new knowledge that she had gained would, he thought, stay
with her.

It was a girl, to be called Erika. Thomas had wanted a boy,
but wrote to Heinrich that maybe watching a girl grow up would
bring him closer to the "other" sex, of which, even though he was
a husband, he had to admit that he knew little.

In the first months of his daughter's life, Thomas saw a good deal of his wife's parents, who doted on the child, enough for him to decide to withdraw the story about the twins, even though the type was set, in case it offended them once they saw it in print and realized that it was about their family. He was still worried, however, when he met a young editor who had been shown the story and breathlessly informed him that others had seen it too.

"How brave, we thought, to write a story about twins when you are married to one!" the editor said. "I have a friend who wondered whether you have a great imagination or have married into the most peculiar family in Munich."

One afternoon, when Katia returned from her parents' house with the baby, she informed him that her father was in a rage. He wished to see Thomas immediately.

He had not been in his father-in-law's study before. The shelves on one wall contained art books from floor to ceiling; on the opposite wall were leather-bound volumes. There were ladders for each. The wall behind the desk was filled with examples of Italian majolica. As Thomas inspected the tiles, his father-in-law asked him what he had possibly been thinking of when he wrote that story.

"Rumors are flying around about its content. I believe it is disgusting."

"It has been withdrawn," Thomas said.

"That is hardly the point. Some people have seen it. Had we known you entertained such views, you would never have been allowed in this house."

"What views?"

"Anti-Semitic views."

"I do not have anti-Semitic views."

"We don't actually care whether you do or not. But we do care about our privacy being invaded by someone posing as a son-in-law."

"I am not posing."

"You are a low form of life. Klaus is going to punch you as soon as he sees you."

For a second, Thomas was going to ask Alfred about his mistress.

"Can you assure me that the offending story will never appear in any rag?" Alfred Pringsheim asked him.

Thomas glanced at him and shrugged.

He accompanied Thomas into the drawing room, where they found that Katia, having left the baby with a maid, had returned to the house. She was standing with her twin brother while their mother sat beside him in an armchair. Katia's eyes were shining. She smiled at him.

"Klaus is rather sorry that the story is not to appear. It would provide him with a reputation. He says he didn't have one before. Isn't that right, my little twin? Everyone might start looking at you strangely."

Klaus started to tickle her.

"I understood you wished to punch me?" Thomas said to Klaus.

"That was just to please Papa."

"Poor Papa," Frau Pringsheim said. "He blames me for not telling him what a horrible story it was after you read it for us. I said that I had listened only to the rhythm. It was like poetry. I didn't really know what it was all about. I actually thought it was quite sweet."

"I listened to every word," Klaus said. "And it was quite sweet. What a great imagination you have! Or maybe you are just a good listener?"

Alfred, who had been standing helplessly at the doorway, now spoke severely.

"My advice to you," he said, pointing to Thomas, "is to stick to historical subjects, or write about commercial life in Lübeck."

He said the words "commercial life in Lübeck" as if he were referring to the tawdriest activity in some far-flung region.

• • •

Their most constant visitor in the apartment was Klaus Pring-sheim, who wondered if Erika did really need to sleep in the afternoon.

"Surely the whole purpose of a girl child is to amuse her poor uncle," he said, "when he comes to see her."

"Leave her sleeping," Katia said.

"Is your husband going to write more stories about us?" Klaus asked, as though Thomas had not just come into the room.

For a moment, Thomas saw Katia hesitating. Since Erika's birth, she had become almost serious. Klaus tried to make her join him in frivolity.

"Perhaps a whole book?" Klaus continued. "So we can all become more famous."

"My husband has more useful things to do," Katia said.

Klaus sat back, folded his arms and studied her.

"Has my princess grown sad?" he asked. "Is that what marriage and motherhood have done to her?"

Thomas wondered if there were a way of intervening to change the subject.

"I really came here to play with the baby," Klaus said.

"I am not even sure Erika likes you," Katia said to Klaus.

"Why ever not?"

"She likes her men less flighty. I think she admires gravity."

"She likes her father?" Klaus asked. "He has plenty of gravity."

"Yes, she likes her father," Thomas said.

"Is she his little darling?" Klaus asked.

Thomas thought it was time to go back to his study.

His mother left Munich and settled in a village to the southwest called Polling. The Schweighardts, whom Josef Löhr had known before his marriage, owned a farm on the outskirts of the village and lived in one of the buildings of an old Benedictine monastery. Max and Katharina Schweighardt offered rooms to paying guests in the summer. Katharina had warmed to Julia and Viktor when they came to see her, agreeing to rent them a house on the grounds of the monastery that they could use all year, promising to introduce Julia to any notables who lived nearby, telling her that the air in Polling and the calm social atmosphere would suit her temperament and that of her son better than Munich.

The village was undisturbed; most southbound trains did not even stop at the station. When Thomas came to visit for the first time, he was taken aside by Katharina.

"I am not sure," she said, "that I understand what you do. I know Herr Löhr and Lula. And I met Carla once, and she is an actress. But I am uncertain about you and your older brother. Are you both writers? Is that how you both make your living?"

"That is correct."

Katharina smiled in satisfaction.

"The idea of two brothers who are writers is new to me. Often, in the summer, we have painters to stay, but I wonder if they are fully engaged with the serious things in life."

She stopped for a moment.

"I don't mean money or ways of earning a living. I mean the dark side of life, its hardships and troubles. Writers understand this, I think, and understanding is perhaps the most important thing in life. It must be a remarkable family to produce two writers."

She had spoken of the dark side of life as if its presence were as normal as the seasons or the hours of the day.

For her modest house in the grounds, his mother brought her best furniture and rugs from Munich, and some pieces taken from Lübeck. Thomas stood in wonder as he saw them in their new resting places; they were like phantoms, signs that the old world had not forgotten them.

In a short time, his mother made herself at home in Polling. She prepared her own lunch, but was happy to be served in the evening by Katharina or by her daughter, just as Viktor was content to spend time in the fields with Max Schweighardt and his son.

Soon Julia began to entertain in the house. She behaved as in the old days in Lübeck, and treated the most ordinary people as though they belonged to some exotic world. If someone came by bicycle, she demanded to be allowed to inspect the bicycle and marveled at its usefulness. Known in Polling as Frau Senator, she started to flourish in the village.

The birth of Thomas's second child, Klaus, was followed two and a half years later by the arrival of Golo. As the two eldest children grew noisier and more demanding, and as Golo developed a habit of screaming at the top of his voice, Thomas found the journeys to Polling to see his mother soothing and relaxing.

But it was the building itself and the sheds and barns, the fruit trees, the pens for animals, the beehives, the whole sense of an undisturbed husbandry that interested him most and made him wish that he knew Bavaria better so that he could, at some point in the future, set a novel in one of its villages.

He liked taking a walk through the grounds and then along the empty upstairs corridors of the old monastery. This became part of his routine. There was one room upstairs that must really have been a monk's cell, he thought. It had a small window looking over the elm tree, whose wavering branches made shadows on the distempered walls. Thomas liked to close the door of this room and enjoy the silence and the changing light, savoring the idea that this had once been a place of prayer and meditation, of self-abnegation, a refuge from the world for a single soul. Downstairs, there was a large room known as the Abbot's Room where he liked to sit and read.

He would have lunch with his mother and discuss affairs of the day with her, including her worry about Carla, who was getting fewer roles as an actress, or parts that did not rise to her considerable ambition.

"She is not an actress," Julia said, "never has been, never will be. But try telling her that! When Lula told her bluntly that she could not act, she stopped speaking to her sister. Heinrich, of course, encourages her, but she depends too much on his support. I think she should get a husband and live a normal domestic life, but she only meets actors, and an actor would hardly do."

Thomas remembered seeing Carla in some minor comedy in a small theater in Düsseldorf. On the stage, she was a tragic heroine, even in scenes where her lines were meant to be funny. At supper after the play, he saw that his sister could not settle. She kept asking him what he thought of her performance. When she had had a few drinks, she reminded him of their mother.

Carla barely referred to his own wife and children. When he spoke of them, she quickly changed the subject. Later, when the topic of marriage came up, she said that Lula was most unhappy in her marriage, despite her lovely daughters. Can you imagine, she asked, being married to Josef Löhr, sleeping with him every night? Thomas had to reply that he could not. They both laughed.

Heinrich wrote to inform him that Carla had a fiancé. His name was Arthur Gibo. He was an industrialist from Mülhausen. He had nothing to do with the theater, and wanted Carla to forsake her career and devote herself to raising a family. Carla, in turn, liked the idea that Mülhausen was French-speaking and had told her mother that she looked forward to having children who would speak French.

"What happened to her famous bohemianism?" Thomas asked.

"She will be thirty in a year," his mother said.

"Has Arthur seen her on the stage?"

"I was so relieved at her news," his mother said, "that I asked her no questions and I have instructed Lula to ask none either. But I do understand that the Gibo family would rather Arthur marry someone without experience of the stage."

When Thomas saw Carla in Polling, he thought she looked older. He was irritated at her constant questions about Heinrich and when he might come to visit. He knew as little of Heinrich's intentions as she did. When he told her that Katia was pregnant with their fourth child, she gave him her petulant look.

"Surely, that is enough," she said.

He shrugged.

"I'm sure Katia is happy," she said. "She is lucky. Of all of us, you are the most constant."

He asked her what she meant.

"I know," she went on, "you imagine Heinrich is more dependable than you, but he isn't. Or you think Lula is more stable than you, but she isn't. And me? I want two things and they are direct opposites. I want fame on the stage, all the travel and excitement. And I want a family and all the quietness. And I cannot have both. You, on the other hand, only want what you have. You are alone among us in that."

He had never heard Carla speak like this, drop her signature nonchalance for something more grave and earnest. He wondered if this was caused by her newfound destiny as a married woman.

Over lunch, his mother spoke with enthusiasm about the plans for Carla's marriage.

"I know Polling is not fashionable and it might be a journey for the Gibos, but they should be informed that the bride's mother longs for the wedding to be here at the lovely church in the village, with the reception in the Abbot's Room. I cannot think of a more pleasant place for a wedding. And the little Löhrs and little Erika can be the bridesmaids or the flower girls."

Thomas watched Carla cringe.

"And I will have no mercy on Heinrich if he does not come. He was almost a father to you, poor Carla, when the senator died. All your tiny problems and secrets were shared with him. I never knew what you were thinking. Do you remember you kept a skull on your dressing table? What a thing for a girl to have! Only Heinrich understood. We should all write to Heinrich and tell him that we expect him on the day."

That summer, after Monika was born, Thomas, Katia and the children moved for the season to the house they had built at Bad Tölz on the Isar, a popular place for citizens of Munich to go for the summer. He liked the swiftly changing sky that cast different kinds of light into the house; the young children enjoyed having friends with whom they could roam under the careful eye of a governess.

One day in high summer he and Katia had had guests for lunch and for a few hours the garden had been filled with the noise of children. The adults had eaten on the terrace, drinking some white wine that he had been saving. When the guests left, the maid took the three eldest children down to the water while Katia went to look after Monika, who was less than two months old.

Thomas was thinking he might have a nap when the telephone rang. It was the pastor at Polling.

"I have to prepare you for bad news."

"Has something happened to my mother?"

"No."

"What, then?"

"Do you have someone with you in the house?"

"Can you tell me what the news is?"

"Your sister is dead."

"Which sister?"

"The actress."

"Where did she die?"

"Here in Polling. Now. This afternoon."

"How did she die?"

"I am not at liberty to say."

"Did she have an accident?"

"No."

"Is my mother there?"

"She is not in any condition to speak."

"Will you tell her that I will come as soon as I can?"

After Thomas put the telephone down, he went to the kitchen. He remembered that one of the bottles of wine had only been half-finished and should be recorked. He put the cork back in with deliberation. Then he had a drink of water and stood staring at objects in the kitchen as though one of them might offer him a clue about how he should feel.

He wondered if he could simply leave a note for Katia to say that he had gone to Polling to see his mother. But that would not be enough. He would need to write that his sister was dead, but he could hardly put those words in a note. And then he realized that Katia was upstairs in the house.

She convinced him to wait until the morning before driving to Polling.

It was before noon when he arrived. He found his mother in the Schweighardts' high-ceilinged living room. She was being consoled by Katharina.

"The body has been taken away," she said. "They asked if we wanted to see her again before they closed the coffin, but I said we did not. There are blotches all over her face."

"Why blotches?" he asked.

"Cyanide," his mother replied. "She took cyanide. She had it with her."

In the hours that followed, Thomas discovered what had transpired. His sister had been having an affair with a doctor who would travel to where she was performing and stay in the same hotel. This man was married and told his wife he was seeing patients who had moved to other cities. He suffered, Carla had told her mother, from intense and unreasonable jealousy. On learning that Carla was engaged, he demanded that she continue to have relations with him. He threatened to write to Arthur Gibo and his family when she refused, informing them that she was not a woman worthy to enter into a state of matrimony with a respectable man. Carla gave in to him, but, having taken full advantage of her, the doctor wrote to her betrothed and his family anyway.

Carla sent a letter to Heinrich in Italy asking him to intervene, to let the Gibos know that the doctor's letter was a pack of lies.

But before Heinrich could do anything, Arthur followed Carla to Polling, where she had fled. Somewhere in the gardens, confronted by him, she told him the truth. On his knees, he begged her never to see the doctor again, or so he told her mother days later. And she agreed. Once he had departed, Carla hurried past her mother and went to her room. A few seconds later, her mother could hear her crying out and then the sound of gargling as Carla sought to cool the burning in her throat. Her mother tried the door but it was locked.

Julia ran out of the house in search of the Schweighardts. Max came quickly and when he couldn't unlock the door, he broke it down. He found Carla lying on a chaise longue with dark spots on her hands and face. She was already dead.

Thomas wrote to Heinrich, knowing that his mother had already told him that Carla was dead.

"In my mother's presence I can remain placid," he wrote, "but when I am alone I can barely control myself. If only Carla would have come to us, we could have helped her. I have tried to speak to Lula, but she is inconsolable."

A few days after Carla's burial, Thomas brought his mother and Viktor back to Bad Tölz.

Heinrich did not appear for the funeral. When he did come, he met Thomas in Munich and they traveled together to Polling. Heinrich wanted to spend time in the room where Carla had died.

They approached her bedroom. Some things had been removed in the immediate aftermath of her death. There was no sign of the glass she had filled with water in order to gargle. No sign either of any clothes or jewelry. The bed had been made. On the bedside table there was a copy of Shakespeare's *Love's Labour's Lost*. Carla must, Thomas thought, have been planning a part in some production of the play. He noticed that her suitcase was in a corner of the room. And when Heinrich opened the wardrobe Carla's clothes were hanging there.

It felt as if she could have walked into the room at any moment, ready to ask her two brothers what they were doing.

"This chaise longue was in Lübeck," Heinrich said as he ran his hand up and down the faded striped material.

Thomas had no memory of it.

"This is where she lay," Heinrich said as though speaking to himself.

When he asked Thomas if he had heard Carla cry before she expired, Thomas had to explain that he was not in Polling when she died, he was in Bad Tölz. He thought Heinrich knew that. In fact, he was sure he had told him again that very morning.

"I know. But did you hear Carla cry?"

"How could I have heard her cry?"

"I did. At the precise time she took the cyanide. I was out for a walk. I stopped and looked around. The voice was clear, and it was her voice. She was in terrible pain. She kept calling my name. I waited and listened until she went silent. I knew then that she was dead. I waited for the news. Nothing like this has ever happened to me before. You know how much I dislike talk of spirits or the dead. But this happened. Do not doubt me that it happened."

He crossed the room and pushed the door closed.

"Do not doubt that it happened," he said again and gazed blankly at his brother, standing there silently until Thomas left him and went downstairs.

Chapter 5
Venice, 1911

Thomas sat alone in an aisle seat in the middle of the hall in Munich as Gustav Mahler began to take the players in the orchestra through a quiet passage, getting a total silence in the hall and raising his two hands as though he wanted it maintained and controlled. Later, he would tell Thomas, whom he had invited to witness the rehearsal process, that if he could get this silence just before the first note, then he could do anything. But it seldom came. There was always some random noise or the players themselves were not able to hold their breaths for as long as he wanted them to. He did not simply require a hush, he said, he wanted moments when there was nothing at all, a pure void.

While fully in command at the podium, the composer was almost gentle. What he was looking for, his movements suggested, would not be achieved by large gestures. Instead, it was about raising the music from nothing, having the players become alert to what was there before they started to play. Mahler, as Thomas watched him, appeared to be trying to lower the intensity of the playing, pointing to individual players, indicating that they should do less. And then he stretched out his arms, as if he were pulling the music towards him. He let the musicians know that they were to play as softly as their instruments would let them.

He had them play the opening bars over and over, moving his

baton to mark the precise instant when they should all begin. He wanted a single, sharp sound.

This was, Thomas thought, like starting a chapter, then erasing sentences, beginning again, adding words and phrases, taking out others, slowly perfecting it so that, whether it was day or night, whether he was tired or full of energy, there was nothing more that could be done.

Thomas had been told how superstitious Mahler was, and haunted by death; he did not want to be reminded that this was his Eighth Symphony and it would be followed by his Ninth.

With this symphony, there was, it struck Thomas, a collision between bombast and subtlety. It was a sign of Mahler's fame and power that he could summon an orchestra and chorus of this size and scope. There was something mysterious and unresolved in the music, a striving for effect and then a melody that exuded a solitary delicacy, sometimes sad and tentative, displaying a talent that was tactful, at ease.

At dinner after the performance, Mahler did not appear exhausted. Rumors of his declining health seemed exaggerated. He had a way of slouching in his seat and looking around him uneasily. And then he would sit up as someone new joined the company. His face would become beautifully alive. Everyone would turn to watch him. Thomas could see an erotic charge in him, a strength that was physical more than spiritual. When Alma finally joined them, her lateness having delayed the serving of dinner, Thomas could see that the composer was intrigued by his wife. It must be part of their game, he thought, that Alma ignored her husband, kissing and hugging minor members of Mahler's entourage, while the great composer kept a seat empty for her, and waited for her as if the whole evening, and indeed the writing of the intricately long symphony, had merely been a preparation for her sitting beside him.

Not long after that event, Katia learned from Klaus that Mahler really did not have long to live. His heart was weakening. He had been lucky a few times, but the luck could not last. Mahler was working feverishly towards his Ninth Symphony and he might not live to complete it.

It fascinated Thomas that Mahler was alive, still writing, imagining the sounds that would come from notation, working in the sure knowledge that his single-minded devotion to music would shortly be nothing. Some moment soon would witness his writing the very last note of his life. This moment was not determined by spirit, but simply by the beating of his heart.

When Heinrich came to visit, he told them that Carla's death continued to haunt him. What had happened to his sister was with him as soon as he woke and was still lingering in his mind as he went to sleep. There was something so free about Carla's spirit that even in death she would not rest. He had been to see their mother, and she too felt the presence of her daughter in the shadowy spaces of the house in Polling.

As Heinrich expressed his open grief, Thomas realized that after his sister's death he had busied himself with writing. Sometimes he even managed to believe that her suicide had not even happened. He almost envied Heinrich his readiness to talk about Carla.

Heinrich when he spoke of the family was easier company than when he spoke of current events. He had become emphatically left-wing and internationalist in his views. In the newspapers, there were accounts of escalating tension between Germany and Russia and France and Britain. While Thomas believed that the other countries were, for nefarious reasons, forcing Germany to increase its military spending, Heinrich saw this as an example of Prussian expansionism. He seemed to be following a set of principles, applying them to each day's news. Thomas found political discussions with his brother tedious.

But he had never witnessed Heinrich suffering before as he did now while talking of Carla's suicide. His brother left long gaps between words, often beginning a phrase that he did not complete.

Katia signaled that she would be happy for them to join Heinrich when he returned to Rome, and Thomas agreed that they should spend a few weeks in Italy with him, seeing if company might console him. They could leave the children in Munich in the care of a governess and some servants, with Katia's mother visiting. Rather than Rome or Naples, Thomas felt he would like to go to the Adriatic. The very word "Adriatic" offered him images of soft sunlight and warm seawater, especially as he contemplated it during a freezing lecture tour in Cologne and Frankfurt and other nearby cities that had become an annual event for him.

In May they booked a hotel on the island of Brioni off the coast of Istria and took the overnight train from Munich to Trieste and then a local train. Thomas liked the formal manners of the hotel staff, the heavy, old-fashioned furniture, the sense of custom and ceremony even on the small stony beach. The food was cooked in the Austrian style, and a reasonably fluent German was spoken by the waiters.

All three, however, developed a pronounced dislike of an archduchess who was staying at the hotel with her followers. When she came into the dining room, all the other guests were expected to rise and not sit down again until this archduchess was suitably seated. And no one was expected to leave the dining room until she did. And they had to stand up again as she departed.

"We are more important than she is," Katia said, laughing.

"I am going to remain seated," Heinrich insisted.

Her presence made them feel comfortable with one another. When Heinrich was formulating some fresh opinion about the need for Prussians to rid themselves of their irrational anxieties, they could discuss the archduchess and the unctuous way in which the restaurant manager approached her table and took her order, walking backwards with decorous care as he personally brought this order to the kitchen.

"I would like to see her in the water," Katia said. "Water has a way of splashing on the mighty in a way that does them no favors."

"That is how empires end," Heinrich said, "a mad old bat being treated obsequiously in a provincial hotel. It will all be swept away."

It was the dullness of the island, as much as the self-importance of the archduchess, that caused them in the end to want to leave the Dalmatian coast. They found that there was a steamer at Pola that would take them to Venice, where Thomas booked rooms at the Grand Hotel des Bains on the Lido.

On the day before they traveled, news came that Mahler had died. It was a headline in all the newspapers.

"Klaus, my brother," Katia said, "was in love with him, and many of his friends were too."

"Do you mean—?" Heinrich asked.

"Yes, I do. I am sure nothing ever happened, however. And Alma was always on the lookout."

"I only met Alma once," Heinrich said. "If I had married her, I would be dead too."

"I remember how she ignored Mahler and that seemed to give him pleasure," Thomas said.

"Those young men loved him," Katia continued. "Klaus and his friends took bets on who would manage to kiss him first."

"Kiss Mahler?" Thomas asked.

"My father, I think, prefers Bruckner," Katia said. "But he loves Mahler's songs. And one of the symphonies. I can't think which one."

"It couldn't be the one I heard," Heinrich said, "because it was so long it lasted from April into the New Year. I grew a long beard listening to it."

"In our house, Mahler was much loved," Katia said. "Even saying Mahler's name gave my brother a funny kind of satisfaction. In every other way he is normal."

"Your brother Klaus? Normal?" Thomas asked.

Thomas had never arrived in Venice by sea before. In the instant that he caught sight of the city in silhouette, he knew that this time he would write about it. In the same instant, it came to him what consolation he would get if he could bring Mahler to life in a story. He imagined him here, in this very spot, having shifted position on the boat to get a better view.

Thomas knew how he would describe Mahler: below middle height, with a head that looked rather too large for his almost delicate figure. He wore his hair brushed back. He had a lofty, rugged, knotty brow and a gaze that was always ready to move inwards.

As Thomas saw him now, the figure in his story was a writer rather than a composer, the author of a number of books that Thomas himself had thought of writing, such as a volume on Frederick the Great. He was a famous figure in his own country, and now he sought a rest from his work and indeed from his fame.

"Are you thinking about something?" Katia asked him.

"Yes, but I am not sure what it is."

Once the engines stopped, gondolas pressed alongside, the landing stairs were let down, customs officials came on board and people began to go ashore. As they sat in their gondola, Thomas noted its somber, ceremonial style, as though it had been designed to take coffins rather than living people through the canals of Venice.

When they stood in the lobby of the hotel, Thomas remarked that it was good to be in a place free of the archduchess. Their rooms overlooked the beach, and the sea, now at full tide, was sending long, low waves with rhythmic beats onto the sand.

At dinner, they discovered themselves in a cosmopolitan world. A party of polite and subdued Americans sat at the table closest to them, and beyond them some English ladies, a Russian family, some Germans and Poles.

He observed the Polish mother, who was with her daughters, sending the waiter away, as there was one more member of the party still to come. Then they indicated to a boy, who had just come through the double doors, that he sit down quickly. He was late.

The boy crossed the dining room with quiet self-possession. He was blond, with curls that stretched almost to his shoulder. He wore an English sailor suit. He walked confidently towards the family table, bowing almost formally to his mother and sisters, taking a seat in Thomas's clear eyeline.

Katia had noticed the boy as well, but Heinrich, Thomas thought, had not.

"I wish to see St. Mark's Square," Heinrich said, "as who does not? And then the Frari, and perhaps also San Rocco for the Tintorettos, and then there is a strange little room, like a small shop, that shows Carpaccio. And that is all I want to see. The rest of the time I want to swim, think of nothing, look at the sea and the sky."

Thomas noted the whiteness of the boy's skin, the blueness of his eyes, his way of remaining still. When his mother addressed him, the boy nodded politely. He spoke to the waiter with seriousness and decorum. It was not merely his beauty that affected Thomas now, it was his way of holding himself, of being quiet without being sullen, of sitting with his family while staying apart from them. Thomas studied his composure, his self-assurance. When the boy caught his eye, Thomas looked down, determined that he would concern himself with plans for the next day and think no more about the boy.

In the morning, since the sky was blue, they decided that they would make full use of the facilities that the hotel provided on the beach. Thomas carried his notebook and a novel he thought he might read, and Katia also had a book. The staff made them comfortable under a sun umbrella, setting up a table and chair so that Thomas could write.

He had seen the boy again at breakfast; once more he arrived later than the other members of his family, as though this were a privilege that he demanded for himself. He walked with the same grace as the night before, moving lightly across the room. The boy charmed him all the more because he knew that he would get no chance to speak to him. All he could do was watch.

For the first hour, as he wrote, there was no sign of the boy or his family. When the boy finally came into view, he was bare-chested, announcing his arrival to a group of others playing on a sand heap, who shouted his name, two syllables whose exact sound Thomas could not make out.

The young people started to create a link between two sand heaps by using an old plank. He watched the boy carry it and, with the help of an older, stronger boy, put it in place. Then the two, having inspected their good work, walked away, their arms around each other.

When a hawker came with strawberries, Katia sent him away.

"They are not even washed," she said.

Thomas had abandoned his writing and taken up the novel to read. He presumed that the boy and his friend had gone on some escapade and the boy would next be seen at lunch.

He dozed in the milky light that came from the sea and woke and read and dozed again until he heard Katia saying: "He has come back."

Her voice was quiet enough, he thought, for Heinrich not to hear. When he sat up and looked at Katia, she was buried in her book, paying him no attention. But she was right. The boy was in the water up to his knees and then he started wading farther out. He began to swim until his mother and a woman who must have been a governess insisted that he come back to shore. Thomas saw him emerging from the water, with dripping locks. The longer and more intensely he watched, the more studiously Katia read. When they were alone later, they would not discuss it, he was sure, since there was nothing to say. Knowing that he did not have to hide his interest in the scene made him feel more at ease, as he shifted his chair so that he could see the boy drying himself under the careful supervision of his mother and the governess.

Even though the weather remained clement enough for the beach, Heinrich convinced them to accompany him to visit churches and galleries the following morning. As soon as the boat took off from the small landing pier, Thomas regretted his decision to come. He was leaving behind the life of the beach, so rich the day before.

When they approached the piazza, Venice appeared at its best. The lukewarm air of the sirocco breathed on him; he leaned back and closed his eyes. They would spend the morning looking at pictures, perhaps have lunch and then return to the Lido for the afternoon when the sun was softer.

He and Katia smiled as Heinrich went into a paroxysm of ecstasy in the Frari over Titian's Virgin ascending into heaven. No novelist, Thomas thought, should like this painting. The central image, despite the sumptuous colors, was too unearthly, too unlikely. Having studied it for a while, he turned his attention to the faces of the shocked figures at the bottom of the picture rooted in ordinary life who had to witness this scene as he did.

He knew, as they walked back towards the Grand Canal, that Heinrich would be inspired to make some large statement about Europe or history or religion. He was not in any mood for this, but he did not want to disturb the cordial relationship he was enjoying with his brother this morning.

"Can you imagine being alive at the time of the Crucifixion?" Heinrich asked.

Thomas glanced at him gravely as if he were now contemplating this question.

"It seems to me that nothing will happen in the world again," Heinrich continued, raising his voice so that he could be heard against the busy morning sounds in the narrow streets. "I mean, there will be local wars and threats of wars and then treaties and agreements. And there will be trade. Ships will be bigger and speedier. Roads will be better. More tunnels will be cut through mountains and better bridges will be built. But there will be no cataclysms, no more visits by the gods. Eternity will be bourgeois."

Thomas smiled and nodded and Katia said that she liked both Titian and Tintoretto even though the guidebook stated that they did not like each other.

They entered the dark space to look at the Carpaccios and it pleased Thomas that no one could see him, no one could discover what his response to these paintings was. He stepped away from Katia and Heinrich. It surprised him how suddenly and precisely Mahler edged into his mind. For a second, it came to him that he himself could be Mahler here in this dimly lit gallery. It was a strange and fanciful idea: to dream that Mahler were present, moving from picture to picture, savoring the scenes.

On the steamer from Pola, when he had imagined a story in which Mahler would figure, the protagonist was to be a lonely man rather than a husband and father. Thomas had toyed with the possibility of reducing all the grand ideas his protagonist had lived with and written about to one idea, or one experience, or one disappointment. It was as if he could take what Heinrich had just been expounding in the street and test it against some pressing, dark emotion. But he had not until now connected this idea with what he himself had been experiencing on the beach and in the hotel dining room.

His figure, whether Mahler or Heinrich or himself, had come to Venice and been confronted by beauty and been animated by desire. Thomas considered making the object of desire a young girl, but immediately, he thought, he would be working in the realm of what was natural and undramatic, especially if he made the girl older. No, he thought, it would have to be a boy. And the story would have to suggest that the desire was sexual, but it would also, of course, be distant and impossible. The gaze of the older man would be all the more fierce because nothing else could happen. The encounter would change the protagonist's life all the more because it would be fleeting and would lead nowhere. It could never be socialized or domesticated or made acceptable to the world. It would break through the gates of a soul that had once believed itself impregnable.

When Heinrich went to the bank to change money, the bank teller warned him not to think of going south, as he had planned to do, since there were rumors of cholera in Naples. The instant this was said, Thomas knew that he would integrate it into his story. He would have rumors of cholera in Venice itself, and the Lido, with the guests in the hotel slowly thinning out. He would mix the desire of the older man with a sense of disease, decay.

In the morning, at breakfast, the Polish table was empty, as it had been the night before. When he found a quiet moment, Thomas asked one of the young men at the concierge's desk if the Polish family had departed. He informed Thomas that the Polish family were still guests at the hotel.

At lunchtime the mother and the daughters arrived in the dining room. Katia and Heinrich were discussing something that Heinrich had read in the morning paper while Thomas kept his eyes on the door. Several times it opened only to reveal a waiter. And then he presented himself, the boy, wearing his sailor suit, moving unapologetically across the room, stopping before he took his seat, acknowledging Thomas for one small second, briefly smiling, and devoting himself to ordering his lunch.

On the beach in the afternoon, Thomas went over the story he now planned to write. Since Heinrich's luggage had been lost, he would incorporate that into the story, making it a reason why his protagonist would delay his departure, even if the real reason was so that he could spend more time in the same ambit as the boy. He thought of the strawberries they had been offered; that moment too could be included in the story.

The emotion his character felt at the sight of such physical perfection would become more overwrought as the days went by. Aschenbach, his protagonist, saw the boy constantly, even in Piazza San Marco, when he crossed the lagoon. Noticing that the family had begun to arrive earlier for breakfast so that its members could benefit from more time on the beach, he took his own breakfast early and tried to be on the beach before them.

Aschenbach, in the story, was alone, a man who had married once and been bereaved early in life, a man with one daughter, to whom he was not close. His Aschenbach was humorless in a way that was expected of a writer. His irony he kept for moments in philosophy and history; he did not allow it to be directed inwards. And he had no defenses against the vision of overpowering beauty that appeared before him in a blue-and-white bathing suit every morning under the brilliant Adriatic light. The boy's very outline against the horizon captivated him. His foreign speech, of which Aschenbach could understand not a word, excited him. What he waited for most were the moments of repose, when, for example, the boy would stand erect at the water's edge, alone, removed from his family, his hands clasped at the back of his neck, daydreaming into blue space.

By the time he and Katia and Heinrich were preparing to leave, having been told that there was now a risk of cholera in Venice,

Thomas had the story in outline. He knew that if he spoke about it to Katia, she would look at him quizzically, suggesting that he was using a preoccupation with a story as an alibi for what he was really thinking about.

Waiting for her in the lobby, he tried to remember when he realized how much she knew about him. He felt it was during that very first meeting with her in her parents' house, when she and her brother Klaus spoke to him. It was as though she had used Klaus as a decoy, or as bait. She saw the man who would become her husband watching her brother.

Thomas had been intent on watching Katia too, but there was nothing unusual about that. At that party, he thought, he had dropped his guard for a few moments, under the teasing eyes of Katia and her brother, and maybe he had done so on other occasions. What was strange, he thought, was how little it seemed to bother her.

In the years of their marriage, under her careful supervision, they had come to an arrangement. It had begun casually, lightly, when Katia found that a particular Riesling from Domaine Weinbach animated Thomas, made him loquacious and attentive. After the wine, Thomas would enjoy a cognac, perhaps even two. And then, having wished him good night, Katia would go upstairs in the knowledge that Thomas would soon appear at the door of her room.

Written into their set of tacit agreements was a clause stating that just as Thomas would do nothing to put their domestic happiness in jeopardy, Katia would recognize the nature of his desires without any complaint, note with tolerance and good humor the figures on whom his eyes most readily rested, and make clear her willingness, when appropriate, to appreciate him in all of his different guises.

• • •

When he had the story written, he gave it to Katia to read. He waited a few days for some response, and, in the end, he had to ask her if she had read it.

"Well, you captured the whole thing. It was like being there, except I was in your mind."

"Do you think there will be any objection to it?"

"You are the most respectable man anyone has ever met. But the story will change things. It will change how the world sees Venice. And I presume it will change how the world sees you."

"Do you think I should withhold it?"

"I don't think you wrote it to withhold it."

When the story was published over two issues of a magazine and then in volume form, he thought it would be a chance for his enemies to round on him. He worried about articles that would imply that the author seemed to know a great deal about the subject of his story, more than was perhaps healthy, especially for a father of four.

In fact, the critics read the relationship between the artist and the boy as standing for what the lure of death and the seductive charm of timeless beauty looked like in an age of estrangement. The only forceful objection came from an uncle-by-marriage of Katia, who was outraged by the story, seeing no metaphors in it at all, writing to Katia's father: "What a story! And a married man with a family!"

On the other hand, Katia's grandmother, now in her early eighties, praised the story in a Berlin newspaper and wrote to Katia to say that she had finally overcome all her previous objections to Katia's husband. Instead of being stiff and unfriendly, she now thought that Thomas Mann represented the new Germany, the one she had been hoping for all her life.

Before the book was published, Thomas and Katia had a more ominous matter to consider. An old tubercular spot on one of

Katia's lungs appeared again. It was decided that she should go to Davos in Switzerland for treatment.

Thomas found it strange how little Erika and Klaus, aged six and five, appeared to miss their mother once she had departed for the sanatorium. While Elise, the maid who was now in control of the children, was strict and performed her duties with diligence, she often had to concentrate on the two younger ones, whose needs were more acute. Soon Erika and Klaus had created a relaxed set of rules for themselves that included a theater show every evening before bed, with both of them dressed up in preposterous costumes and noisy enough to disturb their father's peace as he read by the fire in one of the ground-floor rooms.

In Katia's absence, Thomas installed his mother in Bad Tölz in the summer months. Julia had no experience of dealing with unruly children. Her own brood had been precocious, but always obedient and easy to control. Erika and Klaus, on the other hand, saw their grandmother's eccentricity as another reason why they should do as they pleased. They insisted that they were too old to be kept in the garden of the house with Golo and Monika. They had their own friends, their own routines. Their mother, they declared, always let them go to the river with other children of their age as long as they were supervised by their friends' maid.

When his mother appealed to Thomas, he remonstrated with Erika and Klaus, only to find himself visited later by Erika, who explained to him that they had never been confined in this way before, urging her father to speak to their grandmother and support the case for their freedom.

Golo moved quietly into a world of his own. He made no effort to follow his older siblings, who would, in any case, not have welcomed him. He did not warm to his grandmother or any of the surrogate authority figures put in place during his mother's absence. He barely glanced at his father. If he was in a room, he found a corner and remained alone there. In the garden, he sat in the shelter of a tree. Thomas marveled at his self-command.

Monika was still a baby. She had always been difficult, crying in the night, becoming upset easily. While he had meals with the three older ones, insisting that Erika and Klaus arrive in time, sit up straight, say please and thank you and not ask to leave the table until it was clear that the meal had ended, he was never quite sure what to do about Monika. In Bad Tölz, he left her exclusively in his mother's care. Anytime he passed the room where she was, he could hear her crying.

Katia, especially at the beginning, wrote each day from Davos. The letters were cheerful, and funny about her fellow inmates and the regime in the sanatorium. When Thomas replied, he tried to think of amusing stories about the children. It was easy to make the activities of the first two seem fascinating, offer signs of how clever and original they were, and even Golo's habits could be made into a joke. It was hard to know what to say about Monika.

No matter how long and detailed their letters to each other were, he found, very soon after Katia's departure, that he missed her. Until she was gone, he did not realize how close they had become. Indeed, he did not believe that they spoke to each other very much. They had meals together and went for a walk in the afternoon. But his wife did not come into his study when he was working. And in recent years, as his sleep was lighter, they had separate bedrooms. Now, however, the events of the day, the most ordinary things, had no depth or substance since he could not discuss them with her.

When they returned from Bad Tölz to Munich at the start of the school year, he was aware that Katia's time in the sanatorium could easily be extended. He emphasized, in a few letters, that they longed for her to return. He knew that her mother and grandmother believed that she had had the children too quickly and had been asked to take too much responsibility for the household and her husband's financial affairs. After the first hints that they blamed him for her illness, he carefully avoided the topic of what had caused it. Since her mother and grandmother, unlike his own mother, did not offer to help with the children, then he saw no reason why he should entertain them.

Katia wrote about how much she was looking forward to a visit from him. He made lists of things he wanted to tell her, but even as he added stories about the children, little things they had said or done that might charm her, he realized that, in those first months of her absence, the four had developed in ways that might be difficult to change. The two older were now a source of complaint both from school and from the parents of their friends. When anyone spoke to Golo, it disturbed his strange inward-looking equilibrium. And Monika, no matter what they did to console her, remained upset.

He knew how stark and alarming this could sound in a letter. It would be softer if it were woven into a long conversation. It would be a relief, he thought, when he finally left the children to go to Davos. He had become someone who made rules for them, who attempted to impose order on them. In the past few weeks, he thought, the older three children had come to dislike him. They avoided him when they could and, no matter how eagerly he encouraged them to speak, were often silent at table.

He tasked his mother with informing them that he would be gone for three weeks. On the appointed day, he left the house before dawn and caught an early train to Rorschach, from where he caught a smaller, local train to Landquart in the Alps. From there he waited for the narrow-gauge train whose ascent was steep and dogged and felt as if it would never end. The tracks were squeezed between walls of rock. Even before the train reached its destination, he felt distant from the problems he had faced with the children.

It was not merely that he was a long way from Munich, but

in that day of setting off and waiting at stations and traveling again, Munich itself had receded. He was already embedded in this mountain world, over which Katia would preside. It would be dominated by illness.

Katia came to meet him at the station.

"It's nice to have someone to talk to again," she said to him as they made their way to the sanatorium. He would have his own room, away from hers, and would have his meals in the sanatorium dining room with her and her fellow patients.

She had written to him about many of the inmates. In his first half-hour at Davos he had met the Spanish woman who moved about crying "Tous les deux," in reference to her two sons, who were both suffering from tuberculosis. He had had an encounter as well with the man addicted to chocolates and constantly threatening to shoot himself.

He and Katia talked incessantly over those first days. He learned that a number of patients had died during her sojourn, something that she had omitted to mention in her letters. He was surprised at her casual tone when she spoke of the dead. Soon he found himself telling her about the children, including details that he had promised himself he would not reveal to her.

"You mean there has been no change?" she said.

"No change?"

"All four were as you described before I left, the first two theatrical and hard to handle, Golo solitary and silent and self-involved, and Monika a baby. No one has had an accident?"

"No."

"All that has happened then is that you have begun to notice them."

His room was cheerful and restful, with white practical furniture. The floor was spotless. The door to the balcony stood open to a glimpse of lights in the valley.

At dinner, they were approached by one of the doctors, who was amused when he heard Thomas insist that he himself was perfectly healthy. He was here only to visit his wife.

"Imagine!" the doctor said. "I have never met a perfectly healthy person before."

Quietly, Katia drew for him a picture of everyone who came into the dining room. She pointed to the two tables at which Russians sat.

"One is the good Russian table. It is for superior members of that nation. The other table is for people not wanted at the good table. It is, I suppose, the bad Russian table."

While Katia had warned him that the married couple in the room beside his belonged to the latter table, he put no thought into them and their lowly status until he was woken in the night by the sound of muffled laughter. The walls between the individual rooms, he realized, were thin. He did not need to know Russian to make sense of what was happening. As the sounds they made became unashamedly carnal, he imagined that he would meet these people in the days to come. Surely the intimate knowledge he now had of their love cries would be apparent to them when they were introduced to him. Just at that moment, it did not seem likely that they would care.

When Katia came to take him to breakfast, he decided not to mention to her what he had heard in the night. But, despite his earlier resolve, he found himself describing it to her as though it were urgent information.

Thomas saw how the sanatorium enclosed her. She was interested in the outside world, in stories about her children, in accounts of her mother and her mother-in-law, but she always became more animated when Davos itself was under discussion. Although they spoke more intensely than ever before, and he had no study to retreat to, he felt her distance. A few times, when he raised the possibility of her return to Munich, she grew almost dreamy, she let him know that some problems with her lungs remained. Thus, for the moment, leaving Davos was not an option.

That was the great change in her, he thought. She had become a patient. After a day or two, he noticed that he himself was being carried along by the routine. Like Katia, he had no immediate cares. Observing the inmates, learning about them, began to interest him almost to the point of obsession. While he had brought books with him, he found that he was too exhausted at night to read. During the rest periods in the day, the last thing he needed was a book. He wanted to relax, lie still, ponder on what he had learned so far about the sanatorium.

He loved the rest period in the afternoon when he knew that he would soon see Katia and they could immerse themselves in sharing whatever they had felt in the short time that had elapsed since they had last spoken.

He told her that he had always known that time went slowly in an unfamiliar place.

"But when I look back now, it seems as if I have been up here for who knows how long already and it has been an eternity since I first arrived."

The doctor in charge stopped each time he saw Thomas and Katia on the corridor. He made them understand that, while he had read Thomas's books, Katia was the main focus of his attention. One day, however, having quickly assured Katia that he was thinking of her case, he turned to Thomas, moving him into the light, looking carefully at the whites of his eyes.

"Have you been examined by one of the doctors?" he asked.

"I am not a patient," Thomas replied.

"It might be wise to use your time here fruitfully," he said and, taking Thomas in suspiciously, he departed.

When he made an appointment for Thomas in the clinic, he did not alert him, merely sent two orderlies to his room during the morning rest. Their instructions were, they said, to take him to the clinic. When he intimated that he would need to let his wife know where he was going, they said that his wife's rest could not be disturbed.

In the clinic, the doctor ordered Thomas to take off his jacket, his shirt and vest. He felt exposed and older than his years. He was left waiting for some time before the doctor returned and, without saying a word, set to examining his back, thumping it with his fist, listening to the sound, placing his other hand tenderly on the small of the back. He kept returning to certain spots, one near the left collarbone and one a little below it.

He called a colleague over and they told Thomas to breathe deeply and then cough. They started to move a stethoscope up and down his back, listening to the pressures within. By the slow, intent way that they examined him, Thomas knew that they would have much to say when they had finished.

"Just as I thought," one of them said.

Thomas wished that he were back in his room, having convinced the two orderlies that he was too busy to come with them.

"I'm afraid you are not simply a visitor here," the other one said. "I guessed that as soon as you arrived. It may turn out to be lucky that you came here."

Thomas fetched his shirt. He wanted to cover himself.

"You have a problem with one of your lungs. If it is not treated now, then I can assure you that you will be back here within a few months."

"What sort of treatment?"

"The same as the other patients here. It will take time."

"How long?"

"Ah, that is what they all ask, but soon they tire of asking and they know how difficult it is to answer."

"Are you sure about your diagnosis? Is it not too much of a coincidence that I was diagnosed here and not elsewhere?"

"The air up here," the senior doctor said, "is good for fighting off illness. But it is also good for letting illness emerge. It causes latent illness to erupt. Now you must go to bed. Soon we will take an interior picture of you."

It was the X-ray that woke him from the dream that Davos had induced. He was told one morning that he would be taken to the laboratory in the basement that afternoon. When he asked Katia about it, she said it was nothing, it was merely a way for the doctors to get a clearer image of his chest and lungs.

In a small room, as he waited, he was joined by a tall Swede. In the confined space, he found himself paying the Swede more attention than he had paid anyone since he had come here. He thought about the X-ray penetrating the man's skin, finding areas within him that no one would ever touch or see. When one of the technical assistants came out and instructed them both to strip to the waist, Thomas felt embarrassed and was almost prepared to ask if he could strip to the waist later, when the Swede had already gone into the X-ray room. But instead, hesitantly, he complied.

By the time he had removed his shirt, the Swede, having turned away from him, had already taken off his vest. His skin, in the dim light, was smooth and golden; the muscles on his back were fully developed. It struck Thomas in these few seconds that it would be natural, since the space was so small, to brush up against his companion, let his arm linger casually on the man's bare back. Before he could dismiss this idea, the Swede turned and, unapologetically, put his thumb and forefinger on the biceps of Thomas's right arm to measure his strength. He smiled boyishly and shrugged and indicated the muscles in his own upper arms and then slapped himself gently on the stomach to make clear that he had put on too much weight.

In the inner room, the doctor was standing in front of a cabinet. As his eyes gradually got used to the light in the darkened room, Thomas saw a camera-like box on a rolling stand and rows of glass photographic plates set along the walls. He could also make out glassware and switch boxes and tall vertical gauges. This could, he thought, be a photographer's studio, a darkroom, an inventor's workshop or a sorcerer's laboratory.

Soon a more senior doctor appeared.

"Can you both keep all screams of pain to a minimum?" he asked. There was laughter all around.

"Would you like to see some of our handiwork?" he asked.

He flipped a switch to illuminate a set of plates that revealed ghostly body parts—hands, feet, knees, thighs, arms, pelvises, all phantomlike and hazy. The X-ray machine had peeled the flesh and muscle away and, pushing through what was soft, had focused on the core, what the body would look like once the flesh had begun to rot. As Thomas held his breath, letting his eye roam up and down the inner parts of someone whom he must pass regularly on the corridor, he found that he was leaning against the Swede, his shoulder touching the man's upper arm.

The doctor determined that the Swede should go first. He was put in a sitting position facing the camera, his chest against a metal plate, his legs wide apart. The assistant pushed his shoulders forward and massaged his back in a series of kneading motions. He told the Swede to take a deep breath and hold it. And then the appropriate switch was turned. The Swede, Thomas could see, kept his eyes closed. The gauges sizzled with blue light and sparks crackled along the wall. A red light blinked. Then everything became calm.

It was now Thomas's turn.

"Hug the panel," the doctor said. "Imagine it's someone else, someone you like. And press your chest against the other person and breathe in deeply."

When it was over, the doctor told him and the Swede to wait. They would soon be able to see what the camera had captured. First, they would look at the Swede.

In the image of the Swede held up against the light, Thomas saw the breastbone merged with the spine that was one dark, grisly column. And then his eyes were drawn to something near the breastbone that looked like a sack.

"Do you see his heart?" the doctor asked.

When it was Thomas's turn to see himself, he felt that he had entered an inner sanctum in a holy place. As the screen was illuminated, he thought for a second of his father's body, now reduced to a skeleton in the graveyard in Lübeck. And then he saw his own body as it would be in the grave. He wondered if, among the photographic plates, they had images of Katia, images that might make her more precious to him once he had seen what she would look like in the great eternity.

In a flash, he saw what this could do in a book, how dramatic it would be, the first time a novelist described an X-ray, with all the eerie light and uncanny sounds, the result an image that heretofore had been shared with no one. He had been enticed to Davos, he saw, as if by magic. As soon as he freed himself from its atmosphere, he would, he knew, start to work again. He longed to be back in his study now, ready to complain should one of the children make a sound. He listened respectfully to the doctor, who told him that the X-ray had confirmed what they already suspected. He was tubercular and he needed treatment. He nodded politely and meekly, suggesting that he was ready to put himself in the doctor's hands. But in his mind he was already on the train going down the narrow rails that had been cut into the Alps.

His discussions with the family doctor in Munich released him from the sorcery that had exercised tight control over his dreams and his waking time in Davos.

"My suggestion," the doctor said, "is that you remain in the flatlands. If you start coughing up blood, arrange to see me immediately. I have a feeling, however, that it will be some time before we meet again. And tell your wife, if she will listen, that being away from her family will make her even more ill than she is."

Thomas returned to ensuring that his two eldest children sat up straight at meals and did not leave the table until their plates were clean. Sometimes, after requests from Erika, he made jokes and did magic tricks for them that he had not done since Katia had left. One of them involved pretending that he could not see Erika, who was sitting in a chair, insisting that she was a cushion put there for his comfort. While it made Erika and Klaus scream with laughter, it caused Golo to cover his face with his hands. When the two eldest asked him to do it over and over, he wished Katia were there to decide when the game should stop.

He began to plot out his novel *The Magic Mountain*. The protagonist would be fifteen years younger than he and would be from Hamburg with the mind of a scientist and with a scientist's innocence. He would travel to Davos merely to visit his cousin who was being treated there and he would notice time losing its meaning once he entered into the routines ordained by the authorities. Such novelties would disconcert him until he became used to them.

The ordered days in this imagined Davos replaced the shapeless ones in the lowlands. The slow decline of the patients mirrored a sort of moral illness seeping its way into the life of the plain. But this was too simple. He would have to let life, rather than some theory of life, rule his book. He would have to make scenes full of chance and eccentricity. He would explore the sly persistence of the erotic.

As he dreamed of his book, he was aware of something new happening in Munich. When journalists came to his house, they asked about politics rather than books. They spoke of the Balkans and the Great Powers, presuming that he would have pronounced views on Germany's role in Europe and on what the disintegration of the Ottoman Empire would mean. He wished sometimes that Katia and Heinrich could witness his efforts to sound as if he had put serious thought into these political questions. But he also found that he enjoyed his role as a novelist who kept a sharp eye on a changing world. Slowly, he began to pay more attention to the newspapers, which reported on the growth of the German military and the need for the Kaiser to be vigilant, as his enemies were in every country that surrounded his own.

Thomas wrote to Katia about the novel, but she did not react to that. Instead, she told him that someone from the bad Russian table had died and how in the dead of night they had surreptitiously removed the corpse from the sanatorium.

Even though he asked Katia a number of times how long she thought she might remain at Davos, she did not respond. He saw that she was still bewitched by life there. His visit, his joining in the routine, instead of waking her to reality, had reinforced the illusion.

To break the spell, he wrote to her to say that they would need to build a house in Munich. He was already looking at sites, he said, and thinking about plans. He remembered Katia's involvement in the smallest detail of the house they had built at Bad Tölz. The builder had even jokingly called her the architect. Often, she would wake in the night to make some adjustment to the plans.

He wrote her several letters about what sort of house he was thinking of, drawing a plan to show where his study might be, and how the kitchen would be in the basement. He hoped that this might wake her from her slumber. He imagined, however, it would take time, with more detail about plans for building, to lure her back to them. He was surprised when, having received a number of anodyne letters from her, a brief one came in which she stated that since the doctors had told her that there was no further benefit to be derived from a stay in the mountains, then she would be with them soon.

He did not know whether to tell the children immediately or let her homecoming be a surprise for them. As he waited, he understood that it would not be long before Katia would fill their lives as though she had never been away. He, on the other hand, would, in his imagination, inhabit the life of the very place she was leaving.

Chapter 6
Munich, 1914

Klaus Pringsheim was at the piano, with Erika, who was nine, and Klaus Mann, a year younger, one on each side of him. Katia, sitting on a sofa, was wearing a black brocade dress. Monika had found a spoon and, despite everyone's entreaties, was banging it against a saucepan that she had taken from the kitchen. Golo was watching the scene with mild distaste.

"Klaus," his uncle said, "when Erika does harmony, don't follow her, hold the melody. Sing loud, if you have to."

The song was a music hall number.

Katia, in the presence of her brother, could still change in an instant. Since her return from Davos, she had put energy into dealing with the children's needs and overseeing the building on a site they had bought on Poschingerstrasse, close to the river. In the evening, when the house was quiet, Thomas would find her sitting at the dining room table going over plans. But once her twin came to visit, she became again the girl who had beguiled him at a party in her parents' house. She and Klaus took up their old sardonic poses. They made him feel that they were laughing at him.

"What we want," Klaus said, as he turned to face Thomas, "is an independent Munich that will side with France against the Prussians. That would be a war to win!"

"Would you fight in that war, my pet?" Katia asked.

"In the day, I would be the most fearsome soldier," Klaus said. "And in the evenings, I would be in great demand to make stirring music for the troops."

He played the opening of the Marseillaise.

"We have neighbors," Thomas said, "and these are tense times."

"Some of our neighbors are longing for war," Katia said.

Erika and her brother Klaus began to sing.

> *We hate Johnny Russia with his big smelly farts.*
> *We hate the French for being sly.*
> *We hate the English with their cold, cold hearts.*
> *The Huns will fight them all until they die.*
> *Die, die, die. Until they all die.*

They marched around the room, with Monika following, banging her spoon against the pan. Soon Golo joined them, marching with solemnity.

"Where did they learn that?" Thomas asked.

"There are thousands of songs like that," his brother-in-law said. "You should get out more."

"Tommy likes the world to come to him," Katia said.

"Wait until Marienplatz is renamed Place de Marie," Klaus said. "Then there will be songs. Or when it has a Russian name."

Thomas noticed that some of the servants had congregated on the stairwell. He wished he and Katia had called their elder son some name other than Klaus. One Klaus was enough. He hoped that Klaus Mann might model himself on someone other than his uncle.

In January, they moved into the new house. For some time, out of superstition, Thomas had avoided even passing the site. And when

Katia had tried to consult him about details, he told her that all he wanted was a study where he would have peace and a balcony, if not two, from which he might contemplate the world.

"I would like my own bathroom, but I will not take up arms on the question."

"We must keep my father away until it is done. He would take up arms about the smallest item of furniture."

"I will want the bookcases from Lübeck, and not the ones your father designed, and perhaps a door into the garden from my study so that I can disappear."

"I showed you that. It is in the plans."

He smiled and lifted his arms in a gesture of helplessness.

"All I saw when you showed me the plans was the money it will cost."

"My father—" Katia began.

"I would rather borrow the money from the bank," Thomas said.

The house was too imposing. It looked, he thought, like a rich man's house, a man who had traveled in Holland and in England and taken in the styles, someone who was not shy at his wealth being so obviously displayed. He realized that he was both proud that he owned this house and worried what others might feel, such as Heinrich. Also, he was concerned that it would set the children apart. While they might find friends nearby, they would be the children of parents who took wealth for granted. He did not want his children to have that attitude to privilege. But there was hardly anything he could do about that now. He was careful not to complain to Katia, who delighted in showing the house to her family.

"How grand our little writer has made you," Klaus said to her, winking conspiratorially at Thomas. "From foggy Lübeck to shiny luxury. Don't tell me how much the mortgage is! No writer has that amount of cash."

• • •

When they went to Bad Tölz, Thomas fervently hoped that no one would mention the possibility of war. Once outside the city, he was sure, there would be no jokes about patriotism. In Munich, he had not frequented the cafés since his marriage, and he had no access to political gossip. He thought, however, that war was unlikely. While England, in his opinion, wanted a less powerful and confident Germany, he did not see how France and Russia would join a war from which England, still hungry for spoils in the colonies, would most benefit.

On the road to Bad Tölz, they made a number of stops for refreshments, but they did not hear any news. They arrived in the late afternoon and were too busy putting the house in order to take a walk. However, they allowed the eldest children to look for their friends, accompanied by a maid, with the strict proviso that they had to be back by seven.

Thomas was in his study arranging his books when Erika and Klaus came running in.

"They shot an archduke! They shot an archduke!"

At first, Thomas thought that it was the opening of a song. He was determined that, from the very beginning of this holiday, his two eldest children would not draw too much attention to themselves.

He was glad that Katia was upstairs as he grabbed Klaus and pointed threateningly at Erika.

"I don't want any more songs! No more songs!"

"Uncle Klaus said we can sing what we like," Erika said.

"He is not your father!"

"It isn't a song anyway," Erika said. "It's the truth."

"They shot an archduke," Klaus said. "You are the last to know."

"What archduke?" he asked.

"Who is talking about an archduke?" Katia asked when she appeared.

"They shot him," Erika repeated.

"And he is all dead," Klaus added. "*Die, die, die. Until they all die!*"

The next morning, there were no newspapers to be had. Thomas placed an order with Hans Gähler, the local newsagent, for several of the daily German newspapers to be kept for him each day over the next two months. Gähler prided himself, as soon as the Manns began their summer sojourn, on putting Thomas's books on display in the window.

He accompanied Thomas to the street, looking up and down suspiciously as though some alien army might materialize at any moment.

"The man who assassinated Archduke Franz Ferdinand was not just a Serb," Gähler said slowly and judiciously, "he was a Serb nationalist, which means he was in the pay of the Russians. And if this was done on the orders of the Russians, then the English had to be in on it too. And the French are too weak and too stupid to be able to put a stop to something like this."

Thomas wondered if this were something Gähler had read in the newspapers or if he had heard it from one of his customers.

Every morning, as he came to collect his papers, Thomas found that Gähler combined opinions he had read just hours before with prejudices of his own.

"A short sharp war is the only solution. We should go in after the French like a thief in the night. And the only way to get the English is through their ships. I understand that we have been working hard on a new torpedo. That torpedo will make our enemies shake."

Thomas smiled at the thought of Erika and Klaus singing one of their songs to accompany Gähler's dire prognostications.

The more he studied the newspapers, the more it became clear to him that England, France and Russia were spoiling for a war. He felt proud that Germany had increased its military production. That was, he believed, the best message to send to its enemies.

"I don't think Germany has any appetite for war," he said to Gähler one morning. "But I think the English and the Russians believe that if they don't make one big effort now to crush us, then they never will be equal to us again."

"There is plenty of appetite for war around here," Gähler said. "The men are all ready."

Thomas did not tell Katia about his conversations with Gähler. He knew that she did not want any talk of war in the house.

Since a new bathroom was being built in Munich in their absence, Thomas was forced to go to the city to pay the builders. He was alone in the house on Poschingerstrasse when Russian mobilization was declared.

The builder, when he came to be paid, pointed at the men in the bathroom.

"This is the last day they will be here," he said. "We are working fast so we can finish tonight. Next week, it will be a different world."

"Are you sure?" Thomas asked.

"Next week, we will be in uniform, all of us. Making bathrooms one day and the next day putting manners on the French. I feel sorry for the French, they are a sad race, but if one Russian shows his face in Munich, I can assure you I will teach him a lesson he will not forget. The Russians should know to keep out of here."

That evening, Thomas had an early dinner and went to his study. Every word in every book on these shelves was, he realized, a German word. Unlike Heinrich, he had never learned French or Italian. He could read simple English but his ability to speak the language was rudimentary. He took down books of poems that he had owned since Lübeck by poets such as Goethe, Heine, Höl-derlin, Platen, Novalis. He piled the slim volumes on the floor beside his armchair, aware that this might be the last evening he would have such luxury. He looked for poems that were simple in their structure and melancholy in their tone, poems about love and landscape and solitude. He liked the clanging German rhyme words, the lovely sense of completion, perfection.

It would not be hard to destroy all this. Germany, despite the strength of its military, was, he thought, fragile. It had come into being because of its common language, the language it shared with these poems. In its music and its poetry, it had treasured things of the spirit. It had been ready to explore what was difficult and painful in life. And it was hemmed in now, isolated and vulnerable, by countries with which it had nothing in common.

He went into the drawing room and looked through the records. The phonograph satisfied him only when he could play music that he had already heard in live performance. He remembered, in the early years of his marriage, being taken by the Pringsheims to see Leo Slezak in *Lohengrin*. He found one aria from the opera, "In fernem Land," sung by Slezak. He remembered his father-in-law applauding too loudly when Slezak had sung it at the opera house in Munich, causing those around them to glare.

It was the yearning in the voice that made him think about what could now so easily be lost. And a feeling too of a striving towards light or knowledge in what Wagner had written, something tentative and unsure, but focused too, reaching out into the spirit.

He bowed his head. The war now being threatened, he thought, was not caused by a misunderstanding. It was not as though the representatives of all the parties could meet and slowly find common ground. The other countries hated Germany and wanted it defeated. That would be the cause of war, he thought. And Germany had become powerful not only in its military might and its industry but in its deepening sense of its own soul, the intensity of its somber self-interrogation. He listened to the aria conclude and saw that no one outside Germany would ever understand what it meant to be in this room now, and what strength and solace this music gave to those under its spell.

The next morning, as he went into the city center, people who had read his books came up to him to shake his hand as though he were somehow one of their leaders. Already, men in uniform marched in the streets. In a café, when some soldiers came in, he noticed how young they were, and fresh, and how polite they were to the staff. They moved with dignity and tact, making sure that they did not disturb him as he read his newspaper.

He tried to write something about what war might mean for Germany, but, as the afternoon wore on, he realized that he should return to Bad Tölz. He found Katia openly distressed at the prospect of war. Over supper, she asked him about the builders and the bathroom. He did not tell her about his evening alone with the poetry and the music, or that he had started an essay on the war.

In the morning, he found Gähler standing belligerently at the door of his shop.

"I have all the papers for you. Germany will declare war today. That much is clear. It is a proud moment for our nation."

He spoke with such certainty that Thomas recoiled from him.

"It is right to be nervous," Gähler went on. "War cannot be taken lightly, although there are some who seem to think so."

He looked at Thomas accusingly. Thomas wondered if there was something in one of his books that had offended the newsagent.

"Am I right in thinking that you are the brother of one Heinrich Mann?"

Thomas nodded as Gähler went into the shop and returned with a left-wing Berlin newspaper from two days earlier.

"This sort of thing will have to be censored," he said.

Heinrich's article began by insisting that there was no such thing as victory in a war. There were only casualties, only the dead and injured. He went on to bemoan the rise of military spending in Germany and the lack of spending on things that might improve people's lives. The article ended by stating that if the Kaiser could not pull back from war, then the German people should make their priorities clear.

"Sedition," Gähler said. "A stab in the back. He should be arrested."

"My brother is an internationalist," Thomas said.

"He is an enemy of the people."

"Yes, it might be best if he remained silent until the war is won."

Gähler looked at him sharply to make sure that he was not speaking in jest.

"I had a brother and all this was to be his," Gähler said.

He pointed to the small shop as though it were an estate in the countryside.

"And I was to work on a pig farm. But then he decided to go to America. No one ever knew why. We had one postcard from him. Nothing else. So that is why I am standing here. We all have brothers."

It seemed almost natural that Thomas himself would be declared unfit for active service, as would Heinrich, as, indeed, would Gähler. But his brother Viktor, at twenty-four, was signed up, as was Katia's brother Heinz.

In Bad Tölz, Thomas found that Gähler had been repeating remarks he had made in support of the war. One day, as he and Katia were on the main street, a passing group of middle-aged men saluted him. One of them moved forward to tell him that Germany needed writers like him in this time of crisis. When they heard this, the others cheered.

"What did he mean?" Katia asked.

"I think he means he is glad that I am not Heinrich."

When Thomas and Katia came to Munich from Bad Tölz to attend the wedding of Viktor, who wanted to marry before he went to the front, he found a lightness in the air, a kind of joy. In the train, which was overcrowded, soldiers who were seated immediately stood up if a civilian appeared. Many civilians, including Thomas himself, insisted that, no, the soldiers should take the seats. One soldier, standing on a bench, addressed the carriage.

"We are in the service of Germany. That is what our uniform means. We wish to stand rather than sit to show our determination to serve."

The other men in uniform cheered, as the civilians applauded. Thomas found that he had tears in his eyes.

At the restrained wedding ceremony, his mother told him that Heinrich had met a Czech actress and was also planning to marry.

"She is called Mimi, which I think is a lovely name."

Thomas did not respond.

"I didn't read that article he wrote," his mother continued, "but my neighbors did. This is the time for us all to pull together. I am so proud of Viktor."

Lula and her husband drank too much, Löhr telling Katia to advise her father to invest in war bonds.

"It would be a good way of putting paid to any suspicion that he might not support the war."

"Why would he not support the war?" Katia asked.

"Is he not Jewish? Or was his father not Jewish?"

Katia became an expert on the black market. She developed a network of suppliers and a knowledge of what was available. She said that she could tell how the war was proceeding by the price of eggs, but then her theory was disproved when eggs could not be bought at all, even at exorbitant prices.

Erika and Klaus were under strict orders not to sing any songs or make any comments on the war, even in the privacy of the house.

"They are sending disobedient little boys to the front," Thomas said.

"Indeed they are," Katia said.

The distance between Thomas's study and the living quarters of the house became longer, he thought, in the first few months of the war. He banned children even from the corridor outside. And Klaus Pringsheim visited more freely. He played the piano, amused the children and kept the conversation light, but he always managed to insert some barbed remark about the war effort or a speech made by a military leader. Thomas was careful never to get into an argument with him. Soon, if his brother-in-law was in the house, he did not join the company at all.

In his study, Thomas could return to the books he loved. In the confusion created by the war, however, he could no longer work on the novel about the sanatorium. Instead, he struggled with the article about the meaning of the war for Germany and its culture. He wished sometimes that he knew more, not having read any political philosophy and having a sketchy knowledge of German philosophy.

Since his marriage, he had remained within the family circle, avoiding other writers and literary gatherings. Katia would keep an eye out for anyone who was trying to win his friendship and deal with them suspiciously. Nothing lowered his spirits more than a writer wishing to discuss what might be done for his career.

A few times in the year before the war when he was approached by the writer Ernst Bertram, he thought it was because of *Death in Venice*. Perhaps Bertram, who was homosexual, believed that Thomas was a kindred spirit. And then he thought that Bertram was seeking advancement. But Bertram, it turned out, was interested in Germany and in philosophy. He had read widely and had many strong opinions. He did not want anything from Thomas other than his attention.

Bertram's references, as he discussed current events, were lofty. He seldom made a point without quoting Nietzsche; he could refer to Bismarck and Metternich as much as Plato and Machiavelli. He was precise when he mentioned a source; he could almost summon up the number of the page on which a certain line had appeared.

Katia did not warm to Bertram.

"He is very interested in you," she said. "More than is necessary. Sometimes, he is like a large dog looking for approval, his tongue hanging out. And at other times I think he has plans to run away with you."

"To where?"

"Valhalla," she said.

"He knows a great deal."

"Yes, and he knows how to be polite, and then he averts his eyes. But he only averts them from me. I think he is interested in male friendship. He is too Germanic!"

"Is there something wrong with that?"

"I would imagine so!"

Slowly, Bertram became a regular visitor to the house, getting to know the children and the servants. He was the only one allowed into Thomas's study if he chanced to call in the morning.

Bertram spoke of Germany's destiny, the deep roots that culture had in her soil, the way in which German music expressed and uplifted the German spirit. Gradually, instead of discussing the work of Nietzsche, about whom Bertram was writing a treatise, they began to discuss Germany's singularity, how her very cultural strength caused her neighbors to isolate her. The only solution to this, Bertram believed, was war. Once the war was won, then Germany could exert her influence throughout Europe.

Thomas agreed that the operas of Wagner or the writings of Nietzsche, in all their excitement and sense of longing, were manifestations of the German spirit, a spirit that was all the more palpable and forceful for being unsettled, irrational and filled with internal strife. When Bertram responded by insisting that the German belief in soul could never be easily content with simple democracy, Thomas found himself nodding.

Bertram made no secret of the fact that he had a male partner; he managed to intimate that they even shared a bed. Sometimes, when he spoke, Thomas found himself wondering what this ungainly man would look like naked. He must wake in the morning with this other man beside him. Thomas pictured their thin hairy legs entwined, their lips kissing. The image fascinated him, but it also made him recoil. He would not get much pleasure from sleeping with Ernst Bertram.

Thomas thought that he might write a short book about Germany and the war. Gradually, the projected volume became longer and more ambitious. While he had always involved Katia in his novels and stories, reading sections aloud to her when completed, Thomas could not so easily discuss this political book with her, nor indeed read to her from it.

"Can you imagine if Klaus and Golo were old enough to be in the war and we were here waiting each day for news of them?" she asked. "And all because of some idea."

When their fifth child, Elisabeth, was born, it was natural that Ernst Bertram be asked to be her godfather. By then, he was the only friend that Thomas had.

As he followed the progress of the war and published a number of articles supporting the German struggle, Thomas got comfort from being part of a movement that included workers as much as businessmen, and people from all parts of Germany. How could he have persisted in writing a novel when all the values he cared about were under threat from countries that included Russia, a half-civilized police state, and France, still nourishing itself on the poisoned dreams of its eighteenth-century revolution?

The war, he wrote, would rid Europe of corruption. Germany was warlike out of morality, not out of vanity or glory-seeking or imperialism. Germany would emerge freer and better than it was. But if Germany were to be defeated, he warned, Europe would never have peace or rest. Only Germany's victory, he wrote, could guarantee the peace of Europe.

It pleased him, once this article was published, to receive letters from soldiers at the front to say how much his words had inspired them. And then, encouraged by Bertram, he worked hard to finish the book he had been planning. It was to be called *Reflections of a Nonpolitical Man*.

Before the war, Thomas had viewed Heinrich's internationalism as a result of his living too long in Italy and France. Now, as German fatalities increased, Thomas presumed that his brother would become less nonchalant about the threats to Germany and discard his cosmopolitan airs.

When Thomas went to visit his mother in Polling, he discovered that she had written to Heinrich asking him to stop speaking out against his fatherland. The war, Thomas saw, had put new life into his mother's eyes. She walked about the village, detaining anyone she saw to discuss Germany's progress. She would shout patriotic slogans.

"Everyone stops me to know how my son is doing. And they are asking about Viktor, poor little Viktor. Before it was all Heinrich and Thomas. But now it is the soldier in the family. I go for a walk twice a day, or three times, or more. And everyone tells me to be strong. So I am being strong."

Late in 1915, Heinrich published an essay invoking Zola as a novelist who had, during the Dreyfus case, attempted to alert his fellow countrymen to a wrong that was being committed. Clearly, he was comparing himself to the French novelist.

It was not the argument in the article that offended Thomas. It was the second sentence: "A creator only reaches manhood relatively late in life—it is those who appear natural and worldly-wise in their early twenties who are destined soon to dry up."

He showed the article to Katia.

"This is a personal attack on me. I won fame in my twenties. He is referring to me."

"But you haven't dried up."

He was afraid to argue that not even *Death in Venice* had achieved the same success as his first book, and Heinrich was mocking him for that.

When Bertram came, he felt freer to rail against his brother.

"He has never forgiven me for the fame I won with that book, or for marrying a rich woman, or for setting up house while he grew involved in a series of failed relationships, not marrying until now."

"He is like all so-called socialists," Bertram said. "Filled with bitterness."

Late one afternoon, when Thomas went to see his mother in Polling, the light had already begun to fade. She was sitting in the semidarkness when he entered her living room.

"Who is it?" she called out.

"Tommy," he replied.

As he closed the door behind him, she was in full flight.

"Oh, Tommy? Well, I agree with you that he is like a little general directing the war. Soon he will barge into Belgium with a bugle! How did he become so bellicose? I told that wife of his that he would have to calm down. And she just looked at me! You know, I never warmed to Katia Pringsheim. I much prefer your Mimi."

"Mother, this *is* Tommy."

She turned and peered at him.

"Oh, so it is!" she said.

In Munich, when he told Lula what had happened, she laughed.

"Your mother loves both of you. With Heinrich, she is Rosa Luxemburg. With you, she is Hindenburg. With me, she talks about pincushions and chintz coverings."

While Katia managed to have some relationship with Mimi, Heinrich's new wife, exchanging messages and gifts, the brothers cut each other off. Thomas noted, with disgust, how the Zola article won Heinrich supporters, made him into a courageous public figure, so-called, one of the few brave enough to speak the truth about the war.

Most of Heinrich's early books were out of print. And none of them had ever sold in any numbers. Now, a ten-volume edition of Heinrich Mann's work, with each volume also coming out in a cheap paperbound book, was displayed in the shops. Heinrich's opposition to the war had moved him from obscurity to a sort of literary fame.

Even when Mimi gave birth to a girl, Thomas did not contact his brother. Heinrich's apartment in Leopoldstrasse, he heard, was a haven for those interested in pacifism and new political ideas. On the other side of the Isar river, Thomas's social life was confined to visits from Ernst Bertram. He still could not write any fiction. His book on the war was increasingly labored in its tone, with many emendations and redraftings.

Slowly, it became known that the differences between the two brothers, now that they were openly political, had become more intense. While Heinrich developed a following among young, left-wing activists, Thomas found himself the object of casual deprecation even among those who had been his avid readers. Since much opinion was censored, it was difficult to write openly about the war. Offering views in print, instead, on the relative merits of the Mann brothers came to be an indirect, but powerful, way for writers and journalists to make their position on the war clear.

When they were alone together, Thomas and Katia did not discuss the war, but once they were in the company of her parents and her brothers, Katia in stray remarks let Thomas know that she believed Germany would lose the war and that she did not feel loyal, in any case, to the German cause. She spoke with certainty, but also a sort of lightness and insouciance, so that he could not argue with her.

"It is our duty to love Germany, but it is also our duty to read Goethe's *Faust*, part one and part two," she said. "And all that duty is too much for me. I love my husband and children. I love my family. That takes all my energy. I suppose that makes me a very bad person and people should avoid me."

Thomas became silent not only at the Pringsheims', but in his own house, at his own table. The children, especially Klaus, were noisy and disruptive. Unlike the years before the war, when Thomas would come to the table content with the morning's work, sure about what he was doing, ready to make jokes and pay attention to the children, he found it difficult not to spend the meals insisting that Klaus, now ten, should conduct himself as befitted a boy of his age or ruling that Golo would get no dessert for one whole week if he did not answer his mother when she spoke to him.

Often, however, his efforts to be strict failed him. He still did tricks at the table and had worn a wizard costume to a party that

he attended with Erika and Klaus. A few days later, he had come to
Klaus's room when the boy was having a nightmare about a man
who carried his own head under his arm. Thomas had told Klaus
not to look at the man, but to tell him in no uncertain terms that
his father was a famous magician, and he had said that a child's
bedroom was no place for him and that he should be ashamed of
himself. He made Klaus repeat this several times.

The next morning at breakfast, Klaus told his mother that his
father had magic powers and knew the right words to banish a
ghost.

"Papa is a magician," he said.

"He is the Magician!" Erika repeated.

From being a joke, or a way of cheering the table up, the new
sobriquet for their father stuck. Erika encouraged all visitors to
join her in giving her father this new name.

As the war was waged, Thomas continued to monitor Heinrich's
articles. His brother, he saw, did not often write directly about
the conflict. Instead, he shared his views on the French Second
Empire, leaving enough space for his readers to understand the
connections between France then and Germany now. But as the
antiwar movement grew, Thomas observed his brother becoming
braver. Heinrich agreed, for example, to take part in a meeting
of antiwar socialists in Munich, insisting that war was nothing to
enthuse over, it did not civilize, it did not cleanse, it did not make
anything true or just, and it did not make people more brotherly.

Thomas studied each phrase in the newspaper report, believing that the word "brotherly" referred specifically to him. He
knew that anyone reading what Heinrich had written would recognize that it was part of their feud.

● ● ●

When the war ended, the conversations at the table centered on Katia's continued search for food and her worry about her parents.

"For some reason," she said, "eggs are plentiful, but I can't get flour. And the only fresh vegetable I can get is spinach."

"And we hate spinach," Erika said.

"And I hate eggs and flour," Klaus added.

Klaus Pringsheim explained when he came to Poschingerstrasse that he was trying to form an orchestra made up of returned soldiers.

"Some of them I trained with. They were talented musicians. And now most of them have shaking hands and lungs that are destroyed. I don't know how they will live. I thought they were lucky to survive, but I don't think that now."

He warned Thomas and Katia to be vigilant on the streets.

"A group of young men placed themselves at our street corner two days ago. They were dressed like peasants and they had a cart of apples. When they saw my father on his way home from the university, one of them threw an apple at him and hit him on the side of the head."

Erika began to laugh.

"Did he eat the apple?" she asked.

"No, my mother threw it in the garbage and then she telephoned the police. By which time, having gone out into the street, I discovered that the apple throwers were not peasants at all but socialists and this is their way of showing that they can do what they like."

"Did they throw any apples at you?" Thomas asked.

"They don't know who I am, but you should look out," Klaus Pringsheim said. "And you won't get any help from the police, who told my mother to get private security if she was worried about her safety. And I understand from one of my fellow musicians that the apple throwers will soon be very well armed and will no longer need to throw apples."

"If they are armed," Thomas said, "then they will be dealt with."

"There is no one to deal with them," Klaus said. "In a moment, they could take over the city. That is what losing the war has meant. The police are useless."

"We want to put the whole war behind us," Katia said. "That man Ernst Bertram called a few days ago. He had a bloodthirsty look on his face. And I drove him from the door."

She looked around the table defiantly. Thomas had wondered why Bertram had not been in touch and thought that he should try to contact him by telephone or write to him.

He planned, when the meal was over, to remonstrate with Katia, but she went to bed early and he found himself alone in his study looking around at the shelves for a book that might give him comfort.

The war was lost. His own book was finished and would soon come out in a changed Germany. While as recently as six months earlier there had still been a sense of patriotism and even national fervor, now there was nothing except talk of the wounded and the dead. The newspapers reported on rationing and supplies. The Kaiser was gone, but no one was sure what would replace him. Germany was now a republic, but that, Thomas thought, was a joke.

It was not a night for poetry. Nor did he want to look at any of the philosophy books with which he had been busy. No words by any German would help. If Bertram came, Thomas would like to ask him why this war had been waged since it was so easily lost. And he would want to know what Germany should be proud of now.

If, on the other hand, Heinrich were to appear, he would ask him if Germany was now to be like other places, living under the control of the victorious powers. What would it mean now to write in German, to work in a study whose walls were lined with the great German books, to sit in the evenings listening to German music on the phonograph?

He thought about the young men dressed as peasants throwing apples at wealthy burghers. Was this what it had come to? Parody, futility, foolishness? Was this what the great project that was Germany would finally mean?

Erika and Klaus continued to take an interest in each day's news. When the first elections after the war were taking place, they were delighted at the idea that women could vote for the first time, seeing it as another opportunity to display a general lack of respect for their elders at mealtimes. Erika, when Julia came from Polling, said that she heard that all married women would vote the same way as their husbands.

"They might promise they will, my little one," Katia said, "but the vote is secret. Except my grandmother, who has announced publicly how she will vote."

"How will you vote?" Klaus asked his own grandmother.

"I will vote wisely," Julia said.

"And the Magician?"

For the first time in months, Thomas laughed.

"I will vote the same way as your mother and she will vote wisely also."

"What will the result be?" Klaus asked his father.

Before Thomas had time to respond, Katia interjected.

"Germany will become a democracy," she said.

"But what about the socialists?" Klaus asked.

"They will take part in a democracy," Katia replied firmly.

"Is Herr Bertram a socialist?" Klaus asked.

"No, he is not," Katia replied.

"I am a socialist," Klaus said. "And so is Erika."

"Onto the barricades, both of you, then," Thomas replied. "There is plenty of space."

"They are very young for talk of barricades," Julia said.

"Golo is an anarchist," Klaus said.

"I am not!" Golo shouted.

"Klaus, sit up straight," Thomas said, "or leave the table."

"You know, I never liked that Kaiser," Julia said. "I will like the new people better, I'm sure, as long as they are not telling me that all people are equal. I have learned very little in my life but my views can be trusted on the inferiority of many, including people who think very highly of themselves."

"The working class is going to take over," Klaus said.

"Who told you that?" Julia asked.

"Our uncle Klaus."

"I am sure he is singularly ill-informed," Julia responded.

"The Magician agrees with you," Erika said.

"Erika, be quiet!" Katia said.

"What cause are you supporting?" Julia asked Thomas. "It is so hard to know. I meet people who ask me."

"I am for Germany," Thomas said. "All of Germany."

When he looked over, Katia was shaking her head.

He had planned *Reflections of a Nonpolitical Man* as an intervention in a debate. By the time it was published, however, the debate had moved on. While some reviews were unpleasant, few bothered to go into any detail on why they disliked the book. Heinrich's new novel, on the other hand, was acclaimed.

The family's dining room table had become a battlefield since Erika and Klaus had discovered that their parents did not see eye to eye on political developments. Erika had taken to contacting Klaus Pringsheim by phone for news, and going down into the kitchen when deliveries were being made to inquire about what was really happening in the streets of Munich.

"In Lübeck when I was growing up," Thomas said, "a thirteen-year-old girl and her twelve-year-old brother were silent until they were spoken to."

"This is the twentieth century," Klaus said.

"And there is going to be a revolution in Munich," Erika added.

One evening, as Thomas sat in his study, Katia came to ask him if he remembered a young writer called Kurt Eisner.

"He is a friend of Heinrich's," Thomas said. "One of those fellows who used to get arrested for handing out badly printed seditious pamphlets."

"In the kitchen," Katia said, "they are saying that he has started a revolution."

"Did he write something?"

"He has taken control of the city."

Within a few days, the servants had stopped coming and Katia found it impossible to get any food at all on the black market. Erika and Klaus were banned from even approaching the telephone, but they still managed to follow rumors and speculation.

"It is Soviet-style," Erika said.

"Do you know what that means?" Thomas asked.

"They shoot rich people," Klaus said.

"They will drag them out of their houses," Golo added.

"But where have you heard all of this?"

"Everybody knows it," Erika said.

Thomas was shocked when Kurt Eisner was shot by a right-wing extremist. He felt that Heinrich must be putting himself in danger when he delivered Eisner's funeral oration.

Katia discovered that Hans, their chauffeur, usually had the most accurate information. One morning, she came into Thomas's study with two names on a piece of paper.

"These two have taken over," she said. "They run everything now. But they don't run supplies, because I cannot get flour and there is no milk to be had. The woman I used to get milk from has been warned."

"Show me the names," Thomas said.

He laughed when he saw that she had noted down the names of Ernst Toller and Erich Mühsam.

"They are poets," he said. "They sit in cafés."

"They are on the Central Council," she said. "If you want anything, you go to them."

Later that day, Klaus Pringsheim arrived to visit.

"I had to take a circuitous route," he said, "as there are poets manning blockades and they are ferociously frightening."

"You should have stayed home," Katia said.

"Home is unbearable. Father has been threatened. They have explained that he will eventually have to hand over his house and his paintings, but just now they want the numbers of his Swiss bank accounts."

"I hope he has refused," Thomas said.

"He is in shock. My mother recognized one of the boys and let out a most fearful shout at him. He is from a family of intellectuals, she says. She informed him that there would be consequences if he did not leave."

"What did he do?" Katia asked.

"He pointed a gun at her and said he wanted no further nonsense from her. That is when I slipped out. I tried to look like a servant. I thought we were going to be shot *en masse* like the Romanovs. We would be a *cause célèbre*."

Since they had started hearing news of the revolution in Munich, Thomas had not ventured out. But when he discovered that both of Katia's parents could make their way freely across the city to his door, he did wonder if this revolution was real. His father-in-law's love for the sound of his own voice had, he saw, been much enhanced by the uprising.

"They preach the equality of man, and that means they hate anyone who is not like themselves," Alfred said. "And what they want is for us all to live in one room and spend our time serving our servants. Well, we don't want that and our servants don't either."

"Well, most of them don't," Klaus Pringsheim interrupted.

"I think we should all keep our voices down," Katia said.

"That will come soon enough," her father continued. "But before I am silenced, can I draw your attention to the so-called minister for finance in the new brave, illegal government of Bavaria? He has announced that he does not believe in money. He wants all money abolished! And Dr. Lipp, who is in charge of foreign affairs, is a certified lunatic. I think we should quake in our boots at the thought of these people running Munich. I am indignant that this group of pests has not been arrested and locked away. Thank God for Switzerland, that is what I say. Take me there now!"

"Perhaps we should keep our indignation in reserve," Katia said.

"Indeed," Thomas said. "We might need it before long."

When Erika came into the room, her grandparents rose to hug her, but she stood back.

"I have been told that there is a curfew and if you don't leave now you will be arrested."

The Pringsheims seemed amazed at how solemn she was. She looked at them as though she had some control over their destiny. Even Klaus Pringsheim, Thomas saw, was reduced to silence.

It took Thomas a while to accept that there was a new and functioning government in Munich and that it consisted of poets and dreamers and friends of Heinrich's. He was comforted by the news that no equivalent revolts had happened successfully in other German cities. This meant that the army might see the quelling of this uprising as a way of restoring its own tainted honor.

Sometimes he was sure that all they would have to do was wait. Bavaria was Catholic as well as conservative. It would not quietly accept a group of atheist diehards running things. Also, he believed that while Germany had lost the war, it had not thrown away the ability to mount a measured and strategic attack on anyone who took power in this strange, shocked interlude that came in the war's aftermath. But maybe, on the other hand, they had been fatally demoralized by defeat.

He wished that the state would take action before the poets and their friends had time to realize that they would soon face execution or long prison sentences. Since these leaders of the revolution were still being viewed as absurd by men like his father-in-law, such mockery was likely, Thomas thought, to make them very dangerous if they felt an urgent need to be taken seriously.

When, at last, an attack by state troops was actually threatened, the rebels took hostages from prominent upper-middle-class families. Because Thomas had sold the summer house at Bad Tölz, he had no choice but to remain in Poschingerstrasse, but he discontinued his afternoon walk and did not draw attention to himself in any way.

Katia, he knew, had spoken to Erika and Klaus and warned them not to consort with the servants or telephone their uncle Klaus or spread rumors of any sort. Since the schools had been closed, they were to attend to their lessons under their mother's close supervision.

In some way, however, they found out that men like their father were being arrested and houses like theirs were being ransacked. While they were afraid to be openly disobedient, Golo, whom Katia had not thought of threatening, was found moving about the house shouting: "We are all going to be shot!"

There must be some among the leaders, Thomas thought, who knew about the feud between himself and his brother. He was lucky that hardly anyone had read his book, as armed men wandered the city in search of those who willfully supported the ruling class in word or in deed.

As troops finally prepared to enter the city to end the revolution, rumors came via Hans that the insurgents were summarily shooting some of their hostages. The Mann family and their servants kept away from the windows. Thomas spent as much time as he could in his study. Were the revolution to prevail, then his father-in-law's predictions would be borne out and the family would have to take what they could and make their way to the Swiss border. They would be lucky to escape.

He came close to banging the table with rage as it struck him how little he would actually care for Germany if it were to become a center for disaffection and revolution and mayhem. He cared more, he realized, for himself and his property. This uprising had reduced him to becoming bourgeois; up to then he had merely lived with the trappings.

None of his neighbors came to the house, nor did he visit those who lived close by. He was a man without a country. Germany came to seem like a character in a novel that attracted too much heat and should be dispensed with. He imagined being dragged from the house by armed, myopic, tubercular poets, all the more determined and savage because of their interest in beauty. In those days, he was sure, the prison cells would be full and there would be young men fired up with enthusiasm and they would be left to handle the prisoners. It would not be long before they began to take some of their captives out to be shot. He shuddered at the thought of being in captivity, waking in the dawn to the sound of the names of those to be executed being read.

Every single thought he had had over the previous few years meant nothing in the light of his sense of impending doom. He, who had visualized the end of the war as represented by imaginative energy and social stability, now could not sleep, he was so worried about his own fate and that of his family.

The end of the uprising came slowly, with the noise of shooting frightening all of them except Golo, who was delighted by the sound, clapping his hands in joy. Hans told Katia that Thomas should hide somewhere in the attic, as the revolutionaries could do anything now that they were on the point of being defeated. Instead, Thomas remained in his study, having his meals served there, asking Katia to stay with him as much as she could.

Thomas's only comfort in the aftermath of the Munich Revolution was the baby Elisabeth, who was now learning to crawl. He carried her into his study as soon as breakfast was finished each morning. He followed her with his eyes as she looked around the room, the gaze placid and intelligent, and, having ascertained that there was nothing among the books and the heavy furniture that might entertain her, Elisabeth set about crawling towards the closed door. Only then did she give any sign that she knew her father was in the room. By a turn of her head, she indicated to him that he should open the door for her so that she could depart towards where she thought her siblings might be creating excitement.

Soon after the revolution had been quelled, Thomas was visited by a pale young poet who said that he had been sent by Heinrich. Thomas, summoned by one of the servants to the hallway, did not invite the visitor into the drawing room or the study.

"Could Heinrich not come himself?" he asked.

The young man made a gesture of impatience.

"We need help. I am a friend of Ernst Toller, who admires you and your work. He is in danger of being executed. I have been sent to ask you to sign a petition in his favor, requesting that the sentence be commuted."

"Sent by whom?"

"Your brother told me that I should come to see you. But Ernst Toller also asked if you would sign."

Thomas turned as Katia came down the stairs.

"This young man is a friend of Heinrich's," Thomas said.

"Then surely we should invite him in," Katia replied.

The young man refused to sit down.

"Because of who you are," he said, "you have influence."

"I did not support the revolution."

The man smiled.

"I think we are aware of that."

The tone was almost sarcastic and it created a moment of tension. Thomas felt that his visitor was on the verge of walking out but then thought better of it.

"You were on the list of those to be detained," he said. "I was in the room when that list was read out. And two of the leaders insisted that your name be removed. One was Erich Mühsam and the other was Ernst Toller. Toller spoke eloquently about your virtues."

Thomas nearly smiled at the mention of "virtues," wanting to ask what they might be.

"That was kind of him."

"It was brave of him. There were others in the room who did not agree. He held out against them. I can assure you of this. And I can assure you too that your brother's name was invoked."

"In what way?"

"In a way that saved you."

What surprised him, once he agreed to write a letter, was how much the young man knew about protocols, about how the letter should be worded and to whom it should be addressed. He said that a copy should be made of it, but advised that the appeal for clemency should not, for the moment, be made public. If Ernst Toller needed further help, he would return.

One afternoon, ready to take his walk, Thomas could not find Katia in the house or the garden. Eventually, when he heard shouting from upstairs, he located Erika and Klaus.

"Where is your mother?"

"She has gone to visit Mimi," Klaus said.

"Which Mimi?"

"There is only one Mimi," Erika said. "I answered the call. And the minute she put down the phone my mother got her hat and coat and went to visit Mimi."

She pronounced the name Mimi as though it had been invented to amuse her.

When Katia returned, she opened the door of Thomas's study. She was still wearing her hat and coat.

"Now I need you to write a note," she said. "I can tell you what to say or you can compose it yourself. It is to accompany flowers that are being sent from you to your brother in the hospital. He is out of danger, but he had peritonitis and they thought he might not survive. Mimi is still distraught. The flowers and the note will be a big surprise."

She handed Thomas a pen.

"I have a pen," he said. "I will write a note, but it is not an apology."

Once the note was sent with the flowers, Heinrich, despite his frail state, intimated his pleasure at receiving them.

When Heinrich was home from the hospital, Mimi wrote to Katia to say that her husband would love to receive a visit from his brother.

Thomas went to Leopoldstrasse, carrying flowers for Mimi and a book of Rilke's poems for Heinrich. As the door of the apartment was answered, Mimi introduced herself.

"I am an admirer," she said, "so it is time we met."

Her hair was done in some very current style. Her accent sounded closer to French than Czech. The tone she took was flirtatious, but lightly and elegantly so. She was all presence, all allure, as she escorted him into the sitting room to meet his brother.

"I have brought an old friend," she said.

The apartment was decorated in a way that emphasized its compactness. The rugs were Turkish. The wallpaper was red.

There were pictures everywhere, even leaning against the book-cases, and on the many little desks and side tables there were min-iature statues and oddly shaped vases. The dark blue curtains were made from rough silk.

In the middle of all this pattern and color, in a bank of cushions with covers that looked Arabic, sat Heinrich in a suit and tie and crisp-looking white shirt. His shoes, Thomas thought, were Ital-ian. He could have been a businessman or a conservative politician.

Mimi soon came with coffee. The cups were delicate. The coffeepot was modern. Mimi took in the scene between the two brothers, smiling in a way that was knowing and satisfied before she left the room, which was separated from the study by a parti-tion made up of hanging lines of glass beads.

Katia and Thomas had agreed that, even if provoked by Hein-rich, Thomas would not discuss politics. But Heinrich, he saw, had developed a steely, patrician charm. He said that he wished he had married years before, that there was nothing like family life. His eyes lit up with laughter as he spoke.

They discussed the failing health of their mother and the drop in her income as a result of the inflation. They wondered how long she might survive. In a lighter mode, they wondered at their brother Viktor, who had come unscathed through the war, and how ordinary he was and dull and unbookish.

"If only all of us could have been like Viktor!" Heinrich said. "He has not had his mind darkened by books."

As they chatted and sipped their coffee, a little girl came into the room. She was shy and uneasy when she saw the stranger, moving quietly towards her father and burying her face in his lap. When she finally looked up, Thomas did the little trick with his hands that he had done over the years at home, making it seem that his thumb had disappeared. She buried her face in her father's lap again.

"This is Goschi," Heinrich said.

Her mother joined them and encouraged Goschi to say hello to her uncle. Thomas saw, as she stood up and glanced at him, two generations of his father's family in the girl's dark eyes and her square jaw. His aunt, his grandmother, his father, all of them were gathered together in one small face.

He turned to Heinrich.

"I know," Heinrich said.

"She is a Hanseatic princess," Mimi said. "Aren't you, my darling?"

Goschi shook her head.

"How did your thumb get back to your hand?" she asked Thomas.

"Magic," he said. "I am a magician."

"Can you do it again?" she asked.

He told Katia that he needed to see Ernst Bertram, that too much time had passed.

"It was a mistake to make him Elisabeth's godfather," she said. "If he asks for her, best say that she is with her grandparents."

As soon as they were settled in the study, Thomas let Bertram know that he had been in touch with his brother, adding that he had no illusions about the fragility and difficulty of any revived relationship with him. His own views had not changed, he assured Bertram, but he believed more and more in the idea of humanity and in working out what this idea might mean in the real world, a defeated Germany.

He was irritated when Bertram responded to this with a cold silence.

"We are living in a defeated Germany," Thomas said. "The old ideas will not hold."

"It only seems like defeat," Bertram said. "It is actually a first step towards victory."

"It is defeat," Thomas said. "Go to the railway station and look at the men who were injured who are searching for shelter. The legless ones, the blind, the ones who have lost their reason. Ask them if it was victory or defeat!"

"You sound like your brother," Bertram said.

When Katia had become pregnant again the previous year, her mother advised her to have an abortion and set about making arrangements for this. The official Pringsheim view was that Katia had become exhausted running a house, dealing with troublesome children and managing a husband who had been locked into some dream about Germany while writing an unreadable book.

Thomas went with Katia to the doctor's surgery to discuss the abortion. He noticed how calm she was as she asked detailed questions about the procedure. Having made an appointment and left the building, Katia said quietly: "I am going to have the baby." He linked arms with her as they walked to the car without saying another word.

The birth was difficult. Katia was ordered to stay in bed for some weeks after Michael was born. Thomas, overseeing the children during this period, observed that both Erika and Klaus, in the absence of their mother, had begun to dress differently and to put on the air of adults. Erika, he saw, had budding breasts, and Klaus's voice had deepened. When he asked Katia if she had spotted this, she laughed and said that it had happened some months before.

The family and the servants did everything to encourage Elisabeth, who was a year old, to come with her father to visit her mother and see her new brother. Once she saw the baby in the bed with her mother, however, she recoiled and demanded to be taken from the room. The next time Thomas tried to carry her to Katia's room, she shook her head at the top of the stairs and pointed imperiously to the floor below.

Erika and Klaus as young children had been happy in each other's company. And Golo, as soon as he could read, would find Monika, take her to a quiet part of the house and read to her. Elisabeth, however, decided to ignore Michael. When he cried, she made a fuss as though her day were being destroyed. She sought out Golo, who was the easiest to boss around, and had him accompany her and keep her safe from her baby brother. In the first years of Michael's life, Elisabeth, as far as Thomas could make out, never once looked at him if she could help it. While Katia and her mother, and even Erika, thought that this showed early signs of bad character, Thomas found Elisabeth's determination not to be paired with a baby impressive and fascinating.

Once she could walk, Elisabeth would appear of her own accord in his study in the morning. As soon as she opened the door, she would put a finger to her own lips to make clear that she, as much as he, required total silence. Once she could talk, the others used her to send him messages.

Erika and Klaus had come of age in war and revolution and could speak of little besides politics. They rushed to get the newspapers before their father. Both of them still enjoyed exacerbating the differences between their parents on the future of Germany.

"What is wrong with democracy?" Klaus asked one day.

"Nothing," Katia said.

"We don't want systems imposed from outside," Thomas said. "Let the Germans decide what the Germans want."

"So you are against democracy?" Erika asked.

"I believe in humanity," he replied.

"We all believe in that," Klaus said. "But we also believe in democracy. I do, Erika does, our friends do, my mother does, Uncle Klaus does, Uncle Heinrich does."

"How do you know Uncle Heinrich does?"

"Everyone knows that!" Golo interjected.

"Democracy will come," Thomas said. "And my hope is that

it comes from a German belief in humanity. And I am sure my brother thinks that too."

Katia looked at him, nodding her head.

Some months later, as they were taking a walk, she reminded him of what he had said about democracy.

"Your readers would love to know your views on a German Republic," she said.

"They will have to wait for the novel before they hear from me again. My last effort to communicate with them was not universally welcomed."

"I think you should write an essay or an article or give a lecture. You need not say that you have changed your mind, merely that your support for a German Republic is a direct continuation of your thought as we move into contemporary times. You can say that no one's opinions are stable, especially not now, and that yours have always been dynamic."

"Dynamic?"

"Well, that would be a word you could use. You could also talk about German humanity and that your belief in it has always been fundamental to your thought."

He nodded and thought that he might find a way to do what she suggested. He smiled to himself as he realized that Katia would say nothing more on this subject, having concluded that she might have prevailed. They turned and walked back slowly to the house, relieved that Munich had become quiet again.

Chapter 7
Munich, 1922

"I want to make a new rule!"

Erika looked at her parents defiantly.

"Is it one that you yourself might obey?" Katia asked her.

"I accept," Erika said, "the rule that everyone should wash their hands before they come to the table, especially Monika, who often has very dirty hands."

"I do not have dirty hands," Monika said.

"And I also agree that we should be on time for meals, especially Golo, who is too busy reading to eat."

Golo shrugged.

"But I want a new rule saying that anyone at the table can interrupt anyone else, and that no one has the right to finish what they are saying. If I don't agree with you, I want to interrupt you. And if what you are saying is boring, then I want to stop you speaking."

"Will we have the right to interrupt you?" Katia asked. "Or do you wish to be the exception as usual?"

"My new rule applies to everyone."

"Even the Magician?" Monika asked.

"Especially the Magician," Klaus said.

Sometimes, Thomas's two eldest children intrigued him. They behaved more boisterously than the two youngest in the family. At other times, however, they spoke with seriousness and insight about books and politics. They seemed to have read widely in German and French and English literature. They had buried themselves in all the latest novels, Klaus constantly brandishing copies of the works of André Gide and the novels of E. M. Forster. But Thomas wondered when they actually sat down and read the books they claimed to admire so much, since they devoted all their spare time, as far as he could see, to meeting with their social circle, dressing up before going out and planning elaborate theatrical events with their friends, including Ricki Hallgarten, a handsome and brilliantly clever young man who lived nearby, and Pamela Wedekind, daughter of a fashionable playwright.

While Thomas was often irritated by the shrieks of his two children and their friends, the noisy arrivals and departures, he was also impressed by them. Hallgarten suggested that little in German literature met his exacting standards. He had a way of dismissing entire bodies of work that made Klaus follow his every word. He insisted, for example, that Shakespeare's comedies were better than his tragedies. When Thomas, who thought he was bluffing, asked him which comedies he had in mind, he listed them off.

"*Twelfth Night* and *A Midsummer Night's Dream*. I love the shape of them, the pattern they form," he said. "But of all the plays, I love *The Winter's Tale* most, even though it is not a comedy, although I would cut the middle part with all the shepherds."

Thomas was not sure that he had ever read the play. But Ricki Hallgarten did not notice, too busy now distinguishing between the Greek plays that he loved and the ones he admired but did not quite love. As he spoke, he reminded Thomas of Katia's brother Klaus Pringsheim when he was the same age and filled with opinions about culture. He had the same dark good looks.

Since Erika and Klaus could not fit into the discipline of any ordinary school and were the subjects of constant complaint, Katia convinced Thomas to allow them to go to a more liberal center of education. Once installed, Erika and Klaus made no secret of the freedoms they enjoyed until an edict had to be issued that they could not discuss the details of their untrammeled life at the table in front of the younger children, or if their aunt Lula or any of their grandparents were present.

Thomas was indignant when he discovered that Klaus Pringsheim, on a short visit to the family, had encouraged Erika to confide in him and had found out that at her school she regularly had love affairs with girls, and Klaus, her brother, with boys.

"My niece and nephew have come a long way from their ancestors in Lübeck," Klaus Pringsheim said to Thomas, pronouncing the name of the city as though it were the name of some deformity in nature. "With their lack of inhibitions and the good looks that they have inherited from their mother, I am sure that they will be very popular when they grow up."

"I hope they don't grow up too soon," Thomas said. "And I have always taken the view that their pleasant appearance takes its bearings from both of their parents."

"Do you mean that they look like you?"

"Would that be a surprise?"

"I'm sure they have many surprises left, if what I hear is true," Klaus Pringsheim said.

Thomas amused himself by telling Katia that he thought her brother, with all his pretentions, was a bad influence on Erika and Klaus.

"I have begun to believe that it might be the other way around," Katia said.

Erika, despite many protests, took her *Abitur*, but Klaus refused to become involved in any more study. When his mother asked how she planned to live without any formal qualifications, he laughed at her.

"I am an artist," he said.

Thomas asked Katia how these creatures had emerged from such a staid household as theirs.

"My grandmother was the most outspoken woman in Berlin," Katia said. "And your mother can hardly be described as reticent. But Erika was like that from the day she was born. She brought Klaus with her. She made him in her own image. We did nothing to stop it. That is all we did. Or perhaps we only pretended to be staid."

Lula did not tell them that Josef Löhr was dying. She came to the house as though nothing unusual were happening. She had befriended Monika, who was eleven, and took her into her confidence.

"She is the only one of the children who I can talk to," she said. "The others are too high and mighty. And I tell Monika things that I would tell no one else, and she lets me in on her secrets."

"I hope you are not telling her too much," Thomas said.

"More than I would tell you!" Lula replied.

Heinrich came to tell them that Löhr did not have long to live.

"The house is filled with these peculiar women. Mimi says that they are morphine addicts. They are certainly acting most strangely."

For the funeral, Lula modeled herself on Julia after the death of the senator. She took on, Thomas saw, an otherworldly aura, smiling faintly, speaking softly, wearing powder on her face that made her pale. As she followed the coffin, she wore a black veil and kept her three daughters close to her, but did not speak to them. She looked as if she were posing for a painter or a photographer.

When he and Katia and Heinrich and Mimi approached her at the graveside, she nodded at them as though she were not quite sure who they were.

Afterwards, as Katia and Mimi gathered around Lula's daughters, Thomas and Heinrich lagged behind.

"She has told me," Heinrich said, "that the money Löhr has left her is worth almost nothing."

• • •

Thomas was now living, he believed, in three Germanies. The first was the new one that his two eldest children inhabited. It was disorderly and disrespectful, designed to disrupt the peace. It lived as though the world was to be reinvented and laws to be discarded and remade.

The second Germany was also new. It included a mass of middle-aged people who used the winter nights to read novels and poetry; they would crowd into halls and theaters to witness him lecture or read from his work.

In the immediate aftermath of the war, he had the impression that he was, for many educated Germans, a kind of pariah. His essays and articles had been in tune with popular opinion as the war began, but they were dangerous and old-fashioned by the time the war was halfway through. When the conflict was over, no one wanted to hear from people like him.

Slowly, however, what he wrote about Germany and the war faded from public memory, to be replaced by his novels and stories, which Germans started to read in great numbers. His work was seen to represent freedom; he dramatized change. *Death in Venice* was viewed as a modern book about a complex sexuality. *Buddenbrooks* was a novel about the decline of an old mercantile Germany. How he portrayed the women in that book increased his popularity among women readers in Germany.

Thomas liked receiving invitations, showing them to Katia, looking at his diary, and then making the arrangements. He enjoyed being met from trains or having a car sent for him. Having supper before his event with the mayor or some civil leaders, or with literary editors or publishers, gave him satisfaction. He took pleasure in being treated with reverence. He also appreciated the money he was paid.

He learned that the audiences did not easily tire. He could read for an hour and they were still not satisfied. At Katia's suggestion, he offered long introductions, relishing the hushed silence that descended on the hall as soon as he began. If he could not be easily heard, then Katia would make a sign to him, and he would raise his voice. It felt at times like a religious service, with him as the priest, and a story or chapter as sacred text.

And always there were young men in the audience whom he noticed. Some had come with their literary parents; others, often older, had been stirred by *Death in Venice*. As soon as he stood at the lectern, he would glance at the first rows of seats and always he would find one of them. He would single him out, gaze at him and look away and then gaze more intensely, until the young man was left in no doubt that he was being treated as special. When the reading was over, Thomas would be on the lookout for the young man whom he had observed most directly, but often the object of his attention would have disappeared into the night. Sometimes, however, one of them would approach him shyly, politely, with a book in hand, and they could talk for a few moments before Thomas was asked to direct his attention to the crowd waiting to meet him.

The third Germany was the village of Polling, where his mother lived. Nothing there had changed. Even though young men had fought in the war and many had been killed or injured, life, once the war was over, resumed as though nothing important had occurred. The same machinery was put to work in the fields at harvesttime. The same barns were used for grain and hay. The same food was eaten. The same prayers were said in the churches. Munich seemed as far away as ever. The times of the trains did not change.

Max and Katharina Schweighardt, from whom his mother rented her living quarters, had grown older, but their manners were intact. Katharina's concern about Julia's health was conveyed to Thomas in a tone that was kind and tactful. Even the

Schweighardt children spoke with the accent of the village, having inherited their parents' intelligence and shrewdness.

To come from the company of Erika and Klaus to the village of Polling was to move from a place of chaos, where nothing was settled, to a Germany that felt timeless, secure.

But nothing was timeless or secure. As Lula and his mother complained about their incomes slowly becoming worthless, he saw that the inflation was being blamed on the winners of the war, who had introduced a set of crippling taxes on German exports. Like all Germans, Thomas deplored these, seeing them as vindictive. But it took him time to understand how inflation would not just create misery but foment resentments that could not easily be quelled.

Since income from sales of Thomas's books abroad began to soar as the dollar rose in value, he and Katia had no difficulty paying the wages of their servants, bailing Erika and Klaus out, and helping his mother and sister. They could afford two cars and a chauffeur.

Their wealth was quickly noticed. One day, when there had been several callers, he asked Katia who they were.

"They are people selling things, people who've heard that we have money. They're selling paintings and musical instruments and fur coats. The last woman to call had a statue that she thought was valuable. I didn't know what to say to her."

A few times, coming back from Polling, or from some public event, Thomas saw demonstrations in the streets, and he read in the newspapers about unrest coming this time from anti-Communist groups, but he was working each day on the novel he had abandoned before the war, and he was grateful for the stability in Munich, the sense that things had quietened down. He did not pay any attention to the demonstrations.

• • •

His mother came to stay in Poschingerstrasse and saw Lula every day until Lula tired of her.

"She repeats herself, and then she thinks I am Carla, or pretends she does in order to annoy me. I think she might benefit from a return to her lodgings in Polling."

His mother must have known, Thomas thought, when she handed him some banknotes to cover her expenses, that the notes had no value.

"I'm too old to know what is worth what. I think I have lost the ability to add and subtract. So I am lucky I have you and Katia to work all this out for me. Lula is no use at all and Heinrich made a long speech when I showed him the banknotes. He sounds like your father sometimes."

In Polling, he paid her rent and employed a housekeeper who made sure that the house was warm and that there was enough food. But he could find no way to buy clothes for his mother. She wore slippers, she said, because her feet were hurting her, but Thomas knew it was because she could not afford shoes. When Katia suggested that they go shopping, Julia feigned tiredness.

Sometimes, he saw, his mother was actually tired. After lunch, she often found a place in the sitting room and fell asleep. Like Lula, she warmed most to Monika, and said that she was her only grandchild who was out of old Lübeck.

"Why am I out of old Lübeck?" Monika asked.

"She means that you have good manners," Thomas said.

"Unlike Erika?"

"Yes," Katia said. "Unlike Erika."

Soon after Julia went back to Polling, news came that she had taken to her bed.

Katharina Schweighardt was waiting for Thomas when he arrived.

"I don't believe that there is anything wrong with her," she said, "but there are cases like this in every village around here, especially among women who live on their savings. It started last year. They get into bed and take no more food and then wait to die. And that is what your mother is doing."

"But she is well looked after," Thomas said.

"She cannot get used to having no money. We all love her here. Everyone is ready to help her. But she has run out of money. No one who has been used to money can live with that. That is how the world is."

"Has a doctor seen her?"

"He has, but there is nothing he can do. And she gave him one of those old banknotes."

Julia managed to get through most of the winter, being fed soup and dry bread. Some days she wanted Carla or Lula, and other days she called out for her sons. When Thomas spent an evening by her bed, thinking that she might not last the night, she thought he was someone in Brazil.

"Am I your father?" he asked.

She shook her head.

"Someone you remember?"

She stared at him and began to whisper words that he believed were Portuguese.

"Did you love Brazil?"

"That was what I loved," she said.

A week later, she was still alive. She looked thinner. When she saw him, she asked to be put sitting up. Since Heinrich and Viktor were downstairs, he asked if she wanted to see them too, but she shook her head. She searched his eyes as though puzzled. He told her who he was.

"I know who you are," she whispered.

He held her hand, but she slowly withdrew it. A few times, she made to speak, but there were no more words. She yawned and shut her eyes. When Katharina appeared, she told his mother how well she looked and how she would soon be her old self again, walking in the village. Julia gave her a withering smile.

Outside, Katharina told Thomas that Julia would not last the night.

"How do you know?"

"I nursed my mother and my grandmother. She will fade in the night. It will be very gentle."

Thomas, Heinrich, Lula and Viktor sat by her bed. Julia often indicated that she wanted water. Katharina and her daughter came to change the bedclothes and make her more comfortable. Once midnight had passed, Julia closed her eyes. Her breathing became deep and shallow, then back to normal.

"Can she hear us?" Thomas asked Katharina.

"She might be able to hear until the very end. Who can say?"

In the candlelight, her face was alive. She moved her lips and her eyes opened and closed. When any of them tried to hold her hand, she made clear that she did not want that. An hour went by, and then another.

"It is often the hardest thing to do," Katharina said.

"What?"

"To die."

Thomas was sitting beside her bed when death came. He had never witnessed it before, this sudden change. In one second his mother was alive, and in the next she was no one. He did not know that it could be as quick and decisive as that.

Alone among Thomas's children, Erika came to her grandmother's funeral.

"I have never seen you crying before," she said to Thomas.

"I will stop crying soon," he said.

Heinrich was crying too, as was Viktor, but Lula, paler than ever, stared ahead of her, fully composed. Only when the time came for them to stand in the church did Thomas see how drained and weak she was. Her daughters had to help her walk behind the coffin.

• • •

In the aftermath of his mother's death, all Thomas could do was write. When Katia suggested that they go to Italy, he said that he would go anywhere once *The Magic Mountain* was finished.

In the meantime, he did some readings and lectures in nearby cities. Public appearances gave him energy. He found the hours before and after a reading fruitful, times when new ideas came to him, new scenes to animate the novel.

He let Erika know about the book, but he was careful not to talk too much to Katia about it. She knew it dealt with a sanatorium in Davos, but that was all. He wrote some episodes with only Katia in mind. He dreamed of her as the sole reader of the book, aware that it contained much that was private between them, including scenes and characters that he adapted from her letters. Sometimes, as he read over pages he had been working on, he worried that no reader except Katia would appreciate what he was doing. He was concerned also about the amount of detail, the large cast of characters, the long arguments about philosophy and the future of mankind.

But more than anything, he did not know if his plan to dramatize the passing of time itself, or time slowing down, as if time itself were a character, would mean anything to the readers of the book. He smiled to himself at the thought that this was a volume that came from the most private obsessions and might thrive best in the private realm.

When *The Magic Mountain* was typed and ready, Thomas told Katia that there was a parcel for her. When she expressed surprise, he produced a box with the pages of the book inside.

He studied her as they sat down to meals, but she would only smile at him enigmatically and smile again as she left the table, saying that she was very busy and must return to her work.

Golo had developed an insatiable curiosity about his parents and his older siblings. When no one seemed to know where Erika and Klaus were, Golo would always have the information.

Thomas often found him hovering outside his study. One day, he waylaid Thomas and asked if he knew what his mother was reading.

"Why do you ask?"

"She is laughing all the time. I understood that it was your new book she was reading, but your books are never funny."

"Some people find them funny."

"No, I think you have been misled on that particular point," Golo said, furrowing his brow like a professor.

Since he and Katia went for a walk together in the afternoon, he wished she would give him some response to the book, but she spoke of the usual matters that worried them, such as Lula's financial state and the antics of Erika and Klaus.

When she appeared one morning at the door of his study, carrying a tray with coffee and biscuits, he knew she had finished the book.

"I will have a lot to say," she began. "I love that you turned me into a man in the book, and such a sweet man. But that is a small thing. More important is the fact that you have changed everything for us."

"With the book?"

"Your seriousness has now come to the fore. The book is filled with seriousness. It will be read by every German who cares about books and it will be read all over the world."

"Is it not our private book?"

"It is that as well. But no one cares about that except me. It has taken years for you to be able to do this. And now is the right moment for everyone to read it. It is a book that has found its moment."

In the following weeks, they went through the book. Katia suggested changes and erasures, but she spent most of the time selecting passages that she admired, reading out bits and marveling at details.

"The way time is handled and then how slow the book becomes! And when they play 'Valentin's Prayer' on the gramophone and the figure who is me comes back into the room, back from the dead! And then the good Russian table and the bad Russian table!"

"What are you and my mother doing?" Golo asked.

"We are reading my novel."

"You mean the funny novel?"

The publishers were wary of the book's length but then decided to make a virtue of it. Quickly, foreign publishers bought the rights. Within a few months of publication, when Thomas and Katia went to the opera or the theater, people came up to them to praise the book. Invitations came from all over Germany for Thomas to give readings. In one magazine, readers were invited to submit their favorite passage.

And a rumor came from Sweden that *The Magic Mountain* was being taken most seriously by the Academy, the group that decided on the Nobel Prize in Literature.

When Erika was eighteen and Klaus seventeen, they moved to Berlin, where Erika began to work as an actress and Klaus started to compose essays and stories. They were soon written about widely in the press, becoming famous for their flamboyance. They were spoken about as the voices of a new generation, but also as the children of Thomas Mann. They traded on their father's name, but they wished, they told interviewers, to create a distance between the patriarch's world and theirs; they demanded to be known for their own achievements.

"It is a pity," Katia said, "that they are not being paid for their own achievements. If I read any more interviews with Erika, I shall release her abject letters begging for money to the press."

More and more jokes were made about the confidence and callowness of the two older Mann siblings. A cartoon appeared of a young Klaus saying to his father: "I'm told, Papa, that the son of a genius is never a genius himself. Therefore, you can't be a genius!" And Bertolt Brecht, who disliked Thomas, wrote: "The whole world knows Klaus Mann, the son of Thomas Mann. By the way, who is Thomas Mann?"

Thomas and Katia failed to make sense sometimes of the confusion their two eldest children generated. When it was rumored that Klaus was engaged to Pamela Wedekind, Katia also learned that Erika herself was in love with Pamela.

"Perhaps they are sharing her," Thomas said.

"I have never known Erika to share anything," Katia replied.

Klaus, having written a novel about a homosexual character, then wrote a play about four young people, two boys and two girls, who followed no conventions. Since it was a family custom to have a reading after dinner, it was agreed that Klaus, who was visiting, could share his new work with the family, including his aunt Lula.

When Klaus had finished reading the play, Aunt Lula made plain her objection to the close sexual relationship between the two girls in the work.

"It is most unhealthy," she said, "and I hope the play lives in obscurity. Thomas and Heinrich have written such nice books, and now these children, who should be in school, are writing whatever they like. I am trying to make sure that my daughters don't see any of this."

"The war is over, Lula," Thomas said.

"Well, I don't like the peace."

Lula's views were not shared by the well-known actor Gustaf Gründgens, star of the Kammerspiele in Hamburg, who offered to take one of the parts in Klaus's play, suggesting the other male role be played by Klaus himself and the two young women by Erika and Pamela Wedekind.

Gründgens caused perplexity in the Mann household. Even Golo began to enjoy the different versions of where Gründgens's affections lay. One day, news came via a letter from Klaus himself, who made no secret of his sexual proclivities, that he and Gründgens were in love. Soon afterwards, Erika wrote to say that she was going to marry Gründgens. On a visit home shortly after that, to the bewilderment of his parents and Golo, Klaus confided in them that, while his sister was engaged to Gründgens, she was, in fact, still in love with Pamela Wedekind and, while he himself was in love with Gründgens, he was still engaged to Pamela.

"Is this what everyone does before they get married?" Golo asked.

"No, it is not," his mother replied. "Only Erika and Klaus."

As the play Klaus wrote toured Germany, news of the complicated relationships among the four actors spread among journalists, who hinted in their articles that this theatrical work was based on the actors' own lives.

"We plan a gala Munich opening," Erika said. "And we need everyone there. Our success depends on it."

"Ten horses will not drag me there," Thomas said. "The newspapers can cover your activities with all the fervor in the world, but I will remain in my study and retire early on the evening in question."

Thomas and Katia understood that they could do nothing to stop Erika and Klaus falling in love and getting engaged and acting in plays. For the most part, they found their two children's behavior endearing, but they grew to dislike Gustaf Gründgens and wished they could alert Erika to their disapproval.

Gründgens, when Erika took him to her parents' house, could not conceal how much he knew about them; he had all the details on the rift between Thomas and Heinrich during the war and made reference to the Manns' dollar income. Gründgens was the first outsider to try to penetrate the golden circle that Erika and Klaus had created. While Thomas and Katia knew Pamela Wedekind from when she was a child, and while they were neighbors of the parents of Ricki Hallgarten, they did not know who Gustaf Gründgens was.

"I saw a man like him once on a train from Munich to Berlin," Katia said. "He was all smiles, he could not have been sweeter, but when the ticket collector approached, it turned out he had no ticket."

When Lula came to visit, flushed and excited, and then suddenly angry, she spoke further about the outrageous behavior of Erika and Klaus.

"I read an interview with Erika. It seems that she has no respect for authority. She said so in the interview."

One afternoon, Klaus Pringsheim was sitting languidly having coffee with Thomas and Katia when Lula appeared. As Thomas noticed his brother-in-law taking Lula in, he wished the two of them could be kept apart.

"It is a joy to be alive," Klaus said. "You have the Kaiser one year and then a free-for-all the next. That is called history."

"That is not the name for it," Lula said. "It is an outrage that people from good families are parading around Germany like clowns."

"Erika and Klaus?" Klaus Pringsheim asked. "From good families?"

"Well, our family at least is highly respectable," Lula said.

"Thank God, ours is not," Klaus said, "so maybe a mismatch is at the heart of the problem."

"I think Klaus is joking," Katia said.

Lula's cheeks had become red.

"What exactly do you do for a living?" she asked Klaus.

"I study music. Sometimes I conduct orchestras. I don't do anything for a living."

"You should be ashamed of yourself!"

"Shame is over," Klaus said. "You go out at night in Munich and in Berlin and there is no more shame. It abdicated at the same time as the Kaiser. Since then it has been a feast of shamelessness."

"That will be the end of Germany," Lula said, getting more agitated.

"And would that not be a good thing?" Klaus asked.

Lula announced that she had to leave. She suddenly seemed tired, almost frail. She sat for a while staring straight ahead. For a moment, she looked as if she might fall asleep. Thomas had to help her to the door.

When he came back into the room, Klaus asked him if Lula was being looked after.

"What do you mean?" Thomas asked.

"Your sister looks to me like a woman who is enjoying the benefits of morphine."

"Don't be silly," Katia said.

Soon Erika began wearing a suit and a tie. She and her brother, Thomas thought, resembled each other. They often spoke at the same time, both trying to say the same thing, making clear to Gründgens, if he were present, that he was an outsider in their world, that he would never understand their abstruse references, their intricate jokes or their resistance to any set of moral codes. They spoke in tones, Thomas thought, that deliberately excluded any newcomer. Why Erika wished nonetheless to marry him was something that neither Thomas nor Katia could fathom.

"It might be better if she marries no one," Katia said.

Thomas was tempted to reply that it was a pity Erika could not marry her own younger brother Klaus. It would be one way of keeping Klaus under control. At first, he did not believe that she would go through with her marriage to Gründgens, even when she spoke about it as a task she had to complete, nothing too onerous, like an extra performance added due to public demand. But then an invitation came with a date set.

He and Katia went through the motions of attending the wedding. Thomas could not resist becoming more solemn and formal as the young people around him put on a display of jollity and silliness, giving women's names to men and men's to women, making many jokes that bordered on indecency. When Katia nudged him, he noticed that Klaus had his eyes closed and might have fallen asleep had an overdressed young woman not come up and asked him to dance. The same young woman later joined Thomas and Katia and informed them that Pamela Wedekind had stayed away out of jealousy.

"The honeymoon will be spent in a hotel at Lake Constance where Erika and Pamela recently had a divine love weekend," the young woman said. "Gründgens was so jealous he tore what was to be Erika's wedding dress to shreds. But she didn't mind at all. She laughed, because she didn't even like the dress, and that made it all much worse. In the honeymoon hotel, Pamela posed as a man, calling herself Herr Wedekind, and we all think now that Erika is going to sign the register as Herr Mann, if Gründgens will let her. He can often be very tedious."

Erika started life with her new husband; Klaus remained with his family in Munich. During the day he was exhausted, but then, once supper began each evening, would fill the air with ideas and plans, speaking sometimes, Thomas noticed, to some invisible Erika. Working in the theater with Gründgens, he said, had depressed the three others. In life, Gründgens was dull; he had read very few books. He had no curiosity, no sparkle. But once he was on the stage, he could do anything. While Klaus and Erika and Pamela longed for the performance to be over so they could have supper together, Gründgens seemed greatly diminished once the lights came down. Over supper, he would become ordinary. If they stayed out late, he could be very boring indeed. But on the stage, he was magical. It was uncanny, almost alarming, Klaus said.

As he spoke, it struck Thomas that writing, for Klaus, was a dreary process compared to the excitement of doing other things. Klaus relished outings, parties, new people, chances to travel. He was not naturally drawn to the hard and hidden place where a subject was lured towards the light in a process that was like alchemy. Writing was something he did quickly. Despite his talent, Klaus was not, Thomas judged, an artist. He wondered how his son would live as he grew older, what he would do.

Klaus warned them that Erika's marriage to Gründgens was a disaster from the start. When Klaus had dinner with them in Berlin, he said, Gründgens had produced a magazine cover with a picture of Klaus and Erika and Pamela Wedekind. He reminded them that the picture had, when taken, included him, but some editor, unimpressed by his lack of fame, had erased him. Clearly, he said, he was not important enough; the other three were the great actors, and he was not. Or maybe, he insisted, they were just the spoiled children of famous literary fathers, and he was not.

The entire evening had been spent, Klaus said, listening to Gründgens moan. By that time, Erika was already tired of him. He wanted her to ask her father to make representations to the management of various theaters on his behalf. Gründgens no longer wished to be merely an actor, Klaus told them, he wanted to run his own theater.

"When Erika comes home," he said, "she will feel that she

made a fool of herself marrying this man. We will all have to look after her."

Thomas followed the news about Adolf Hitler without much interest. There had always been cranks and fanatics in Munich. It hardly mattered whether they were left-wing or right-wing. People spoke of Hitler when he was in prison and when there was speculation about releasing him and then deporting him to Austria. In the December 1924 elections, his party won only three percent of the national vote.

Thomas saw the German defeat in the war as the end of something. Since he himself had entertained views about the specialness of the German soul, he felt it his duty now to ban such phrases from his lexicon and from his mind. The more time he had spent on the novel, the more he was certain that he needed to become ironic and speculative about his own heritage.

When Heinrich and Mimi came to dinner, Thomas knew that Heinrich would declare Hitler a looming menace. His photograph, haranguing a crowd, was starting to appear regularly in many newspapers.

"There is something offensive about his face," Thomas said.

"About all of him," Mimi replied.

"Money is no longer money," Heinrich said. "And this is unimaginable for most people. Anyone who can cast blame with a shrill voice will be listened to."

"But no one is listening to Hitler," Thomas said. "His so-called putsch was a disaster. He is a failed demagogue."

"What do you think of him, Katia?" Mimi asked.

"I would like this Hitler to leave us alone," Katia said. "Bavaria without him is bad enough. I can't imagine what Bavaria with him would be like."

• • •

Mimi reported that she now knew for a fact that Lula was taking morphine.

"She is still in that circle of women and what binds them together is the drug. They look out for each other, and make sure that supplies don't run out. I have a friend whose sister was in the group."

The next time Lula was in the house, she sat with glazed eyes and a nodding head. For a while, she slurred her words, but then, with a start, appeared to realize where she was and began to talk animatedly.

When she was accompanied by her daughters, she made sure that they paid as much attention to social niceties as she did. If she found one of them sitting in a pose that seemed to her less than formal, she immediately reprimanded the girl. She was strict about what to do on arrival and departure, demanding that others follow her in traditional words of greeting and number of kisses.

One day, when she was invited to lunch, she corrected Golo's relaxed way of holding his knife and fork, as though she were a reverend mother. The smallest breach in how things should be done made her shake her head in sadness or raise her voice to deplore the general fall in standards.

"You can blame the war," she said, "or the inflation, but I blame people themselves. It is people themselves who have bad manners. And sometimes the parents are worse than the children."

"Do you mean my parents?" Golo asked.

"That is an example of the new rudeness I am talking about."

When there was any possibility of Erika and Klaus being present, Lula would announce that she had forbidden her daughters from coming to Poschingerstrasse in case they would be influenced by their cousins' lack of social seriousness.

"Erika has no feminine qualities," she said. "How will she live? She looks like a man."

"That is how she wishes to look," Katia said.

"She is a very bad example to her sisters, to her cousins, and to young women in general."

Since Heinrich moved in many levels of Munich society, he was informed that, even before Löhr's death, Lula was having affairs with married men. She had been spotted making a scene at the front door of a well-known apartment building. At first, Thomas thought this was the sort of gossip that would surround the widowed sister of two famous writers. People could not content themselves, he believed, with saying nothing, knowing nothing, about Lula. In the place where literary Munich and its more respectable counterpart met, Lula would be noticed all the more not only because of her opinions, but because she was conspicuously running out of money.

Heinrich told them that he knew for certain that Lula had a lover who was being unfaithful to her. The man was married, but he could be seen in public places with a number of women other than his wife and Lula.

"His wife has long ceased to care," Heinrich said, "but it is an open humiliation for Lula."

Soon Heinrich told them that Lula had been seen following this man in the street, or entering cafés and restaurants checking if he was at one of the tables, and then sitting alone in a state of despondency as she gave his name and insisted that she would wait for him.

And then the news broke that Lula had taken her own life. When Heinrich arrived at the house to tell Thomas and Katia, she and Golo immediately went to comfort Lula's daughters, but Heinrich and Thomas stayed behind, finding refuge in Thomas's study.

Heinrich reminded him of the nights when their mother would tell them about her childhood in Brazil.

"Can you imagine on one of those nights if someone had come into the room and told our two sisters how they would die?" Thomas asked.

"When Carla went," Heinrich continued, "part of me followed her. And now Lula. Soon we will all be gone."

In 1927 and 1928 there were reporters outside his house on the day that the Nobel Prize in Literature was being announced. The first year, Katia had the servants make them tea and give them cake, but the second year, she closed the shutters and ordered everyone to use the back entrance to the house.

"I detected a note of glee last year when it was announced that you hadn't won."

By 1929, Thomas and Katia dreaded the possibility that he might be awarded the prize. Since unemployment had once more gone over two million and since the name Hitler was on everyone's lips, his meetings in Munich attended by thousands of people, they did not want to become public recipients of a large amount of money, nor did they want to add to the attention drawn to them by Erika and Klaus, whose invective against Hitler and his friends grew in proportion to the rise of Hitler's popularity.

Thomas did not fully trust Erika and Klaus, or indeed his brother Heinrich, when they expressed alarm about Hitler and made clear their hatred of his followers. His brother and two eldest children, he felt, needed an enemy in Germany to rail against. In the morning, when he read the paper, he often found himself skimming over the news about Hitler, whose party was declaring a triumph in the local state and district elections having won just a few percent of the vote.

Golo, however, had begun to keep a file of cuttings about Hitler and the SA. After the Nuremburg rally in August 1929, he bought all the newspapers, some of which estimated the numbers in attendance at forty thousand, others at one hundred thousand. He put all the cuttings on the dining room table and invited his father to look at them.

"This is growing," he said, "and it is disciplined. They are fighting elections and running a semi-official army at the same time."

"They have no support," Thomas said.

"That is not true. I can show you every day what their support is. It is not happening in secret."

Thomas and Katia made a pact not to mention the Nobel Prize and to silence anyone who raised the subject. But the night before the announcement, he lay awake thinking how much he wanted this prize and how much he saw that as a defect in his own character. He should not want it, he told himself; it would perhaps bring him readers, but it would also bring him trouble.

In the morning, he heard the telephone ring and he waited for Katia or Golo to appear. When they did not, he smiled at how sure he had been that the prize was his. When Katia came to the door with a tray and coffee for both of them, he presumed that she was preparing to console him. She did not speak until she was sitting down, with the door closed.

"The phone will start ringing in about two minutes and the journalists will be at the door. I thought we'd have a quiet time until then. We won't get another chance for a while."

He was already engaged to do readings in the Rhineland; other events were now added, including a celebratory dinner in Munich and a ceremony at Bonn University. The crowds who filled the hall were the same people who had come to his readings since the war, but now the atmosphere in the halls was high with expectation, as though he could deliver the audience from the fear and failure all around them.

In his introductions, he did not speak of politics, but his very presence as a German who stood above the fray and wrote books that were admired all over the world made these events feel like shadowy gatherings of the opposition, where the untainted soul of Germany could find respite.

In the liberal newspapers, as Golo told him, the prize was seen as a vindication not only of his work but of the idea that he represented the life of the mind in his own country. The celebrations were a rebuke, one of the papers wrote, against dark forces that were threatening his native land.

When Golo showed him the *Illustrierter Beobachter*, which was controlled by Hitler, he read a more incendiary version of something he already knew. The award marked him further for the Nazis. The very culture he had represented since the war—bourgeois, cosmopolitan, balanced, unpassionate—was the very one that they were most determined to destroy. The tone he used in his prose—ponderous, ceremonious, civilized—was the precise opposite of the tone they wielded.

The battles they were fighting included one for cultural hegemony. A lyric poem written by a Jew or a left-wing writer could offend them as much as a thriving Jewish business. A famous novelist could come into their sights as much as an unfriendly foreign country or a Jewish banker. Not only did they want to control streets and government buildings, banks and businesses, they wanted to re-create the Germany of the future. If they could not hold the lyric poem to account, or the novel, then the future of German culture could easily slip from their hands, and it was that future that concerned them as much as the present.

These conclusions struck him most forcefully when he sat alone in his study in Munich in the evening. He did not think for a moment that the Nazis would ever take power. Some days they were merely a nuisance, representing a coarseness that was entering every aspect of life. Waiters were not as polite in restaurants as they used to be. The staff in the bookshops he favored were not as compliant. Katia complained much more about finding suitable household help. The post, he was sure, was slower.

But these were minor irritants. He did not think too much about the uniformed thugs on the streets because he spent little time on the streets. The presence of the Nazis in any German polity of the future was hardly worth arguing about. As they had come from nowhere, he believed, they would soon fade away. He believed that the struggle would be between socialism and social democracy.

A few years earlier, when Golo became interested in political philosophy, he had enjoyed debating with him how the gap between the two might be reconciled. Now the discussions with Golo were all about the differences between the Nazis and the Italian Fascists, about the slow and insidious way the National Socialists had moved to the very center of the public imagination without winning any elections or softening their tone in order to win more support. When he tried to interest Golo in socialism and social democracy, Golo shrugged and said:

"Just because Heinrich and Erika and Klaus think that Hitler threatens us all does not mean it isn't true."

"I never said it isn't true."

"I am glad to hear that."

Erika and Klaus, he saw, got energy from the vulgarity and viciousness of their enemies. They had traveled to the United States, where they were met by a horde of curious journalists who wished to interview them. They were given shelter by their friend Ricki Hallgarten, who was living in New York and introduced them to the pleasures of the city—some of which, Erika wrote in a letter, could not be revealed even to her own dear parents. They crossed America by train, and then made their journey into a trip around the world, visiting Japan, Korea and Russia, writing a book together about their experiences, a book that ended with their gloomy arrival home, into a Prussian landscape in the pale light of dawn when, under the watchful eye of the police, they had to stop laughing and take life seriously.

In fact, they were not met on arrival, Thomas remembered, by the police, but by their parents and their siblings. They did not return to Berlin, but to Munich. In their first days home, they were almost children again. While usually he or their mother had to remind them to censor themselves at the family table, this time all their stories of their escapades throughout the world were filled with innocent adventure, as though they had been a couple of siblings from a folktale let loose in a world where they were looked after by many kind strangers and avoided all calamity by a stroke of luck.

Soon they disappeared to become adults again. When Ricki Hallgarten returned from America, Erika wrote a children's book that he illustrated, and, Katia informed Thomas, Klaus and he became lovers. Klaus was now publishing one or two works of fiction every year. Erika became famous throughout Germany for her short articles about what being a new woman meant. She loved being photographed driving a car, flashing her short hair and expressing opinions on sex and politics that were combative and controversial. She and Ricki took part in a ten day car race that they won, Erika writing articles from their resting places.

Just as Thomas and Katia were settling into a serene late middle age, Erika and Klaus were finding life more exciting. They were planning a trip in two cars from Germany to Persia in the company of Ricki and Annemarie Schwarzenbach, a friend of Erika.

For Thomas, the change from complacency to shock was a swift one. The year after his Nobel Prize, the Nazis got six and a half million votes compared to eight hundred thousand just two years earlier. But their support, he believed, could dissolve as easily as it had surged. The emptiness of the National Socialist promises, in his opinion, would surely come home to people. If only Golo could stop showing him lurid and portentous articles in obscure publications, then he could get on with his work in peace.

A few months later, however, the transformation that had taken place in Germany while he was busy writing and traveling to give lectures and readings came to him as an unforgettable image. He had agreed to deliver a lecture at the Beethovensaal in Berlin called "An Appeal to Reason." The title might not have been provocative at any other time, but it was now. He prepared the lecture carefully, becoming angrier as he wrote, and also more certain that these words needed to be spoken.

He still believed that he was speaking to the middle one of the three Germanies that he had identified. He expected the Beethovensaal to be filled with thoughtful people who spent the winter evenings reading books. He presumed that they would deplore, as he did, the turning away from the principles that made a civilized society, which were, as he named them, "liberty, equality, education, optimism and belief in progress." He took the view that his audience despised what he called "the gigantic wave of eccentric barbarism and primitive, populist fairground barking" and that they agreed with him that National Socialism offered "a politics of the grotesque, replete with reflexive mass paroxysms, amusement-park chiming, cries of hallelujah and mantra-like repetitions of monotonous slogans until everyone foamed at the mouth." He called on the audience to support the Social Democrats, as the most rational and progressive party in German politics.

It was a full house and the response as he began was appreciative. He was glad that Erika and Klaus were in the audience as well as Katia. When he described the state of feeling in Germany that might become "a menace to the world" and added that Nazism was "a colossus with clay feet," a man in the audience stood up and demanded to be heard.

Thomas had never been interrupted before. He was unsure

what to do. He hesitated and then pointed to the man, encouraging him to speak.

Shouting loud enough to be heard all over the hall, the man called him a liar and an enemy of the people. There were murmurs of disapproval from the audience. Thomas was relieved that he had a script. He was determined not to falter. He knew there were sentiments coming to which the audience who admired his work would assent but that would further enrage the man who had interrupted him.

He saw that there were dissenters all over the hall, and they were ready to shout abuse and catcall at every chance. It was clear that they were organized, and had come here to prevent him speaking. They now started to shout him down. Several of them moved from their seats towards the podium as the majority of the audience sat silently. His interrupters had been strategically placed. They were all young men. What he noted every time he looked up from his speech was their belligerent presence in the hall.

As he continued to speak, Thomas was handed a note, warning him to shorten his speech, to finish before tensions rose further. He decided that he could not do that. It was not merely that such a retreat would be reported widely as an ignominious capitulation but he could not see how he and Katia and the others might depart if the protesters felt that they had made him afraid of them.

He went on to attack Nazi ideology with greater vehemence as the heckling became even more widespread in the hall and more heated. Instead of individuals shouting abuse, groups of them began to sing songs and hurl insults. As he came to the end, Thomas could barely be heard at all.

Once he had finished, it was obvious that it would not be easy to make a safe exit. He saw Katia signaling to him to go over to the side. There he found the conductor Bruno Walter and his wife, who, familiar with the elaborate system of stairs and corridors in the building, carefully guided him and Katia to the neighboring building, close to which Walter had left his car.

Thomas understood that he would never be able to speak in Germany again without fear of a repetition as long as the Nazis were in the ascendant. No one who wished to hear him would deem it safe to attend one of his events. He agreed to have his speech printed and was pleased that it went into three editions, but knew that it made no difference. He was marked. When Golo offered to show him the reports of his lecture in the National Socialist newspaper, he declined. He knew what they would have to say about him.

He carried on writing, but he was aware that he would be noticed were he even to venture onto the streets of Munich. When he and Katia took their walk by the river, they were wary. He thought the task of opposing the Nazis a worthy one and believed that they would be defeated. Inflation had unsettled the country, he saw, and there would be many swings from one faction to another, from one ideology to another, before there was stability. But that night in Berlin had alerted him as nothing else did to the fact that his own exalted literary reputation did not place him in an unassailable position. He would not be allowed to speak his mind when he wished. His Germany, the one to which he addressed his readings, had lost its place at the center.

Erika and Klaus were stirred into further bursts of eloquence by the danger all around them. While being shouted down in Berlin had made their father unwilling to partake in more events, they became even braver as the Nazi menace grew more intense.

Klaus wrote a second play for four actors, two men and two women, but this time the tone was darker, more ominous; there seemed more at stake than love as a game of pleasure. Now the young characters were fighting for their lives. Drugs for them did not offer release but suggested doom. Love was a tangled attempt to possess the other, death a sort of freedom.

Klaus and Erika and Ricki Hallgarten continued to make final preparations for their trip to Persia. Thomas and Katia had come to admire Ricki, who spoke to them with the same debonair ease as he did to their two eldest children. Klaus, in Ricki's company, became more thoughtful, less prone to offering extreme opinions that might irritate his father.

In those months, however, all of them harbored extreme opinions about the National Socialists. At meals Thomas listened to heated invective. Nonetheless, he was surprised by Ricki's tone as he denounced Hitler.

"Everything is lost! We are doomed! The whole lot of us. They will destroy everything. Books, pictures, everything. No one will be safe."

He then did an extreme imitation of one of Hitler's interminable rants.

"Don't you see what is happening?" he asked, his voice shaking.

The day before the planned departure, Ricki, Erika, Klaus and Annemarie Schwarzenbach went to a Bavarian newsreel company to make a film about their journey. For the cameras, Klaus and Erika sat in the car; the other two set about repairing some imaginary damage. They laughed so much when Ricki suggested that Klaus should be filmed mending a puncture that the filming had to be stopped.

It was arranged that, after spending a final night with their families, they would set out at three o'clock the next afternoon. At noon, however, news came that Ricki had shot himself in the heart, having traveled to Utting on the Ammersee, where he kept a small apartment. He left a note addressed to the local police station giving Katia's name and phone number with the suggestion that the police contact Frau Mann so that she could break the news to his parents.

That night, Erika and Klaus were speechless at the table. For some time, they had been in a state of elation. Klaus had been worried that the trip would put pressure on his delicate relationship with Ricki, but Ricki had managed to reassure him by making love, Erika told Katia, in a new way that had excited them both. Klaus was to embark on a journey with the two people in the world that he loved most. In the days beforehand, he could not sit still. Every time Thomas saw Erika, she had the map of their route in front of her and a pile of guidebooks and dictionaries. She was issuing commands to an empty room. She had already worked out the titles of articles she would publish and had plans for a book all four travelers would write together.

When they went to the apartment where Ricki had died, they saw that the wall above his bed was splattered with blood. Confronted with his dead body and the blood, Erika began to scream. She was still screaming when Klaus took her home.

Katia found Thomas in his study.

"I don't know why Ricki gave my name to the police. As soon as my knock was answered, I knew that I would destroy the Hallgartens' lives. And Erika must stop screaming. You must come out of your study and insist that she stop!"

In the days that followed, Thomas tried to talk to Erika and Klaus about the deaths of his own two sisters, how those two suicides were also shocking and inexplicable, but they seemed unable to understand. They could not connect Ricki's death with any other death. Even when he went into detail about where he was and how he felt when Carla and Lula died, neither of them paid attention. It was as though their own lives had a brightness, a richness, a vividness that no other life could measure up to. Ricki could not be compared to their aunts whom no one had ever heard of.

"You don't understand," Erika said to him over and over. "You don't understand."

Chapter 8
Lugano, 1933

When the Reichstag fire happened in February 1933, Thomas and Katia were in Arosa in Switzerland on holiday. Each day, they heard further news of mass arrests and attacks on people in the street. When the National Assembly elections took place a week later, Thomas's first instinct was to return to Munich as soon as possible to make sure that the house would not be ransacked. If it became necessary, he thought, they could make plans to rent the house, or even sell it, and quietly remove their assets to Switzerland.

He was shocked to hear Katia tell a fellow guest in the hotel that they could not go back to Munich.

When he suggested that they decide what to do only when they had spoken to Erika, Katia insisted that calling the house would be dangerous. They should not even say where they were. He sat close to her as she put in a call. He listened as Erika answered. Katia spoke in code, asking her daughter if it would be a good time for spring cleaning.

"No, no," Erika replied, "and besides the weather is terrible. Just stay there for a little while; you're not missing a thing."

Erika and Klaus left Munich as soon as they could. Only Golo was now in the house. It puzzled them that his letters had an air of normality, as though the rise of the regime was no longer news. He told them that he had heard a rumor that Erika had been arrested and was being held in the concentration camp at Dachau, but he now knew that this was not true. Golo added that he had also met his uncle Viktor, who told him how pleased he was to get a promotion in the bank where he worked. He wondered if his uncle might have taken the job of a Jewish colleague.

Katia found them a house for rent in Lugano, where they were joined by Monika and Elisabeth. Michael was at a Swiss boarding school. Soon they were also joined by Erika, who smoked more than usual and drank a lot at night and was first up in the morning to get the newspapers. Her voice filled the house; she was more like a relative sent to scold them than their eldest daughter who had become, like them, a refugee. Since Erika knew the names of even the most minor regional governors in Germany, she took them through the changes that were being ruthlessly implemented. She spent the rest of the morning writing to friends and allies all over the world. She made many phone calls. The rumor of her incarceration in Dachau was conveyed by her with a strange relish to everyone. She threatened to defy the authorities by driving back to Munich to rescue the manuscripts of her father's books, but, at her mother's insistence, she agreed not to attempt such a dangerous mission. Later, however, Thomas was amused to hear her describe the journey as if she had actually made it, outwitting Nazi border guards and returning with a tranche of precious papers under the driver's seat of her car.

He was less amused when Erika began arguing that the family would have to get used to the idea that they would never go back to their house in Munich again, they would lose it, just as they would have to forfeit all the money they had in German banks. Erika spoke as though she had learned this by heart and was reciting it as a way of forcing him and her mother to deal with a reality they had been avoiding.

Erika wanted Thomas to make a statement that would break

his connection with Germany for good. When a lecture he had given on Wagner was denounced by a long list of eminent figures in the Bavarian musical and cultural world including Richard Strauss and Hans Pfitzner, who had been a friend of his, Thomas felt it wisest not to respond. He presumed that they must have been put under pressure by the new regime. Erika, on the other hand, believed that he should use this opportunity to declare his loathing for the new government. He should call on his compatriots to oppose Hitler in every way. When Thomas finally did issue a statement, which was published in the Swiss press, he made sure that Erika did not see it before it was sent. He was not surprised when Katia told him that his daughter viewed its tone as ingratiating and spineless.

At the beginning of the Great War, Thomas had a clear sense of his German audience. And when he gave his lecture in Berlin, he believed he was speaking to the people who shared his views about liberty and democracy, and also about what it meant to be German. These people had now become silent. There was no forum where he could address them. If he denounced Hitler from the safety of Switzerland, he would be denounced in turn. His books would be removed from bookshops and libraries. He would not be allowed to speak again.

His views on the Nazis were known. He saw no value in repeating them while Golo and Katia's parents were still in Germany, while he owned a house in Munich and had money in German banks. Also, attacking the National Socialists when they were no more than a fringe movement, a kind of nuisance, was different to attacking the German government, which was seeking legitimacy all over the world.

As each letter came from Golo, they worried about his safety. But he did not seem frightened; instead, he wrote as though all Munich were a sort of theater or a spectacle that it was his duty to report on. Some of his news was sad, especially his accounts of visits to his grandparents, still living in their beautiful house but increasingly anxious about their future. His grandfather, he wrote, kept saying: "That we had to live to see this!" As far as the authorities were concerned, the Pringsheims were Jewish. Peter, Katia's brother, had been dismissed from his job at Humboldt University in Berlin and, like his brothers, was making plans to leave Germany.

Katia's father wrote to her, and had the letter delivered by hand, to say that she should not write or call. She showed Thomas the passage that read:

> I am never sure, my little one, that everyone knows that you, my daughter, are the mother of Erika and Klaus Mann and the wife of Thomas Mann. Once it might have been a matter of pride in Munich. Now that you are in exile, I know that your children and your husband will need to speak out against the new order, and I understand that. But it will make our lives more precarious. We have always tried to be loyal Germans. I have loved the music of Wagner and I have done everything to support him, including helping to create Bayreuth. The only glimmer of hope in all this darkness has come from Winifred Wagner, and that is most unlikely as she is an ardent supporter of the man whose name I will not spell out. She has told us that she will help us, but we do not know what this means.

Thomas noticed that while Elisabeth read the letter, it was not shown to the others. At meals, Katia let Erika do all the talking. She retreated to her quarters each evening as soon as she could and seemed relieved finally when Erika left to be with Klaus in France.

Michael, who was fourteen, joined them in Lugano. Thomas

remembered how reluctantly he had attended his violin lessons in Munich, and how his piano teacher refused to give him any more classes because of his surly response to instruction. But in his boarding school he had found an Italian teacher of the viola and the violin whom he did not alienate.

"But how was he different to all your other teachers?" Katia asked.

"He's Italian and the other teachers laughed at him," Michael said.

"Is that why you liked him?"

"His father and brother are in prison. If he goes back to Italy he will be arrested. And no one really needs a violin teacher. So he looked sad."

Michael spent several hours a day practicing, especially on the viola, and arranged to have his teacher come to Lugano two days a week to work with him.

When Thomas told him that the music he played sounded beautiful, Michael scowled.

"My teacher has told me that I have talent, that is all."

"What more do you want?" Katia asked.

"Genius," Michael said.

It was Michael who suggested that Thomas take English lessons from his viola teacher.

"His English is perfect, and he needs the money."

"He is Italian. I don't want to speak English like an Italian."

"Do you want to speak English like a German?" Michael asked.

Thomas agreed that he would take lessons, and he would try to read a simple book in English.

In one of Golo's letters he described a lunch in Munich with Ernst Bertram, who insisted that while he was all in favor of freedom, it was only for good Germans. And when Golo said that his father might never return to Germany, Bertram replied: "Why not? He is a German, after all, and we do live in a free country."

Bertram, he added, had tried to make excuses for not going to visit Thomas when he was in Lugano. He was not alone at the time, he had said, suggesting that he was under pressure not to maintain his friendship with Golo's father.

Golo added that he had given a dinner party in the house so that the best bottles in his father's wine cellar could be consumed. He was slowly packing up books and sorting papers.

Each time he heard such news, news that suggested he would not be seeing his old house again, it almost surprised Thomas. He was still following daily reports in the hope that Hitler's power would fade or that he would be assassinated or that a rebellion would take place within the ranks of the army against the Nazi leaders.

At first, when books that offended the Nazis were burned in Berlin, Thomas was relieved that his own were not among them. But when Erika returned, she pointed out that all the important German writers, including Heinrich and Klaus, and Brecht and Hermann Hesse, had their books tossed into the fire. It was hardly a badge of honor, she insisted, to be excluded from this. Thomas noticed Katia nodding silently. When Golo wrote to let them know that although Ernst Bertram had fully supported the burning of the books, he had seen to it that Thomas's work was not included, Katia read the letter first before handing it to him and leaving the room.

It proved easy for Golo to have furniture and paintings and books removed from the house in Munich and taken to Switzerland by pretending that he was selling them. Golo also managed to withdraw large sums of money from his father's bank account. While there were manuscripts and letters, including all the letters from Katia written from Davos, that he would like to have transported out of Germany, the most important set of papers, Thomas knew, were his diaries. They were in a safe in his study in Poschingerstrasse. No one had ever seen them. Katia, he supposed, knew of their existence and must have realized, since they were always locked away, that they contained private material. However, she would never have envisaged that peppered through pages that dealt with banalities such as the weather and where he gave lectures were references to his intimate dreams and his erotic life.

He needed to get the diaries out of Munich. He had to plan a way to have the safe opened, and the diaries sent to him without being read.

His dreams about sex had made their way into stories and novels, but in fiction they could easily be interpreted as literary games. Since he was the father of six children, no one had ever openly accused him of private perversions. If published, however, the diaries would make clear who he was and what he dreamed about. They would show that his distant, bookish tone, his personal stiffness, his interest in being honored and attended to, were masks designed to disguise base sexual desires. While other writers, including Ernst Bertram and the poet Stefan George, had let the world know of their homosexuality, Thomas had locked his sexual interests inside a diary that was, in turn, locked in a safe. If he were now exposed, he believed, he would be despised all the more because of his duplicity.

Katia was resigned, he thought, to the loss of the house and the possibility of a long exile, but not to her husband being disgraced.

"How strange it is," she said, "that we are now Jewish. My parents never went near a synagogue. And I thought of the children as pure Manns, but now they are Jewish because their mother is Jewish."

She worried that Golo was staying too long in Munich. She also worried about how Erika and Klaus, now in their late twenties, would make a living since Germany was closed to them. She had no idea, Thomas thought, that there was another danger. It was something he could not share with her without actually revealing the content of the diaries. She would be appalled at how idiotic he had been to offer such a hostage to fortune.

Of all his children, he thought, Golo, even when he was a child, was the best at keeping a secret. At the table, he liked to watch carefully and give nothing away. Thomas was confident that when he sent him the key for the safe, asking him to remove the oilcloth-covered notebooks without reading them and put them in a suit-case and send them by freight mail to Lugano, Golo would do as he was asked.

When Golo indicated that this had been done, Thomas felt relieved. All he had to do now was wait for them to come.

Slowly, things became more difficult for Golo in Munich. The banks refused to allow him to withdraw any more money. He believed that he was being watched and could be detained at any time. He was unable to prevent the authorities from confis-cating both of the family cars, and as the confiscation took place he realized that Hans, the family chauffeur, was the one who had informed the Nazis that he had plans to drive one of the cars to Switzerland.

On being accused of informing, Hans grew arrogant and began to strut around the house, threatening the cook and the maids that he would have them arrested. It was clear, since Golo was in earshot, that he meant him to know that he could be arrested too.

Golo, arriving in Lugano, told his parents this story and added casually: "And I trusted Hans with that suitcase, which he prom-ised to take to the post office for me. God only knows what he did with it. He probably handed it over to the Nazis."

When Katia left them, Thomas asked Golo if the suitcase he had trusted Hans with was the one containing the diaries.

"He offered to take it. I thought that he would attract less attention. I felt I was being watched. It seemed like the best solu-tion. I might have waited and carried it with me, but I thought you wanted it sooner."

"Did he bring you back a receipt or a piece of paper to say that he had put it in the mail?"

"No."

For one second as Golo glanced at him uneasily, Thomas realized that Golo had a sense of what was in the diaries. He wondered if he had flicked through the pages or read some passages. If he had done so, he would have quickly deduced why they were kept in the safe and why they, and not other papers, had needed to be sent to Lugano.

As Golo and he sat down on armchairs facing each other, it was the closest Thomas had ever been to his son. The fact that it might be best to say nothing seemed to make Golo more comfortable. Unlike his two older siblings, he had an ability to take an interest in a mind other than his own. Now, Thomas imagined, he perceived what was preoccupying his father. After all, he had been in the house, silently watching, throughout the years.

What would also be strange, he thought, to anyone who might read the diaries was how remote his household had been from the common lives of Germans. While his fellow citizens owned banknotes that were worthless, he earned dollars. He had spent that time living in a luxury he took for granted. In politics, he had become more liberal, more internationalist, but in how he lived he was more insulated.

At the beginning, in the 1920s, he had disliked the Nazis because there was something low about them; he thought that they would remain, at most, a thorn in the side of a struggling Germany. He imagined a group of them now reading his diaries page by page, irritated by his self-absorption, and then coming across passages that would make them sit up. Instead of following his aimless days, they would, with fire in their eyes, find scenes and phrases to mark and note.

His two eldest children, he understood, could not be damaged as he could be. Their standing in the world depended on their open dismissal of easy sexual categories. Any effort to undermine their reputation would be banished by their own careless laughter and that of their friends. But no one would be amused if sections of his diary were to be published.

In the mornings, when he woke, he imagined that this would be the day the suitcase would come. He was not sure if it would be delivered by the post office van or by some other official vehicle. As soon as he got dressed, Thomas began to watch from the upstairs window. Downstairs, since his makeshift study overlooked the front of the house, he could see anyone coming or going. He noted the postman when he showed up but he only ever had letters and small packages.

Since the house was quiet, Thomas believed that he would hear the van that would deliver the suitcase. He listened out for the sound of an engine. The more he learned about the Nazis, the more he understood their talent for publicity. Were Goebbels to be handed the diaries, he would know what treasure he now possessed. He would select the most damaging details and make them news all over the world. He would transform the reputation of Thomas Mann from great German writer to a name that was a byword for scandal.

Having found a bookseller in Zürich, Thomas added a request for any book on the life of Oscar Wilde to the list of books that he wished to buy for his small provisional library. While he did not expect to go to prison as a result of any disclosures, as Wilde did, and he was aware that Wilde's life had been dissolute, as his had not, it was the move from famous writer to disgraced public figure that interested him. How easily and quickly it happened to Wilde, and how ready the public was to accuse!

Over and over, he went through in his mind what was in the diaries. Some of the personal content was harmless. He wrote, he remembered, about his tender love for Elisabeth, feelings that would befit any father. No one, not even the most malevolent Nazi, could have the slightest objection to his tone when he wrote about Elisabeth. What made him wince, however, were his memories of what he had written about Klaus. As a youth, his eldest son had struck him as being especially beautiful. Once, on coming into the bedroom that Klaus shared with Golo, he had found Klaus naked. The image had remained with him, enough for him to record in his diary how strangely attractive he found his son.

There must have been, he thought, a few more times when he wrote in his diary about the allure of Klaus's body, or how aroused he was by the appearance of Klaus in a swimsuit.

These were thoughts that not many fathers must have felt, he imagined. He was sure that he could not be completely alone but he was aware that the few other fathers, perhaps very few, who found their son sexually attractive had not been foolish enough to share what they were feeling. He himself, of course, had told no one, and he was certain that neither Klaus nor any other member of the family had the slightest idea what was going on in his mind.

Instead, he had noted it all in his diary. Now, somewhere in Germany, it was possible that those pages were being examined by people who had every reason to want to wreck his reputation.

If the phone rang in the house, Thomas worried that it would be someone to tell him that sections of his diaries had appeared in some newspaper. He paced up and down the road outside the house hoping for the sound of an engine that might belong to a van that might deliver his suitcase. If they had fallen into the hands of the Nazis, he wondered if he could deny that the diaries were his, insist that they were a clever forgery. But they were too detailed, he knew, they contained too much day-to-day information that no one could invent.

And they contained accounts of moments that he treasured but could share with no one. Casual glances at young men who had come to his lectures or whom he encountered at a concert. Glances that were sometimes reciprocated and then became unmistakable in their intensity. While he enjoyed the homage he received in public and appreciated the large audiences he attracted, it was always these chance meetings, silent and furtive, that he remembered. Not to have registered in his diary the message sent by the secret energy in a gaze would have been unthinkable. He wanted that which had been so fleeting to become solid. The only way he knew to make this happen was to write it down. Should he have let it pass so that it would have faded completely, this, the story of his life?

The section of the diaries that most worried him described his feelings for a boy called Klaus Heuser, whom he had met six years earlier, in the summer of 1927, when he and Katia had gone, with their three younger children, to Kampen on the island of Sylt in the North Sea.

On the first day, when the weather was blustery and no one could use the beach, Thomas sat on his balcony watching the white clouds racing across the sky. He tried to read, but, whatever heaviness was in the air, he felt too sleepy. Katia, having bought some rainwear, had rented bicycles and gone cycling with the children.

Thomas walked down to the lobby, noticing how scarce the light had grown, even though it was still the afternoon. How different it would be now, he thought, if they had gone to Sicily or even Venice. Or how much emotion it might stir in him had they gone to Travemünde.

From the front porch of the hotel, he saw an elderly woman battling against the wind. With one hand she carried a heavy shopping bag, and in her other hand she had a walking stick. When a sudden gust came, her hat blew off. As he was about to go out to retrieve it, he saw a boy, tall, slim, with blond hair, who had been walking behind the woman, quickly turn and run to get the hat.

He could not hear what the boy said to the woman, but it was good-humored enough to cause her to laugh and shout words of thanks. The boy responded by offering to carry her shopping bag for her, but the woman refused. His dress and his confident air suggested that he was not from the island. As he passed Thomas to go into the lobby, he smiled.

On the first evening, as supper came to an end, their table was approached by a man who said that he was an art professor from Lübeck; he told the family how much he admired *Buddenbrooks*, a novel that he felt lifted his city from its provinciality. His name was Hallen. Since he was in the habit each evening of having a drink with his friend Professor Heuser, who was also an artist, from Düsseldorf, he wondered if they could be joined by the author this evening or some other evening. He pointed to a table, where a man raised his hand to them in greeting. He was, Thomas presumed, Professor Heuser. Beside him, watching the proceedings with interest, was the boy he had seen earlier, obviously the man's son. Thomas nodded to the professor and then moved his attention to the boy, who was staring back at him. As they all stood up, he thought the boy must be seventeen or eighteen. The boy spoke to his father for a moment before leading his mother, who was a tall, fine-boned woman, from the room.

As they sat over drinks that evening in the hotel lounge, it was clear to Thomas that the two art professors had decided not to question him about his books. Instead, they discussed artists they knew and admired, names that were new to Thomas. They spoke with relish of nightclubs and scenes from the German side streets becoming worthy topics for painters.

"A millionaire's face in a time of inflation," Professor Heuser said. "That makes a great portrait."

"Or a philosopher who has not yet begun his book," the Lübeck professor suggested.

"Perhaps he has written 'I am' and is now unsure how he might proceed."

Since Thomas had his back to the door, he did not see Heuser's son entering. What he noticed first was the father's fond smile. He introduced his son Klaus to Thomas.

"My son has read *Buddenbrooks*, *The Magic Mountain* and *Death in Venice*. Can you imagine how he feels on finding his favorite author staying in the same hotel?"

"I'm sure the writer has other things to do than imagine my feelings," Klaus said. He curled his lip in amusement and then smiled broadly.

"Are they telling you about paintings?" he asked Thomas.

"That is what we normally do at night," his father said. "We are tremendously boring."

By lunchtime the next day, Elisabeth had made friends with Klaus Heuser.

"He told me," she whispered, "that there is a man on the island who always knows when the weather is about to change. And the man says that it will soon be sweltering."

"How does this Klaus know the man?" Katia asked.

"He was on his bicycle," Elisabeth said, "and he met the man."

"And where did you meet Klaus?" Thomas asked.

"When the chain fell off my bicycle, he came and fixed it."

"He is obviously very obliging," Thomas said.

"And he knows all our names," Monika added.

"How?" Katia asked.

"He is friends with the man at the desk and he checked our names on the register," Monika said.

In the afternoon, when the others had once more ventured out on bicycles and as the weather worsened, Thomas stood on his balcony and looked at the high waves breaking, the rushing whiteness of the foam. When a knock came to the door, he thought it was one of the staff and shouted "Come in," but no one entered.

The knocking resumed, so he went to the door and opened it to find Klaus Heuser standing there.

"I am sorry if I am disturbing you. Your daughter told me that you work only in the mornings, so I hoped you would not be writing now."

He managed to seem polite without being timid. There was an ironic edge to his tone that reminded Thomas of how his own son Klaus often dealt with his mother. Thomas invited him into the room, and when Klaus went directly to the window, Thomas did not know whether he should leave the door open or close it. As Klaus, without turning, began to admire the view, Thomas quietly closed the door.

"I came because my father, in his enthusiasm last night, told you that I have read *The Magic Mountain*. I was very embarrassed, as I have read only the opening. But I have read *Buddenbrooks* and *Death in Venice* and I admire them greatly."

He sounded confident, but, once he had finished, he was blushing.

"*The Magic Mountain* is very long," Thomas said. "I often wonder if anyone at all has read it."

"I love the opening, the part when Hans meets his cousin."

When a gust of wind rattled the window frames, Thomas joined him to look out.

"The weather is going to change," Klaus said. "I met a man who is considered the island expert. He has arthritis and he can judge what is coming by the quality of his pain."

"Do you study art?" Thomas asked.

"No, I study commerce. I have no talent for art."

The boy looked around the room.

"Is this where you write?"

"In the mornings, as you say."

"And in the afternoons?"

"I read, and, if the weather improves, I will go to the beach."

"I must get going now. I must not disturb you. Tomorrow will be the first sunny day. Perhaps I will see you at the beach."

Soon Klaus Heuser's arthritic informant was proved right. The days became warm and there was no wind. In the mornings, there were hints of gray among the white clouds over the sea, but by noon the sky was completely blue. As soon as he went to the beach, Thomas needed the shade of a beach umbrella. While he read, or looked out at the water, Katia was forced to help Michael make sandcastles or accompany him to the water. Monika and Elisabeth had been shown a beach farther down the coast by Klaus Heuser.

"We promise to be careful," Klaus said when he appeared.

Elisabeth demanded that Klaus sit with them at lunch. When he told her that his mother would miss him, she tried to arrange for her family to start lunch later than the other guests so that Klaus could eat first with his parents and then join the Manns.

Klaus Heuser began to visit Thomas at noon, as he finished his morning's work.

"My father and Professor Hallen were talking about your books. They say that you wrote a story about a professor and his family."

Thomas was amused by the earnestness of Klaus's tone.

"It is called *Disorder and Early Sorrow*," he said. "And yes, the father is a professor."

"Like my father. But it would be hard to put my father into a story."

"Why?"

"Because he sees himself too clearly as a man in a story. It would be too obvious. He is like an artist in a story about an artist. That is why he does self-portraits."

"Has he ever painted you?"

"He did drawings of me when I was a baby. But I don't want him to paint me now. Anyway, when he is not painting himself, he prefers to paint circus performers and people who stay out too late."

Klaus emphasized each day that he would not outstay his welcome, often going to the window to look at the pathway that led to the beach. He liked to examine Thomas's handwriting in a notebook on the desk, following a paragraph or a long sentence, reading it aloud. If he joined the Manns for lunch, or came to their table when the meal was over, he never alluded to the conversations that he and Thomas had had, nor indeed did he refer in any way to his visit to Thomas's room. Instead, he paid attention exclusively to Monika and Elisabeth.

"I see that Klaus has made a conquest," Thomas said.

"The boy has made many conquests," Katia said. "He has won over the entire dining room, perhaps even much of the island, with the exception of poor Michael, who doesn't pay him any attention at all, and perhaps myself."

"You don't like him?"

"I like anyone that can make Monika happy."

One evening, when Professor Hallen had gone to bed early, Thomas had a late-night drink with Professor Heuser.

"I see you have made a conquest of my son," he said.

Thomas was surprised to hear the same phrase as he himself had used earlier in the day.

"He is very clever and quite grown-up for his age," Thomas said. "And then he plays so well with our daughters."

"Everyone has always liked Klaus," the professor said, "and wanted him in their game."

He looked at Thomas, smiling. Thomas saw no mockery or disapproval. The professor seemed relaxed, like a man enjoying his evening.

"Isn't it strange," he asked, "that no matter how well we paint the face, we struggle to paint hands. If the Devil came here now and asked me what I would want in exchange for eternity under his reign I would ask him to let me paint hands, hands that no one would even notice, perfect hands. Do novelists have a problem like our problem with hands?"

"It is sometimes hard to write about love," Thomas said.

"Ah yes, that is why I cannot paint my wife or my son. What colors would you use?"

One afternoon on the beach, when Michael had fallen asleep under the shade of the umbrella, Katia interrupted Thomas as he read.

"Elisabeth is insisting that we invite Klaus Heuser to Munich. This morning, after breakfast, she went to speak to his mother. She had Monika in tow. Did she consult you about this?"

"Not at all," he said.

"Nor me. She is headstrong. Monika, I could see, was worried that they had not checked with us first. But not your darling Elisabeth. She is not worried at all."

"Did the boy accept?"

"He stood close by, as he often does, in full control."

That evening, after dinner, they were approached by Klaus Heuser's mother.

"Your daughters are the two most charming girls," she said.

"Your son has been a delightful companion," Katia replied.

"All three have appealed to me to allow Klaus to visit you in Munich, but I have told him that what happens on holidays does not last into the winter."

Thomas saw the expression on Katia's face darken at the suggestion that her daughters might somehow be fickle.

"Your son would be very welcome in Munich," she said.

"I had best discuss the matter with my husband," Klaus's mother said. "Klaus does have free time, but I would hate to feel that he was imposing himself on you."

"But he is not," Katia said.

Monika and Elisabeth promised that they would look after Klaus Heuser if he came to stay.

"There is plenty of room in the house," Elisabeth said.

"It will all be perfect," Monika said. "Please let him come!"

"But it is unusual," Katia said, "for a boy to stay with two girls."

"I am seventeen," Monika said. "When Erika and Klaus were this age, you let them go to Berlin. And all we want is to have someone nice staying with us."

Soon it was agreed that Klaus Heuser would come in the autumn. Although Thomas listened carefully to see how long Klaus planned to be with them, he noticed that it was not mentioned.

At the end of lunch one day he heard Monika and Elisabeth in low voices appealing to Katia on some matter, with Katia shaking her head as Monika insisted.

"Why the whispering?" he asked.

"They want Klaus to stay on when his parents leave in two days' time."

"Surely that is for his parents to decide? Or Klaus himself?"

"Klaus wants to stay. His parents have agreed. But they say that since he will be our responsibility, then we must agree too."

"I agree," Monika said, "and so does Elisabeth."

"Is that not settled, then?" Thomas asked.

"If you all say so," Katia said.

Thomas found that he benefited from the routine that had been established. His work each morning was progressing to his satisfaction. At meals, he enjoyed watching his daughters respond to Klaus, and on the beach in the afternoon Michael, now eight, once left alone with his parents, was much calmer and more amenable than normal. He had become used to the water and wanted his father and mother on each side of him to hold his hands as they lifted him above the breaking waves. While Thomas had given Klaus and Golo piggybacks, he had never played like he did with Michael, who squealed with pleasure each day when he saw his father appearing on the beach after lunch.

On the day his parents left, having accompanied them to the ferry, Klaus returned to the hotel and knocked on Thomas's door. It must be strange, Thomas thought, to be seventeen and left behind in a hotel by your parents. He and Katia would now have to stand in for the departed professor and his wife. When his own son Klaus was seventeen, he remembered, he lived unsupervised and made no secret of the advantage he took from the lack of parental supervision. But this boy, this other Klaus, had none of Klaus Mann's interest in ideas or current affairs. He did not want to write novels or go on the stage. He could speak to Thomas, and question him, as if they were equals. Thomas supposed he dealt with Monika and Elisabeth in the same way. He would merely adjust his tone.

"I don't feel any different now that my parents are gone," he said. "I was just as free when they were here. Because my father was in the war, he hates orders. So he never gives any. My parents have never in my life told me what to do."

"I try to tell my children what to do, but they ignore me, especially the two eldest," Thomas said.

"Klaus and Erika," Klaus replied.

"How do you know their names?"

"My parents saw them on the stage in Düsseldorf, in that play about four young people, and they told me about them. But everyone knows who they are."

Klaus looked at a paragraph Thomas had been writing. As he traced his fingers along the lines of handwriting, Thomas stood beside him. When Thomas pointed to a word that had been crossed out, Klaus, in frustration, put his hand on Thomas's and brushed it away from the line so that he himself could see the erased word.

Instantly, Thomas could feel the heat of Klaus's hand against his own knuckles. He remained still and said nothing, allowing Klaus to leave his hand in place for a few seconds more than was necessary.

Neither of them spoke. Thomas saw that it was open to him to seek to turn and embrace Klaus. But he also understood how unlikely it was that such an approach would be welcomed. Klaus had come to his room, he supposed, in all innocence. He was used to being with adults and being treated as their equal. But he, who recently had been playing and cavorting on the beach with Monika and Elisabeth, hardly expected to be embraced by their father, a man three times his age.

Thomas tried to think of something to say that would lessen the tension in the room, a tension that Klaus, he thought, must also sense. Klaus glanced at him and then looked at the floor. He was blushing and seemed younger than his years. Thomas would have given anything now to get this boy out of the room. He was sure that Katia or the children would arrive or someone from the hotel would suddenly knock at the door. Even if Klaus left, he thought, he would be bound to meet Katia in the corridor.

"Do you mind me coming to Munich?" Klaus asked.

"No, and my daughters are especially excited that you will be coming."

"I hope I will not interrupt your routine. Monika says that no one can even speak when they are anywhere near your study."

"She exaggerates," Thomas said.

"I hope to read all of your work," Klaus said. "But I must leave you in peace."

He put a finger to his lips, suggesting that he was involved in some furtive action. And then he made his way across the room and slipped out, closing the door quietly behind him.

• • •

When Klaus Heuser came to Munich in the autumn, he managed never to be in the way. If no one required his company, he was to be found alone in one of the reception rooms reading a book. If Monika were free, then he would spend time with her. So too with Elisabeth. Soon Golo began to pay attention to him; the two were often to be seen in deep discussion.

Klaus Mann, when he came, made no secret of his admiration for the younger Klaus, flirting with him openly and asserting that he believed the two had a great deal in common. Thomas watched as Klaus Heuser kept his distance from Klaus Mann.

Once Thomas had returned from his afternoon walk with Katia and had had his nap, he was usually visited in his study by Klaus Heuser, who listened carefully as Thomas told him what he had been writing that morning. Always, Klaus would want to see the handwriting and he became fascinated by the erasures. Each time Thomas pointed out a word to him, he would repeat what he had first done in the hotel room, he would place his hand over Thomas's and let it linger there before moving Thomas's hand out of the way so that he himself could see the erased word.

Erika arrived and insisted that she was so pleased to be home that she would not complain even if she were forced to take a daily walk with Monika and listen to all her sister's woes.

"Monika doesn't have any woes," her brother Klaus said. "No one in this house does. Even Golo smiles. And the Magician has taken to wearing brightly colored neckties. This is all because on that island in the North Sea they found a little angel from Düsseldorf and they had him packaged and delivered fresh to our door. He lives in the attic. My mother loves him too. Only Michael scowls when he appears."

"And I am sure your feelings about this boy are simply indescribable?"

"Yes, that is a good summary of my feelings," Klaus said.

Over dinner, Erika ignored Klaus Heuser, discussing various theater shows she had seen and talking of the need for an anti-Nazi cabaret that would draw crowds.

"I should do it, but first I want to go on a tour of the world. I want to see every place before civilization falls asunder!"

"Erika," her mother said, "you are such a fine example to the younger ones that I think we will have your portrait painted and put up in the hall."

"Klaus Heuser's father could do it," Monika said.

Klaus smiled shyly.

"Oh, you are the golden boy," Erika said, turning to Klaus Heuser. "Oh, I had not noticed you! Well, look at the golden boy!"

"Yes, that is what I am," Klaus said and lifted his head to gaze at Erika, as though ready to outdo her if she chose to continue being provocative. Thomas had never seen him look so beautiful.

Klaus Heuser, on one of his afternoon visits, asked Thomas about his early life. As Klaus listened with close attention, Thomas found himself recounting the death of his father. He told Klaus then about the years of rancor between himself and Heinrich. When Klaus asked him about his mother, Thomas became emotional and could not answer. He stood up and went towards the bookcases and remained there, with his back to Klaus. As he waited, he knew that Klaus would have to decide whether to come near. Thomas determined not to turn, not to speak. He held his breath so that he would be able to hear if Klaus was crossing the room.

He sensed him moving, and then he must have stopped. He imagined Klaus asking himself what he should do. Even if he coughed, he thought, or made some whispering sound, even if he shifted his weight from one foot to another, then he would rescue Klaus from having to take a risk.

Later, he wondered if he was being manipulated as Paul Ehrenberg had once manipulated him, but he was sure that Klaus Heuser was not playing with him. Rather, he presumed that the boy
was in awe of him and had no idea that this elderly writer's days
were filled with thoughts of him, and his nights too. He believed
that Klaus was utterly unaware that a fond glance, or a brushing of
the boy's hand against his, or even the sound of his voice, excited
Thomas in ways that he thought would never come to him again.

Erika proposed that they invite their uncle Klaus Pringsheim to
dinner so that they could celebrate the presence of three Klauses
among them. It was seen as a joke until it was taken up by Monika
and Elisabeth and arranged for some days later.

When Klaus Pringsheim arrived, Katia asked him to sit beside
her at the table. Erika, in turn, insisted that she be seated beside
her brother Klaus. Monika and Elisabeth wanted Klaus Heuser
between them. Thomas smiled as he observed that just as he,
Golo and Michael expressed no preference, no one, it seemed,
made any special plea to be put near any one of them.

As the food was served and the talk grew animated, Thomas
was left out of the conversation. Monika and Elisabeth, he saw,
became irritated by the amount of attention Erika and Klaus
Mann were paying to Klaus Heuser, asking him questions, telling
him jokes, teasing him. All the time, Katia and her brother Klaus
spoke to each other quietly. They were amused by each other,
Katia shaking her head in wonder at something that Klaus said.
And then the talk between them could become serious, Klaus
Pringsheim listening intently to something Katia told him.

Watching them, Thomas saw his fictions taking on life. Klaus
and Katia were back in the setting he had imagined for them in
The Blood of the Walsungs; they were the twins in thrall to each

other. He was the dull interloper become magician, the one who had given substance to this amorphous family of his.

His eyes caught the eyes of Klaus Heuser and he realized that he himself had been changed in his turn, transformed into Gustav von Aschenbach in *Death in Venice* and Klaus into the boy he had observed so intensely on the beach.

All Thomas could do was watch. If he left the table, no one except Klaus Heuser would see him depart. Even Golo and Michael were having a lively conversation. As he shifted his gaze from one face to another, he noticed that Klaus Heuser, while pretending to listen to Monika, was actually regularly glancing in his direction. Since everyone else was so preoccupied, he used this chance to stare openly at Klaus. While Klaus attended to Monika and then to Elisabeth and replied to something that Klaus Mann had said to him, he sometimes lifted his eyes towards Thomas and silently acknowledged that he was fully alert to him, that everything else that was happening at the table was barely impinging on his consciousness.

The household knew that he could never be disturbed in the mornings but it was understood that this rule did not apply to the afternoons. Despite this, no one ever came near his study during the time Klaus Heuser was with him.

At some point in the conversation, Thomas would stand up and go to the bookshelves. He would not take down a book or change his position. Instead, he would wait for the sound of Klaus approaching.

On an afternoon in his second week with them, Klaus told him that he had had a conversation with Katia.

"It was strange," he said. "It began by her saying that I must stay here as long as I wanted. I was not sure how to reply, so I thanked her. I was going to say that I do not have any urgent need to go home but then she repeated how welcome I would be to stay. She is, I think, a very subtle person."

"What do you mean?"

"I mean that by the end of the conversation, without my being sure how this had happened, it was agreed that I would leave at the end of the week."

Thomas had to swallow hard. They sat in silence for some time until he spoke.

"Would you like me to come to Düsseldorf to see you?"

"Yes."

Thomas stood up and went to the bookcases. Before he had time to compose himself and listen out for Klaus's breath, Klaus had moved swiftly across the room, grasping Thomas's hands for a moment and then edging him around so that they faced each other and started to kiss.

Since Erika and Klaus were to leave, they had a final dinner with the family and Klaus Heuser. Klaus Mann sat next to him at table. Thomas watched as they made plans to meet in Düsseldorf when Klaus Mann was visiting. Soon it was decided that Erika would come too, and all three of them might go to Berlin together. When it was apparent that Monika and Elisabeth were feeling left out of these arrangements, Klaus Heuser turned away from Klaus and Erika and spoke to the two younger ones for the rest of the evening.

Thomas wrote about Klaus Heuser in his diaries, describing the culmination of their time together in precise detail. He saw no danger in doing that. The danger would be in not noting it down, in letting it fade.

One day, the week after Klaus Heuser had left, when Thomas and Katia were taking a walk through the autumn leaves by the bank of the river, Katia spoke about their visitor.

"I think we live such a sheltered life," she said. "I liked having six children because I thought they would be company for each other. But I often wonder if it doesn't mean that we are more enclosed, less open to the outside world. Young Klaus brightened up all our lives, including mine. All our children except Golo think only of themselves, and maybe we do too, but Klaus seemed to consider everybody. It is a remarkable gift."

Thomas listened carefully for a hint of irony, but there was none.

"What did your brother think of him?" he asked.

"The third Klaus? My brother only notices me," she replied.

"Monika loved Klaus Heuser."

"We all loved him. We were lucky we chose to go to Sylt. Otherwise, we would never have met him."

In the diaries, he remembered, he did not just record what had happened between him and Klaus Heuser. He had, each day, written down what his dreams were, what it meant for him to have the boy in his study, what he thought about in the morning when he woke, knowing that Klaus was in bed in one of the upper rooms. In some office, he thought, men in uniforms could be nudging each other and sniggering as they read of his relationship with someone younger than his two eldest sons. He imagined the moment when they might hand these pages of the diary over to their superiors. And among these superiors there would be someone who would know how to use the diaries. He pictured himself walking the streets of Lugano with Katia, dressed with his usual formality, only to find that people were coming to the doors of shops to peer at him as he walked by.

When he and Katia and Golo had a meeting with Heins, his lawyer, who had traveled from Munich to Switzerland, their main preoccupation was that the Nazis might seize the house on

Poschingerstrasse. It was now agreed that Heins would do what he could to prevent that and take what papers were in the study, including letters and the manuscripts of the novels, to keep in his own office.

Finally, Thomas raised the matter of the suitcase. Having questioned Golo closely about the role of the chauffeur, Heins said that he would make inquiries.

One morning a week later, he heard the phone ringing. It was Heins.

"I have the suitcase. It is here. What should I do with it?"

"How did you get it?"

"It was not difficult. Some things work in Munich as they always have. Officials are still official. I simply complained to the post office about the delay. And when they found the case, they were quite penitent and at a loss to explain why it had not been sent."

"Can it be delivered now?"

"You can rest assured that you will have it, unless you want to keep the contents with the other papers in my office."

"No, I do not. There are notes for a novel I am working on."

As he waited for the delivery, he looked forward to reading one more time what he had written about Klaus Heuser.

And then, on a night when he was alone in this rented house, he would put those pages, and perhaps some others, into the fire. In having the diaries delivered to him, he had, he knew, been lucky. He wondered now, in the first year of his exile, if he would ever need to be so lucky again.

Chapter 9
Küsnacht, 1934

Nothing had prepared him for fleeing his own country. He had failed to read the signs. He had misunderstood Germany, the very place that was meant to be inscribed on his soul. The idea that if he were to set foot in Munich he would soon be dragged from the house and taken to a place from which he would not ever return seemed like an event in a dream.

Each morning, as they read the newspapers over breakfast, one of them would share an item, a fresh outrage committed by the Nazis, an arrest or confiscation of property, a threat to the peace of Europe, an outlandish claim against the Jewish population or against writers and artists or against Communists, and they would sigh or grow silent. On some days, while reading out an item of news, Katia would say that this was the worst yet, only to be corrected by Erika, who would have found something even more outrageous.

At first, he had found his Italian English teacher's poverty and neediness so apparent that he could not concentrate on the lessons. The study of grammar and the constant repetitions were also tedious. The bespectacled teacher, clearly irritated, produced an English translation of Dante's *Inferno* and offered to take Thomas through the poem line by line, making him note down all the new words and remember their meaning for the next class. When Thomas mentioned at dinner that he was studying Dante in the original English, both Erika and Michael rushed to correct him.

"I won the Nobel Prize in Literature," Thomas said. "I know what language Dante wrote in!"

Katia decided to join the class; but she was more a teacher than a pupil, Thomas thought. She had already studied an English grammar book and demanded to be taken slowly and methodically through the rules, starting with the present tense. Each morning, she handed Thomas a list of twenty words in English with the German meaning opposite and said he had to learn them by evening. In the class, she tried to be better than the teacher, often becoming exasperated and breaking into German, a language the Italian did not speak.

After some months, Katia found a young English poet living nearby and invited him to come for conversation classes, with no grammar, announcing that she was more comfortable in the past tense and would like to talk about history.

"History is all in the past tense," she said, "so that will help us. He was. It was. She was. They were. There was. There were."

From the safety of outside, Thomas knew he would, at some stage, have to denounce what was happening in Germany. But for the moment, despite the pressure on him, he did not want to put Katia's parents in any more danger, nor did he want his own books to be taken from the shelves. Also, his publisher Gottfried Bermann remained in Germany. If Thomas's books could not be distributed there, Bermann would go out of business and all the effort he had put into keeping Thomas's work in print would serve only to make his position more precarious. Ignoring Katia's and Erika's arguments to the contrary, Thomas still believed that Hitler would be removed by his generals, or that there would be a massive uprising against him. Each morning, as he opened the papers, it was in the expectation that there would be some news that the power of the Nazis was waning.

When he saw that his passport and that of Katia were shortly to expire, the efforts he made to renew them were rebuffed by the German authorities at first and then ignored. It was foolish, he saw, to have believed that the Swiss would step in and grant him and his family citizenship. The country that had taken him in, he understood, was as much a fortress as a sanctuary. In the end, Switzerland offered him provisional leave to stay and provisional papers with which he could travel.

By this time, the Swiss newspapers were calling Hitler the Führer without any irony. Thomas began to lose hope that the regime might fail in Germany. The Nazis, he realized, were not like the poets of the Munich Revolution. They were street fighters who had taken power without losing their sway over the streets. They managed to be both government and opposition. They thrived on the idea of enemies, including enemies within. They did not fear bad publicity—rather, they actually wanted the worst of their actions to become widely known, all the better to make everyone, even those loyal to them, afraid.

At first, he had been so surprised at being uprooted from the stately house he had built in Munich, with its air of solidity and permanence, that he believed he needed to find just one secure spot and stay there. But once his Swiss papers came through, he felt restless, as though Lugano had merely been a first stop, a provisional refuge. Being away from home frightened him. There were days when he thought of a book and could see where it might be found in his study. Not being able to take it down and open it came to him with sadness but also, at times, with panic. On the other hand, living in Switzerland, listening to the amusing dialect the locals used, reading local newspapers, offered him a lightness, a sense that he had embarked on an adventure.

Thus, the decision to move to the south of France was made on what seemed like a whim. Once it was decided, however, neither he nor Katia tried to justify the change by listing the reasons. There had been no reasons. He smiled at the thought that, since they felt they needed to do something, they had determined to do this. He told anyone who asked that he believed he might feel more comfortable in the south of France, where many other German exiles were. The family traveled first to Bandol and then, following other writers, they went to Sanary-sur-Mer, where they rented a large house.

In Lugano and Arosa, Thomas had had access to the German newspapers. In Sanary, all was rumor and there were many factions and feuds. Most of the German exiles went to the cafés each morning. The Jewish ones, he saw, were interested in the fate of the Jewish population that had remained in Germany and was under more intense threat as each day went by. The Social Democrats busied themselves hating the Communists, who, in turn, hated the Social Democrats. Bertolt Brecht, he saw, was a great troublemaker, moving from one café to another spreading dissent. It amazed him that Ernst Toller had also turned up in Sanary and was being listened to as though his opinion mattered. Others came and went, including Heinrich, who was based mainly in Nice and wrote a regular column in French for one of the local newspapers in which he excoriated Hitler and his regime.

It was easy for Thomas to follow his usual morning routine, but in the afternoon it was tempting to take a walk into the town center, check at the newsstand to see what foreign newspapers had come in and have a late coffee in one of the cafés. Thomas was quite happy to find himself at a Jewish table or a Social Democrat table but he tended to avoid the Communist table.

One afternoon, when he was sitting alone, he became aware that he was being closely observed by a number of young men nearby who were speaking German. When one of them approached and invited him to join them, he smiled and stood up and greeted each young man. His arrival, he saw, caused suspicion among a couple of thin-faced fellows in the company. Whatever they had been talking about, his appearance had put an end to their conversation. He noticed that the one who had invited him to join them was on the point of saying something and then demurred.

"Are you a poet?" he asked him.

"No. Sometimes I write a line or two and then I cross it out. I don't even keep the paper."

"So, what do you do?"

He realized that the question sounded like criticism.

"I feel sorry for myself," the young man said.

One of the others began to laugh.

"He doesn't like Germany," he said, "but he hates France even more."

"Do you still have your big house in Munich?" one of the thin-faced young men asked.

"I believe it is to be confiscated," Thomas said.

"I was in charge of watching you during the Munich Revolution." Thomas looked puzzled.

"Don't be so surprised. I was sixteen then and I looked innocent. I saw all your comings and goings and reported back."

"Why?"

"For writing all those books," another one said and sniggered.

"You might have been shot," the young man continued.

"It would have done wonders for my reputation," Thomas said.

"Toller was the one who stopped it."

"I know that," Thomas said.

"And now here he is without a penny, but you and your family are in a big house. Someday, all of that is going to change."

"Do you mean under Hitler?" Thomas asked.

"You know what I mean," the young man answered.

Thomas swore to avoid the cafés completely, but he could not decline every invitation that came from fellow émigrés. What was strange, he thought, was that even the most political among them became more animated when they discussed their own plight, such as the loss of their property or problems with visas. When he studied them, he belicved them to be a group already defeated, suffering from ailments, real and imaginary, waiting for news or money, their clothes becoming shabbier.

Part of the reason he wished to avoid them was that he saw in them what he himself was slowly becoming. Like them, he waited each day for news, knowing that a headline in one of the papers or a story inside could dictate how soundly he would sleep and how darkly he would dream.

All of the others had, in one way or another, denounced the regime. He was the only one who had not. He knew that, led by Brecht, they were watching him, the best-known among them. He and Katia had to be careful when they did decide to take a walk on the esplanade in the evening not to wear clothes that might appear new or expensive.

One evening, at the end of an émigré dinner he had attended alone, Katia being indisposed, he found himself face-to-face with Ernst Toller.

He had never understood how this unformed youth managed to become the leader of a revolution, ending as so-called president of the Bavarian Soviet Republic, if only for six days. He had no idea what had impelled Ernst Toller to want to turn Munich upside down.

As Toller shook his hand with nervous enthusiasm and asked him if he had time for a coffee or a drink, it struck Thomas that the poet needed money. He had some cash with him, and thought he might offer it to Toller as soon as they were sitting down and perhaps suggest that if he owed money at his hotel, then his bill might be paid.

Instead of mentioning money, however, Toller asked him what he thought of the work Klaus was doing to galvanize the opposition to Hitler outside Germany.

"It puts the rest of us to shame," Toller said.

Thomas said that he had not been in touch with his son for a while.

"He is brilliant," Toller said. "He works tirelessly. Perhaps he will only be recognized in the future."

Thomas was used to hearing such remarks about Heinrich, but this was the first time he had heard someone speaking in this way about Klaus.

"There is a reason I wanted to see you alone," Toller said.

He was even more nervous than before. Thomas wondered if he was going to ask for a large amount of money.

"Erich Mühsam is being held by the Nazis. They arrested him after the Reichstag fire. I know he has been tortured. He is not like the rest of us. As you know, he is a playwright and a poet, but he is also an anarchist of the old school. He would not do himself any favors in prison."

Thomas remembered that Mühsam had been another of the unlikely leaders of the Munich Revolution.

"Do you mean he would remain outspoken?"

"Yes."

When their drinks came, they sat in silence.

"He always spoke about you warmly," Toller eventually said. "May I ask if you could help him?"

"In what way?"

"You are one of the most powerful Germans alive."

"Not now."

"But you must still have friends and associates?"

"Among the Nazis?"

"Among those who have influence."

"If I did, why would I be here?"

"I am asking you because I am desperate. I cannot sleep think-ing about him. There must be somebody you can contact."

"I have no friends among the Nazis."

Toller nodded sadly.

"He is doomed, then. I can think of nothing else."

Walking home, Thomas asked himself if the émigrés really believed that he had enough influence to have a man released from prison. Toller's request, he thought, had not been casual. He had put thought into it. The only Nazi that Thomas knew was Ernst Bertram and he could imagine Bertram's surprise were he to receive a missive from Thomas Mann asking him to exert his influence to have an anarchist who had been involved in the Munich Revolution freed from prison.

Even though he could do nothing, his very powerlessness made him feel uneasy. As he sat alone in his study, it struck him that he could stir up interest in Mühsam's case in the wider world, maybe even in America, but this might make things worse for him. It might be best to do nothing. By the time he went to bed he knew that. But he did not know if his own motives were pure or not, if he had decided not to act to avoid trouble for himself, or for better reasons.

More and more German writers and artists and their families were leaving the country, including Heinrich's new girlfriend, Nelly Kröger. Heinrich and Mimi had split up some years before. Mimi and Goschi were now living in Prague. Heinrich often wrote to Thomas about his guilt at leaving them and his worry about their fate. He could not invite them to Nice, since he could barely make ends meet for himself. When Nelly came, it would be even harder.

Heinrich also sent cuttings from the French newspapers to Thomas, with passages underlined. Thomas and Katia planned to reciprocate but then forgot. Thomas decided that he should write to his brother every Saturday, even if there was no news. He could let Heinrich know the novels and poetry he was reading, aware that Heinrich was more interested in political developments.

When Heinrich came from Nice to stay with them, he was intrigued by the number of exiles living in Sanary. He usually woke early and went into the center to get the newspapers and see who was in the cafés. By the time Thomas and Katia came down for breakfast, Heinrich had all the fresh news. While Thomas thought that most of the Germans in Sanary, including Brecht and Walter Benjamin and Stefan Zweig, met merely to grumble in congenial company, Heinrich said that he discussed art and politics with them.

"No matter who is in power in Germany," Thomas said, "these men will feel left out."

"You should spend more time with them," Heinrich said. "They see beyond the war, and even beyond the peace. They meet to discuss ideas. Important books will come from this."

"They want to make a new world," Thomas replied. "And I rather liked the old one. So I would hardly be any use to them."

Heinrich poured more coffee and settled back into his chair.

In the evening, they took walks on the esplanade before depositing Heinrich at one of the cafés, Thomas and Katia relieved to go home without him.

When he was with Heinrich, he listened, he smiled, and he made sure, if they were in a restaurant, that he paid the bill. He asked after Mimi and Goschi, and he asked after Nelly Kröger.

It was agreed that, once she came to Nice, Nelly and Heinrich would visit Sanary and stay in one of the small hotels. Thomas and Katia would take her and Heinrich for a celebratory dinner when she arrived.

In the lobby of the hotel, when they went to collect them, Thomas saw a young blond woman sitting beside his brother. He believed for a few seconds that she was someone from the hotel, or from the bar. He noticed how formal Katia became as Nelly stood up and clapped her hands and let out a whooping cry, causing those around to stare at her.

"Oh, a big lovely dinner, with bubbles and then wine and soup and then lobster or will we have duck? Do you think they will have duck, my little duck?"

She fondled one of Heinrich's ears.

"For you, they will have everything," Heinrich replied.

Nelly directed her gaze to Katia as they walked towards the restaurant.

"When it's hot I'm cold and when it's cold I'm hot. I don't know what that says about me! I hope I'm not frigid after my long journey. But the rattling of a train, they say, is a tremendous warm-up."

Katia looked coldly into the distance.

At the table, when Heinrich sought to inform Thomas about something he had read in an afternoon paper, Nelly interrupted.

"No politics, and no talking about books."

"What would you like to talk about?" Thomas asked. "You are the guest."

"Oh, food and love! What else is there? Perhaps money, perhaps the chance of us ladies getting fur coats before the winter. And fur hats, and silk stockings."

There was a long table in the restaurant occupied by a group of staid and middle-aged French people. They were speaking quietly to one another and seemed surprised when Nelly, having ordered cognac at the end of the meal, demanded that the evening not end before she was allowed to toast France and all the French.

Since she did this in German, she did not, Thomas saw, endear herself to the long table.

She persisted, even when Heinrich suggested that she sit down, even as waiters hovered, looking concerned.

"To France," she said. "I drink to France. Do you not want to drink to France?"

When, finally, she sat down, she turned her attention to Heinrich.

"Darling, I want a night on the town. I would like to start in a plush bar and end in a dive by the port. Shall we?"

"This is why I have been longing to see you," Heinrich said.

"Katia," Nelly asked, "do you know the best places for a real night out?"

"I have never been on a real night out in my life," Katia said.

"Oh, then you must come with us. You can leave Bismarck at home. I am sure he has another book to write."

The more émigrés who came to Sanary, the more the locals appeared to resent them. Thomas did not enjoy being singled out as a German as he walked in the streets, nor did Katia take any pleasure from entering a shop and being glared at once her nationality became clear. Elisabeth and Michael, at sixteen and fifteen, who were still going to school, wished they could live in a place where the language they spoke did not set them apart.

Thomas decided that they would go back to Switzerland, where Elisabeth and Michael could go to German-speaking schools once term began. They hoped that Monika, who had grown depressed in Sanary, might find something useful to do in Switzerland.

As soon as they returned, Katia set about finding them another English teacher to supplement the work of the Italian.

"Yes, I know about Dante," she said to Thomas, "the middle of the journey and the dark wood and all that, but it won't help me to buy carrots in a grocery or to tell a plumber about a leaking pipe. We need to learn proper American English."

When the first issue of *Die Sammlung*, a literary magazine edited by Klaus, arrived from Amsterdam, where he was living, Thomas saw his name in the list of future contributors. While he had not given specific permission for his name to appear, he had, he supposed, agreed to write for the magazine at some point. But no one had told him, least of all Klaus, that it was going to take such a strident political line. Both Heinrich in an article and Klaus in an editorial vehemently attacked the Nazi regime, Klaus writing that, although the publication was not exclusively political, it had a political mission that was unequivocal.

Since his lecture in Berlin in 1930, Thomas had still done nothing to provoke the authorities. In France and in Switzerland in these first years of exile, he had been careful to give no interviews. His reticence, he understood from Bermann, his publisher, was noted in Berlin. The Nazis might be inclined to confiscate his property and refuse to renew his passport and the passports of his family, but they continued to allow his books to be sold.

He contemplated the idea that someday in the near future his books would be withdrawn in Germany, and it frightened him. He thought back to *Buddenbrooks* and *The Magic Mountain*, the books for which he was most famous, and realized that they would have been paler books, less confident, less intense, had he known when he was writing them that no German would be permitted to read them. At the time he wrote those books, he did not have to think of them as imaginative interventions in the fraught public life of his own country. Such high-flown thoughts were not necessary. The relationship between his words and the German reader had been calm and natural. There would come a time, he knew, when that relationship would have to be broken, but he wanted to postpone it for as long as he could.

And now Klaus, by printing his name as a future contributor to the magazine, had dragged him into the net of émigré disaffection, putting everything at risk.

"Yes," Katia said, "I agree that it was a misjudgment. He should perhaps have included a chapter from the novel Heinrich is working on instead of an attack on Hitler. And the editorial is, you are right, too strident, although no one could disagree with it. And it might have been better to have left out the names of future contributors."

"Klaus has deliberately sought to include me in his pantheon of dissidents."

"Klaus is hotheaded and inconsiderate," Katia said, "but he is not devious or sly. I suggest a gentle letter, but one that emphasizes that this must not happen again."

It might have been left like that, Thomas thought, had not a trade magazine in Germany published a warning to booksellers from the Office for the Furtherance of German Writing that they should not handle Klaus's magazine. When Bermann, alarmed by this, contacted Thomas to say that his association with this troublemaking publication could involve the removal of his books from circulation, Thomas, without consulting Katia, sent a telegram to the trade magazine to confirm that the character of the first issue of *Die Sammlung* did not correspond to its original aims.

His telegram, in turn, was attacked in German-language newspapers in Prague and Vienna. He knew, because Golo told him, how upset Klaus was and how he had taken to calling his mother collect late at night to say that his life was blighted, as his father had no respect for what he did. Klaus could not believe, Golo said, that his father would betray him in this way.

"He likes to use my name when it suits him," Thomas said. "And he has no problem about compromising me at the same time."

"Denouncing Hitler is hardly a way of compromising you," Golo said.

"Decisions about my denouncing Hitler will be taken by me and by no one else."

Golo stood up and left the room.

Soon Katia appeared.

"No telegrams in future without consulting me," she said sternly. "But it was a great help that you sent it."

"I don't think—"

"Oh yes it was, it allowed me to tell Klaus that his father is as hotheaded as he is, and that seemed to please him."

Thomas was expecting an avalanche of criticism from Erika and was prepared to ask her if she would spare him much of it. He and Katia were busy moving into a three-story villa in Küsnacht, on the lake close to Zürich. When Erika came to stay, she went with her mother to purchase new furniture and she oversaw the arrival of books and paintings that they had managed to rescue from Munich. It looked as if this engaged her, for the moment, more than the plight of her brother, who remained in Amsterdam.

Having received permission from the Swiss authorities to restage *The Peppermill*, the anti-Nazi cabaret that she had produced in Germany before her departure, she began to rewrite the songs to make them connect with current events. The phone was busy all day as she made bookings and hired new performers.

"I want them to hate me," she said as the date of her opening neared.

"Well, that won't be hard," Monika said.

"I want the Swiss to hate me, but nonetheless to stay until the end of the show. I want the Nazis to know that I am still in business. And if everyone did what I am doing, then Hitler would soon be painting our hallways at less than the going rate."

"If there was no Hitler, what would you do?" Golo asked.

"I don't think in 'ifs,'" Erika said.

"But you just said 'if everyone did what I am doing,'" Golo pointed out.

"Golo, I am too busy to be consistent. I have too much to do."

The Peppermill played to packed houses. Thomas was amused when Katia told him that when the cabaret went on tour, Erika and a lady friend traveled first class and stayed in the best hotels, while the rest of the cast traveled in second class and stayed in cheaper hotels.

"She has never been a socialist," Thomas said. "Even when she was a baby she believed in the free market."

In Amsterdam Erika met Klaus, who had been officially

declared stateless by Goebbels, causing Thomas to realize that his own semi-stateless position should not continue for much longer. He considered applying for Czech citizenship, as Heinrich had done. Thomas had met Edvard Beneš, the Czech foreign minister, at a conference and was informed by him that his application would be warmly received. Since her own German passport would soon reach its expiry date, Erika explained to her parents on her return, she had decided to strike out on her own and look for a foreign husband.

"The minute I saw a man called Christopher Isherwood," she said, "I knew he was for me. He is small, English, a writer and homosexual. I enticed him into a corner in some bar that Klaus favors in Amsterdam and I immediately came to the point. And I presumed that he would just say yes. But to my horror, Isherwood said no, and mentioned his boyfriend or his mother or both as impediments. And then he offered to contact his friend, who is even more famous and more English and more homosexual. He is called Auden. And this Auden said he would be delighted to marry me. So I put on my best suit and flew to England and he was so sweet if slightly hard to understand. And not only am I married, but I am English, so everyone has to pay even more attention to me now."

"Will we be seeing your husband?" Katia asked.

"I am not sure that he grows in soil that is not English," Erika replied.

When Erika informed her family that Christopher Isherwood delighted in being known as "the pimp" for his services to her, they warned Monika that, since she too was about to become stateless, then she would also have to find a husband of the English persuasion.

"They don't wash," Elisabeth said. "There is no English word for soap."

"You will have to marry Isherwood," Michael told her, "if he will have you. He wouldn't have Erika."

"He longed for me," Erika said. "But the circumstances were not right."

"The Magician," Monika said, "is going to make us all into Czechs."

"I think I would prefer to be Danish," Elisabeth said.

"Or Brazilian, like my grandmother," Monika added.

"If Uncle Heinrich has his way, we will all be Russian," Michael said.

"Why can't we be Swiss?" Monika asked.

"Because the Swiss don't give citizenship to just anyone," Thomas said. "In fact, they give it to no one, least of all Germans fleeing Hitler."

"Is that what we are?" Michael asked.

"Wake up, my boy," Erika said. "Hitler is looking at your file as we speak. He sees a nasty, spotty, petulant youth."

She made a theatrical grimace and stretched her arms out towards Michael as though to attack him. And then she followed him around the table.

They tried to make the rented house overlooking the lake in Küsnacht feel like their own. It wasn't simply that the candelabra they placed on the dining room table came from his grandmother's house in Lübeck, or that the 143-volume Weimarer Sophienausgabe edition of Goethe's works was on his bookshelves. Rather, Katia had a way of creating intimate, comfortable corners and then larger, more impressive spaces. She had done this everywhere they had been, in Sanary as much as in Munich.

He began to dream about the other houses where he had lived. In each dream he was himself, now. Through some mysterious arrangement, he had been allowed back for a brief time to wander in the emptied-out rooms. In Lübeck, he saw where the piano had been, where his mother's dressing table once was, how the oil painting of the woman on the stairwell had been removed, leaving a raw mark on the wallpaper.

He walked through his grandmother's house on Mengstrasse in the sure knowledge that it would one day be his.

But in the other house, the house on Poschingerstrasse in Munich, there was, in another dream that came often, no one in the rooms, and no furniture, no books, no paintings. He had come back to find something that had been left behind. It was vital that it be retrieved. It was night and he had to make his way by touch. He grew more distressed when he could not remember what it was he should take with him. And when he began to worry that he would be found here, he heard stomping feet on the stairs and shouts and he was arrested and led away helplessly out of the house to a military car that made its way at speed through the streets of Munich.

In the spring of 1935 when he and Einstein were offered honorary doctorates from Harvard, he presumed that Katia would be too worried about the fate of her parents in Munich to want to travel far. On the days when her father was determined to pack up what they could and depart, Katia's mother became uncertain. And on the days when her mother called, it was to say that her husband, in turn, had changed his mind. Since they did not run a Jewish business, they were not under orders to close. They were private people, she said, and they continued to be reassured by Winifred Wagner that they would be protected. And they had never liked Switzerland, she said. Why would anyone want to go to Switzerland?

But despite her worry about her parents, Katia insisted that he should accept the doctorate.

"At a time like this, we need allies," she said. "And it will help me sleep knowing that Harvard is on our side."

The ship was more comfortable than he had expected, the

journey smoother. He amused himself watching American movies in the small cinema, and he avoided other passengers.

Alfred Knopf, his American publisher, made an enormous fuss when the ship docked, demanding, to the surprise of the other passengers, that journalists be allowed on board to do interviews with the great man and that Thomas and Katia be given special treatment by the authorities.

At the Harvard event there were six thousand people. Einstein seemed delighted that the cheering for the writer was, to his ears, louder than that for the scientist.

"That is as it should be," he said. "If it was otherwise, there would be chaos."

Thomas wondered what he meant, but was too distracted by admirers wanting books signed to think any further about it. Over lunch and later during drinks before dinner, he noticed that Einstein was trying to make Katia laugh.

"He is funnier than Charlie Chaplin," she said. "I was so worried that he would want to talk about science. My father has some theory on his theory, but I'm afraid that I have forgotten what it is. He will never forgive me."

"Who?"

"My father. He said that if only Einstein would listen to him, things would be different."

Thomas was ready to say that this was typical of the Pringsheims, but he did not want to take from the sweetness of the occasion.

They had many invitations to stay at grand houses that lay between Boston and New York, but all their plans had to change when an invitation came to dine at the White House. Since he was to meet Roosevelt, Thomas had to decide what view on Germany he would share with him. Perhaps, he thought, he could have most influence if he spoke to the president about what was facing the Jews in Germany, and how many Jewish people had no choice but to seek refuge elsewhere. He wondered if America could still become a safe haven for them. But he should be careful not to let the president feel that he represented any particular group, or that he was here to lobby him or hector him.

One day in New York, Katia picked up the phone in their room to find someone from the *Washington Post* looking for Thomas. He knew that the German embassy was monitoring his movements. In the few interviews he had given, he had said as little as possible, insisting that he wanted only to talk about literature. He did not wish to be caught off guard so shook his head when Katia held the receiver out.

"I'm afraid he is not giving any interviews," Katia said in her best English.

He saw her frowning and then heard her replying in German to whoever was on the line. She was apologizing profusely.

"She is the owner of the *Washington Post*," Katia said, putting her hand over the receiver. "She says she has been trying to contact you. Her name is Agnes Meyer. She speaks German."

He remembered receiving a note at Harvard from someone of that name, but he had replied to no one.

"What shall I do?" Katia asked.

"What does she want?"

Before he could advise her not to, Katia asked the woman on the line what she wanted. From where he sat, Thomas could hear this Agnes roaring.

"Either I hang up, or you speak to her," Katia said, once more with her hand over the receiver.

When Thomas took the call, the woman was hurling abuse at Katia, whom she thought was a secretary.

"You were speaking to my wife," Thomas said.

There was silence for a while, and then Agnes Meyer welcomed him to America and claimed immediately that his invitation to the White House had been her idea.

"He needs to know about the middle ground," she said. "Up to now he sees Nazis, whom he doesn't like, and malcontents, whom he likes even less. I assured him that you would take a fresh line on the whole matter. We are being so vilified in Washington."

"We?"

"Germans."

"Quite rightly, perhaps," Thomas said.

"This is not what the president will want to hear," she replied.

He did not like her tone.

"Who are you?" he asked.

"I am Agnes Meyer, the wife of Eugene Meyer, the owner of the *Washington Post*."

"And what is the reason for your call?"

"Do not speak to me in that way," she said.

"Perhaps if you answer my question?"

"I am calling to say that we should meet in Washington, where I am now. I will not be at the dinner, which will be an intimate affair. I am calling because there are two things you need to know. One, Roosevelt will be in power for a very long time. Two, I will be very useful to you."

"Thank you."

"When I see your schedule, I will add a meeting with me in our Crescent Place house. It will be a private meeting. Now I must go. Thank you for your time and give my regards to your lady wife."

The White House was smaller than he had imagined. The side entrance to which they were directed was not imposing. In one of the drawing rooms, with wallpaper that he judged too colorful and curtains that were like something in a theater, he found Mrs. Roosevelt and a few other guests, all of whom wished to ask him and Katia about their journey and their plans to return to Europe.

He tried out his English, but was more comfortable when the translator took over.

In the dining room, they were joined by the president, wheeled in by a male assistant. He was wearing a velvet dinner jacket and seemed to be pleased to see them.

"Europeans find me strange," he said. "I am both president and prime minister. But I mean no harm."

Over a very ordinary dinner, the president asked no questions, but made many wry comments. He was as amused as his wife at the news that the Manns had been telephoned by Agnes Meyer.

"In person, she is fearsome," he said. "But down a telephone line, she is an opera singer."

"We had to sit through an opera recently," Mrs. Roosevelt said, "so the president is still haunted by the terror of it all."

After dinner, they were taken to watch a movie, and then, as the president pleaded urgent matters as an excuse to be wheeled away, his wife showed them his study.

Thomas had presumed that there would be a one-to-one discussion between him and the president at some point, a time when they might speak about Germany, but obviously this was not something the president wanted.

The next day, Agnes Meyer assured him that this was the Roosevelts' way of being friendly.

"They do this for very few people," she said. "The less they say and the plainer the food, the more they like you. And the fact that they invited no one of any importance is a sign they trust you. You see, I told them to trust you. The First Lady wished to get the measure of you, and my understanding is that she actually liked your reserve. In Harvard, they found you stuffy, but the Roosevelts are more perceptive. You see, they both approved of your wife, and that means a lot to them. They are, more than anything, family people."

Thomas hardly knew what to say in reply.

"At any time, you can send me a sign," she went on, "and I will open doors in America for you. The Knopfs know only a slice of New York. They deal in books. They have no real influence. If you don't send me a sign, I will know when the time is right and I will send you one."

"A sign to say what?"

"That you must settle in America. In the meantime, you must do something urgent about your command of English."

Thomas returned from the United States still having made no public statement against the regime. When Erika saw how strong his determination remained not to make life unduly difficult for Bermann, his German publisher, by denouncing Hitler, she wrote to him, suggesting that it was time he made his position clear and emphasizing how little she cared for Bermann.

"She doesn't understand the precarious position of your parents," Thomas said to Katia.

"With Klaus and Erika and Heinrich in full flight," Katia said, "any damage that could be done has been done. Your speaking out would hardly matter to them. But it's time in any case that they left Germany."

"My speaking out would matter to Erika, it seems."

"It would matter to us all."

When Thomas issued a statement in support of Bermann, who was under fire from the émigrés for continuing as a publisher within Germany, Erika wrote to him in a tone of controlled rage.

Probably you will be very angry with me because of this letter. I am prepared for that, and I know what I am doing. This friendly time is predestined to separate people. Your relation to Dr. Bermann and his publishing house is indestructible—you seem to be ready to sacrifice everything for it. In that case, if it is a sacrifice for you that I, slowly but surely, will be lost for you—then just never mind. For me it is sad and terrible.

When he showed the letter to Katia, Thomas presumed that she would have much to say about the many ways in which Erika, since the day she was born, had attempted to control their lives. But Katia said nothing.

He was aware that the shunning of him that Erika threatened would possibly become widely known. He knew also from Alfred Knopf that the reading public in the United States were coming to see him as the most significant German writer alive, and one who was in exile because of his opposition to Hitler. It would not be easy to explain his silence to them.

Up to now, he had seen himself as exceptional, and that was why he had not wanted to join the dissidents. But more than anything else, he had been afraid. This was something that Katia understood, but not Erika nor Klaus nor Heinrich either. They did not understand timidity. For them there was only clarity. But this, Thomas believed, was a time of clarity just for the brave few; for the rest, it was a time of confusion. And he belonged to the rest in a way that did not, now, make him feel proud. He presented himself to the world as a man of principle, but instead, he thought, he was weak.

When a telegram arrived from Klaus adding fuel to Erika's fire, Thomas went for a walk by the lake on his own. It was so typical of Klaus to wait until Erika had sent her letter! He was inclined to write to both of them to suggest, since they were so astute, that they add up the amount of money they had received from him during their time in exile.

What irritated him more than anything was the knowledge that Erika and Klaus were right.

He was working each day on the next volume of his long work based on the story of Joseph in the Old Testament; he still felt that there would be readers for such a book, even as the sound of warmongering became shriller in Germany. Once he spoke out against the regime, however, he would lose his German readers. The words he was writing would lie dead on the page. They would depend on translators. And he would be forever on the Nazi blacklist, and Katia's parents would be hounded by them further. But as he faced towards home, he told himself that this was happening to all the other writers, and to many other people.

He had been loyal to his publisher; he had wanted to keep his German readership. He had prevaricated and delayed. He had tried not to think about what he should do. He lived in dread of facing the fact that Germany was lost to him already. If he spoke out, he would have no choice.

Of course he would denounce Hitler! But doing so at the behest of his daughter, with all the family watching him, made him feel powerless. If only Erika could be quiet, then he would act.

Katia wrote to Erika expressing sorrow at her tone; she was careful not to distance herself from Thomas as she emphasized how hurt they both were that Erika would write to her father in this way. Thomas himself composed a gentle, appeasing letter to Erika some days later saying that the day might dawn when he would speak out.

The two letters served only to exasperate Erika further.

He watched from his study window as Katia, standing in the drive, was handed the post a few mornings later. As he saw her opening a letter and reading it with a frown on her face, he knew it was from Erika. He was surprised that Katia did not come immediately to his study to show it to him. At lunch, they discussed the events of the day without any reference to Erika. It was only later when he came in search of Katia, asking if she would accompany him on his afternoon stroll, that she showed him not just the letter, which was filled with acrimony, but a draft of a statement that she herself, in her old-fashioned handwriting, had prepared for him to issue: a statement denouncing the Nazis.

"Have you all turned against me?" he asked.

"There is no rush," she said. "And what I have here is merely an outline. I am sure you will do it better yourself. There is nothing in this that you do not think."

"Does Erika decide for me?" he asked.

"No, I do," she replied.

"Do you agree with her letter?"

"I have no interest in her letter. I read it quickly this morning. I have already forgotten what was in it."

His statement, published some days later in the *Neue Zürcher Zeitung*, while roundly denouncing the regime, lacked any real sharpness. It had been written with Katia looking over his shoulder.

At first, his statement was mainly ignored. He received a warm note from Heinrich congratulating him on his stance, but no one else got in touch, nor was he threatened in any way by the regime. The Nazis had, he supposed, more important things to do. The only real consequence of his letter was that Bonn University rescinded his honorary doctorate.

The more he pondered on that news, the more the idea came to him for a longer, more passionate letter, one that could be reprinted in newspapers all over the world. If Erika could be angry, then he would show her what anger really looked like. If she could be eloquent, then he would outdo her. He did not tell Katia what he was preparing. He would do this on his own.

Often, readers had complained about the length of his sentences, the high tone of his style. This time, he determined, he would make his style even more exalted. He would speak to the Nazis using all the systems at his command; he would speak to them from a commanding German place, using tones that had served writers before the Nazis were ever imagined. He would shower clause and subclause upon them, those who were regarded with fear and cold aversion by anyone who believed in liberty and progress. He would ask, as though he had the right to a reply, how the state to which these so-called leaders had reduced Germany, in less than four years, could ever be accurately described. He would ask, as though no reply would ever be good enough, how a writer, accustomed to a responsibility to the word, could be silent in the face of the frightful danger to the whole continent presented by this soul-destroying regime.

And he would underline, because he knew that his letter would be read in Paris and London and Washington, that the only reason for the repression and the elimination of every stirring of opposition was to prepare the German people for war.

He was well aware, as he worked, that this performance had been enacted too late, and that its very tone, so haughty and certain of itself, appeared to come from a pen that had written many other denunciations of Hitler. Thomas realized that he was moving too fast from silence to speech, but writing the sentences themselves gave him confidence, and reading the piece over gave him relief. He should have written this on the night that Hitler came to power.

While Heinrich's response to Thomas's first letter had been polite, it had also been mild. This time, he wrote with patent enthusiasm, delighting in how his brother had said everything there was to say in one fell swoop and with the greatest effect. He assured him that the world had lost nothing by his long silence because what he had said now was the final word.

Erika wrote to her mother to express her delight. Now the Magician has put everything right, she said. Klaus also wrote to praise his father's proud provocation of the Nazis.

"It might help," Katia said, "if you wrote to Klaus."

"To say what?"

"I'm sure you will know what to say. Perhaps you could write that you're looking forward to reading his next book. Erika says he is writing a modern version of the Faust story."

• • •

Their visit to the United States had made them conscious of how much more work they needed to do to become fluent English-speakers. Katia found a woman who could help her to translate sentences and phrases from German to English that she learned by heart. She knew every tense by now, and every rule, and had learned five hundred words, but she was still not confident speaking. The English poet did an hour of conversation with them every day and then, noting errors they had made, he did an hour of grammar.

"This 'did,'" Thomas said, "will be the end of me. You can actually say 'he did do' and then the opposite is 'he didn't do.' No wonder the English are so warlike."

"What about 'does'?" Katia asked.

"Should it not be 'do'?" he asked.

"It's both. And then there are phrasal verbs," Katia said. "I have ordered a book on them."

Thomas noticed that fewer people were taking a walk by the lake. If the Nazis really wanted to repatriate him, he thought, it would not take much to snatch him from this sylvan pastoral. Once the thought struck him, it preoccupied him. The border between Switzerland and Germany was porous. It would be easy to drag him towards a car, bundle him into the trunk and inject him with some sleep-inducing serum. As he wondered if he should share these worries with Katia, it occurred to him that she must already have thought of them too. They would have to start taking the invitations they received from America more seriously.

On approaching the house late one afternoon, they spotted a man standing beside a car that was almost blocking their driveway. Thomas motioned to Katia that they should turn back.

"I have a bad feeling about him," he said.

"I have that feeling every time someone comes to deliver something, or even when the postman comes," she said.

They took a more circuitous route to the house. When it was in full view, they saw that the man had gone.

The next morning, Katia came into his study.

"He is outside our house again," she said.

Thomas went to one of the upper windows and peered down. The man was in his thirties. He was standing casually, with his hands in his pockets, directly in front of their drive.

"If we call the police," Katia said, "it will be hard to know what to say to them. And we will be drawing attention to ourselves."

If Erika were here, Thomas thought, she would be able to drive this outsider away, whoever he was.

After lunch, he decided to go out and see who it was, with Katia watching from the window, ready to phone the police if necessary.

When he confronted him, the man took his hands out of his pockets and smiled.

"I have orders not to disturb you, so I thought I would wait for you to come in or out of the house."

"Who are you?"

"I am a friend of Ernst Toller's. We met once in a café in Sanary. I am a colleague of the fellow who told you that he used to watch over your house. But it was Toller who sent me."

"What does he want?"

The man appeared taken aback by his tone. Thomas tried to smile to soften the tension.

"He has asked me to pass on a message to you."

"Would you like to come in?"

In the house, he introduced himself to Katia, saying that he had seen her the previous year on the street in Sanary.

"Are you one of the exiles?" she asked him.

"Yes," he said, "that is one way to describe me. I used to be a Communist and I was even an anarchist, but now I am one of the exiles."

"You seem young to have been all those things," Katia said.

"I served under Ernst Toller in the Munich Revolution, but I didn't get a prison sentence. I worked for him while he was in jail."

"You must have been a child during the revolution," Katia said.

"I was."

In Thomas's study, once they had been served coffee, he could see a hardness in the man's expression that was not apparent before. He was amused at the idea that this fellow, despite his initial gentleness, was once a revolutionary. Perhaps, he thought, Lenin had once looked like this too.

"I need to tell you how Erich Mühsam died," the man began abruptly. "That is what Ernst Toller has asked me to do. I understand that you sent money to Erich's widow after his death. We have now pieced together all the details of what happened."

"He was from Lübeck," Thomas said. "I did not admire his politics, but I was appalled to hear of his death."

"You need to know how he died, the facts, because what happened to him is now happening to many others, to anarchists and Communists but also to Jews. To anyone the Nazis set their sights on. People are being detained in camps. Mühsam was held at three different camps. He was tortured almost continuously. We have clear evidence of this. It was said that Hitler hated him because of his involvement in the Munich Revolution. But they could have charged him. Or even executed him. But they did neither of those things. Toller asked me to inform you that this is now widespread, this new brutality. In these camps, the guards behave without any restraint, but in Mühsam's case there was something like a plan. They broke his teeth, and that may have happened on the spur of the moment. But they also stamped a swastika on his scalp with a red-hot brand, and that must have been planned. They made him dig his own grave and they did a mock execution. Finally, they invited him to hang himself in the latrines and when he refused, they killed him and dragged his body across the parade ground so that his skull was shattered and then put him hanging up in the latrines. We have witnesses to this. During Erich's incarceration, we have evidence that he was beaten every day. All this happened over a period of almost eighteen months."

"Why have you come to tell me this?"

"Toller thinks that you do not understand what is happening. He spoke to you about Erich before. But no one could save him. Now there are others."

"What can I do?"

"Be very careful. This is not like anything we have seen before. All of us who were involved in Munich that time are on a list."

"I did not support the Munich Revolution."

"I know. I was in the room when Mühsam and Toller prevented the rest of us from detaining you and taking your house. And Mühsam said you would be needed in the new world we were ready to make. But there won't be any new world, except the one being created in the camps."

As he stood up, Thomas detected a bearing that was almost military.

"Where will you go now?" Thomas asked.

"Toller plans to go to America, and I will follow him if I can. He believes that we might be safe there, or he does sometimes. There is great despair. No matter what, all of us will have to leave, there is no safe place for any of us. And that includes you."

Thomas showed him out and stood at the door as he walked down the drive.

"Who is he?" Katia asked.

"Ernst Toller sent him to speak to me," Thomas said. "He is a man from the past, or maybe from the future. I don't know."

Chapter 10
New Jersey, 1938

In the back seat of the car as they left New York Katia was silent and seemed distant from him. When the driver stopped at traffic lights, Thomas heard her muffle a sigh. It must be on her mind, he thought, as it was on his, that even though they were now going home, their destination was a rented house in Princeton.

His study there, even though he had his books and the old desk from the house in Munich, and some items that were tokens of his former life, was a pale replica of his real study. In the mornings when he worked, he could act out the role of himself, write as if he had never left Germany. Since he had taken the language with him and the cast of mind, he could, in theory, write anywhere. But outside his study was a foreign country. America did not belong to him, or to Katia either; they were too old to make the change. Instead of adapting to novelty, or learning to appreciate the virtues of the new country, they were living in a time of loss.

At least they were safe, he thought, and he should be grateful for that. He would breathe easier, however, once all the children and Heinrich and Katia's parents were away from danger too.

He moved towards Katia for a moment. She squeezed his hand in reassurance but then took it away and hugged herself as though she were cold.

The night was dark and there was little traffic. At first, he could see nothing except stray lights from the few oncoming cars. He was tired. The dinner the previous evening had been exhausting. His speech, delivered in English, about the looming catastrophe had been respectfully received, but his tone, he felt, was at times faltering. It was not merely that he lacked fluency, but rather his delivery masked his uncertainties with too much earnestness.

Each afternoon, the young wife of a graduate student in the German Department at Princeton came for two hours to give him and Katia an English lesson. In the evening, they went through what they had learned, trying to add twenty new words each day to their English vocabulary. They read children's stories in English that Katia viewed as more instructive than Dante's *Inferno*.

He closed his eyes and thought that he might sleep.

When he woke, he could see lights from houses on a hillside. Perhaps it was a village or a small town. He tried to imagine the interiors of those houses, the American life that was being played out within their walls, what words were spoken, what thoughts entertained. Instead of people, however, he saw well-scrubbed emptiness, silence broken only by the humming of electrical appliances. He simply did not know how people lived here or what thoughts they had, what they did at night.

If this were Germany, there would be a church and a square, some narrow streets and other streets that had been widened. Houses with attic windows. There would be old stoves in the kitchens and tiled stoves in the living rooms. And books in some of the houses, and a sense that these books made a difference, just as legends and songs had, and poems and plays. Maybe even novels.

The past would be evoked by the names of the streets, or by the names of families, and continuity by the bells that rang softly, as they had for centuries, to mark the passing of each quarter-hour.

He would give anything if the car could turn and enter noise-lessly into one of those squares, a space enriched by the work of Gutenberg or the writings of Luther or the images made by Dürer. Enriched by a thousand years of trade, a stability broken at times by plagues or wars, by the clattering of cavalry horses and the boom of cannon, until a time of treaties when peace was restored.

It would almost satisfy him if this journey would go on through the night, if he and Katia could be driven in silence down through America and not have to face the unfamiliarity and fragility they would meet on arrival in Princeton, where their house, he believed, could be as easily flattened as it was quickly made, despite its ostensible opulence.

It occurred to him then—and the thought made him shiver—that this new alien space they lived in was actually innocent in a way that the air in the German villages was poisoned now. He shuddered at the thought of what was coming; and then he actually wished the journey to Princeton would end so that he could walk through the brightened rooms of his new house into his study and find comfort there, feel enclosed and safe, and then emerge to have a quiet supper with Katia and Elisabeth, who was waiting for them.

In the settled life he had once known, such sudden swings in his mood would have been unusual. But that was how his mind worked now, even in the daytime, but more often at night.

He saw lights of other houses on a rise in the landscape ahead and thought that he should ask about them.

"Excuse me," he leaned forward in the car, "what is this place called, where we are now?"

"This is called New Jersey, sir," the driver said drily. "New Jersey. Yes, that's what it is called."

The driver was silent for a moment and then spoke again.

"NEW. JERSEY." He intoned the words as though he were making an important announcement.

Thomas heard Katia gasp slightly. As he turned, he saw that she was trying to control her laughter. His question and the driver's response would be a story that Katia would tell Elisabeth, who would force her father to ask the question again and have her mother repeat what the driver had said as accurately as she could. Elisabeth or Katia would then probably write to Erika, who would shortly arrive in New York with Klaus. And Erika would dine out on the story, offering it to anyone who would listen as a typical example of her father, the puzzled magician, his inability to find the right tone in America, despite his constant efforts.

New Jersey. Yes, that was where they were.

The only consolation, Thomas thought, was that Monika was not there; she was in Italy, with plans to marry a Hungarian art historian. When Monika came into possession of any anecdote at all about her father that set him in a comic light, she would repeat it *ad nauseam*. Eventually, Katia would have to speak crossly to her. But the only person who could exert real control over Monika was her younger sister, Elisabeth, the calm, patient, watchful one, the one whose intelligence seemed to be all-embracing, his daughter who was ready to treat the world on her own measured terms.

Elisabeth reminded him of the old world. She had an aura that had wafted down from three generations before her. Thomas looked forward to seeing her now, as the car was nearing Princeton.

It came into his mind that they would soon be visited in Princeton by Erika and Klaus. Klaus had a way of suggesting that he cared more deeply about politics than anyone around him, including his father. All fired up, often with the help of some illegal substance, he would talk uncontrollably about some piece of news, some further act of cruelty committed in Germany or Italy, before asking how novelists could possibly write stories in a time like this. Were they not aware of the tragedy that was unfolding? How could novels matter? Klaus would enunciate all this even in front of guests, eminent people in Princeton, who would of course repeat it to others.

As they arrived into the main street of Princeton, Thomas determined that they would not have guests for dinner during Klaus's next visit. Klaus would have to relay his views on current affairs and the peripheral nature of fiction solely to the immediate family circle.

He must mention this to Katia, but he must choose the right moment so that she would not be offended at how exasperating and irritating he found his eldest son, who happened also to be his mother's favorite.

Elisabeth had laid a small table in a corner of the sitting room. She told them that she had allowed the cook to depart early and had herself prepared for them a cold supper with cheeses and cured meat with a salad and pickled cucumbers and onions.

"I hope you were not expecting a large supper. In that case, I have made a mistake."

"My dear, you always know what we want," Thomas said as he kissed her and let her help him remove his coat and scarf.

"At least it is warm here," Katia said as she fussed in the hallway. "Now it will take me a while to organize myself."

"Once I wash my hands, perhaps you can join me for a glass of wine while your mother is getting ready?" Thomas whispered to Elisabeth.

"The wine is already open," she whispered in reply.

"I can hear you both," Katia said, and laughed. "As I get older, I really believe that I hear whispers more clearly than I hear shouting. So have a drink, the two of you, and I'll join you as soon as I am ready."

Thomas sat on the sofa with his daughter as she asked him in detail about his trip to New York. She was ready to be amused at the slightest thing.

After supper, as Katia poured more wine for him, Thomas

noticed her glancing knowingly at Elisabeth and felt a sense of strain or unease between them. For a second, it struck him that there could be news about Golo or Monika or Michael or even Klaus and Erika.

He looked up again and saw Katia nodding to Elisabeth. They were, it seemed, involved in some private communication.

He sipped his wine and pushed his chair back.

"Can I be included?" he asked.

"The plan was that you would go to your study and I would call you when we wanted to give you the news," Elisabeth said. "But my mother appears to have forgotten that is what we arranged."

"My worry is that your father won't go to his study this evening," Katia said. "That he will go straight to bed."

"So, there is news?" Thomas asked.

"Well, Elisabeth has news."

If the news were merely about Elisabeth, he thought, then there was nothing significant to worry about.

"News concerning my favorite child?" he asked.

When Elisabeth lifted her eyes and took in her mother mischievously, it was, for a split second, as if his own sister Carla, long dead now, were sitting at the table.

"Perhaps your mother can tell me if you won't do so," he said in mock severity.

"Elisabeth is to be married," Katia said.

"To the president of Princeton University," Thomas replied. "Or to President Roosevelt."

"As far as I am aware, both of them already have a wife," Elisabeth said.

Her tone had become dignified suddenly, almost sad. She put a hand over her mouth and gazed into the distance. She seemed older than her twenty years.

Thomas tried to recall if any young man had been visiting the house, but all he could remember was Elisabeth's encounter in a colleague's house with some Princeton students who had not appreciated her diffidence nor she their sense of entitlement. A young man had asked her if it would be safe for him and his family to go hiking in Germany over the summer as they had planned. When she had told him that it would be perfectly safe unless he and his family were Jewish, he had replied: "Hell no, we are not Jewish!" The atmosphere had not been helped when Elisabeth followed this by asking the young man if he and his family were by any chance Communists. When he had denied this vehemently, she had then suggested that he and his family might have a very pleasant time in Germany if they made sure to keep away from places where people were being dragged from their houses and beaten up on the street by thugs in uniforms.

Elisabeth had insisted that she had said all this calmly, but she had to agree that her conversation with the young man may have been the cause of the evening ending early. No further invitations had been issued to her to spend time with Princeton students.

When neither Katia nor Elisabeth spoke, and both remained gravely at the table, Thomas asked his daughter if she had changed her mind and become fond of that very student, who wished to visit Germany with his family, the "Hell no" boy.

"She is marrying Borgese," Katia said.

Thomas caught Katia's eye and knew immediately that this was not a joke. Giuseppe Borgese, a professor of Romance languages in Chicago, a leading anti-fascist, had recently come to the house to discuss politics, having also visited when the Manns moved to Princeton first.

"Borgese? Where did she meet him?"

"Here. Where we all met him."

"He has only been here twice."

"She has only met him twice."

"'She' is sitting at the table, if you both don't mind," Elisabeth said.

"This has happened with great speed," Thomas said to her.

"And with great decorum," she replied.

"Whose idea was it?"

"I think that is a private matter."

"Is that why Borgese came here again? To see you?"

"I am sure it must have been part of the reason."

She smiled coyly, self-mockingly.

"I thought he came to see me!"

"He managed to see both of us," she replied.

Thomas was about to say that although Giuseppe Borgese was slightly younger than he was, he looked much older, but then he stopped himself, saying instead: "I thought he devoted himself entirely to literature and the cause of anti-fascism."

"He does."

"Perhaps not as single-mindedly as he liked us all to think!"

"I am engaged to him. And if you seek single-mindedness, you can take it that I am the one in possession of that precise quality."

Elisabeth's acerbic tone, often kept in reserve, had appeared now in a flash.

"Have you been writing to him?" he asked.

"We are in regular communication."

"So, Erika married Auden and you marry Borgese."

"Yes," Elisabeth said, "and Monika will marry her Hungarian, and Michael, who is even younger than I am, will marry Gret. That is what people often do, they grow up and they marry."

"You are twenty and he is . . . what?"

"Fifty-six," Katia interjected.

"Just seven years younger than your poor old father," he went on.

"It will make everyone happy," Elisabeth said, "if you refuse to play the role of the poor, upset old father."

"I wasn't thinking of that," he replied. For a second, he was close to tears.

"Then what?"

"I was worried about losing you. I was thinking entirely of myself and your mother. Now we will have no one to talk to."

"You have five other children."

"That is what I mean. You are the one . . ."

He wanted to say that she was the one who had such good sense and good humor and such a sardonic distance from things that he had imagined she would never meet a match but would remain with them throughout their lives.

"My mother and I have decided that you will behave impeccably when my fiancé comes to visit," Elisabeth said.

He almost laughed.

"Did it take you both long to decide this?"

"We walked as far as Witherspoon Street and then back while you were busy writing."

"You do actually intend to marry him?"

"Yes, here in Princeton, in the university church, and soon."

"I wish my mother were alive," he said.

"Your mother?"

"She loved weddings. She always did. I think that is the only pleasure she ever got from marrying my father."

Elisabeth ignored what he had just said.

"I asked Borgese if he was nervous about visiting now," she said. "And he replied that, strangely, he was not nervous at all."

"Then it is simple. Everything is settled."

"We don't have the date yet."

"Who else knows?"

"Michael knows," Katia said. "We wrote to him, and we will tell Klaus and Erika when they arrive and then write to Golo and Monika."

"Tell me something," Thomas asked. "Has Borgese been married before? Or will this be his first venture into the holy state of matrimony?"

"I don't," Elisabeth said, arching her eyebrows, "detect a note of sarcasm in your tone. Although some lesser creature would. And that pleases me. But Giuseppe will ask me if you congratulated me when you heard the good news. And I will say yes. Since I have not yet told him anything that is not true, then . . ."

"I offer you, my beloved child, my heartiest congratulations."

"As I do," Katia said.

"You both planned all of this," Thomas said. "Not telling me before now."

"Of course we did," Katia said. "You had enough to think about in New York."

"And this is usually the moment," Elisabeth said, "when you stand up from the table with a preoccupied look and go to your study."

"Yes, my child," Thomas replied.

"So, I will clear the table and we can discuss this further in the morning."

"What a new sort of daughter you are becoming now that you are engaged," Thomas said, smiling. "I thought Erika was the bossy one."

"We all have our moments. I am sure Monika will have hers too when we see her."

"I was hoping that you would protect me from all of them," he said and sighed.

Elisabeth stood and bowed ironically to him.

"Was that to be my purpose in life?" she asked, stepping away from the table and leaving the room before he could respond.

"What an old goat!" Thomas said when he was sure his daughter was out of earshot.

"When I went for a walk with the two of them, Borgese barely spoke," Katia replied.

"That is often a sign."

"He gave no sign. He just muttered and complained of the cold."

"That, too, is often a sign."

Katia smiled.

"I intend to glower at him, even if just briefly, when he comes to see us again," she said.

"He will find me in my study if he is looking for me," Thomas said.

He stood up.

"It has been hard for Elisabeth," Katia said. "We have moved around so much. She has lost those years."

"She would not be marrying an old man had things been different and we had stayed in Munich," Thomas replied. "She would have found someone her own age."

He was almost hoping that Katia would question his description of Borgese as an old man, but she accepted it as a melancholy fact.

"There is nothing we can do, I suppose?" he asked.

"Nothing."

While he was preparing for bed, Katia came into his room.

"There was something I didn't say," she began.

"Something else?"

"No. About Elisabeth. I do really believe that she will be content in her new state."

"Perhaps we should have told her how warm the welcome would be, were she to change her mind at any point and come back to us."

"She won't come back," Katia said.

He smiled at her and sighed.

"And I had a letter from Klaus," Katia said.

"From where?"

"I think it was sent before he set sail. It was confused. Even some of the handwriting was hard to read. It must have been written in a hurry. But I'm concerned about him."

"When I was his age, I wrote four hours in the morning and then had a light lunch and afterwards went for a walk."

"He has lost his country."

"We have all lost our country."

"We must be careful when he comes."

"Did Erika write too?"

"No, she just sent her love."

"She will look after him."

Katia closed her mouth and fixed her jaw firmly. It was a look that she had learned, he knew, from her father.

"We must be careful with him when he comes," Katia repeated.

And then she gently kissed him and wished him good night and returned to her own room.

In the morning after breakfast, they went through phrasal verbs in English. Katia had written each one out on a piece of paper with a sample sentence in which it might appear on the other side. She began to examine Thomas by randomly selecting one.

"Put up with," she said.

"I cannot put up with Agnes Meyer."

"Put on."

"I will put on my new coat."

"Go over."

"I will go over my new novel one more time."

"Get over."

"I cannot get over the news that Elisabeth is marrying Borgese."

"Give up."

"I will soon give up to be pleasant to anyone in Princeton."

"Give up being, not to be!"

"Are you certain?"

Since he was scheduled to present himself at the office in Princeton that dealt with visas and foreigners, Katia had drawn him a map so he could locate the building. She had offered to go with him, but he assured her that he could best deal with these matters on his own. He had the impression that a German writer coming with his wife, both of them speaking heavily accented English, would be treated with less warmth than the writer coming alone, a writer who had just a decade earlier received the Nobel Prize in Literature. Also, Katia's valiant efforts to comprehend the regulations might antagonize the Princeton authorities, who would, he felt, be more sympathetic to someone who knew nothing at all about them.

Although he was sure that he had followed Katia's directions, he found himself at the very center of the campus walking toward Nassau Street when he realized he should, in fact, be heading in the other direction. He would now be late for his appointment. He asked a student for assistance, and was told to walk down a sloping path that passed close to the university gymnasium and swimming pool.

When he heard through an open window a sudden shout and an echoing whoop of pleasure as someone dived into the water, he remembered that Klaus had once told him that the students actually swam naked in this pool. And now, as he hurried along, he thought of the scene, the young men gathering in groups, each one tensing his back, lifting his arms, opening out his legs slightly as he got ready to dive. And others edging themselves out of the water, all the muscles of their legs and buttocks on display.

It would not do for an elderly German professor to be seen among them, or even to think too much about this scene. As he moved along, nonetheless, he saw himself in the water, doing a lap and then turning to find a group of students freshly naked preparing themselves for the plunge.

In his study, he had Hofmann's painting *Die Quelle* hanging opposite his desk, having managed to rescue it from the house in Munich and taken it with him to Switzerland and then to America. The painted image of the three naked youths on the rocks, two of the young men bending, so that the full heft and curve of their lower bodies could be seen, the slim beauty of their legs, gave him energy in the mornings, even more than coffee did, and offered him some stimulus as he tried to fill pages with sentences.

Should he find the meeting about his visa status irritating, he resolved, he would summon up the image of that painting to soothe himself and then, if that were not enough, he would imagine the very students he was passing now—tall young Americans fully dressed—and have them appearing naked from the doorway of the dressing room into the enclosed space of the swimming pool.

He found the visa office and pushed open the door. There was no one at the reception desk. After a while, he took a seat. When, eventually, a woman came, she looked at him for a moment and then made a phone call. Once she was finished on the phone, he stood up and approached the desk.

"I have an appointment with Mrs. Finley," he said.

"For what time?"

"I am afraid that I am fifteen minutes late. I lost my way."

"I'll see if she is still available."

She left him standing at the desk while she went to an inner room. Having returned, she led him into another waiting area and motioned him to sit.

He watched people coming and going, none of them paying any attention to him, until a middle-aged woman appeared with a file in her hand, calling out his name loudly, even though he was the only one waiting. When he identified himself, she indicated that he should follow her into an office where she looked through the file. Then without a word she stood up and walked out of the room, leaving him alone.

Through the open door he could see this woman, whom he supposed to be Mrs. Finley, chatting to a colleague of hers. He wondered if Katia should not have accompanied him. Katia would have a way of letting Mrs. Finley know that she should attend to her work rather than engage in idle talk. All he could do was stare into the distance, checking now and then that Mrs. Finley was still out there, laughing and talking.

For a second, he thought that he might just slip out, make his way home unnoticed and wait to see what the authorities in Princeton would do in response. But since the president's office had phoned the house several times insisting that he would have to deal with his visa status or he could no longer be paid and his very position in the United States would be in danger, then such an action would be merely petulant and foolhardy. He would have to wait while Mrs. Finley enjoyed her morning.

Finally, she returned and sat at the desk opposite him. She brusquely began to go through the file.

"No, no," she said. "This makes no sense. I have here that you are a German citizen, but then I am looking at your passport details and they say that are you a Czech citizen. The problem is that both forms are signed by you, and this could have serious legal implications. I will have to send this file to another department."

"I have a Czech passport," he said.

"So it says here."

"But I was born in Germany."

"But no one asked you where you were born. It is only your citizenship that matters."

"I lost my German citizenship."

"We have so many people," she said, looking through the file again, "coming here from those countries, and all I get is confusion."

He stared at her coldly.

"And, yes, here it is, your wife, she has created the same confusion. I suppose she is Czech too."

"Like me—"

"I know," she interrupted, "you don't need to explain about the German thing. And I'm not sure what the regulations are for Czech citizens. This letter says that you and your wife are both Germans."

She pulled a letter from the file.

"As I said, we were Germans until—"

"Until you were not," she said.

He stood up.

"We'll have to schedule another meeting," she said. "Now, will you be at the same address?"

"Yes."

"The same phone number?"

"Yes."

"I don't know how long this will take. Make sure that you do not change address or phone number. We may need to see you at very short notice."

He tried to look distant and proud, but also sad and offended, as he waited for her to let him know that he could leave.

"In future, you are Czech," she said. "Czech. Czech. Czech. And your wife is the same. You don't write the word 'German' down anywhere. The best thing might be to go back to the very beginning and simply put these forms in the bin. Now let me see if we have duplicate forms."

She left the room again.

He found that he was shaking with rage.

"No, of course we don't," she said when she came back. "Of course we don't! I'll have to put in a request for them. So I will be in touch with you. But I have to warn you that if you fill in forms incorrectly another time and then sign them, it will be a very serious problem. Immigration does not take kindly to this. You could be on the next boat back to Czechoslovakia."

He was about to tell her that Czechoslovakia was, in fact, land-locked until he realized what a great story this would make for

Katia and for Elisabeth, and indeed for one or two of his colleagues. He had to concentrate to stop himself from laughing.

"I presume you see the gravity of this?"

He nodded.

She started to look through the file again.

He was not sure whether he should go or stay. He stood there awkwardly. When she looked up at him, she frowned.

He bowed to her and left, thinking that he should walk more slowly as he passed the swimming pool on his way home. Even a single sound from one of the swimmers or a splash of water would be enough to offer him consolation.

On the morning that Klaus and Erika were to arrive he asked Katia what train they were taking.

"I think they are coming by car," she said.

"They are driving?"

"They are getting a driver."

He smiled at their extravagance. Despite the fact that they had no money, he did not suppose that public transport would do for them. Erika was worse than Klaus, he thought.

When he heard a car pulling into the drive, he was at the front window in time to see Katia paying the driver in cash. He watched Klaus getting out of the car slowly, like someone who was in pain. As Katia and Erika busied themselves removing the luggage, Klaus stood idly by.

Thomas moved back from the window, and retreated to his study.

Within a short time, Erika knocked on his door. Since he had become used to Elisabeth's shy and tactful presence, Erika's forthright way of entering, closing the door behind her and making herself at home in his armchair was amusing, almost refreshing.

She immediately wanted to know about the book he was writing and asked to see the opening chapter. As he rummaged among his papers, she raised the subject of Elisabeth's engagement to Borgese.

"I asked Elisabeth about it just now and she simply turned and walked out of the room."

"She has made up her mind," he said.

He handed her a sheaf of papers and she looked through the pages.

"Your handwriting has not improved. I am the only one who knows how to read what you write."

"The Knopfs have found me a typist," he said, "but she makes terrible mistakes."

Erika was already reading the opening page.

"You are a magnificent old magician. But you know what I am going to say now?"

"Yes, my darling, I do."

"You will have to write a novel set in the present, if only so that it can tell us about the future."

"I can make no sense of the present. It is all confusion. I know nothing about the future."

"Write about the confusion."

"After this, I have another Old Testament book to write."

"Start taking notes for a novel about the years in Munich when everything led to his rise, but when few of us noticed. You were there."

"I was busy watching my children growing up."

"My dear father, none of us saw you much, except at meals. So you must have been doing something else. Why don't you write a novel about my mother's family?"

"I know nothing about them."

"No, but you watched them."

At supper, when he asked where Klaus was, Katia and Erika gave each other an uneasy look.

"He is not well," Katia said.

"Perhaps he was out late in New York?" Thomas asked.

"We were seeing old friends," Erika said, "and there is talk of a new magazine. But he has not been well."

"He will be better by the time the journalist from *Life* magazine comes and the photographer," Katia said. "He knows he has to be better by then. So he is getting some rest."

"Yes, to prepare for the feature article about our happy and united family," Elisabeth said drily.

"We will all smile," Thomas said. "It is the least we can do."

"Is Borgese an American citizen?" Erika asked Elisabeth.

"Yes," Elisabeth replied.

"Wonderful. I met him at some conference years ago. If I had thought of it, I would have married him myself," Erika said, "and then you could have married Auden."

"I didn't want to marry Auden," Elisabeth said gravely.

"Neither did I," Erika said, "but he will be here to have his photograph taken as a member of our happy family. O Lord, if only they knew!"

"I am sure we are as happy as any other family," Katia said.

As Erika glanced at Thomas, they both managed a surreptitious laugh.

Thomas was glad Erika was home, but, by her very restlessness at the table and then in the sitting room afterwards, he was aware that she would not be with them for long. She had come, he supposed, to see them, but also to get money for some journey or project, and to make him feel guilty for not being more intensely involved in the anti-fascist movement. Once all that had been completed, she would set out again. It struck him for a moment that he would like to go with her, leave Katia and Elisabeth here in the quietness of Princeton. He would enjoy traveling with his daughter, basking in the glow of her energy, staying up late with her and being with new people.

But he knew that this urge would pass. Soon he would long for his last hour alone in the study and then his solitary bed.

In the night, Klaus woke them all by knocking over a piece of furniture in his room in the attic and then stumbling clumsily down the stairs. Thomas listened as Katia remonstrated with him. He got out of bed only when Klaus began to shout at his mother, and then at Erika as she intervened.

"I'm just going downstairs to get a sandwich because I am hungry," he said. "I don't see what all the fuss is about."

"The fuss is that these floors are thin and you have woken the entire household," Katia replied.

"Is it my fault the house is badly built? Is that another thing I have done?"

"Klaus, get your sandwich," Erika said sternly, "and then go quietly upstairs to bed."

"I didn't want to come here at all," he said. "I'm not a child, you know."

"You are a child, my love," Erika said, almost unpleasantly. "You are an unruly youth. So be quiet and let us all sleep."

Thomas returned to bed but did not sleep. He asked himself what might have happened to Klaus and Erika if Hitler had not come to power. There was a moment, he remembered, when they were in their late teens and the war was over, when both of them seemed to match the very time they lived in, in their open bisexuality, in their flair for publicity and notoriety, in their tireless enthusiasm for fame.

They had regularly come back to the house in Munich, much as they did now, exhausted and excited, filled with strong opinions and a zest for the next adventure that made him envious.

If Germany had remained stable and hospitable to such difference and restlessness, would they have thrived, he wondered. Even in their late teens, they were both outside his control. Klaus barely acknowledged his existence in those years when he was publishing his own first books and articles, and Erika treated him as old-fashioned and staid, too conservative and pessimistic. Klaus spent more time with his uncle Heinrich, whom he admired greatly.

His two eldest children had only returned into his orbit now, Thomas thought, because they were short of money, but perhaps they also needed to know that there would be a refuge for them should everything in their own world fall apart.

They were living outside their own language, outside their own country. In Amsterdam and Paris, it had been easy, but once their novelty value wore off in America, the country would not embrace them further, he was sure of that. The freedoms they supported, the vehemence of their politics, would be frowned upon.

They were in their thirties now. They could no longer be written about as the fiercely talented young Manns, but rather as people who had failed to make a substantial mark in the world, who wanted the world to pay them a homage that they did not quite merit. As the danger of Hitler became more apparent, Klaus and Erika would seem tedious as they carried a banner saying "I told you so." Soon, he was certain, no one would have much interest in what these two former *wunderkinder* had to say.

On the day that the reporter and photographer were due, it was agreed that Auden and his friend Isherwood would come to lunch in Princeton with the family before the interview and the photographs. Klaus and Erika would collect them by car at Princeton Junction railway station.

When Erika returned alone her father was in the hallway.

"Where are our visitors?" he asked.

"They have gone for a swim," she said.

"Where?"

"In the Princeton pool. Auden says he gets the train down here from time to time to use the pool and Klaus says he knows it too. When I asked if they had their swimsuits, they assured me that they did. But I'm sure Klaus did not."

"Perhaps they will borrow swimsuits," he said.

"That is hardly hygienic."

"I understand that hygiene is not high among your husband's priorities. I know he has many other good qualities, but not that, I think."

When lunch was ready, the three men had still not arrived. For a time, Thomas and Katia and their two daughters sat at the table waiting, but soon they moved into the large-windowed drawing room.

"The people from *Life* will be here immediately after lunch," Katia said. "I have had some woman from the president's office calling twice a day about arrangements. It really will not do for Klaus and Auden to be late."

"You had someone on from Roosevelt's office?" Erika asked. "How exciting!"

"No, don't be silly," Katia replied. "The president is the president of Princeton. He is much more important than the mere president of the United States. It seems that the university wants to gain as much publicity as possible from our presence here."

"Before they return us to Czechoslovakia," Thomas said.

"By boat," Erika added.

When Klaus finally appeared with their two guests, all three were out of breath and almost giddy.

Thomas studied the poet now, noting how much he resembled one of those lean dogs one saw in the Bavarian countryside, russet-colored, watchful, always on the verge of pleading for some food or mildly barking as a way of drawing attention to himself.

He smiled at Auden and shook his hand, and then bowed to Auden's friend Isherwood.

"Sorry we are late," Klaus said. "We needed some exercise."

"I am a new man," Isherwood said, "after my swim. Ready to take on the world."

Auden was peering around the room as though some of the objects in it would soon belong to him.

"It is always marvelous to see the different types of boys," he said.

"That would be a good first line for a poem," Isherwood said. "An alexandrine."

"No, the stresses in 'marvelous' would not fit at all," Auden replied.

What Thomas noticed over lunch was how relaxed the two Englishmen were. They must go out to lunch quite often, he thought, or perhaps they believed they were back in one of their famous public schools. Klaus, on the other hand, was jittery and nervous, leaving the table several times, attempting when he returned to tell Auden about his plans for a new international literary magazine that would have an anti-fascist agenda.

He wanted to know if Auden knew Virginia Woolf well enough to ask her to contribute to the first issue.

"Know her? Do I know the Virgin Queen?" Auden asked.

"I wanted top-notch writers for the first issue."

"In that case," Isherwood interjected, "just write to her at Virginia Woolf, England. I mean, there couldn't be two of her."

"Can you imagine," Auden asked, "if we found other versions of her writing for the weeklies? Where would it end?"

"You don't admire her?" Erika asked.

"Oh, on the contrary, I rather do!" Auden said and then started imitating a woman's high-pitched English accent: "She would get the flowers herself, Mrs. Walloway, because her maid Letitia would have her work cut out for her. Oh, yes she would! What a day, as fresh as the curl-fold of the waves, all those waves, flowing untidily, as untidily as cabbages, with all their unnecessary leaves, lying raw and unplucked in the fields, the fields strangely silent and queerly humming in all their dark, sweet, sweeping, vertiginous verticality or, wondered Mrs. Walloway greenly, should that be horizontality? Oh yes, I really admire her."

"Did you write that or did she?" Elisabeth asked.

"I am being unfair," Auden replied. "Mrs. Woolf would be perfect for an anti-fascist magazine. In fact, I cannot think of anyone who would be more perfect. You know, I do really admire her."

Klaus had put his knife and fork down and was busy once more trying to get Auden to listen to him. It was clear to Thomas that Auden did not take Klaus seriously.

"I mean, an essay from her would be splendid. And there must be some young English writers we could ask. And then some international ones."

"Yes, international," Auden said.

"We could launch it in New York and London at the same time."

"It would all be in English?" Katia asked.

"We could also do a French edition," Klaus said. "And maybe an edition in Dutch. I have friends in Amsterdam."

"Oh, don't be so daft," Auden said.

Thomas thought it was time to change the subject.

"Do you know Princeton?" he asked Auden.

"Only the pool," Auden said. "I like the pool."

Thomas was not ready to be mocked at his own table.

"It would perhaps be best if you did not tell the journalist from *Life* about the pool. He will be here soon. So discretion might be advisable."

He took in Auden witheringly.

"Is there something wrong with the pool?" Elisabeth asked.

"It is a normal swimming pool," Thomas said, "of which the Princeton authorities are justly proud."

He glared at Auden, daring him to contradict.

"Muhammad here and I," Auden said pointing to Isherwood, "were discussing something on the train and I did want to ask about it. We think there are three important German novelists, Musil, Döblin and our host. Are they all friends?"

"No," Erika said. "They are all different."

"Enemies, then?" Auden asked.

Thomas was certain that he was being ridiculed. He let his gaze wander to a spot in the garden.

"We just wondered," Isherwood said.

"Once my husband has that look on his face, you may wonder all you like," Katia said.

"We saw Michael in London," Klaus interrupted. "He has developed an intense dislike for Hitler. A real, personal dislike."

"He is not in favor of Hitler at all, then?" Auden asked.

"Any special reason?" Isherwood inquired, looking at Auden, seeking his approval.

"Yes," Klaus said. "He told us that throughout his childhood he promised himself that he would go to America at the earliest opportunity in order to get as far away as possible from his father, and now, because of Hitler, when he finally makes it to America, his father is already here. And will be waiting for him at the dock."

Klaus began to splutter and laugh.

Thomas was about to inform the table that he was paying not only Michael's fare but that of his fiancée, and also arranging their visas, but instead he looked stonily down the table at his wife, who raised her eyes to heaven in exasperation as Klaus started some other story.

After lunch, as they waited for the reporter and photographer, Isherwood approached him and began to speak in German. Thomas listened to him for a while, concluding that Isherwood's way of speaking German would be perfect for anyone trying to learn English. He simply took all the structures of the English sentence and put in German words instead of the English ones, pronouncing these words in a pained manner. Despite his lack of height, he was not short of confidence.

It occurred to Thomas that since 1933 he had not often felt free to be very rude to anyone. Part of the daily grind of exile was that it was necessary to do a great deal of smiling and to say very little. He saw no reason, however, not to be rude now. He was in his own house and there was something so insolent about this little Englishman that he thought required a response.

"I'm afraid I cannot hear you at all," he said in German.

"Oh, do you have problems with your hearing?" Isherwood asked.

"None. None whatsoever."

He spoke slowly so that Isherwood could take in every word.

"Now, could you and your friend, my son-in-law, whatever he is called, be on your best behavior when the journalist and the photographer get here? Could you make an effort to behave like normal people?"

Isherwood looked puzzled.

"Do you get my point?" Thomas asked in English. He poked Isherwood gently in the chest.

The expression on Isherwood's face darkened; he moved quickly away and chatted to Elisabeth.

Thomas was fascinated by the change in both Isherwood and Auden when the journalist and the photographer came. There were no more jokes or smirking glances. They stood up straight. Even their suits seemed to have become less wrinkled and their ties less eccentric. He could see, as they were all gathered for a group shot, that these two were used to being photographed and appreciated the experience. Publicity appeared to make them more agreeable, more settled, less mischievous.

The magazine wanted a formal picture of the family. They all posed accordingly, Auden and Erika as young husband and wife, Klaus and Elisabeth as a devoted and contented son and daughter, and Thomas and Katia as model parents.

The photographer asked them to share a joke and they duly obliged. And then he asked Thomas to stand up and place himself at the center as the paterfamilias, so that, with Isherwood included, he had three on the sofa to his right and three on low stools to his left. Many photographs were taken as they were all encouraged to look relaxed.

When the reporter asked them what relationship Isherwood had with the family, Erika replied under her breath that he was their pimp.

In his study, they photographed Thomas's desk, but although they glanced at the Hofmann painting of the naked youths hanging on the wall, they did not ask about it. Such a picture would hardly enhance the image of stability and harmony that he wished to display. Instead, photos were taken of Thomas's record collection and his walking sticks and the medals and awards he had received.

Thomas let the reporter know, as the photographer listened and took more pictures, that he was seeking American citizenship. He spoke of how pleasant he found Princeton and how often he traveled to New York with his wife and daughter to go to classical concerts. He spoke enthusiastically of the literary evenings that they organized in Princeton, but emphasized his own personal discipline and the need, which he had long had, to spend the entire morning working alone in his study.

He did not demur when the journalist suggested that he was the most important anti-fascist writer and speaker in the world today, but insisted that what he sought in America was peace so that he could write more novels and stories, even though he knew that he had other duties as well, now that so many of his fellow countrymen were in danger and so much was at stake. But he would not get involved in party politics, he stressed. His task was to remain distant from many arguments so that he could make the most important argument of all, the one that simply proposed freedom and firmly insisted on democracy. That would for him be the only argument worth winning, he said.

He was glad when this was over that he had kept the door of his study closed. He did not want Klaus or his two guests listening to talk that sounded pompous and self-important even to himself. But he knew this article would be read in Washington, D.C., as well as in Princeton and New York, and he had reason to be taken seriously in Washington.

He liked how earnest the reporter was. He was relieved at being in the presence of someone who did not bathe every remark in irony or mockery, as Auden did, egged on by his friend Isherwood, and did not exude a permanent aura of nervous petulance, as his son did. It was as though he were speaking to students at Princeton, many of whom were earnest and thoughtful too, all of whom were respectful. With this reporter, also, he did not feel that he had to be on his guard. The questions were easy; there were no traps set. Thus, it was not hard to present himself judiciously for the consumption of Americans.

When they returned to the drawing room, Katia and Elisabeth were no longer there. Klaus, Erika, Auden and Isherwood were engaged in a spirited discussion about something, but when they saw him with the photographer and the reporter, they began to laugh uproariously. He would be glad, he thought, when the two Englishmen left for New York.

They had to wait until the reporter and photographer left, since the two men from the magazine had been told that Auden, as a dutiful husband, was staying in Princeton with his wife, while Isherwood was a guest. They had insisted that the happy extended family was looking forward to supper together, followed perhaps by some literary readings.

They would therefore remain until it was fully safe, Auden whispered, as the journalist and photographer departed.

Thomas went to his study, telling Katia, whom he met in the

hallway, that he would not need to say any farewells. When he heard the guests taking their leave, however, he went to a front window and saw them getting into the car. Erika was going to drive them to the station. Even as they closed the doors and shouted out goodbyes, he could see that they were laughing at something. It was not far-fetched, he thought, to believe that the object of their laughter was not only the entire charade of family life that they had just been engaged in, but him, their host. He might find himself comic too, he thought, were he to visit. Instead, he was resigned to return to his study and find the silence more soothing than usual now that his guests had departed.

When a month had gone by and he had heard nothing more from the visa and immigration office, he told Katia that he was worried about it.

"I have been dealing with that," she said.

"With the woman who thinks that Czechoslovakia is on the sea?"

"I have had nothing to do with her. I went to see the president himself. I gathered up some ammunition before I went. I called to renew my old acquaintance with Einstein. And I discovered that he too has been pushed around by that woman. And, with his blessing, I went to the president's office, unannounced, and demanded to see Dr. Dodds. When they asked me why I wanted to see him, I said I was on urgent business representing both Albert Einstein and Thomas Mann."

"Did he see you?"

"They insisted he was away. So I said I would wait until he returned. And they said that he was away for some days, and so I told them to contact him by telephone. And they kept me waiting for about an hour until I informed them of the gravest consequences for the president and indeed for Princeton University itself if President Dodds was not informed forthwith that I was waiting to speak to him. And after a lot of scurrying around, one of his assistants arrived on the scene. A young man in a suit who introduced himself as Mr. Lawrence Stewart. And he led me into an office and I explained what I wanted."

"'I'm afraid,' Mr. Stewart told me, 'that Princeton has to live within the rules.'"

Katia, who had been sitting down at the dining room table, stood up and pointed at Thomas, thus adding to the drama of her story, as though he were Mr. Lawrence Stewart, and she an even more formidable version of herself.

"'Mr. Stewart,' I said, 'I am representing Albert Einstein and Thomas Mann. Do you know who they are?'"

"'Yes, Frau Mann.'"

"'Now, do you have a better suit than the one you are wearing?'"

"'I'm not sure what you mean.'"

"'And do you have a good barber?'"

"'Frau Mann, I cannot see why you are asking me this.'"

"'Well, I will explain. You should go home and put on your better suit and also get a proper haircut because a journalist and photographer from *Life* magazine will shortly come to Princeton to write about you and photograph you as the man who is making the lives of Albert Einstein and Thomas Mann a misery in America. Do you have a wife and children?'"

"'Yes, I do.'"

"'They will not be proud of you when they see the article. The photographer and the reporter were with us recently, and it would just take one call from me for them to return and pounce on you. Just one call!'"

"Did you actually say 'pounce'?" Thomas asked her.

"Yes, I practiced my speech with Einstein's secretary, a Miss Bruce."

"And what happened next?"

"This Mr. Lawrence Stewart asked me to come back the next day when one of his colleagues would be there. And I agreed. And so I returned the next day and they could not have been more polite. From now on, visa inquires all come to me and to Miss Bruce. We deal directly with the president's office and with no one else, and soon application forms will come for us for citizenship and the most you will have to do is sign them. Miss Bruce and I have checked every detail thoroughly. Last week, I was even invited into the president's office to meet him."

"So, it is all settled, then?"

"Except for one thing," she said. "Einstein had been kept awake at night by the whole business and now is very relieved. He hugged me. And then he said that if I was ever thinking of getting divorced then I should keep him in mind."

"He proposed to you?"

"Well, almost. Miss Bruce was in the room for that part so he implied that rather than saying it out loud. But when she left, he moved closer and whispered in my ear that since I had solved this problem so efficiently, perhaps we could also make some other arrangement, one that would suit both of us, if I understood what he meant. And then he looked into my eyes. And then he winked at me. I think he is a real genius."

"E equals old goat," Thomas said.

"Yes, that is what I thought too on my way home."

"We must have him to supper. I'm sure I would enjoy his company again. And since we are to have that old goat Borgese in the family, it would be good to meet another, so we can prepare."

"Yes, I think Einstein is lonely. And we might have Miss Bruce too. She is passionate about literature. She has read your *Buddenbrooks* three times, she says, and longs to meet you. But it would be best, I think, not to leave me alone with Einstein for too long. He is very sweet. But the family has enough problems."

"Without you running away with a scientist?"

"Where would we go?" Katia asked, as if she were already contemplating a future in the wider world. "But perhaps we should not think about such matters until all our documents are in order. I did quite like Einstein's mustache and his eyes, but, for me, his hair is too untidy. The first thing I would do is have him tidy his hair."

She crossed the room and kissed Thomas affectionately on the cheek before making her way out of the room.

Chapter 11
Sweden, 1939

In the weeks before the war broke out, Thomas, accompanied by Katia and Erika, gave lectures and interviews in Holland and then in Sweden. The audiences and journalists, and even the waiters in restaurants and the hotel staff, were light and almost jolly. Hitler's name was in the headlines, but so it had been for the past decade. Despite his initial misgivings, Thomas was glad that they had come back to Europe for this short trip.

In his mind, he went through where each member of the family was. Elisabeth was safe in Princeton, waiting for her wedding, Klaus was still in New York, trying to raise funds for his magazine. And the other children were being looked after: Michael and Gret, his fiancée, had visas for America; he hoped also to get visas for Monika and her husband. When he returned, he would set to work getting papers for Golo and also for Heinrich and Nelly, whom Heinrich had married, so they could leave France. Katia's parents, having lost their house and their paintings, their precious ceramics and all their money, were finally safe in Zürich. Her brothers had left Germany, Klaus going to Japan to be a conductor with the Imperial Orchestra. Klaus Heuser, who wrote to Thomas regularly, was now in Dutch India working for a trading company and had no intention, he said, of returning to Germany as long as the Nazis were in power.

Between events, Thomas had enjoyed the August sunshine on

the beach at Noordwijk in Holland, savoring the shallow water and the long tides, working on an introduction to a new translation of *Anna Karenina*. Now, from the vantage point of this luxury hotel at Saltsjöbaden in Sweden, the only ominous sign, he felt, was a seasonal chill wind from the sea as the sun was going down.

The previous evening, over supper, he and Katia had discussed the possibility with Erika of moving from Princeton to Los Angeles. They had found the winter hard in Princeton and felt isolated there.

"Surely Los Angeles is the most isolated place on earth!" Erika said.

"We liked it when we were there," Katia said. "I dream of waking in the morning and seeing only sunshine. And we saw so many foreigners when we were there, so we would not stand out as much. In Princeton, people respond to me as if I were personally threatening to undermine the American way of life."

"Do you really want to go where the German writers and composers are living?" Erika asked. "And Brecht is there. You hate Brecht."

"I hope to have a house with walls high enough to keep him out," Thomas said. "But I would not mind hearing German voices."

As the end of August approached, they did not believe that war was imminent; nonetheless, they followed the news closely. After breakfast, which they each had in their room, they waited downstairs for the foreign newspapers to arrive. While they had to labor over the French, they managed to work out what the headlines said. The English papers tended to be a few days out of date, but there was nothing in any of them that suggested immediate war.

"But there is a crisis," Erika said. "Look at the papers. There is a crisis."

"There has been a crisis since 1933," Katia said.

Thomas, as usual, wrote in the mornings, and enjoyed a long lunch with Katia and Erika and then a walk on the beach.

When Katia came to his room to tell him that war had broken out, Thomas was sure it was not true. He telephoned Bermann, his publisher, who was in Stockholm. Bermann confirmed what Katia had said. By this time, Erika had come to Thomas's room.

"We have to get back to America," she said.

Thomas realized they could quickly find that they were trapped in Sweden.

On hotel notepaper, Thomas wrote out a telegram to be sent to Agnes Meyer in Washington, D.C., asking her to telephone him. He also prepared another for the Knopfs in New York asking for their help. When he called to reception to have the telegrams sent, there was no reply. Erika offered to deliver them personally to the front desk and wait until they had been dispatched.

Thomas called Bermann again and suggested that he contact the Swedish government asking that they offer Thomas urgent assistance to return to the United States.

He began to panic only when the hotel informed him some hours later that his telegrams were still in a batch of others waiting to be sent. They had assured Erika that they had gone out. When he tried to telephone Washington, the hotel said that international lines were down.

He went to the front desk a number of times to insist that his telegrams be treated as urgent. Soon there were many people hovering in the lobby and more and more guests demanding attention at the front desk. The hotel manager stood apart, severely issuing instructions, putting his hand up to signal that he could not be approached by anyone except the hotel staff. Thomas saw porters with an air of concern carrying suitcases and trunks to waiting cars outside.

As the day passed and the air of frenzy remained in the lobby, the rest of the hotel operated as if nothing had changed. Meals were on time. In the evening the orchestra played some light waltzes and gypsy music before dinner and then romantic tunes afterwards.

His breakfast was brought to his room in the morning at the appointed time, the eggs cooked as he had requested, his coffee freshly made, the napkin crisply folded, the waiter placing the tray carefully on the table near the window so that he would have a view of the salt flats, and then bowing politely, his uniform perfect and his demeanor unhurried, his blondness almost exquisite in the rich morning light.

Waiting for news, they continued to have lunch and dinner together at the same table close to the windows and away from the orchestra. In Thomas's room before they descended to the dining room, Katia and he went over what other calls they might attempt to make, or what further telegrams they would try to send. Katia had found a hotel porter who spoke German and he translated the Swedish newspapers for her.

"It will be total war," she said. "Nowhere in Europe will be safe."

He wondered if Katia and Erika blamed him for taking them on this trip. He had been misled by the surface of life, which had seemed to him, for the moment, stable. He had been warning others about Hitler's intentions, but he had not imagined war would come so soon, despite all the signs. Thus, while he had been busy taking a stroll or reading, or having a drink before dinner with Katia and Erika, men in uniforms with maps in front of them and murder in their eyes had been planning invasions. There was nothing secret about what they aimed to do; they had given interviews that made everything clear, so clear indeed that he himself had managed to pretend that it was not about to happen.

Once back in Princeton, if they managed to return, he would use every connection that he had made to get the members of his family still in Europe across the Atlantic. How they would live, or where, or what they would do, he would think about when they were safely home.

He spoke by phone to a diplomat in Stockholm who Bermann

had located. He was assured that he would be helped in every way possible to leave Sweden. He should be ready to depart at short notice.

Katia stayed with Erika in her room and waited for a call. They had their visas for the United States; all they would need was a flight from Malmö and then a berth, perhaps from Southampton in England.

Thomas stood with a forced ease in the lobby of the hotel, keeping close to the front desk and listening in case a call came or a telegram arrived, aware also that it was essential that no one sensed his panic.

Over meals, he noticed that Erika had grown brighter and was filled with plans and possibilities. As he and Katia grew silent, Erika, since she had British citizenship, spoke of what she might do once they were in London, how she might join some propaganda unit or work as a reporter.

"I might even join the British Army."

"I am not sure you can just join the British Army," Katia said.

"Now that there is war, I am certain I can."

"What would you do in the British Army?" Thomas asked.

"I would work in some area to do with information and disinformation," Erika said.

It struck Thomas that, until now, Erika had been generally unsure what she might do at all in the future. Her days as an actress were over; she was not really a writer. While she had published books about the evils of the Nazi system, they had not sold well and had caused some people to suspect her of being a Communist. Her time as a public speaker in America had been exhausting. Now, however, with war declared, there would be a need for clever young women. All of the skills Erika had—her energy, her knowledge of German, her command of English, her commitment to democracy and the fact that she was single and not actually attached to Auden in any real way—would mean that she would now be in demand. The realization of that made her eyes brighter and her voice louder.

Only in the reaches of the night did Thomas fully consider what would happen to them were they to be actually stranded in Sweden. If Hitler could so easily take Czechoslovakia and invade Poland, it would not be long before he and his generals looked towards Scandinavia. Were they to invade, Thomas Mann would be high on the list of those to be detained and repatriated to Germany. No one would be able to intervene on his behalf. He saw his name in the American newspapers and imagined the appeals to the Germans to furnish information about his whereabouts. He foresaw writers signing a petition for his release. He had signed such petitions himself. He knew how worthy their intentions were and how ineffective most of them proved to be.

It was essential then that they leave Sweden. But all the flights were either full or grounded or no information about booking was available. The diplomat was not returning his calls. An appeal to the Swedish Academy as a Nobel Prize winner had been met with silence. He was not sure that his daily telegram to Agnes Meyer was even leaving the hotel. There had been no reply from the Knopfs either. The staff at the front desk barely looked up when he approached.

One day when the phone in his room rang before lunch, he presumed that it was Katia or Erika to let him know that it would soon be time to eat. When he heard a woman's voice in heavily accented English asking for him by name, he presumed it was someone from the hotel, whose staff had the habit of calling to ask if he wanted his room cleaned or his bed made.

Thus it took him a moment to realize that Agnes Meyer was speaking on a clear line from Washington.

"I don't know why you have not replied to my telegrams," she said, switching to German, having discovered that she was talking to him.

"I have received no telegrams."

"I have been informed otherwise by the hotel."

"The hotel has not delivered any telegrams to me."

"This has been most difficult. Most difficult. I had to deal with the Swedish authorities both here in the embassy and in Stockholm and then I had to use up valuable contacts among the higher echelons of the British diplomatic service. My husband is exasperated and wonders what you are doing in Europe."

"We need to leave."

"Leave? You need to be ready to flee at a moment's notice. As soon as you get a call, there will be a car to take you to the airport in Malmö and then you will fly to London and you must make your own way to Southampton. I will have a berth booked for you on the SS *Washington*. I have been in touch with the management of the shipping company. You will have to pay when you arrive at Southampton. The booking is for first class. But don't expect any comfort."

"I am most grateful to you."

"And come and see me the second you arrive in America. Do not continue ignoring me."

"I can assure you that I have not been ignoring you. Will we get a call from the Swedish authorities about the flight to London? Do you know the name of the person who will call?"

"I found a diplomat. And he assures me you will get a call. I did not bother him by asking about the details of who would actually make the call."

"So I should wait in my room?"

"You should be ready to go at a moment's notice. As I said, this has been most frustrating."

"We are very grateful."

"Indeed."

"Do you have a number or a name I can call if we don't hear from anybody?"

"Are you doubting me?"

"As I said, I am grateful."

"Pack, then, and tell your wife and daughter to pack too. Don't think anyone will wait patiently for you. Those days are over. I have told them that your visas are in order. Is your daughter still married to that Englishman, the poet?"

"Yes, she is."

"Advise her to stay married to him. At least until she arrives safely in America."

He did not respond to this. Her tone made him remember why he had been avoiding Agnes Meyer.

"Do not miss this flight," she said.

"We will not. I will let my wife know immediately."

"And come and see me, as I said."

"I will do that."

Early the next morning they waited with their luggage in the lobby as they had been told to do by a caller from the Swedish Ministry for Foreign Affairs. When a young official arrived and saw all their suitcases, he shook his head.

"These will have to be sent on," he said. "We can allow you only the bare minimum."

When Katia remonstrated with him, the official turned away from her and spoke to Erika.

"If you want to board this plane to London, you must store this luggage. I cannot keep the car waiting. You have ten minutes to organize that or you will miss the flight."

They went through their suitcases, removing items that were deemed fully necessary for the journey. Thomas already had a book of Hugo Wolf's letters and a biography of Nietzsche and all his notebooks in a large briefcase. Katia packed some of his shirts and underclothes in a case with some of her own clothes and shoes. Several times, as the official looked on, Erika had to reopen suitcases to find some item she insisted was indispensable. Only when her father assured her that his publisher would be certain to send on their luggage did she close the cases and stand up with one small bag in her hand.

Thomas and Katia went to the front desk asking to have their luggage stored and were told they would have to wait for the manager to see what could be done as the storeroom was full to the brim with suitcases belonging to guests who had departed over the previous week. When Thomas produced a large banknote, he was coldly informed by the tall Swede working at the desk that they did not accept money in this way and that Herr Mann should wait for the manager as he had been told to do.

The young official was becoming more and more impatient.

"I need you to get into the car," he said. "We must go to the airport."

Thomas was told that the luggage could not simply be left in the lobby. They would have to make some arrangement with the manager, as the staff had no authority to accept luggage for storage by departing guests.

Katia insisted that Thomas and Erika and the official go to the car, whose engine was running. They should take all the hand luggage with them. She would find the manager, she said.

They sat silently in the car as the official said that if Frau Mann did not soon join them, then she would be left behind. It would not be easy to get her a seat on another flight.

"My mother is looking for the manager," Erika said.

"Your mother is putting the journey in jeopardy," the official said.

When Katia appeared, she got into the car angrily.

"The manager, who was of course there all the time, actually said: 'There are too many people like you staying in this hotel.' And when I informed him that my husband had won the Nobel

Prize in Literature, he shrugged. I did not know that there were people like that in Sweden. I left our address and Bermann's name and told him that the king of Sweden will hold him personally responsible if a single item of our luggage goes missing."

By then the car was already moving. Thomas nudged Erika at the mention of the king of Sweden, but he did not look at her or smile.

From the front passenger seat, the official addressed the three in the back.

"I have been told to inform you that because the plane will fly over German territory for some of the journey, it will be forced to fly low. This brings dangers and risks."

"Why will it fly low?" Erika asked.

"That is a condition that the Germans have imposed. Yesterday, a German plane flew alongside this flight."

"Do we have a choice?" Katia asked. "I mean, can the plane take some other route?"

"I'm afraid not. Not if you want to leave Sweden now. The plane will land in Amsterdam for refueling, but no one will get on or off."

Once on board the plane, Katia insisted on sitting at the window seat and said that Thomas and Erika should take aisle seats.

"I am an ordinary-looking middle-aged lady and of no interest to anyone," she said. "Could you two bury your heads in books, but not in a way that makes either of you appear in any way conspicuous?"

The plane was full, with passengers trying to stuff their belongings in the overhead compartments. When one woman screamed that her suitcase would not fit, she was told that it would have to be abandoned. When she began to argue with the flight attendant, other passengers warned her that she was delaying the takeoff.

Eventually, with a great sweep, she opened her case, took out a pair of shoes and a bottle of perfume and some clothes and threw them on her seat.

"Take all the rest and do as you please with it," she said dramatically. "I will be traveling with only the underclothes I am wearing, if that is what you want."

"Let us hope that lady is not crossing the Atlantic with us," Katia said.

The propellers had begun to turn even before the doors were closed. Thomas believed that if one more day had passed it would have been too late. They had not asked if the Germans had a list of passengers, but such a list would not be hard to acquire, or indeed it would not be too difficult for someone with Nazi sympathies on the Swedish side to alert the Germans to his presence on the plane. A good number of officials must know he was traveling.

As the plane flew out of Malmö, it struck him that if he were ever to contemplate prayer, now would be a good time to do so. But since he did not pray, then he would read his book. He would continue reading with fierce concentration, he thought, until they reached London.

Only once, when the plane suddenly dipped for a moment, did he allow himself to tremble. He reached across the aisle towards Erika, who held his hand. When he caught Katia's eye, she motioned to him that he should keep his head down, return to his reading.

The anxiety he was going through, he recognized, had been shared by many others. And they had not been lucky enough to be spirited by a government official from a luxury hotel to a plane flying west. They had no one to call on. What he was feeling was only a pale shadow of their terror.

The plane started its descent and Erika went towards the cockpit. Thomas watched her questioning the attendant. Soon she returned to reassure them that they were close to Amsterdam and well out of German airspace. The plane would stay on the tarmac at Amsterdam for less than an hour.

Passport control in London went smoothly, but when they arrived at customs, the official asked Thomas to open his brief-case, calling two of his colleagues over. Erika and Katia began to speak, but they were instructed to be silent. The men studied his two books first, flicking through the pages, and then set about examining the notebooks and the pages of handwriting.

"My husband is a writer," Katia said.

Ignoring her, the officials whispered to one another before taking the contents of the briefcase and Thomas's passport to an inner room. As they stood waiting, the hall emptied out.

"I hope that lady with only one set of underclothes will eventually find happiness," Katia said.

Thomas looked at Erika and they both laughed, their laughter causing Katia to become more solemn.

"It is no small matter," she said. "I think the experience of being deprived like that may have marked her for life."

By the time the three officials emerged from the inner office, Katia had joined in the laughter, which Thomas now sought to control.

"We must ask you, sir, what the writing in these notebooks and pages contains."

"It is a novel I am attempting to complete."

"In German?"

"Yes, I write in German."

One of the officials opened a page of the notebook and asked him to translate it.

"My daughter is a better translator than I am."

"But you wrote this, sir?"

"Yes."

"Then we need you to translate it."

Thomas slowly began to translate.

"What does it mean, sir?"

"It is from a novel I am writing about the German poet Goethe."

"And when was the last time you were in Germany?"

"1933."

"And where are you going now?"

"Southampton," Katia said, "and then America. We have our visas here and we will miss the boat if we have any further delays."

When the customs men found a map that Thomas had drawn of a room, with a table in the center and names hastily scribbled around the oblong outline of the table, they grew concerned.

"It is for my novel," Thomas said. "It is a sketch of the dining room in Goethe's house. See, this is his name here, and these are the other people at his table. This was in the early nineteenth century."

"How do you know who was at his table?" one of them asked.

"I do not. I am imagining where they sat so that I can imagine their conversation."

One of the officials looked at the map, concerned, turning it around as though it might be of some strategic importance.

"He is a novelist," his colleague said.

"A novelist who draws maps," another interjected and then smiled.

"There is a bus to Waterloo," the official who appeared to be in charge said. "And then you get the train from there to Southampton."

"And you have nice weather for the journey," the other added, as he smiled and waved them towards the exit.

Thomas was surprised by the sense of peace and plenty that he observed from the bus as it wound through the English countryside.

It was greener than he had expected, the roads narrower, the sky bluer, the late afternoon heat more intense. In the distance, he saw a farmhouse. Even the modest houses on the side of the road, or in the few villages through which they passed, exuded ease and freshness. Nothing seemed too old, or worn. When they approached London itself, however, he marveled at the extent of the suburbs, the dismal rows of houses, the small shops. This felt even more foreign to him somehow than Princeton or New York. He was glad that he did not have to settle here. Perhaps it would be different in the grand squares and the big shopping streets, he thought, but they would have time to see nothing, just find the train for Southampton once they reached Waterloo Station.

It was strange traveling without luggage. There was a freedom in alighting from the bus without having to supervise the moving of all their suitcases to the train. He felt also a lightness in himself, as though he had been released from school for the summer, and was prevented from smiling and making jokes as they entered the station only by the expressions of determination on the faces of Katia and Erika.

As he waited while Katia and Erika purchased train tickets Thomas saw that people were carrying gas masks, many displaying them prominently over their shoulder. England was at war. He studied each person who passed, trying to see if he could find in their faces some sign that freedom and democracy did indeed matter to them. These people here had decided, practically without dissent, to resist Hitler, to live in permanent danger.

Soon, he thought, they would know real fear. Their cities would be bombed; their sons would die in uniform. All he could do was watch them. There was nothing he could tell them about Germany that they did not know or feel. He was a double outsider, a German exile on his way back to America.

• • •

When they went to the office in the port at Southampton, they were informed that the SS *Washington* would be days late. They should find a hotel, they were told. As they walked through the warm evening, with seagulls overhead crying out as though in panic at their very presence, Katia said that they would now be able to make contact with Michael and his fiancée, and encourage them to cross the Atlantic as soon as possible, and perhaps they would be able to speak to Monika and her husband to let them know that they should follow suit as soon as their visas were issued.

In the morning, having convinced the hotel to move a desk into Thomas's room so that he could work, Katia and Erika ventured out to visit the shops of Southampton, hoping to buy new suitcases and at least enough clothes for the journey. When they returned, Thomas could hear their laughter as they ascended the narrow stairs.

They had bought the suitcases and some clothes and underclothes and shoes. In each shop, she said, they explained immediately to the shopkeeper that they were fleeing from Germany, and not only the shopkeeper but other customers had been very kind. They had bought newspapers and told him that Goering had made an offer of peace that the British government had summarily rejected. Everyone they met, Katia said, supported the government.

"One woman even approached us in the street saying that they would free Germany just like they did in the last war. I hardly knew what to say to her, so I told her I was very grateful."

In Erika's room, as they opened their parcels they began to laugh again.

"We thought of that poor woman who lost all of her clothes," Katia said, "and is walking the world now with no change of underwear. The thought of her made us laugh so that one very serious woman behind a counter selling handkerchiefs thought we were laughing at her."

"I would not be surprised," Erika said, "if she reports us to the police as undesirable aliens."

She produced a wooden tea towel rack with a picture of the royal family engraved on it.

"I bought this for Auden," she said. "To let him see what he is missing."

"But look what else we bought!" Katia said.

She held up a woolen vest with sleeves and a pair of long johns. The wool was almost yellow.

"We have never seen anything like this," Erika said. "And we started laughing again when I said that it would be perfect for Klaus."

"Oh, and English women's underwear!" Katia said.

"It is even worse than German underwear," Erika added. "Some of the inner garments are open invitations to lice. I don't know how the English tolerate this!"

After lunch all three of them walked down to the port to find out if there was any news of the SS *Washington*. They were told that it would arrive in two days, but that it was vastly overbooked. The company would try to fit everyone on, but there would be no such thing as private cabins, and men and women would have to be segregated. When Katia asked if, by paying more money, they could secure two first-class berths, one for her husband and the other for herself and Erika, she was told that such requests would not even be considered.

"There would be a riot on the ship. This is an evacuation, madam. We will try to get every person who has a ticket to America on board. It will be over in five or six days. You can get all the first-class accommodation you want once you arrive in New York."

On the day the boat was scheduled to set out there was a long line and there was much confusion, with passengers pushing ahead and rumors that the boat might not even sail that day, and other rumors that not everyone in the line would be allowed on. As people looked around at them when they spoke German, they attempted to speak English to one another until Thomas wondered if their foreign accents and errors in grammar might cause even more suspicion. The morning was hot and there was nowhere to sit. When Erika, in exasperation, pushed her way through the crowd, hoping to find someone from the authorities who would help her parents jump the queue, Thomas turned to Katia.

"This is not how we thought we were going to live, is it?"

"We are the lucky ones," she said. "This is what good fortune looks like."

Erika came bustling back with two members of the crew in uniform.

"This is my father. He is ill," she said. "And he has been standing for two hours now. This could kill him."

The two men examined Thomas, who tried to appear fragile. All around there were murmurs from the crowd that they too were accompanying elderly people to the ship.

"My mother and I can wait," Erika said loudly. "But if you could take my father onto the ship now."

Thomas looked distracted, as though he could not quite fathom what was happening. He could see that the two crew members had expected someone much older. They were hesitating.

"Come with us, sir," one of them eventually said, and gently they took him through the crowd and then made him wait for a pilot boat. He carried his briefcase with him.

"He has a bad heart, his daughter says," one of them shouted. They gave instructions that he should be ferried out to the ship. After much difficulty and to shouts of advice and encouragement, he managed to get from the boat to the ship. With as much dignity as he could muster, he sat in the first public space he could find, noting that many others had already been allowed on.

He rummaged through his briefcase and found a notebook. Slowly, as he waited, he took out his pen and began to add some paragraphs to his Goethe novel, letting his mind move far away from where he was, picking up the rhythm of the sentences he had been working on the day before, imagining that a novel about the poet's love in old age for a young girl might comfort a reader in a time when his books would be read in Germany again.

He kept working even as announcements through loudspeakers were made and crowds that had been kept in line were finally being let onto the ship. He realized that, if he stayed where he was, Katia and Erika would be bound to find him.

They gave him a first-class berth that he had to share with four other men. Since Thomas had the bed, and the others merely cots and mattresses, there was muffled animosity towards him, exacerbated when they discovered that he was German. Two of the men were English and spoke as though he could not understand them.

"Who knows who these Germans are?" one asked.

"In flight from Hitler," his companion said, "given a bed, and, before we know where we are, he'll be cabling code messages home."

"They will sing a different tune in short order. I was there when they surrendered the last time, and it was a sight to behold. I told one of them that he was now free to kick the Kaiser, and I repeated it several times, but I was wasting my breath. He hadn't a word of English, or so he said. You can never tell with them."

All Thomas wanted to do was work. Each morning, once Katia and Erika found a place for him to sit, they walked around the deck, checking on him each time they passed. When, one sunny afternoon, he offered his seat to Katia, she was almost indignant, saying that she had put all that energy into securing a seat for him so that he could write, not so that she could lie about in the sun.

The idea of his own life merging with the life of Goethe had not occurred to him before, but it must have been there as an undercurrent. It must have been why the book had become longer and he had put so much care into it. It was a story of impossible love, desire in old age. As he lifted his head and looked out at the vast expanse of water, names came to him, and then faces—Armin Martens blushing, Willri Timpe standing naked, Paul Ehrenberg leaning towards him earnestly, Klaus Heuser's soft lips.

If Paul were in front of him now, or even if Klaus Heuser were to be on this boat as a passenger, what would he say to them? If they stood in the darkness of the deck after dinner, with so many other passengers around, what would be the message in their eyes? He sighed and thought about holding Klaus Heuser, feeling his heart beating and his breath coming faster.

Katia and Erika approached; Katia asked him what he was thinking about.

"The book," he said. "If I could get this section right."

On the last few days of the voyage, the congestion on the ship grew more and more unbearable, and water for washing grew scarce. The two Englishmen in his berth became more loquacious.

"Have you seen the way the German is mollycoddled by that wife and daughter?"

"I wasn't sure if that girl was a man or a woman. I'd be surprised if they let her into America."

Thomas wrote the word "mollycoddled" in his notebook, but neither Erika nor Katia could tell him what it meant.

Erika had demanded that they be given precedence as the boat docked. As they walked from the ship to the customs shed, watched by the exhausted passengers who were being held back so that Thomas, his wife and his daughter could get ahead, Thomas felt their hostile gaze. It reminded him of those nights in Munich in the years after the revolution when he and Katia had descended the stairs of the opera house to find their chauffeur waiting, Katia's mink stole and Thomas's greatcoat on his arm. As they emerged, the crowd outside, impoverished by galloping inflation, watched them with a smoldering resentment.

It had occurred to him more than once that Adolf Hitler could have easily been among that Munich crowd. He might not have been able to afford an opera ticket, but perhaps he was waiting to see if there were tickets that someone could not use. In the Munich winter, he would have been cold standing on the street. And then he would, Thomas imagined, have seen the Manns coming with their chauffeur, both of them stately, distant, dignified, alert to their status in the city, nodding to some, greeting others, as their position dictated. On the nights when Wagner was playing, Hitler would have been desperate to hear *Lohengrin* or *Die Meistersinger* or *Parsifal*. And he would watch as the people who had paid for their tickets well in advance, or who had their own box in the theater, alighted from their cars dressed perfectly for the occasion, while he was turned away into the night.

As he thought about this, Thomas followed Katia and Erika towards passport control, their luggage carried behind them by a porter. Once their passports and visas had been checked, their suitcases were not even inspected. A car was waiting, as arranged by the Knopfs. When they had put their cases in the trunk, Erika told them that she was going to stay in New York. She needed to see Klaus, she said. Now that Britain was at war with Germany, they would have to make plans.

"Do you know where Klaus is?" Katia asked.

"Auden is in Brooklyn. He will know where Klaus is."

Erika had already packed a small case for her stay in New York; the rest of the luggage could go with them to Princeton. Thomas realized that she was going to miss battling on his behalf. Instead of Erika, so busy and brittle, Elisabeth would be at home calmly waiting for them. Tears came into Thomas's eyes at the thought that this would be the last time they would find Elisabeth at home.

"Don't cry," Erika said. "We have arrived safely. I did not enjoy that flight over Germany."

"Can you tell Klaus that he should call?" Katia asked. "Or better, come to stay. If he has time."

"I have that funny yellow underwear for him. I will tell him that it is a present from us all."

A few days later, Thomas took the slow train to Trenton in order to catch the express going south from Boston that stopped there en route to Washington. The car Agnes Meyer had sent for him was waiting outside the station. The day before, Mrs. Meyer had wavered between demanding that he and Katia come to her country house for a lengthy stay and insisting that Thomas travel alone to Washington and lodge with her and her husband for just one night. In the end, she had decided on the latter option.

"Agnes Meyer is the sort of person who emerges when there is a war or threat of a war," Katia said. "But they usually work as matrons or snipers."

Thomas knew that, on this visit, he would need to ask Agnes how visas could be secured for Golo and for Heinrich and his wife, and how the visas for Monika and her husband could be expedited. He wanted to talk to Agnes too about his own position and how it might be improved were he to receive American citizenship. He had a list in his pocket of writers in Europe who desperately needed help, sometimes just financial help, but also assistance in getting to the United States if Germany were to invade Holland or France. When he had returned to Princeton, he had found many heartbreaking letters from frantic German artists, many of them Jewish, all of them appealing for help. Some had been sent to him at Princeton, others redirected from Knopf. All the senders believed that he had the power to rescue them.

No one knew that he was, in fact, mostly powerless. His vague association with Roosevelt and his job in Princeton could not be used to get visas for anyone. But his friendship with Agnes Meyer might make a difference. He could at least ask her to help, which he did not feel he could do with Roosevelt. If he had to flatter this woman, he would do so, as he would willingly spend time with her, allow her to translate his speeches, listen to her as she told him what he should write. He would even entertain the idea that she might write a book about his work.

But, in return, he determined that she would have to listen to him today and provide the requisite assistance. Since Agnes did not ever listen to anyone, making her pay attention would be no simple matter.

Agnes was waiting for him in her large drawing room. As she started to speak, it was clear to Thomas that she had spent the morning preparing what she was going to say. He was placed opposite her, he felt, as audience rather than as visitor.

"Now, you must be careful not to speak about America entering the war. It is something no one wants to hear about, least of all from someone who is not American. And I hope you will convey this also to your eldest daughter and your eldest son. America will decide itself what course of action to follow. For the moment, it has decided to watch and wait, and that therefore is what we all must do. In the meantime, I think a novel about Goethe will be welcomed here. Not by everyone, of course. I do long to see it myself, but I hope the translation is not going to be marred as usual by that woman, that Mrs. Lowe-Porter, your so-called translator. I wish she would devote herself to some lesser writer, Hermann Broch, for example, or Hermann Hesse, or Hermann Brecht."

"I don't think Brecht is called Hermann."

"Nor do I. It was a joke."

"My wife and I and Erika are very grateful for your help in getting us back to America."

"Don't eat too much now, as there will be lunch. Although I know you like marzipan. Well, who doesn't? But not before lunch. Perhaps just one, and some tea."

"I know that you must be tired of me asking you for favors," he began.

"Fundraising is now the new American industry," she said. "I said that to my husband just last week. This museum, that museum, this committee, that committee, this refugee, that refugee. All worthy, of course."

Thomas would have preferred if Agnes's husband had joined them for lunch. Despite the fact that he was obtuse, having Eugene Meyer in the room distracted Agnes, making it slightly more difficult for her to interrupt so quickly or to change the subject so precipitously.

He was disappointed when Agnes told him that her husband was out of town and they would be dining alone, as well as just having lunch *à deux*.

He could not face spending all afternoon with Agnes, or near her. He told her that he would need to work for several hours in his room, as his novel was very near completion.

"Well, this house is perfect for you. No one will disturb you. I will issue strict instructions, and silence will be imposed. The servants know already that a famous writer is staying here. I assembled them all this morning and told them. You should always consider coming here when you need to get work done. I should send a note to your wife and let her know that. The modern luxuries are here, as you can see, and you will be in complete seclusion. My husband often works late."

Over lunch, Thomas made no progress with her. She wanted to talk about the book she might write setting his work in the context of German history and culture.

"So few people here know anything about European culture in any form, so imagine how little they must know about Faust or Goethe, or the Hanseatic League indeed."

All he could do was nod and agree and make brisk, solemn interjections. He started to long for the solitude she had promised him. When he stood up while Agnes was still in mid-sentence, he hoped she would not take offense, but he could not bear it any longer. And he decided now that just as she had prepared every word she spoke at lunch, he would do the same at dinner.

Walking down the great staircase for dinner, he realized that he rather appreciated the opulence of this house, the rich fabrics and the heavy furniture, the early American paintings that Agnes had so carefully collected, the rugs, the polished wood. And it struck him for a moment that he almost liked Agnes. In her bossiness, she reminded him of an old Germany, of his aunt and grandmother, of gatherings in Lübeck in the house where his father had been raised. Because they controlled so little, the women there exercised a fierce grip on what was within their reach. Servants lived in fear of them and they kept a close watch on the cook.

In the future, he thought, perhaps when this war was over, women like Agnes would have more power. Erika, it occurred to him, would be a good companion for her as they set about some noble task. He smiled at the idea of Agnes and his daughter in each other's orbit. Together they could run the world.

Over dinner, he saw once more just how formidable Agnes Meyer was, as she directed the conversation towards topics that interested her and her alone, allowing no deviation. She spoke about her parents, who had emigrated from Germany, how conservative her father was and how difficult life had been for them in a cramped apartment in the Bronx with German as the only language used among them. Her father took the view, she said, that she should remain at home honing her domestic skills until she married. He had opposed her going to Barnard College to study. So she had applied for a scholarship and taken part-time jobs to pay for her own education. She had not asked him for any help.

"I owed them nothing," she said, "and this meant I could do what I liked. I could go to Paris. I could work for a newspaper. I could get married without consulting them. Anything I wanted."

Thomas understood that interrupting Agnes, attempting to move the subject onto the question of visas, would simply not succeed. He wondered if he should write her a note and have it delivered to her room when she had retired and then try to talk to her in the morning before he left for Princeton.

Once the meal had ended, she said that perhaps she had spoken enough.

"I do not usually have the company of the most distinguished man of letters in the world," she said. "Generally, it's Eugene's friends, and they are dull men with even duller wives. Recently, when I was left with a group of the wives, I wanted to ask the servants to send out for mustard gas."

Thomas smiled.

Agnes stood up and went to a desk in the corner of the room and returned with a pen and a folder.

"Now, you think I don't listen. I do listen. Today when you came you mentioned favors."

Thomas nodded.

"Your son Michael is in London with his fiancée, and they have visas for the United States. I believe he is a viola player and I can probably help to find him work in some American orchestra. Your daughter and her Hungarian husband are in London and I can assure you that their visas will come through very soon. But your son Golo is in Switzerland, and your brother and his second wife are in France, and they do not have visas?"

"That is all correct. You have a marvelous memory."

"I can get a visa for Golo without any difficulty. You'll have to sign forms to say that you will be fully responsible for him financially. That's all. As long as he remains unmarried."

"I will convey that to him."

"With your brother, we can get him a contract with Warner Brothers. Once that is signed, then we can deal with the visa question."

"Has Warner Brothers agreed to offer him a contract?"

"Didn't your brother write *The Blue Angel*?"

"He wrote the novel on which the film was based."

"In that case, Warner Brothers will see him as an asset. For a one-year contract at least."

"Are you sure this can be arranged?"

"Have I ever failed you?"

She folded her arms and smiled in satisfaction.

"Now join me in the drawing room, where we will have coffee served."

In the drawing room she sat close to him on the sofa. The folder was on her lap.

"I know you will want a check. Everyone who comes here wants a check. Who is it for?"

"There are many writers who need help."

"I can write one check to cover them all. I will write it in your name and you can imburse the neediest."

"Some of them are in real danger."

"Please do not ask for anything else on this visit. The check will be sent to your room later."

"I am truly very grateful to you."

"In the New Year, I think you should go on a lecture tour. I can make contacts for you, but the essential thing is that you don't call on the administration to declare war on Germany. That is what you must not do. America is not at war. You can talk about anything you like, but the president does not want you stirring people up. He has an election to win next year. So he wants you to be silent on America entering the war."

"The president? How do you know that?"

"Eugene and I know him. And that is how he feels. And, once more, can I ask you to remind your daughter of that too? People here associate me with you and I am blamed for every word she utters. And utter she does! She is a tremendous utterer."

"She has her own opinions."

"Does she ever see that husband of hers?"

"She is in New York."

"New York is the source of all trouble. My husband often says that. People here disapprove of your daughter, even more than they do her brother."

"They are both committed."

Agnes sighed in exasperation.

"I think they have made that plain."

She sipped her coffee.

"Is all that agreed?" she asked.

Thomas behaved impeccably at Elisabeth's wedding in November. He shook Borgese's hand and kissed the bride in full view of those who attended the service in the church on the Princeton campus.

The only irritant had been Auden, who had written a poem for the occasion that Thomas had scarcely understood, and then after the ceremony, while walking with Thomas back to the house on Stockton Street, had remarked, as they spotted Klaus ahead of them: "For an author, sons are an embarrassment. It must be as if characters in one of your novels had come to life. You know, I rather like Klaus, but some people call him the Subordinate Klaus, but that is too cruel, far too cruel."

Thomas was not quite sure what this meant, but he avoided Auden for the rest of the day.

Katia had warned Erika to be kind to Elisabeth and say nothing that would cause even the slightest offense. Erika had told her parents that a friend of hers had seen Elisabeth in New York dining with a man whom the friend presumed was the man she was soon to marry.

"It was all candles and whispering and romance," Erika said. "Until my friend went over to congratulate them and found that the man was none other than Hermann Broch. They were most upset at being seen together. Elisabeth obviously likes elderly émigré writers. If she had just stayed at home with her father, who is chief among them, then she could have saved us all a lot of trouble."

"She is in love with Borgese," Katia had said. "I am sure your friend was entirely mistaken."

For Christmas, Thomas had asked that Elisabeth and her husband be placed on the attic floor of the house so that he would not have to encounter Borgese in the corridor near his bedroom.

On the first morning, lying in bed, he heard Borgese in a room above clearing his throat loudly and coughing, and then a tap being turned on. He realized that the bathroom assigned to the newly married couple was the one directly above his own bedroom. At first, it was just the noise of the tap, but soon the unmistakable sound of a man urinating into a toilet bowl and doing so with some vehemence and at some length came to him through the floorboards.

The image of Borgese feeling free in this regard nauseated him. Even when he heard the toilet being flushed, he could not get the picture out of his mind of Borgese standing in his night attire urinating. His own sons, he thought, had always been discreet in the bathroom. This Italian, it seemed, was only too ready to make his presence felt.

On the second morning of their stay, when Thomas was in his study, Borgese knocked on the door and came in to have, as he said, a little chat with Thomas, adding that he was at a loose end since the women had gone shopping. He asked Thomas if he would like tea. Thomas wondered what he should do.

In the four hours before lunch, going back over a period of thirty-five years, he had remained fully undisturbed in his study. Now this man was sitting on the chair opposite him, asking him again if he wanted tea and then inquiring casually if his work was progressing as planned, as though Thomas's writing were something that could benefit from such a query. When Thomas did not reply to either question, Borgese took up a book from the table and began to flick through the pages.

"What do you think will happen in France?" Borgese asked him.

"I have no idea," Thomas said, barely looking up.

"I think the Germans will wait to invade until the spring or early summer. But invade they will. Mark my words. Invade they will. And they will get through."

Thomas glanced up at him sharply.

"Who has told you this?" he asked.

"It is a feeling I have," Borgese said. "But I am sure I am right."

As Thomas studied Borgese, it struck him that Elisabeth must really be well tired of him by now. He wished she and her mother and Erika would return from shopping so that this old man could be quickly ejected from his study and told never to return.

On Christmas Eve, as the table was being prepared for supper, he heard Erika talking loudly to Klaus on the phone in the hallway.

"You must go to Penn Station now and be on the next train. I will be at Princeton Junction waiting. No, the next train! I don't care who you are with. You can miss supper, but you must be here for the opening of the presents. I have bought your presents for you. That's what I said I would do. They are all wrapped. You don't have to worry. Klaus, I said now!"

When the phone rang again a few moments later, he heard Erika telling Klaus once more she would be at the train to meet him and he must not worry about missing supper.

As time for supper came near, and the family got ready, the house was quiet and the smells from the kitchen wafted through the rooms. Approaching the drawing room, Thomas heard the sound of someone moving within. Katia was standing with her back to him at the Christmas tree. She was gently rearranging the decorations, and then bending down to make the piles of presents assembled under the tree more orderly. She did not realize he was watching her. He knew that the news that Klaus was arriving after supper and would be with them the next day had come as a relief to her.

He thought of clearing his throat or making some sound, but he decided instead to withdraw, to go to his study until he was called to the table. Katia would, he thought, be more content alone like this. He would talk to her later, when the night was over. He would put the good champagne he had been saving in the refrigerator. The two of them would, he hoped, raise a quiet glass to each other at the end of the night, when everyone else had finally gone to bed.

Chapter 12
Princeton, 1940

When the telephone rang, no one answered it. Katia and Gret had taken Frido, just six weeks old, for a walk. Michael had found three young musicians in Princeton and had taken his viola with him to meet them. And the woman who came to cook and clean had not arrived yet. When the ringing continued, Thomas went to answer, but it rang out before he got there.

Calls often came from the university, asking him to attend dinners or receptions. Katia had a special way of dealing with such requests. Among their own people, only Klaus in New York, Elisabeth in Chicago, Agnes Meyer in Washington and the Knopfs in New York had the Princeton telephone number. They could, he thought, always call again.

Before lunch, he was upstairs changing his shoes when the phone rang once more; he heard Katia answering it. He listened as she intoned the number in her best, most studied accent in English. Then she did not say anything for a while. Suddenly he heard her issue a loud gasp before she repeated several times: "Who are you? How do you know this?"

By the time he reached her, Michael and Gret were already by her side. When he tried to speak, Katia brushed him away with her hand.

"Where are you phoning from?" she asked the caller.

"I have never heard of that newspaper," she then said. "I have never been in Toronto. I am a German woman and I live in Princeton."

When Michael moved to take the receiver from her, his mother ignored him.

"Yes, my daughter is Mrs. Lányi, yes, Mrs. Monika Lányi. Yes, her husband is Mr. Jenö Lányi. Could you speak more slowly?"

She gasped again.

"The *City of Benares*? Yes, that is the ship. But we have firm news that it set out safely. It is going to Quebec."

Impatiently, she motioned to the others to step farther away from her.

"But we have had no news of that. Someone would have contacted us if anything had happened."

She listened intently to the reply.

"Can I ask you to tell me something clearly," she said more loudly. "If you do not know, say so. Is my daughter alive?"

She took in what was said carefully, nodding her head. She looked gravely at Thomas.

"Is her husband alive?"

Thomas watched the expression on Katia's face harden.

"Are you sure?" she asked.

She became irritated with the caller.

"What are you saying? Do I have any comment? Are you asking me if I have any comment? No, I have no comment, and no, my husband has no comment either. No, he is not here."

Thomas could hear the voice of the caller still speaking as Katia put the receiver down.

"A man from a newspaper in Toronto," she said. "Monika is alive. The boat was torpedoed. Monika was in the water for a long time. But he is dead, her Jenö is dead."

"Did the ship sink?" Michael asked.

"What do you think happened? Monika's ship was torpedoed

by the Germans. We should have made her take the journey earlier when it would have been safer."

"But she is safe," Gret said.

"That is what the man says," Katia replied. "But Jenö has drowned. In the middle of the Atlantic. The man was certain about it. He knew their names."

"Why has no one else phoned?" Michael asked.

"Because the news is fresh. It won't be fresh for long and then the phone will ring forever."

She moved toward Thomas and stood beside him.

"How strange it is that we are not prepared for this," she said. "How strange that we are surprised."

They should telephone Elisabeth immediately, Katia added, to let her know the news before someone else called her. Erika should be sent a telegram in London asking her to help her sister in whatever way she could, although they were not sure whether Monika had been taken to Canada or had been returned to England.

When asked what to do about Klaus, Katia sighed. They had not heard from him in some time. She had phoned the hotel in New York where Klaus had been staying but was told that he had left. Thomas suggested that she try to contact him using Auden's address.

When Michael left to send the telegrams, Thomas and Katia decided to get some air. They would call Elisabeth later.

They walked in the grounds of the university in the soft autumn weather.

"Imagine being in the middle of the ocean," Katia said, "holding on to a plank for twelve hours. Imagine seeing your husband sinking in front of you and not coming up again."

"Is that what the Canadian told you?"

"That is what he said. I will never get it out of my mind. How will Monika ever recover from that?"

"We should have taken her with us when we sailed from South-ampton."

"She had no visa for the U.S."

"I presumed that once the ship sailed, she was safe. I actually felt relieved."

Katia stopped for a moment and bowed her head.

"That is how I felt too. And how foolish it was!"

In the morning there was a reply from Erika saying that Monika would be taken to Scotland and Erika would locate her there and see that she was being well looked after. The telegram added that she did not know where Klaus was. Before lunchtime, there was a telegram from Auden saying that he would seek to contact Klaus.

Elisabeth phoned a number of times during the day and spoke to her mother and her father.

Each time the phone rang, all of them became alert to the possibility of news and listened closely from doorways. Although the news that Monika had been on the ship had appeared in the newspapers, no one from Princeton called them or came to the house. It was as if they had brought the war with them to this peaceful university town.

Before dinner, as they gathered in the sitting room, Michael asked them if he could play something. He introduced it as the viola part of a slow movement from a quartet by Arnold Schoenberg. As he began to play, Thomas thought, it sounded like a set of cries pitted against a much more implacable sound, a sound that he could barely manage to listen to, it was so intense.

A few days later a telegram arrived from Erika in London: "Monika recovering. Will stay in Scotland. Weak. Klaus safe in New York. Sad."

"I presume she means that Monika is weak and Klaus is sad," Michael said.

Within an hour another cable had arrived, this time from Golo.

"Sailing on *Nea Hellas* from Lisbon to New York on 3 October. With Heinrich and Nelly and the Werfels. Varian a star."

"Who are the Werfels?" Michael asked.

"Alma Mahler is married to Franz Werfel. He is her third husband," Thomas said.

"She will be marvelous company," Katia said. "Better, I imagine, than Nelly. I was hoping Nelly would have found some other refuge."

"I presume that the Werfels will have somewhere to go once they arrive," Thomas said.

"I presume that too," Katia said.

"Who is Varian the star?" Michael asked.

"He is Varian Fry from the Emergency Rescue Committee," Thomas said. "He has done all the work to get them out. He is a most extraordinary young man. Even Agnes Meyer praises his efficiency and his cunning."

Thomas glanced at Katia and realized that she was having the same thoughts. Since the Germans were attacking transatlantic shipping, then they could also direct their malice against whatever ship Golo and Heinrich and Nelly traveled on. It made a difference, he supposed, that the *City of Benares* had been on its way to Canada. The Germans would feel less ready, he felt, to attack a ship on its way to New York. But the sinking of Monika's ship made the Atlantic seem more dangerous. The sigh of relief that Golo and the others were safe would have to wait until they had actually arrived in New York Harbor and disembarked. He hoped that Golo had not heard that Monika had been on the *City of Benares*.

They decided to go to New York and stay in the Bedford for a night before meeting Golo, Heinrich and Nelly from the ship and taking them to Princeton.

When Thomas said that he wanted to arrive by lunchtime, Katia expressed surprise that he was ready to break his morning work schedule.

"I want to buy some records," he said.

"Add something to surprise me," she said.

"Give me a clue."

"Haydn, maybe," she said. "Some quartets or his piano music. That would be nice, and they do no harm."

"Is that why you want them?"

She smiled.

"They remind me of summer."

"I felt ice in the wind today," Thomas said, "and thought it would be good to live somewhere warmer."

"Michael and Gret and the baby are moving to the west coast. And Heinrich will be in Los Angeles."

"And Nelly?" Thomas asked.

"Do not mention Nelly. I dread the thought of sharing a roof with her."

After lunch at the Bedford, Thomas made his way alone by taxi downtown, instructing the driver to let him off at Sixth Avenue so that he could walk the few streets to the store. In Princeton, he was generally on his guard, aware that he would be noticed and recognized everywhere. Here, however, in these narrow streets that reminded him of some European city, he could let his gaze linger freely on anyone at all. While most of those he passed were preoccupied and distant, eventually, he knew, he would see some young man coming towards him and, catching his eye for a second, become unafraid to look at him directly and deeply, not disguising his interest.

The teeming commercial life of the street had its own sensuality. He could idle at shop windows, or bathe in the general busyness, stepping aside as goods were delivered from a truck to a store. Most people in these streets were men. Thomas derived such pleasure from observing them that he almost passed the record store without realizing.

He remembered on his previous visit to the shop that he was like a child surrounded by things that he dearly wanted, an almost unimaginable richness of them. And he recalled too the close attention that the owner and his assistant, both English, had paid to him.

The stirring of desire that had occurred on the street found a focus now among thousands of records that he could choose from.

Even though a bell rang when he opened the door, no one appeared for some time. He noticed how cluttered the big square room was, with boxes of records piled up everywhere. When the owner emerged from an inner room wearing, Thomas thought, the same loose-fitting gray suit as he had on the first time Thomas had come to the shop, they both looked at each other and said nothing. The man must be half his age but this did not lessen the connection. As he glanced around again, he was sure that there were many more records here than on his previous visit.

"Why all this?" Thomas asked, indicating the extent of the merchandise on display.

"Business has never been as good as it is now. It means that America will soon be at war. People are stocking up with music for the war."

"Cheerful music?"

"No, they want everything. From opera buffa to requiems."

Thomas looked at the man's full-blooded lips against the whiteness of his face. He seemed amused about the war. Thomas wondered where his assistant was.

He turned and began to examine a shelf of records.

"Those are not for you," the man said. "Unless you have suddenly become interested in swing."

"Swing?"

"They used to help pay the bills, but now they are only in the way. It is all Bach Masses and cello music and Schubert songs. I have a man who is collecting all the recordings of Hugo Wolf songs. A year ago, I had one Wolf record here that had spent five years gathering dust."

"I never warmed to Wolf."

"An interesting life, nonetheless. Composers have more interesting lives than writers. I can't think why that should be. Unless yours is interesting."

He was reminding Thomas that he knew exactly who he was.

"Buxtehude?" Thomas asked.

"No change there. Just the boring organ music. No one has made a recording of the vocal music. I expected *Membra Jesu Nostri* to appear, but there is no sign whatsoever of it. I sang in it, you know."

"Where?"

"Durham Cathedral."

His assistant now appeared.

"I have a friend who went to one of your lectures in Princeton," the assistant said without any greeting.

Thomas took in his rosy cheeks and his blond hair.

"I don't think we have been introduced by name," he said.

"Henry," both the owner and Henry himself said at the same time.

"Are you both called Henry?"

"He is Adrian," Henry said, pointing to the owner.

The owner's gaze was even more ironic and penetrating now that he had been named.

"Schoenberg?" Thomas asked.

"Is all the rage," Adrian replied. "Last week an old couple of deep Episcopalians came in here and bought *Pelleas und Melisande*."

"We have a new box of records with the lieder, what's it called?" Henry said.

"*Gurrelieder*. Fourteen records."

"What else do you have by him?"

"Quite a lot. He is almost popular."

"Can you deliver any records I buy to my hotel?"

"When?"

"My wife and I are at the Bedford until tomorrow morning."

"They can be delivered by the end of the day."

"There is a contralto aria from *Samson and Delilah*."

"'Mon coeur,'" Henry said in a perfect French accent.

"Yes, that."

"Just the aria, or the entire opera?" Adrian asked.

"Just the aria."

"We'll find something good."

"And I have a recording of Beethoven Opus 132 but it is scratched. I would like another."

"I also favor Opus 131," Adrian said.

"I have a reason for wanting 132."

"I have a number of recordings. Why don't I include what I deem to be the best?"

"Yes, I can write you a check now. Maybe I should take all the late quartets and some Haydn and Mozart quartets and a *Magic Flute*. I presume I get a reduction for buying in bulk."

"Is bulk a German concept?" Adrian asked.

When the amount owed was agreed on and a check was written, Adrian accompanied Thomas to the door.

"Does your wife always stay with you when you are in New York?" he asked.

"Not always," Thomas replied.

As he shook Adrian's hand, he saw that the record seller was blushing. It occurred to him that he himself was too old for his blushes to be fully apparent, but he hoped that he had shown how stirred he felt nonetheless.

• • •

The next day they ordered two cars to wait for them at the docks. It was a warm October day as they set out walking through the crowds. Thomas was relieved that there was no large group of journalists to greet Alma Mahler and Franz Werfel. He had been reading a volume of the letters between Gustav Mahler and his wife and had found Alma's epistolary style unconstrained by any form of reserve. It would be best, he felt, if the New York press were spared a sample of her tone.

"My mother loved her," Katia said, "but then, she loved anyone who was famous. I can't imagine Alma Mahler traveling with that Nelly. But maybe Heinrich and Golo made peace between them. I still don't understand how all five ended up traveling together."

"Neither do I," Thomas said. "They must have met Alma and Werfel in France and decided to exit together."

They asked several passengers if they had sailed on the *Nea Hellas* and were assured that the ship had docked an hour earlier.

"It's her luggage that is delaying her," Thomas said. "Alma Mahler will have luggage."

"And Nelly, your sister-in-law," Katia said, "is bound to have said something untoward to a customs official."

When the crowds thinned out, they moved close to the door from which passengers emerged. Eventually, led by Golo, all five appeared, and Thomas was shocked at how old and tired Heinrich seemed and how disgruntled Franz Werfel was. Nelly, on the other hand, looked like someone's young and flighty daughter.

Alma Mahler moved ahead to embrace Thomas and Katia. As the others offered hugs and kisses or shook hands, Golo stood aside.

"All I want is a hot bath, a pink gin, and a good piano tuner waiting beside a baby grand," Alma said, addressing the wider air and the city of New York itself as much as Thomas and Katia. "But I will start with the hot bath. Why is the hotel maid not running it now?"

"I would like so to join you," Nelly said, touching Alma's shoulder. "Yes, a hot bath!"

"Well, you won't be joining me. I can assure you: of all the unlikely things that might occur in New York during our stay that will not be one of them."

Nelly tried to smile.

"I have had quite enough of you," Alma continued. "We all have had our fill of you."

She turned to Heinrich.

"Tell this Nelly woman to be off with herself. There will be plenty, I'm sure, for someone like her to do in New York."

Thomas noticed Golo watching him intently as Alma edged towards Werfel and cradled her head against him, putting one hand around his neck while holding an old leather briefcase firmly in the other hand. She began to purr in satisfaction as she snuggled in close to him.

"It is so good to be safe," she said.

"I think it is time we all went to the cars," Katia said. "We have two cars waiting. Your luggage can come later. We asked one of the drivers to arrange that with the shipping office."

"We don't have any luggage," Heinrich said. "Just what you see here."

He pointed to a few small shabby-looking cases.

"We lost everything," Nelly said.

Having examined the suitcases, Thomas saw that Nelly's stockings were torn and one of her shoes had a loose heel. Werfel's shoes were coming apart. When he glanced up again, Golo was still staring at him. He stepped towards him and embraced him.

"A man from the New York Philharmonic," Alma said, "promised to meet us. He has reserved a hotel for us. And if he does not materialize in the next thirty seconds, his orchestra can say goodbye to performing Gustav's music ever again."

Moving towards the cars, they found a man with a sign with the word "Mahler" written on it.

"That is me," Alma said to the man. "And that also would have been me, a better-humored me, if you had placed yourself at a more convenient spot. This convinces me more than ever that America might be well advised to keep out of the war. It would be more of a hindrance than a help."

Katia indicated to Thomas that they should hurry to the cars.

Alma walked along by his side.

"Don't pay any attention to the stiffness and antisocial pouting of that son of yours. He just did not believe we would ever make it. There have been such adventures."

She linked her arm with Thomas's.

"Everybody likes Golo," Alma went on. "Even though he does nothing to deserve it. He doesn't talk and he doesn't even smile. But no one seems to mind all that. The waiters on the ship liked him. The border guards liked him. Complete strangers liked him. Even that dreadful Nelly likes him. Now I hope I have seen her off. It would take me a week to go through all the elements of her ghastliness. And Heinrich, on the other hand, is so sensible. But we all have our moments of madness. Thus, Heinrich married Nelly. And look at me, marrying all these Jews."

Katia, who was walking ahead, having heard the last remark, looked behind her in alarm.

Alma let out a large laugh.

Once they reached the cars, Alma and Werfel promised to come and visit soon in Princeton. Before saying goodbye to all of the others, Alma kissed Thomas on the lips.

When the Alma car, with the disconsolate man from the Philharmonic in the front passenger seat, had pulled away, Heinrich said that he would like to travel to Princeton with Thomas and Katia, and perhaps Nelly and Golo would follow in the car behind.

As soon as they had gone through the Holland Tunnel, it became clear to Thomas why Heinrich had wanted to be alone with them.

"I want to rescue Mimi and Goschi," he said.

Heinrich's daughter Goschi must be, Thomas thought, in her early twenties.

"Where are they?" Thomas asked.

"They are still in Prague."

"What are their circumstances?"

"Things are closing in on people like them. Mimi is Jewish, and they will also be singled out because of me. I have had desperate messages from Mimi, messages that Nelly doesn't know about. I spoke to Varian Fry about it, and he said I should speak to you. He seems to think you have great power."

Thomas knew that it would not be easy to help his brother's ex-wife and his daughter.

"If you give me all their details, then I will make representations. But I'm not sure—"

"Sometimes," Katia interrupted, "things happen very slowly and then very quickly. So you mustn't worry."

Thomas wished that she had not said that. It suggested that something really could be done for Mimi and Goschi.

"How long is it since you have seen Mimi?" Thomas asked.

"It is a while," Heinrich said. "I should have known all this was coming ten years ago. I warned everyone else."

"We are lucky to be here," Katia said.

"I am too old to change country," Heinrich said. "And I was too old to stay in France. We learned that they came for us the day after we left the hotel. They missed us by a day."

"The French police?"

"No, the Germans. We would have been taken straight to the homeland. You write your books, little novels, and you make some speeches, and then you become a golden prize for fascists. The horror is that I led Nelly into this, and that I have abandoned Mimi and Goschi."

They told Golo about Monika as soon as they arrived. He kept coming back to the image of her husband drowning in front of her.

"You have just been through that journey," Katia said. "You might be the best to write to her. We have all written, but Erika says that the poor child still can't sleep or settle and she cries out all the time."

"I would cry all the time too," Golo said. "The idea of being torpedoed! It is unimaginable."

Before supper, Golo found Thomas in his study.

"Is America going to declare war?" he asked.

"There is strong opposition to war here," Thomas said. "Maybe the bombing of London will change that, but I am not sure."

"They have to join. Have you made your position clear?"

Thomas looked at him quizzically.

"You have been silent again?" Golo asked.

"I am biding my time."

He was on the point of saying that he had not wanted to risk the safe passage of Golo and Heinrich and Nelly by criticizing the American government, but he presumed that Golo might realize that.

"Why has no one mentioned Klaus?"

"He is in New York."

"Why did he not come to meet us?"

"He has not been in contact for some time. He moves from hotel to hotel. When your mother tried to locate him, she did not succeed."

• • •

Thomas had forgotten how close Michael, now twenty-one, was to Golo, ten years his senior. As soon as Golo arrived, the two huddled together, ignoring everyone else. When they were joined by Gret and the baby, Golo put his arm around his sister-in-law and then examined the baby with a look of pride and good humor. He asked to be allowed to hold the child, and once he had little Frido in his arms he rocked him back and forth.

With the baby fast asleep in the other room, Thomas watched Golo speaking attentively to Gret over supper to make sure that she did not feel left out. He was, Thomas thought, the considerate one, the dutiful son, the one who looked after Monika when his mother was recovering from her time in the sanatorium, when his father, preoccupied by the war, was writing a book, and when Erika and Klaus were doing whatever they pleased.

"The best thing about Princeton," Michael said, "is that our father has access to the library. He can take out any number of books. The German holdings are good."

Katia encouraged Michael and Gret to go out for lunch the next day, leaving her with Frido. She forbade Golo to lift him out of his cot.

"How will I get to know him if I don't lift him up?"

"Your father likes to sit staring at him. That is what he does if we can get Michael and Gret out of the room."

"Does that not frighten the poor child?" Golo asked.

"Unlike other members of the family," Thomas said, "Frido is sweet-natured."

"All the more reason why I want to lift him up," Golo replied.

He bent down and whispered into the cot.

"I am your uncle who has been rescued from the Nazis."

"Don't say that word in front of the baby!" Katia said.

"I am your uncle who is back in the bosom of his family."

Thomas waited for Michael and Gret and the baby to leave for New York before he unpacked the new records. When he put on the Schoenberg, it was even more affecting than the music that Michael had played on the viola. He wished he had the sheet music so that he could see what was happening technically. Usually, when he bought something new, Katia would stay in the room to listen, but this time she came to the doorway for a few moments and then went back to the kitchen.

In the days that followed, it rained and the house was noisy. Nelly, instead of staying in her room, looked for someone to talk to. Thomas was amused at how skilled Katia was at avoiding any lengthy engagement with her. If Thomas himself heard Nelly's heels on the floorboards, he did not emerge from his study; Nelly had been warned by Katia not to disturb him under any circumstances. When she joined Golo a number of times and flicked through the pile of books he kept close to him, Golo moved himself and his books to the attic.

After a while, Nelly was found talking to the servants.

When Franz Werfel phoned, Thomas invited him and Alma to dinner. The news that they had accepted was met with a groan from Heinrich, Nelly and Golo.

"We were having a very peaceful time," Golo said.

"It will be good for us all," Katia said, "to be on our best behavior."

Alma was dressed all in white, with an expensive string of pearls around her neck. Werfel walked behind her. He looked to Thomas like someone who believed that he was soon to be deported.

Alma began to talk even before her first drink arrived.

"It has been hectic in New York. Night after night. Lunch after lunch. Outing after outing. In Vienna, as you know, I am famous because of my first husband, but in New York they are familiar with my own work, my songs especially. I mean, not everyone, but people in the know. And they flock to our hotel. Puddings here is exhausted."

She pointed to Werfel.

When the drinks came, she stood up.

"Now I need to see your study," she said to Thomas. "I always like to see where my men do their work."

As he passed Katia on his way to the study, she gave him a look as if to say that she was impressed by the quality of the company he was keeping.

"Oh, this is marvelous," Alma said. "And the door seems strong. American doors are often made of the cheapest wood. You need good doors, what with that Nelly."

Thomas felt he should change the subject.

"I met you and Mahler just before he died," Thomas said. "I don't know if you remember. I attended rehearsals of his Eighth Symphony in Munich."

"I knew you then. Or I knew you to see. You and your wife were fixtures at the opera in Munich. Everyone pointed you out. He felt lucky that you came. I always call that Eighth Symphony the Apple Symphony, as it is filled with apple blossom and apple pie. And plenty of cinnamon and sugar with all those choirs. I had no peace during that time."

"I thought it was a remarkable work."

She approached him and held his hand and then stood with her back to the door. She seemed to be excited.

"And it struck me then," she went on, "that we could have made a real match, you and I. I would have loved a proper German to marry, someone outward-looking, as you are, not in a permanent state of gloomy introspection, like Gustav and Werfel. Even Gropius, although he wasn't Jewish. Thousands of years of sadness can wear one down eventually."

Thomas thought that perhaps he should warn her not to repeat these views in public anywhere in New York.

"And I would love keeping house for you," she went on. "I

always thought you were more handsome than your brother. And now that I am close to you, I feel even more certain about you."

The gallant thing to do might be to say something in return. Instead, he tried to make sure that he would remember every word she said so that he could recount it later to Katia.

At the table, Alma spoke freely, hopping from one topic to another.

"I think people who say they are sick have a duty to actually be sick," she said. "If Gustav had a pimple on his nose, he was sure it was the end. And I suppose he had the courage of his convictions since he died young. He was, indeed, sick. But it did come as a shock because he was sick so many times before he was really sick."

Thomas thought how strange it was that she should speak of Mahler in this way. Thirty years after his death, he was already among the pantheon of great composers. Alma spoke of him in such a casual way as this helpless creature to whom she had been married. He studied the light in her eyes. She must have brightened up Mahler's life with her darting, chirping talk.

"Gustav used to go silent as you have just done. It was an energetic silence. And when I asked him what he was thinking of, he would reply: 'Notes, quavers.' What are you thinking of?"

"Words, sentences," Thomas said.

"Puddings and I want you and Katia to come and live in Los Angeles. That is where we have decided to settle. Puddings is going to write screenplays, or at least that is the idea. And we have gone through a list of everyone there and, except for the Schoenbergs, there is no one to talk to."

"What are the Schoenbergs like?" Thomas asked as a way of distracting attention from the fact that Heinrich and Nelly, also planning to live in Los Angeles, were not on Alma's list of people to talk to.

"They are pure Vienna."

"What do you mean by that?"

"He cares only about his music. Nothing else matters. Oh, except posterity. He cares about that too, and so does she. They are single-minded people and everything they say is interesting. That is Vienna."

Across the table Thomas noticed that one of the straps of Nelly's dress had slipped from her shoulder, making part of her brassiere visible. Just as he found that Alma Mahler's provocative tone reminded him of a Germany he had lost, he was intrigued by Nelly's brashness. Whereas Alma was like the young bohemian women in those cafés in Munich, Nelly had carried with her across the Atlantic the tone of German women who worked in shops or bars, a tone that was flirtatious but also had an edge of contempt, a tone that suggested its owner could see through most forms of pretension.

He listened to the accents of the two women in the same way as he might have eaten different kinds of food that came from his childhood.

"I am longing for some California sunshine," Nelly said. "Aren't we all? Los Angeles will be filled with cars, and I adore cars. People talk of America as exciting. Well, they haven't been in Princeton, that is all I have to say! Last week I really would have liked a drink. Not just a drink, but a drink in a bar. So I went down the road. And what did I find? Not a bar in sight. I asked a man and he told me that there were no bars in Princeton. Can you believe that?"

"You went out on your own looking for a bar?" Alma asked.

"Yes."

"In Vienna, we have names for a woman who does that."

Nelly stood up and moved slowly out of the room, leaving her food half-finished.

"Of all of the Second Viennese School composers," Alma said, addressing Thomas directly, "the most talented and original is

Webern. But, of course, he is the one who isn't Jewish so he gets the least attention."

"But he hasn't written an opera," Golo said.

"Because no one has asked him to. Why haven't they asked him to? Because he is not Jewish!"

Katia put her two hands on the table and sighed loudly. Both Heinrich and Werfel looked uncomfortable.

"My wife," Werfel said, "when she has some drinks, likes to speak ill of the Jewish race. I was hoping she would not carry this with her to America."

From the other room, there came a crash. The needle of the record player had landed on a piece of metal and, since the volume had been turned up high, the noise was unbearable. Soon there was a jagged scratching as the needle was placed carelessly on a record and the sound of a jazz melody went through the house.

Katia shouted: "Turn that off!" as Nelly came into the dining room with a drink in her hand.

"I decided to put some oomph into the evening," she said.

She walked unsteadily to the back of Heinrich's chair and put her arms around his neck.

"I love my Heinri," she said.

Katia went into the other room and turned off the record player.

"I think it is time my wife went to bed," Heinrich said.

He stood up with some difficulty, as though he were in pain, and took Nelly's drink from her, leaving it on the table. And then he caught her hand and kissed her on the side of the face before they both proceeded out of the room without saying good night to anyone.

Their steps could be heard on the stairs as they made their way to the floor above.

"As I was saying," Alma said, as if she had been interrupted, "I

have simply never warmed to Schumann. I don't like his symphonies. I don't like his piano music. I don't like his quartets. And,
more than anything, I don't like his songs. And I believe that you
can always judge a composer by his songs. My husband's songs
were exquisite, as were Schubert's. And I love some of the French
songs. And the English songs. And there are a few Russian songs.
But nothing by Schumann."

"My parents loved his *Dichterliebe*," Katia said. "It was often
played in our house. I would love to hear it again."

Golo began to recite:

> "From my tears burst
> Many full-blown flowers,
> And my sighs become
> A nightingale chorus."

"Ah, Heine," Alma said, "he was a wonderful poet, and how
clever Schumann was to use him. But it does not sing to me, sighs
or no sighs. If Los Angeles is free of Schumann, as I think it is
likely to be, then I will be a happy woman."

There was no mention of Nelly's putting on the record. Alma
and Werfel left when the car Thomas had ordered came for them.
They made the Manns promise they would consider moving to
California and living near them.

"But no Schumann, mind!" Alma shouted. "No Schumann."

She sang the opening of one of his songs while getting into
the car.

As Golo prepared to go to his room, Katia asked him and
Thomas to follow her into the dining room, where they could
close the door and not be easily heard.

"I have three words for her," Katia said. "And I cannot think
of the shame that will be brought on this house when news leaks
out, as it will, that Mrs. Heinrich Mann was seen wandering alone

on the streets of Princeton looking for a bar. She is a trollop and she is a slattern and she is a barmaid. And to make matters worse, she put on a display tonight in front of Alma Mahler. I don't know what Alma will think of us."

"Alma had her own moments," Golo said.

"She has always been larger than life," Katia said. "But she has been through so much."

"You mean, losing her two husbands?" Golo asked.

"She was devoted to Mahler, as far as I know," Thomas said.

"Well, it will be a while before she agrees to come to our house again," Katia said. "We were so looking forward to having them. You know, it's lonely here, Golo!"

The next morning Thomas was in his study when Katia opened the door and closed it behind her. She looked worried. She had just dropped Heinrich and Nelly at the station so they could go to New York to buy clothes. Thomas presumed that she was coming to tell him something Nelly had done.

"No, it's not Nelly, it's Golo. I had a cup of tea with him just now and he said things that I thought you should hear. I have asked him to wait in the morning room."

Golo, who was reading a book, did not look up when his parents came into the room, even though Thomas was sure he must have heard them.

"I didn't seek all this drama," Golo said. "My mother asked me what I thought of last night and I felt that I had no choice but to let her know."

His tone, Thomas noted, was like that of a much older person, perhaps even a clergyman. He sat in an armchair with his legs crossed and looked at them both severely.

"You don't know the details of how we got out of France

because none of us wants to go over them," Golo said. "But there are things you should know. When we met Werfel and Alma, she had twenty-three suitcases. Twenty-three! She, Werfel and the suitcases had been in Lourdes. Her sole preoccupation seemed to be the fate of those suitcases. When Varian Fry told her that she would probably have to walk over the Pyrenees and should try to make herself as invisible as possible, she asked him who would take her suitcases."

He stared into the distance before he began again.

"In a briefcase, the one she had with her when she disembarked, Frau Mahler had the original score of Bruckner's Third Symphony and a lock of Beethoven's hair that had once been presented to her husband. I don't know what she intended to do with the hair, but I know what plans she had for the Bruckner. She wanted to sell it to Hitler. And Hitler wanted to buy it. When I say Hitler, I mean Adolf Hitler. They had even fixed on a price. The issue was that she wanted cash and the German embassy in Paris did not have enough cash to satisfy her. But she was ready to sell it to Hitler, who remains concerned, apparently, about the fate of Bruckner's papers."

"Surely that was just a story she told?" Thomas said.

"Ask her. She will show you the correspondence," Golo replied. "She feels no shame. And she felt no shame on the journey from France into Spain, which was more arduous than any of us had foreseen. It involved climbing sheer rock. Our guides were nervous. I was never sure they were not taking us on a circuitous route so we could be arrested before anyone knew. We were all wearing the wrong clothes but Alma looked as if she were going to some ball. Her white dress looked like a flag of surrender to be seen billowing for miles. Once we set out, she began to scream that she wanted to go back. She called Werfel names. Her names for Jewish people were worthy of an Austrian."

Golo stopped and stared at them both. While Thomas, for a moment, had thought he was holding back tears, he now saw that he was fully collected.

"It is appalling," Golo said, "that we had to be in Alma's company last night. On that journey over the Pyrenees, Nelly could not have been more kind and more careful. She loves Heinrich, she really does, and she made that obvious all the time. She even helped me to lift him and at times carry him when he was too weak to go on. She was so sweet to him. As we rested, she reassured him. She is a most graceful, tender person. On the journey by ship as my uncle lay in his cabin making drawings of women, Nelly told me that he had actually left her behind when he fled from Berlin to France. He left her to take money from his bank account and settle his affairs, all of which put her in grave danger. She was even arrested at one point and was lucky to escape. Alma, in the meantime, was still worried about her luggage. Varian Fry crossed the border with some of it, which she then sent separately to New York from Barcelona. Varian was infinitely patient with her on the luggage question, as he was wise all the time in how he saved us. In the future, the world should know what he did, just how brave he was. But now, here in this house, I insist that what Nelly did should also be understood and her warm heart suitably appreciated. I do not want to hear her being called a trollop or a slattern or any other word. She is a good woman. I want that to be known. Yes, she was indeed a barmaid, and I trust that, since we are in exile now, we have not brought with us the snobbery that so maimed our lives when we lived in Munich."

Thomas decided to leave it to Katia to respond, but when she remained silent, he saw that he had to speak.

"I'm sure Nelly is very fine. And she is a member of the family," he said.

"As long as that is fully understood," Golo said. "I insist that she be treated with respect."

Thomas was tempted to ask Golo under whose roof he was living. Who had arranged his safety? Who was supporting him as he read library books? And he wanted to ask him further in what way his life in Munich had been maimed?

Instead, he gazed at him coldly and then smiled in a forced way. He led Katia from the morning room back to his study. They closed the door and sat in silence until Katia eventually departed, leaving Thomas alone to continue his morning's work.

Chapter 13
Pacific Palisades, 1941

When Monika arrived in Princeton from England, neither Thomas nor Katia was sure how to console her. On seeing her first, Thomas had expected someone broken, shocked, still suffering. He took her close to him and hugged her. He was ready to say how unimaginably terrible her ordeal must have been, and how tragic her loss. But as he was preparing to speak, she cried out: "This house is far too big. It's another example of our family. I wish we had a smaller house. A house like other people have. Mother, could we please have a smaller house?"

"In time, my dear," Katia said. "In time."

"I suppose there are servants?" Monika asked. "While the world is at war, the Manns have servants."

Katia did not reply.

"I have been dreaming about a kitchen. A refrigerator filled with food."

"I am sure there is food," Katia said.

"Are you not tired?" Thomas asked her. He wished Elisabeth were here, or even Michael and Gret. It was typical, he thought, of Michael not to be where he might be useful.

When Golo appeared in the doorway, his sister recoiled from him.

"Don't approach me. Don't hug me," she said. "My father has

just done that. It was like being embraced by a dead trout. It will take me years to recover."

"Worse than being torpedoed in the Atlantic?" Golo asked.

"Much worse!" Monika said and began to shriek with laughter. "I need to be rescued. Help me. Send for the fire brigade. Mother, do they have fire brigades in America?"

"Yes, they do," Katia said calmly.

As Thomas got ready to leave Princeton and abandon this world of bare trees and scarce sunlight, the prospect of moving house again, perhaps for the last time, excited him.

Once he had announced his decision to leave the university, fewer invitations for lunch or dinner arrived. His refusal to accept Princeton's hospitality was seen by his colleagues as a sort of betrayal, and they did not want him, a prize example of their concern for what was happening in Germany, in their homes as much as they had before. Katia told him that she felt the same when she encountered their wives.

He was amused at the suggestion that he was moving to some great American wilderness. On their visits to Los Angeles, he and Katia had noted how cheap it was to buy or rent a house near the ocean, how spacious the gardens and how glorious the weather.

Every report they received on the city was good. Heinrich and Nelly had found it easy to rent a house and a car. Even though he was having trouble with Warner Brothers, which had no interest in any of his ideas for films, Heinrich wrote to say that he felt some days he had arrived in paradise.

"The presence of so many German exiles there will be a gift and a nuisance," Katia said, "but you can leave me to deal with the troublesome ones."

"They will all be trouble," Thomas said.

"Not as much trouble as our neighbors in Munich turned out to be!"

Thomas was surprised to receive a short note from Eugene Meyer, asking him to meet at the Knickerbocker Club in New York at a time that could be arranged by telephone with Meyer's secretary. When Thomas and Katia had stayed with the Meyers, Eugene had remained in the background while Agnes dominated the table. Alone together, Eugene and Thomas had discussed the awkwardness of train times between New York and Princeton and between Washington, D.C., and New York. Even on these mundane matters, he noted, Eugene had nothing interesting to say.

Thomas arrived at the Knickerbocker Club at the appointed hour and was directed to a large, light-filled room with many sofas and armchairs. At first, he thought the room was empty, but then he saw Eugene Meyer sitting alone, inconspicuously, in a corner. Eugene stood up and spoke in a low voice.

"Perhaps I should have seen you at Princeton. But I felt we might be too easily noticed there."

Thomas nodded. He stopped himself from pointing out that whereas he might indeed be noticed, Eugene Meyer would not.

"I have been asked to speak to you," Eugene began and then paused like someone waiting for a reply.

"Who asked you?" Thomas inquired.

"I am not at liberty to say."

For a moment, Thomas wished that Agnes Meyer were here to encourage her husband to be less cautious.

"You can take it that I am referring to very powerful people," he added.

They sat silently as a waiter came with tea.

"They need you to know that the United States will eventually enter the war. But public opinion is against it and Congress is against it. The loudest voices are declaring that we should stay out of the war. This means that public opinion cannot be aroused too much nor Congress made too suspicious, and so the plan to close the country, for the most part, to refugees is not merely a response to a single crisis. It is part of a larger strategy. And this strategy is to enter the war when the time is right and win over public opinion that will only harden if the country fills up with war refugees. The expectation is that the United States, at some point, will be provoked to enter the war. It may not work out like that, but that is the plan. What we don't want, in the meantime, is any serious protest against the refugee policy or any strident calls either for us to join the war."

As Eugene spoke, Thomas saw the newspaperman using plain language directly, without shyness or reserve. He wondered if Eugene dictated the *Washington Post* editorials in the same monotone as he used now.

"You want me to keep silent as events unfold?" Thomas asked.

"They want you to become part of the strategy."

"Why should I do this?"

"They take you seriously. You speak in public and do interviews, and people pay attention. I have not myself attended any of your public speeches, but my wife says that you are making two things very clear. One, that we have to defeat Hitler. And two, that German democracy will have to be restored. You have been inspiring American audiences. That is why we need you to know what our strategy is."

"Thank you for telling me."

"You could be the head of state in a new Germany. I can't be the first to tell you this."

"I am merely a poor writer."

"That is not true. You have become a public figure. You must be aware of that. You stand for the future as no one else does. We can hardly consider Brecht or your brother in the same light. And I don't think your son could be thought about in this way either."

Thomas smiled.

"No, I suppose not."

"Your silence is not required, merely that you are alert to the broader plan. No one asks you not to oppose policy, and no one wants you not to speak in favor of American entry into the war. All that is asked is that you are aware that there is a strategy."

"Does this message come from the president?"

"Mr. Roosevelt would like to see you and your wife again. A stay in the White House is being discussed. He will know that you have been spoken to so that he will not need to repeat to you anything that I have said. In the meantime, as you know, any personal requests you have made through my wife were considered and, if at all possible, granted."

"The German émigrés, including my brother, are having trouble in Hollywood. There is talk of contracts not being renewed. Could anything be done about this?"

"We control Washington only with difficulty. We have little influence in Hollywood."

"None?"

"Yes, some. My wife was able to secure the contract for your brother with Warner Brothers, it had a sort of novelty value and it was patriotic, but she cannot demand that a contract be renewed. She had to exert extraordinary pressure the first time. She cannot come back a year later to do the same. They are running a business."

"Could you mention it? Perhaps see—"

"No, I could not. It would not do at all."

For the first time, Thomas saw a toughness in Eugene Meyer that had been kept carefully hidden until now. He almost enjoyed the look of worldly control and canniness that had come over the newspaper owner's face. He wondered if it would have been wiser not to have mentioned Warner Brothers and have asked him instead about helping Mimi and Goschi. But it was too late now.

As they stood up to depart, Eugene moved close to him.

"Blanche Knopf was in D.C. recently and we had her to supper. She told us that your books are selling remarkably well, bringing in a tidy income. And there is a lecture tour planned, she says, that will pull in a year's salary. We were pleased to hear you are doing so well."

Thomas did not respond.

He parted from Eugene feeling ever more certain that the move to California was essential. If power was in Washington, then the farther he was away from it, and from all the machinations and half-said things associated with it, the better for him and his family.

Without saying so, Eugene Meyer had let him know that he was being watched, his speeches listened to, his interviews studied. He liked Roosevelt, what he knew of him, but he liked him less when he thought that he had asked Eugene Meyer to speak to him without actually using Roosevelt's name.

The idea of being a temporary head of state would serve only as a story to tell Erika when he saw her; perhaps her old father was not as unreliable and dreamy as he seemed, at least not in the eyes of some. He smiled at the thought that anyone who believed that he could become a useful head of state must have some other ideas too; not all of them could be wise.

Thomas was surprised at how brisk the furniture removers were, how carefully they handled each object, and how they worked out a system for packing his books so that they would be in order when he got to California. As they edged his desk out of his study, he was tempted to tell them that it had come from the house in Munich. And as they wrapped the candelabra, he could have added the story of how they had been brought from Lübeck. But removers did not want to listen to stories. The furniture was going to be driven across America. Within a few hours, the house was hollowed out, as though they had never lived in it.

Once they were installed in Los Angeles, he and Katia agreed to look at a site that was for sale in Pacific Palisades, close to Santa Monica. They had been renting a house, but now decided that they would build. They chose Julius Davidson to be the architect because they saw a conversion he had done of a house in Bel Air, but, more than that, because they liked his aura of cool competence. He had a habit of looking away when they spoke, as though what they had said required consideration, and then staring soulfully into the distance while they waited for a response.

"Our architect has a mysterious inner life," Katia said, "and that can only be good."

Thomas and Katia walked around the foundations with Davidson, imagining the house that would soon rise here. Thomas dreamed of his study, where the desk would be and the bookcases.

He noticed how beautifully dressed Davidson was, and was tempted to have Katia ask him where he had bought his suits. Instead, he reminded him that he did not want floor-to-ceiling windows in his study.

"I want shadows," he said. "I don't want to look out."

He did an imitation of a man writing at a desk.

"I need to talk to you also about that built-in record player you mentioned," Thomas said. "In the high summer, I thought, I would like to have sad chamber music on loud and clear, thus evoking the winter."

Although they did all their business with him in German, Davidson seemed American. Even his way of walking around the site had nothing of German hesitancy and watchfulness about it. He behaved like a man who had spent his childhood on the prairie. He had become an American. He knew the planning laws and those who implemented them as if Los Angeles were a kind of village. He also had a way of speaking freely and easily about money that no German would risk.

It struck Thomas that maybe one of his own children would soak in America like this, although, as he pictured them one by one, each of them seemed stubbornly in possession of a Teutonic spirit and Teutonic virtues, if any still existed.

"It all seems too small until I measure it with my steps," Katia said. "And then it is big."

"It will be a modest house," Davidson said. "But comfortable and bright. Big enough for the family."

As they walked around the site, which had views of the sierra and Santa Catalina, Thomas noticed a small bare tree in a corner with dark rotting fruit hanging from the upper branches. He asked Davidson what it was.

"It's a pomegranate tree. What you can see is the high fruit that the birds hollowed out. The tree will flower in the late spring with the help of hummingbirds and then in the early winter you will have pomegranates."

Thomas moved away from Davidson and Katia and made as though to inspect the back of the house. In Lübeck, pomegranates came from the cargo ships that normally carried sugar; they were in wooden boxes, individually wrapped in rice paper. For months on end, his mother would find a way to incorporate the fruit in every meal, in salads or in sauces or as dessert. And then they would disappear. She would ask their father to make inquiries, but no one could ever predict when the pomegranates would come again to Lübeck.

He knew how to open a pomegranate and fill a bowl with the rich, red seeds. If that was all he had learned from his mother, it would be enough, he thought. She, in turn, had learned it from the women in the kitchen in Paraty in Brazil. The trick was not to scoop the seeds out, but to nudge the skin backwards and push the seeds up gently but firmly, removing the white fleshy mass that surrounded them.

He loved the dry edge that mingled with the sweet taste of the pomegranate, and he loved the color. But now it was his mother's gaiety that he recalled, her voice, her pleasure at the news that a fresh consignment had arrived from Brazil, her assertion that a small piece of home, perhaps the best piece, had reached out to her across the ocean and would delight her days.

In moving to California, he thought, he had unwittingly chosen to live close to the weather that had made Julia Mann. He imagined for a second that he could tell Heinrich about the tree and see whether he too might remember the bowls full of red seeds. But he had refrained from saying too much about this new house he was building, afraid that he would further depress his brother, who had finally been informed that his contract as a screenwriter would not be renewed.

Walking across the lawn to where Davidson and Katia stood by a single tall palm tree, he remembered that somewhere in Greek mythology the pomegranate had significance. It had to do with death, he thought, the underworld, but he was not sure. As soon as his books were unpacked and on the shelves of his study here, he would find a volume that had come from Munich, a dictionary of Greek mythology. He would wait until the house was built and they were living there, enjoying the thought, in the meantime, that by the end of the year he would be eating the fruit that he had almost forgotten about.

One day after lunch, he had his customary short nap and then he read for a while. At four, Katia was ready with the car. They drove to Santa Monica and walked on the path overlooking the beach and then down to the pier.

"I find it strange," Katia said, "that our youngest child, who is still a boy as far as I am concerned, is the first to have his own baby. But I was around Michael's age when I had Erika, so I should think it's normal. But I don't. I wonder if Michael will be the only one to have children."

"Elisabeth will," Thomas said.

"Borgese is too old to have children," Katia said.

They stopped and looked at the high curling waves and, farther out, the blue water under the clear sky. Thomas's eye was captured by a scene closer to them. There were two young men in shorts doing gymnastics on the beach. They were facing the water, so Thomas could study their muscular backs and legs. He could happily have stayed there until darkness fell.

When one of them turned, he appeared sensitive, serious. As Thomas stood for a while and watched, Katia silent beside him, the young man started to glance regularly in his direction. Thomas observed him—the smooth chest, the light hair on the legs, the short blond hair, the blue eyes. But also a sense in the face of thoughtfulness, perhaps even of someone whose sensibility had not been brightened too much or made too blank by California.

Over the days and nights that followed, he imagined this young man coming into his study as Klaus Heuser had done, maybe to talk about books, or the conflict, or the German heritage. He would tell him what he could, try to talk about how tentative his own beginnings as a writer were, and how long it took to complete some of the books. He would lend the visitor some volumes by himself and others, knowing that this would ensure that the boy would return. Thomas would accompany him to the door and watch him walking away, down the path through the garden.

• • •

Life in their rented house was more peaceful once Monika had left for northern California to stay with Michael and Gret, who was pregnant again. But then Michael wrote to Katia to say that Monika was too much of a burden. The smallest thing would set her off talking and then she could not be stopped. She did not want to talk about her ordeal at sea, he wrote, but about something as inconsequential as a delivery boy who had dropped some of the groceries or a dog that trespassed on their lawn. He hoped his mother would understand if Monika returned to the family house.

As he went from his study to the living room one day, Thomas found Katia and Monika and Golo passing around a set of photographs that Monika had taken of Frido, now a year old. Katia, he knew, was upset at not being asked to spend time with Michael and Gret and Frido.

When they passed him the freshly developed photos, he had expected to see nondescript images of the baby he remembered from Princeton. Instead, the child emerged as fully alive, amused by the attention of the camera, unafraid, nearly defiant. Thomas saw the same square jaw that Elisabeth and Golo and Goschi had, the same strong face that he associated with his father's family, as well as an ironic, quizzical gaze that was solely Katia's. What surprised him was how much Frido was formed, ready for the world, demanding close attention.

"Why don't we invite them to stay?" he asked.

"This house doesn't have enough room," Katia said.

"Why don't we write to say that we would like young Frido to be the first guest in the new house? Or maybe use our charm and see if they would invite us to stay with them?"

"My mother has already used hers," Monika said, "but it didn't work. No invitation to visit Frido was forthcoming."

"That, I am afraid, is true," Katia said. "But I did ask Monika not to share the news with anyone."

"I don't like secrets or lies," Monika said.

"Maybe the less you reveal them or spread them, the less you will dislike them," Thomas replied.

"Do you want us to be quiet while you write your books?" Golo asked. His tone was sarcastic, bordering on aggressive.

"Hunger is not improving the atmosphere," Thomas said. "I think we might all benefit from lunch."

The painters were working on the new house and the furniture was beginning to arrive, including an elaborate Thermador range for the kitchen. Erika, having flown back from London to New York, took a train across America to visit them in the house they were renting. She ignored any talk about blinds and color schemes for the new house, and instead was filled with excitement about the war.

"I know I am prejudiced, but the English women are so splendid now, so efficient. With the men gone to fight, it is an ideal society. Visiting a munitions factory, with the young women concentrating on their work, is such an inspiration. I wish the Americans could witness it."

When Katia asked her if she had seen Klaus during the few days she had spent in New York, she shrugged.

"He is planning to visit," she said.

"For how long?" Katia asked.

"He has nowhere else to go, and no money."

"I sent him money."

"He spent it."

Thomas spotted Katia indicating to Erika that she should not discuss this further in front of him and Golo and Monika.

Later, when he was reading in his study, Katia and Erika appeared and closed the door behind them.

"Klaus has been visited by the police," Katia said.

"Arrested?" Thomas asked.

"It's not exactly that," Erika interjected. "He wants to join the

United States Army and he has to be investigated because he is German-born. And, of course, they found that he is a morphine addict and a homosexual. He has denied everything. He will ask you to intercede for him."

"Intercede with whom?"

"Don't ask me. And there is also something I didn't tell you, Mother. One of the other questions that they asked him was about incest."

"Incest?" Katia asked and started to laugh. "And who do they think his lucky partner is or was?"

"Klaus told them that they are mixing him up with characters in his father's fiction."

"Yes, I remember your father's story about incest," Katia said.

"And they think," Erika added, "that Klaus and I are twins."

"Surely he can just tell them that you are not," Katia said.

"You see," Erika said, standing up and looking directly at her father, "Klaus is broken. I couldn't wait to get away from him."

"But he wants to come here?" Katia asked.

"There are other matters we have to keep in mind when he comes," Erika said. "It would be best not to mention the possibility of your further visit to the White House."

"Why not?" Thomas asked.

"Because he feels that he should be included in any party to advise the president about Germany. And also he is sensitive, to say the least, at the idea that you are planning a Faust novel."

"Who told him that I was planning a Faust novel?"

"I did," Erika said.

"Maybe the quietness here will do him good," Katia said. "And Golo is so well-balanced that he might have a good influence on Klaus."

"Golo? Well-balanced?" Erika asked and laughed.

"Oh dear. Is he taking morphine too?" Katia asked. "Or is it incest?"

"He is in love with a librarian that he met when he was in Princeton," Erika said.

"Isn't that nice?" Katia asked. "They were always very kind, the librarians in Princeton. Did we ever meet her?"

"Him," Erika said.

"Him?" Katia asked.

"Him," Erika repeated.

"I asked him about those letters from Princeton," Katia said. "But he told me they were about library books that were overdue."

Thomas noticed that Erika's cheeks were flushed. She was enjoying telling them all this news. He was tempted to reveal to her that he was fully aware that she was in Los Angeles not only to see her parents but because she was having an affair with Bruno Walter, a married man just a year younger than her father.

This information came to him courtesy of Elisabeth in Chicago. He had formed the habit of phoning his youngest daughter, who was pregnant with her first child, on a Saturday evening. The rule was that they could only stay for fifteen minutes on the line. He realized that Elisabeth was also in regular touch with the rest of the family, even Klaus, although, as far as he was aware, she did not know about the interview with the police.

Elisabeth and he spoke with a frankness that was made easier, it seemed, because of the distance between Los Angeles and Chicago. However, she told him most things with the strict agreement that they would not be shared with Katia. Elisabeth also confided in her mother, to whom she wrote regularly. Katia thus found out some things about her children that Thomas, up to then, had presumed secret.

When Elisabeth told him about Erika and Bruno Walter, Thomas thought at first that she was mistaken and that perhaps Erika was having an affair with one of Walter's daughters, who were friends of hers.

"No, it's the father," Elisabeth said.

"I didn't think she liked men," Thomas replied.

"She likes Bruno Walter. She is the second of your daughters to like a man close to you in age. Be flattered!"

"And Monika?"

"Gerontophilia appears to have escaped her up to now."

"And how is your marriage?"

"Perfect."

"Would you tell me if it were not?"

"I tell you everything, but you must not say anything to my mother about Erika. She will think she has been a failure as a mother. Three homosexuals, or two homosexuals and one bisexual. Two daughters who enjoy the company of old men. And then there is Monika."

"And Michael," Thomas said.

"Yes, the normal one."

"He bears grudges."

"So he should. You were never kind to him."

"Neither were you. How often does Erika see Bruno Walter?"

"When she can."

"Does his wife know?"

"Yes. But no one else knows."

"You are sure this is true? I really thought Erika preferred women."

"So she does. But she has made an exception for the famous conductor."

Thomas watched Erika now, posing as the voice of sanity within the family, and felt further tempted to ask her if there was any news from her own love life. But he could not betray Elisabeth. That evening, he smiled as he saw Erika asking her mother for the keys of the car, saying that she had to see friends who lived on the east side of the city. He saw how stylish she looked and how she had put her hair in an elegant chignon.

He had to stand up and quickly leave the room to stop himself calling after her: "Think of me as he holds you in his arms." When he got to his study, he could not control his laughter.

As 1941 wore on, Thomas began to work on a new speech that he might give on a lecture tour, a speech that would include the tone of high idealism that he had been using in other talks he gave, but that might also become more pointed, more personal and more political. He liked the idea that his task was to spread a higher kind of propaganda, but as the argument raged over the possible American involvement in the war, Erika insisted that he needed to be more direct, and this view was shared, in quieter voices, by Golo and Katia.

By September, Roosevelt, after the sinking of American ships in the Atlantic by German U-boats, had come close to declaring a naval war against Germany, only to be vehemently attacked by Charles Lindbergh, who spoke of the warmongering of the English, the Jews and Roosevelt. Thomas determined that he would never mention Lindbergh by name, nor Roosevelt. But he would let the audience know that, speaking as a German, as a democrat, as a friend of America and an admirer of its freedoms, he believed that the world now looked to America.

He wrote the speech out in German and had it translated and then, with help from a young woman whom Katia had found, he started to work on delivery in English, speaking slowly, trying to pronounce words clearly.

After the first few cities, he had to make rules. He was not to be welcomed with fanfare at the railway station but to be discreetly taken to a car, his name not to be anywhere visible. At the beginning, he wondered if the crowds would come to see any Nobel Prize winner at all, but gradually he came to understand that his audience was political and well-informed. They read newspapers every day; they read books. And they understood that they needed to know more about the crisis in Europe.

By the beginning of November, when he spoke in Chicago, he was managing to make fewer mistakes in pronunciation. Also, he realized, as the audiences grew bigger, how much was at stake not only for democracy itself, but for himself and other German exiles. If America entered the war, there would be a movement to have all Germans interned. He needed to make clear that he represented a significant German opposition to Hitler, a large group in America whose loyalty in any war would wholeheartedly be to America.

In Chicago, he and Katia stayed in a hotel, agreeing to have lunch with Elisabeth and Borgese downtown on the day of his speech and then go home with them to see Angelica, Elisabeth's baby daughter.

Over lunch, Borgese informed him that Thomas would need to be cautious in Chicago as there was much anti-German feeling.

"People don't even want to hear attacks on Hitler. They don't want to hear his name at all. So if you denounce him you will win no friends, and of course if you don't denounce him you will make people feel that all Germans are in this together."

"I am sure the Magician will know exactly what to say," Elisabeth interjected.

"Rather you than me," Borgese said.

Angelica, in her cot, had no interest in the visitors until Katia produced a large box and signaled to her that she could help open it. She responded with an intent that made them all laugh.

"She has the family lack of patience," Thomas said.

"Your family, not mine!" Katia replied.

"Nor my family either," Borgese said.

Thomas glanced up at Borgese, wondering for a moment at what his family had to do with this.

In the car back to the hotel, Thomas turned to Katia.

"Do you think the child will continue to resemble her mother more than her father?"

"I am sure she will," Katia said. "Let's all pray that she will."

In the hour before the organizers came to collect him, Thomas went over the speech. The words that were difficult to pronounce he had marked, with a phonetic spelling in the margin. As the time approached, Katia came to his room to make sure that his tie was straight and his shoes suitably polished.

He was warned that the audience was much larger than they had planned for. They would try to find space for everybody.

Outside, there was chaos, with long lines and people shoving and shouting. When a few recognized him, they started to cheer, and the cheer was then taken up by all the people outside. He lifted his hat and waved and then went inside.

He knew the effect that his opening could have on an audience. He had tried it first in Iowa and then in Indianapolis. At the beginning, partly because of the money he was being paid, he felt fraudulent. He did not represent any group. There was nothing he could promise his audience. But, as the tour went on, he found the crowd became responsive, sometimes silent, other times emotional, if he used certain words or expressed strong opinions about the Nazis.

As always, the introduction was too long and too effusive. The man at the microphone roared out that the greatest living man of letters was about to address the crowd. And then he said it again, gesturing to the audience that they should cheer in approval. But finally, the microphone was his.

"We are told that much divides us, but one thing unites us. In America now, there is one word that stands for many other words. It is at the core of the American achievement; it is at the core of American influence in the world. That word is 'freedom'! Freedom! In Germany now, freedom has been replaced by murder, by threats, by large-scale prisons, by attacks on the Jewish population. But like all storms, this one will pass, and in the morning, when the wind has died down, Germans will once more cry out the word, the word that knows no borders and no limits. And that word will be 'freedom.' We cry out for freedom now, and there will come a time when our cry will be heard, when freedom will once more prevail."

He stopped and took in the crowd, which had fallen completely silent.

"I am one of the many Germans who has known fear and who has sought freedom in America. Just as Germans learned to fear Hitler and his henchmen, the whole world, the free world, has reason to fear the Nazis too. Fear is a natural response to violence and terror. But soon our fear will become our defiance, will be replaced by our courage, by our determination. Because there is a second word that matters to us now, a word worth fighting for, a word that unites Americans with free people all over the world. That word is 'democracy.' Democracy!"

He shouted the word and knew that the response would be instant cheering and applause.

"I am here not to tell you of the dark times that are ahead, of the struggle. I am here to tell you of the coming victory of democracy. I am here to represent the human spirit, and I stand proudly in Chicago as I invoke the sanctity of the human spirit, as I invoke freedom, as I invoke democracy, as I tell you that democracy will return to Germany as a river flows towards the sea, because democracy is in our spirit. It is not a gift, something that can be given or taken away. It is as essential to our well-being as food or water.

"I stand here not merely as a writer, or as a refugee from the most ruthless dictatorship that history has known, I stand here as a man and I speak to the men and women here about the dignity we share, the inner light that shines in each of us, and the rights we have, and the rights that we, as humans, have struggled for, rights that we deserve. I stand here because I believe that these rights will be returned to Germany. The Nazis cannot last. They cannot last. They must not last. They will not last."

At the final use of the word "last," the crowd were on their feet.

In New York, he had a meeting in a private room at his hotel with Agnes Meyer, who had traveled from Washington to see him. He knew that she was still intending to write a book about him and his work and he did not look forward to discussing it with her. Nor did he want to discuss his lectures with her. Since their content and the size of the audiences had been widely reported, he presumed that she would have opinions on what he should include in future and what he should leave out. He was determined that she would not dictate to him what he should and should not say.

"Now, I will need your acceptance in writing," she said, as soon as they were sitting down.

"My acceptance?"

"You will be offered the position of consultant in Germanic literature at the Library of Congress, at a salary of four thousand, eight hundred dollars a year, plus one thousand dollars for an annual lecture. You will be required to live in Washington for two weeks of every year."

"How has this come about?"

"I have been working quietly to make sure that, when war is declared, there will be no support for action against Germans in America. It is essential that this appointment happens before war is declared. You can hardly intern a consultant to the Library of Congress as an enemy alien. And you can hardly intern others like the consultant and not intern him. It is a small thing compared to your lectures, which are seen as the essence of good sense in very powerful places. 'High-minded and helpful' were the words he used."

"Who said that?"

"It was said in confidence, but I would not report it were the speaker not in the most important office."

"So I should expect a letter?"

"Yes, but I need your acceptance now, so let us go and have it typed. War could break out at any moment and I want this in place before then."

Thomas was in his bedroom in the rented house in Los Angeles, which they were soon to leave, when news came of the Pearl Harbor attacks. Since Golo normally never came to his bedroom door, he knew something serious had occurred. Downstairs, they found Katia and Monika sitting by the radio. Over the next three days, they waited for war to be declared against Germany.

On the second night, as they were preparing to leave the supper table, Monika said something in passing about her dead husband. Until now, she had not spoken about him without bursting into tears, but this time when she said his name she smiled.

"What was he like?" Golo asked. "I have wanted to ask you this for so long, but none of us wanted to upset you."

"Jenö was a scholar," Monika said. "I saw him one morning in Florence in both the Uffizi and the Pitti. And then in the afternoon when I went to the Brancacci he was there too. And he had noticed me each time, and that is how we met."

"He was writing about Italian art?" Golo asked.

"That was his subject," Monika replied. "He could remember the smallest detail in a painting or a piece of sculpture. But that is all lost now. It doesn't matter anymore what he could remember."

"I wish we could have known him," Erika said.

"If he had lived," Monika went on, "he might be here now. His book on Italian sculpture might even be finished. All of you would admire him."

Monika looked around the table, at her parents and at Erika and Golo.

"When I see you going for walks, Golo," she continued, "I often think that Jenö might join you, because you could talk about books. Even the Magician would have liked Jenö."

"I can only regret not knowing him," Thomas said.

For a second, Thomas thought Monika was going to cry, but she took a deep breath and lowered her voice.

"I cannot imagine what it was like for him to die like that. But I know that he would love to have lived. He would love to be here now, knowing that America was going to join the war."

Katia and Erika embraced Monika, as Thomas and Golo watched.

"I don't know why he was drowned and I was saved. No one will ever be able to explain that to me."

Two months later, once they had moved to Pacific Palisades, Klaus came from New York. Thomas and Katia met him at Union Station and drove him to the new house, which he appeared barely to notice. Even when Katia said that this would be their last refuge, he did not respond. Like his sister, Klaus was in his mid-thirties now. But unlike her, he seemed worn out. His hair was thinning. All the brightness had left his eyes.

The real change, however, was in how Erika reacted to him. She could hardly look at her brother. At the table, she spoke about her application to work for the BBC and her plans to cover the war. A few times, when Klaus started to offer some opinion about the war, she turned to him, interrupting: "Ask us, Klaus. Don't tell us. Monika lost her husband in the war. I have been in London. Your father is kept well-informed by the administration. We know about the war. Someone like you, living with artists and writers and God knows who else in New York, cannot know what we know. So please don't tell us about the war!"

When they were in their late teens and early twenties and flying high, Thomas remembered, Erika and Klaus would dominate the family table on their visits home. Now Golo and Monika watched silently as Erika alone dominated the table. Thomas noticed Klaus giving in to her, offering opinions that might win her approval. But when her brother began to explain how he believed that now more than ever culture, especially literature, was an essential weapon in the battle against fascism, Erika cut him short.

"We have heard this before, Klaus."

"That is because it cannot be said enough."

"The best weapons against fascism are weapons," she said. "Real weapons."

She glanced at her father, seeking his agreement. Thomas did not want to encourage her to continue, but he also did not want to get involved in an argument with her.

Erika said she was going out, adding that she would be with her friends until quite late. When Klaus asked her if she could drop him off at an address nearby, Thomas saw the expression on Katia's face darken.

"I can drop you off," Erika said. "But you will have to make your own way home."

"Where are you going?" Klaus asked her.

"To spend time with friends."

"What friends?"

"People you would not know."

She said this in a tone completely dismissive. Thomas could see the hurt look on Klaus's face.

Later, Katia came into his room.

"As if Klaus were not in bad enough shape," she said. "Erika is determined to make little of him in front of all of us."

"Where are they both going?" he asked.

"Klaus has a friend who is in some hotel nearby."

He took it that the friend was somehow unsuitable. He believed also that, unless Katia were afraid to share the news about Bruno Walter with him, she had taken Erika at her word. She was seeing friends. For a second, he had a vision of Bruno Walter, fresh from a concert, removing his trousers and folding them over a chair in some deluxe downtown Los Angeles hotel room while Erika watched him, smoking. He remembered Davidson telling him that he could not work for Walter, as the conductor could not stop boasting about his own greatness. No house would be good enough for such a man, Davidson had said.

On Saturday, when he called her, Elisabeth told him that Klaus did indeed have an unsuitable lover installed in a hotel and that both Klaus and the lover represented a considerable expense, both needing a constant supply of morphine and other drugs.

When Thomas mentioned his vision of Bruno Walter and Erika, Elisabeth told him that, in fact, they enjoyed their trysts in the Walters' own house in Beverly Hills. Elisabeth presumed that her mother knew even more details, but, since Elisabeth had made the error of sounding too interested, she had not disclosed them.

"Katia knows about Erika and Walter?"

"Nothing escapes my mother."

"Does she know about Klaus and the drugs?"

"It was she who told me."

In these early months of the war, Thomas actually looked forward to phone calls from Agnes Meyer. She, in turn, seemed to relish having news for him, although often she called merely to inform him that she knew something before it had been printed in the newspapers. When news came that Japanese people on the west coast were to be removed from their homes, she called to say that she had hinted to him when they met in New York that this would happen.

"But there are many things I cannot say," she added.

"Is there any discussion about taking action against Germans in America?"

"It has been quelled," she replied.

One morning, as he was working in his study, Klaus came to see him. Over the previous week he had appeared increasingly disheveled. His face was thinner and his teeth were stained. He had a way of moving that was edgy and uneasy. He began by admiring his father's study.

"This is all I ever wanted," he said. "A study like this."

Thomas wondered if he were being mocked. Should any other of his children speak to him like this, their words would be sardonic, to say the least. But perhaps not Klaus. He was the earnest one.

"I think you enjoy your freedom," Thomas said.

"I take that as a rebuke," Klaus replied.

"You are much admired as a writer. If there is ever a new Germany, you will be needed there."

"I mean to join the U.S. Army," Klaus said. "At the moment, there are some obstacles to my being accepted. Life has not been simple in New York. There are many spies and rumormongers."

"I'm not sure life is simple in the army either."

"I'm serious about it," Klaus said. "My mother does not believe me. Erika does not believe me. But I will come here the next time in an army uniform."

"Are you asking me to help you?"

"I am asking you to believe me."

"I can imagine what the obstacles are."

"They are going to need men like me."

Thomas was tempted to ask him if he meant drug addicts and homosexuals and men who ask their mothers for money, but he saw that Klaus was on the verge of tears. He thought he should say something supportive.

"I would be proud and happy to see you in a U.S. Army uniform. I cannot think of anything that would make me happier. This is our country now."

He looked at Klaus as a father in a movie might.

"Do you believe I can do it?" Klaus asked.

"Join?"

"Yes."

"I think you would have to make significant adjustments in your life. But I cannot see any reason . . ."

Thomas hesitated as Klaus watched him closely. He noticed how pale his son was.

"As I say, significant adjustments," Thomas said, looking directly at Klaus.

"You, too, have been listening to all the gossip," Klaus said.

"You live as you want to live," Thomas replied.

"As you do, in your grand new house."

"Indeed. A house in which you are welcome at any time."

"I have nowhere to go once I leave here."

"What do you want?"

"My mother has said that she cannot continue paying for me."

"I will speak to her. Is that what you came to see me for?"

"I came here to ask you to believe me."

"It is inconceivable that the army would accept you in your current state."

"What is my current state?"

"You tell me."

"I promise that the next time I see you I will be in uniform."

"The army will make no allowances for you, but I do not want to argue about that. It should be clear enough."

"So, I take it I am being dismissed," Klaus said.

Thomas did not reply. Klaus stood up and brusquely left the room.

Once Klaus had returned to New York and Erika had gone to England, Michael and Gret came to stay, bringing Frido and their new baby, a boy, with them. Michael would spend his stay in Pacific Palisades practicing with three other musicians who were planning to form a quartet.

There was more raw charm in Frido, Thomas saw, than even the photographs had suggested. As soon as the boy saw new people, he brightened and smiled.

Frido gazed at his grandfather, intrigued first by his glasses, then by the intense interest with which Thomas was gazing at him in return, doing tricks with his hands, trying to make Frido laugh.

Seeing that Michael and Golo had gone for a walk in the garden, Thomas followed them. They heard him coming behind them and both looked around suspiciously. They stopped, but neither of them smiled.

"Golo was explaining that Heinrich is in a most dreadful situation," Michael said.

"In what way?"

"He has run out of money. His rent is already two months in arrears, and they are threatening to evict him and Nelly."

"And the car has broken down," Golo added, "and the garage won't even begin repairs until they are paid."

"And Nelly has some medical problems, but can't afford to go to the doctor."

"When I went there yesterday," Golo continued, "they were both desperate. Heinrich could barely speak."

"Does your mother know?"

"I told her last night."

Instantly, Thomas understood why Katia had said nothing. The only solution to Heinrich's financial problems was a regular stipend, and that would be a large commitment.

"I will speak to her," Thomas said.

"I think it needs a long-term solution," Golo said.

"I know what it needs," Thomas replied.

He turned to Michael.

"Gret told me that you and your friends have been rehearsing the Beethoven Opus 132 quartet. I would love if you could play it here as soon as you can. We will invite Heinrich. I know he would like to hear it as well."

"It is the most difficult," Michael said. "We are a new quartet."

"I know it is hard. But it has a special meaning for me and your mother."

"Spare us the exaggeration. It does not have a special meaning for my mother," Michael said.

Thomas immediately regretted having invoked Katia, who had never expressed any opinion on any Beethoven quartet. He would have to reach her before Michael did and ask her to insist that she had a special reverence for Opus 132.

"Will you see if it can be done?" Thomas asked.

"The second violinist I am working with does not speak English. He is Romanian."

"But he can read music?"

Michael glanced at him contemptuously.

"In a rehearsal for a quartet, there is a great deal of discussion."

"Do your best," Thomas said.

As Thomas walked away from his two sons, he knew that if he looked back he would see them both staring after him coldly. He wanted to tell Golo, who was now thirty-two, that Elisabeth had declared that after the age of thirty no one had the right to blame their parents for anything. And then he could turn to Michael, who was twenty-two, and tell him that he had eight years left and he should use them wisely.

When he found Katia, he made her swear that she would say she had strong personal reasons for needing to hear that Beethoven quartet played in her own house, with Michael on the viola.

Heinrich and Nelly came early, as arranged, on the day the quartet was to be played. Thomas had sent his brother a check. He noticed how impeccably dressed they were. While Heinrich was frail and walked slowly, his suit was perfectly pressed and his shoes were shiny. Nelly was wearing a red dress and red shoes with a white cardigan. Her handbag and hat matched the cardigan. No one would have guessed, he thought, how badly they had needed money just a few days earlier.

The night before at supper when the subject of Nelly came up, Katia had emphasized that, while Nelly was welcome in her house, she would prefer not to be left alone with her.

"If I discover that my husband and his two sons, not to speak of his daughter, are leaving the wives together in the deluded view that the two Frau Manns must have so much to talk about, then I will release mice in all your bedrooms."

"What about me?" asked Gret. "I, too, am a Frau Mann."

"You are exempt from criticism," Katia said. "But I will not be left alone with Nelly. From the moment she sets foot in this house to the moment she leaves, I am depending on all of you to ensure that."

While Golo sat at the garden table with Nelly, Thomas and Heinrich strolled around the property. With the check, Thomas had included a friendly note saying that they should discuss Heinrich's finances as soon as possible. It should be easy, he thought, to do it now. Slowly, however, as Heinrich spoke about a novel whose first chapter he had written, it was as though they were in Munich again, or in Italy as young writers, with Heinrich always confident, ready to assert his greater knowledge of the world and of books. If Thomas were to tell him now that he was planning a novel based on the Faust story, Heinrich would say that this had been done too many times already. If Thomas were to add that his protagonist would be a modern composer, Heinrich would insist that it was impossible to write about music. Thomas remembered that he had not told Heinrich much about *Buddenbrooks* while he worked on it, too afraid that a single, withering remark might be enough to make him doubt its worth.

He let Heinrich talk about his novels about Henry IV of France, and how he believed they would make a good film.

They turned towards the main entrance to the house and Gret appeared with Frido, who focused all his attention on Heinrich.

"It is marvelous to meet a Mann who does not look suspiciously at one," Heinrich said.

Since none of the others was present, Thomas took this as aimed entirely at him. Its tone arose, he supposed, from his having sent his brother a check. It struck him that he was going to be made to suffer even more as he provided for his brother in the future.

When Gret took Nelly to see the baby, Heinrich suggested that he and Thomas take another stroll around the gardens. This time, Thomas imagined, they could talk about money.

"I wake every night," Heinrich said, "and think about Mimi and Goschi. Perhaps Mimi is safe, I can't find out. She could be singled out because of me. And Goschi too. She is twenty-five, a time when she should be at her happiest. I have abandoned her in a hellhole, as I have abandoned her mother."

"Do you have a precise idea what is happening to them?"

"They are in Prague, and if the Germans have their way, they will be arrested. We walk on manicured lawns under blue skies. We build new houses. We live in a place of plenty. I have left them behind and they call to me in the night. I cannot even begin to share with Nelly how concerned I am."

Thomas realized that this too was directed at him; the manicured lawns were the very ones they were walking on, his house was the place of plenty. But he determined that he should ignore his brother's efforts to make him feel guilty. Instead, he should offer to intensify previous efforts to locate Heinrich's ex-wife and his daughter and agree to use his influence to have them brought to America. For a second, however, he wanted to tell Heinrich that, in reality, it would be almost impossible to rescue anyone now from Central Europe and get them visas for America. He knew how wrong it was to build up Heinrich's hopes, but still he could not tell his brother the truth.

"I have asked and asked again. If I hear anything, I will tell you. And I will keep up the pressure."

"Can you ask the president directly?"

"No," Thomas said. "That cannot be done."

Even though he did not speak, his brother made clear to him that he saw this as a betrayal.

"Carla and Lula were lucky that they took themselves out of this world," Heinrich said.

They had supper with Michael's colleagues, the musicians, all three handsome and young, Thomas doing what he could to disguise his interest in them. They were dressed in the same kind of loose-fitting suit and had matching haircuts, even the Romanian, who spoke French. With Gret on one side of him and the lead violinist on the other, Thomas had to force himself to be sufficiently polite to his daughter-in-law. They discussed Frido and his baby brother for a while, but then he could not think of another topic. He turned to the violinist, who asked him why he had especially wanted Opus 132.

"For the third movement," he said. "I like the idea of *Neue Kraft fühlend*."

"Do you feel new strength?"

"When I think of the book I must write, I do. Or I hope I do."

After supper, they moved to the main room, Gret excusing herself to feed the baby, Nelly going back to the dining room to fill her wineglass to the brim.

"Heinrich warned me that this is going to be long and tedious," she whispered to Monika, who let out a laugh.

The four young men were putting their music stands in place. Once seated, they started to tune their instruments, following the Romanian, whose instrument was already tuned. Thomas liked the Romanian, who looked around at the small audience with calm wonder, but it was the two Americans who really held his attention. The cellist had a softer face than the lead violinist, and brown eyes. His delicate beauty would fade in a few years, Thomas thought. The lead violinist was not as obviously handsome, the face was too thin, he was already balding, but his frame was the strongest of the four, his shoulders the broadest.

When the music began, Thomas was struck by its daring, the quiet release of a sort of anguish, followed by a tone that suggested struggle, with hints that the struggle brought both pain and joy, immense joy. He must, he knew, stop thinking, give up trying to find simple meaning in the music, but instead let it enter his spirit, listen to it as though he might never get another chance.

It was hard not to look at the players, however, not to study their seriousness and concentration. Thomas watched them taking their cues from the lead violinist. The lead violinist and Michael on the viola seemed to spar, taking energy from each other; the music edged towards resolution and held back for a moment before it soared.

He glanced over at Katia, who smiled at him. This was the world of her parents, who had hosted many such chamber concerts in their house in Munich. Out of this old world from which they had been forced to flee, Michael had emerged as the one with musical talent. Thomas watched him playing with slow care, showing no emotion as, handsome and self-possessed, he let the viola's dark sound hit against the sweeter sound of the two violins.

As the music continued, the lead violinist and the cellist shed some of their Americanness. The rangy, friendly, masculine openness, apparent earlier, was replaced, he saw, by vulnerability, sensitivity, until they could have been Germans or Hungarians from decades before. Maybe, he thought, it was merely something he imagined, something caused by the force of the four instruments playing together, as they found moments of pure connection with one another, and then went silent or played solo, but Thomas could entertain the idea that ghosts from an earlier time, ghosts who had once walked the streets of the European cities carrying instruments, ghosts on their way to rehearsal, were present here in this new house overlooking the Pacific Ocean in southern California.

The second movement ended and Thomas vowed that, from now on, he would listen more keenly, stop letting his mind wander into idle speculation. He tried not to notice as Nelly left the room. He remembered this Beethoven quartet as being sad, sometimes mournful. What was surprising now was that, while the undertone was melancholy, the way the instruments stopped and started and then moved into melody made it uplifting. The suffering in the music was buried in every note, but so too was something almost stronger, some sense of an unyielding beauty that after a few minutes rose, as though surprised at its own vigor, into a sound that made him stop thinking, stop trying to find meaning in this, and simply listen, let his spirit absorb what was being played.

Katia had her eyes closed now, as did Heinrich. Both Golo and Monika were watching the players with intense concentration, Monika sitting forward in her seat. To move from the bombast of the symphonies to the unearthly loneliness of this quartet, he thought, must have been a journey that even Beethoven himself could not easily comprehend. It must have come as though some strange, tentative, shivering knowledge emerged suddenly into clarity.

Thomas wished he had been able to do this as a writer, find a tone or a context that was beyond himself, that was rooted in what shone and glittered and could be seen, but that hovered above the world of fact, entering into a place where spirit and substance could merge and drift apart and merge again.

He had made the great compromise. As he sat, perfectly washed and shaved, in his grand house, in his suit and tie, his family all around, his books arranged on the shelves in his study with the same respect for order as his thoughts and his response to life, he could have been a businessman.

He bowed his head. For one moment, the players faltered; Michael had come in too early. Thomas looked up as Michael stopped playing and waited for a signal from the lead violinist and then gently brought his instrument in, letting the sound go under the sound the violin made, like a backdrop for the drama. Just then, he noticed that Gret had come into the room and taken Nelly's seat.

When all four players got ready to play the notes that lifted the quartet out of plaintive reverie into something close to song, Michael looked at Golo, who nodded to him in appreciation. His timing in this section was perfect.

On a few occasions in his own books, Thomas thought, he had risen above the ordinary world from which the work emerged. The death of Hanno in *Buddenbrooks*, for example, or the quality of the desire described in *Death in Venice*, or the séance scenes in *The Magic Mountain*. Maybe in other parts of other books too. But he did not think so. He had let dry humor and social settings dominate his writing; he was afraid of what might take over if he did not exercise caution and control.

He could imagine decency, but that was hardly a virtue in a time that had grown sinister. He could imagine humanism, but that made no difference in a time that exalted the will of the crowd. He could imagine a frail intelligence, but that meant little in a time that honored brute strength. As the slow movement came gravely to an end, he realized that, if he could summon the courage, he would have to entertain evil in a book, he would have to open the door to what was darkly outside his own comprehension.

There were two men that he did not become and he might make a book from them if he could conjure up their spirits properly. One was himself without his talent, without his ambition, but with the same sensibility. Someone fully at ease in a German democracy. A man who liked chamber music, lyric poetry, domestic quietness, gradual reform. A man, all conscience, who would have stayed in Germany even as Germany became barbaric, living a fearful life as an internal exile.

The other man was someone who did not know caution, whose imagination was as fiery and uncompromising as his sexual appetite, a man who destroyed those who loved him, who sought to make an art that was austere and contemptuous of all tradition, an art as dangerous as the world coming into shape. A man who had been brushed by demons, whose talent was the result of a pact with demons.

What would happen if these two men met? What energy would then emerge? What sort of book would that be? What sort of music would surface from that?

He must, he knew, stop thinking about books he might write and characters he might invent. He was aware from experience that listening to music with any intensity brought emotions that he could not harness, intentions that he could not carry out. Often, since they had moved into the new house, ideas for novels and stories came to him as he listened to Schubert or Brahms. When he stood up to go to his study immediately afterwards, he was sure that the idea could be transformed into something solid, only for it to dissolve once he was sitting at his desk with a pen in his hand.

Music made him unstable. But as he followed the short movement with its lovely march beats and dance beats, and then the final movement with its lack of hesitancy, its flowing elegance, he felt that the two men he had imagined, the two shadow versions of who he was, would not leave him, as other such imaginings had left him. They would fit into what he had already been dreaming of, his book about a composer who, like Faust, formed a pact with the devil.

As the quartet was close to the end, he forced himself to listen, and do nothing else. No musings on character or on novels! Just the sound, its rhythms held by the viola and cello and then interrupted by the two violinists, who darted in and out of each other's orbit as though the other two musicians did not exist. Now Michael started to play the viola with more and more confidence, determined, it seemed, that his sound would not merely be an undertone, even if it could not dominate against the high emotion coming from the violins, which were now playing with ferocious zeal.

If music could evoke feelings that allowed for chaos as much as order or resolution, Thomas thought, and since this quartet left space for the romantic soul to swoon or bow its head in sorrow, then what would the music that led to the German catastrophe sound like? It would not be war music, or marching music. It would not need drums. It could be sweeter than that, more sly and silky. What happened in Germany would need a music not only somber but slippery and ambiguous, with a parody of seriousness, alert to the idea that it was not only desire for territory or riches that gave rise to this mockery of culture that was Germany now. It was the very culture itself, he thought, the actual culture that had formed him and people like him, that contained the seeds of its own destruction. The culture had proved defenseless and useless against pressure. And the music, the romantic music, in all the heightened emotion it unleashed, had helped to nourish a raw mindlessness that had now become brutality.

His own confused state when he listened to music was a kind of panic; the music was a way of absolving him from remaining rational. In creating confusion, it inspired him. Its untrustworthy sound gave rise to the conditions in which he could work. For others, including some who now ruled Germany, it stirred emotions that were savage.

He listened as the musicians began to speed up under the direction of the lead violinist, who was smiling, goading the others to follow him, to play more loudly, to soften, then come back in with more force.

As the players drew near the final stretch, he felt the excitement of having been taken out of time and also a resolve that on this occasion the thoughts and ideas that came to him would mean something, would fill a space that he had been quietly creating. For a split second as the playing ended, he was sure that he had it, he saw the scene, his composer in a house in Polling, the place where his mother had died, but then it faded as he stood up with the others to applaud the quartet, who bowed in unison, making clear that this final gesture, like their playing, had been rehearsed.

Chapter 14
Washington, 1942

Eleanor Roosevelt led them briskly along a corridor.

"Some of this is not to my taste, but I am not allowed to spend money on unnecessary redecoration."

Thomas noticed that she addressed Katia more directly than him. He had been told that the president might be able to see him, but since Mrs. Roosevelt had not mentioned the meeting, he deduced that it had been canceled or postponed. That morning, there was news of the Russian counteroffensive at Stalingrad against the German Sixth Army. He wondered if Roosevelt was not devoting his full attention to the outcome.

They were to have tea with Mrs. Roosevelt, even though they had just had breakfast in the house of Agnes and Eugene Meyer, where they were staying.

"I wish," Eleanor said when they were seated in a small side room, "that we had all listened to you when you warned us that force would have to be met with force."

Thomas did not want to interrupt her to say that he never issued any such warning. It struck him that she was trying to flatter him by pretending that he had been prescient about the threat that Hitler posed.

"We really want you," Mrs. Roosevelt went on, "to continue making those broadcasts that are relayed into Germany. You have been a beacon of hope. When I was in London, it was talked about. They are so happy to have you involved, and so are we. They were more than impressed that you agreed to do them even when Hitler was in the ascendant."

Katia asked Mrs. Roosevelt about her involvement in the war effort.

"I have to be careful," she said. "In wartime, you cannot criticize a sitting president, but you can attack his wife. I have had to retreat. I thought my journey to England would be helpful. I liked the king and the queen, they are so dedicated, but I found Churchill very difficult to talk to. My main interest was to meet as many ordinary people as possible and our troops."

"You are much admired," Katia said.

"So many of our young men are now seeing England for the first time. It will, I hope, stay with them all of their lives."

Eleanor shook her head in sadness. Thomas could see that she had refrained from adding that this would be the case only with the ones who survived the war.

"We will win the war," she continued. "I am sure we will win the war, no matter what the cost. Soon we must begin to concentrate on winning the peace."

She glanced at Katia, who responded by smiling in assent. Thomas wondered if something important were happening at this very moment in the Oval Office, something that was keeping the president from seeing them.

"When we met before," Eleanor said, "we were all so awed by your husband, by his great humanity, and his books, that I'm afraid we did not pay you enough attention."

She addressed Katia as though she were a teacher dealing with a student.

"And now I discover that you are a marvel, a real marvel. And I am longing to hear all you said last night, but I want to hear it from you personally rather than secondhand on the telephone from Agnes Meyer."

"She telephoned you?" Katia asked.

"She calls once a day and I take her call once a week," Mrs. Roosevelt replied.

"Yes, she calls my husband too."

It struck Thomas for a moment that he now had a chance to ask the First Lady if she could do anything for Mimi and Goschi. Even though he believed that it was too late, the very act of asking might result in new information or even some reassurance that would console Heinrich.

When he told Mrs. Roosevelt about them, she looked concerned.

"Are they Jewish?" she asked.

Thomas nodded.

"The news is not good," she said. "Not good for anyone. It is why we must . . ."

She stopped. There was a catch in her voice.

"There is nothing I can do. I am sorry. I did what I could before the war broke out, but I can do no more now. We have to hope."

In the silence, Thomas knew that it would be best maybe to keep the news from Heinrich that Eleanor Roosevelt did not think there was anything she could do for Mimi and Goschi. He bowed his head.

Their visit with the Meyers had not begun well the previous evening. While their house in Crescent Place was grand and imposing, some of the walls were very thin indeed. Prior to dinner, he and Katia heard most of the heated argument between Agnes and her husband. It was about some letter that had not appeared in the *Washington Post* despite his assurances that it would be published in that day's issue.

"Someday I will leave you and then there will be sorrow!"
Agnes roared several times. "Then what a fool you are you will
come to know!"

"I think she is translating from the German," Katia said.

"She does this when she is excited," Thomas replied.

"She is excited now," Katia said.

At dinner there was a senator who stated categorically, as soon
as he was introduced to Thomas and Katia, that he did not support America's involvement in the war. When Thomas smiled
coldly and shrugged, making it plain that he could not be bothered to become involved in an argument with a nonentity, the
man scowled. Thomas could not think why this politician had
been invited or why he had come, but he presumed that Washington must be a lonely place, especially for senators with limited
social skills and political views that were obsolete.

Then there was a man whom Agnes introduced to him as
Alan Bird. He worked, she said, at the German desk of the State
Department. His clear blue eyes and the square set of his jaw,
the neatness of his dress that bordered on the military, interested
Thomas, but when he realized that he was staring too much at the
man, he switched his focus to the man's wife, who seemed startled
by the attention, saying that she wished she had more time to
read, but it was hard with young children.

The other guests included a very glamorous and confident-
looking elderly woman who wrote a syndicated column and was,
Agnes said, one of Eleanor Roosevelt's staunchest supporters.
They were soon joined by a poet, meek in manners, who was
translating Brecht's poetry for a small press. The poet's wife was
a tall, formidable-looking woman whose antecedents were obviously Scandinavian. She told Thomas that she had read all of his
novels and followed his speeches.

"You will save Europe," she said. "Yes, you will be the one."

Eugene Meyer sat sullenly at one end of the table while Agnes sat imperiously at the other. The row with her husband seemed to have made Agnes eager for further argument, and even before the first course was served she set about provoking her guests.

"Do you all not agree," she asked, "that people who opposed Hitler too early might have missed the chance to have real and steady influence in Germany?"

Thomas glanced at Katia, who had her head down. He decided to pretend he had not heard Agnes and was relieved when no one at all responded to her question.

Thomas wished that Agnes had briefed him on Alan Bird. If the man had not been strategically placed opposite him, then he gave the impression that he had. He watched Thomas closely, suspiciously. It occurred to Thomas that he would be wise tonight not to be goaded by Agnes into expressing any opinion at all. He would endeavor to remain silent or react with amusement and diffidence to whatever Agnes had to say.

"I often ask myself if the war could not have been prevented," she said. "And I am not alone in that. I mean by true vision when the clouds showed signs of darkening."

The senator signaled to the waiter that he would like a second helping of the soup. He had tucked his napkin into the neck of his shirt. He made a single, loud sound, a clear warning that he had something emphatic to say, and then spooned some soup into his mouth. Having swallowed it, he looked up, the table waiting for him to speak.

"We did ourselves no good over there in that last war," he said. "And we will do ourselves no good over there now. It's not our dogfight. We have our own struggle, especially against that awful woman. She will bring the country down."

The man from the State Department glanced at Thomas, who tried to look as though he did not understand that the senator was referring to Eleanor Roosevelt.

"She does nothing but good," the columnist said.

As the second course was served, Agnes attempted to find other topics that might create controversy at the table, but even the senator and the columnist, who appeared to know each other well, were tired of sparring. Eugene did not speak at all. The poet also stayed silent. His wife, several times, when there was a gap in the conversation, mentioned the name of one of Thomas's books and went into a kind of swoon.

"They did not merely change my life," she said. "They taught me how to live."

"After the war, of course," Agnes said, "there will have to be huge investment in Germany. That's when America will have to spend money, real money."

"I do not think that would be desirable or possible," Katia interjected.

"Well, it will certainly be possible and I believe it will also be desirable," Agnes replied.

"Yes, I agree," the columnist said. "From the rubble, something will emerge, and all, I hope, with America's help."

"I have heard enough," the senator said. "Where I live, no one wants to give a cent to Germans at peace or at war. It's not our war. And there's no guarantee we will win it."

"But of course a new Germany will have to be created," Agnes said, ignoring the senator. "And we may even have someone in the company who will be the first president of a new Germany."

"We do not want Germany to be built again," Katia said.

"Why not, my dear?" Agnes asked.

"The German people voted for Hitler," Katia said, "and the thugs around him. They are supporting the Nazis. They oversee the cruelty. It is not simply that there is a group of barbarians at the top. The whole country, and Austria too, is barbarous. And the barbarity is not new. The anti-Semitism is not new. It is part of Germany."

"But what about Goethe, Schiller, Bach, Beethoven?" Agnes asked.

"That is what disgusts me," Katia said. "The Nazi leaders listen to the same music as we do, look at the same paintings, read the same poetry. But it makes them feel that they represent some higher civilization. And that means no one is safe from them, least of all the Jews."

"But surely the Jews—" the poet started to say.

"Don't tell me about the Jews, if you don't mind," Katia interrupted.

"I wasn't aware that you yourself—" Agnes began.

"Were you not, Mrs. Meyer?" Katia again cut in.

Thomas had never seen Katia become heated like this in the company of strangers. Nor had he ever heard her claim her own Jewishness in public in such an open and defiant way. Her English was more fluent than normal; her command of the language suggested that she had actually prepared what she was going to say.

He noticed Alan Bird fixing his attention on Katia as Agnes asked her, in the event of an Allied victory, what might be done with a defeated Germany.

"Suppress it," Katia said. "The very thought of it makes me shiver."

"But will you and your husband not return there if Germany is defeated?" Alan Bird asked.

"The war will never be over for us. We will never live in Germany again. The idea of mingling with Germans who complied, who stood quietly by, or who took part, is horrifying."

"But aren't you German as much as they are?"

"The thought that I ever might have been German fills me with shame."

"But do you not feel—?" Agnes began.

"I feel pity for my parents. That is what I feel. Everything they owned taken from them. Reduced to paupers. Their children all fled. My father was stripped naked at the Swiss border. But they were lucky. They had old friends who helped them, including a rich Swiss family who rescued them, but also old friends whose names are now among the great dishonored Germans."

"Who helped them escape?" Agnes asked.

"Winifred Wagner did," Katia said. "My father loved Wagner's music. He and his parents were the first patrons of Bayreuth. That might seem like a fantasy now—Jews paying for Wagner—but that is how we lived. And she remembered it, Wagner's daughter-in-law. My father accepted help from her. He had no choice. I hope not to thank her if ever the chance comes. Too much has happened for that. I despise her."

Katia sounded grand and everyone at the table was impressed by her tone. Katia and he, Thomas thought, had become so used to being Germans in America, always aware how much casual suspicion they could provoke. Now Katia had discarded any humility or caution she might have worn. She caused the table to fall silent. Even the senator studied her with a look of mild, Midwestern awe.

They returned to California to find Klaus there waiting for his call-up. He had been, to their surprise, finally accepted into the army. The winter days were warm and they were heartened to see him up early, reading the newspapers in the garden. In the evening, he was relaxed, ready to argue with Golo and his father about the progress of the war without becoming ill-tempered.

Earlier in the year, 150 tons of incendiary bombs had been dropped on Lübeck, resulting in many civilian casualties. The medieval center had largely been destroyed, including the cathedral and the Marienkirche, and also the Mann family house on Mengstrasse.

"There has to be a stronger movement," Klaus said at the dinner table, "to denounce these bombings of civilian targets."

"The people of Lübeck," Thomas replied quietly, "have been among the most devout Nazis."

It was easier to make this argument than try to describe what it meant for him to have the actual streets in which his parents and grandparents walked, streets that were etched in his memory and came often to him in dreams, obliterated in one night.

"And so you incinerate them? You burn their children too?" Klaus asked. "You fight the war like Nazis?"

Thomas pictured Mengstrasse at night, how calm and prosperous it looked. He wished Katia would intervene to stop Klaus talking.

"If we use their tactics, what is the difference between us and them?" Klaus asked.

Thomas put down his knife and fork.

"The difference is in me," he said. "I am from there. Those are my streets. But it grew barbarous and I have fled from there. And I don't know what to say, and I don't know what to feel. I wish I had your certainty."

"I wish you did too," Klaus replied.

The house in Pacific Palisades, Thomas often believed, was a mistake. Even before a visitor entered the building itself, it was evident that too much money had been lavished on the gardens.

And then the house was like something from a magazine, a showcase. He felt most embarrassed by it when he considered it from his brother's perspective. Heinrich and Nelly were living in a dingy apartment. They had bought their secondhand car on a hire-purchase scheme and were frequently behind with payments, as they were with rent. While Thomas gave his brother a stipend, he knew it was not enough. A few times as they sat in the garden, he noticed Heinrich lift his gaze towards the large building and look around. Heinrich did not need to speak. The distance between his brother's conspicuous comfort and his own misery was all too apparent.

Thomas blamed the poet, the one who had barely spoken at Agnes Meyer's in Washington, the one with the Scandinavian wife, for spreading the news about what Katia had said at the Meyers' dinner table. Greatly exaggerated, it was repeated to Thomas as an argument that had occurred over dinner in the White House itself, with the Roosevelts both at the table. It was reported that Katia had said that Germany should be left to burn and then reduced to producing vegetables. It could become the farm of Europe, she was reported to have said, with all its industrial zones cemented over.

Even Heinrich, when he heard the story, thought it was true.

Agnes Meyer continued to correspond with Thomas, announcing in one letter that all three of his sons should be fighting on behalf of the Allies. She was perplexed as to why Klaus had not yet seen combat. And Golo, she was informed, was working in propaganda. It was the least the Manns could do, she said, to become more actively engaged, considering how generous the United States had been to the family. When Thomas replied to her sharply, she wrote back as if she had just received one of his regular admiring letters, adding her delight at the defeat of the German forces in Stalingrad and the announcement by Churchill and Roosevelt that they would only accept unconditional surrender.

Soon afterwards, Agnes called and asked him to see a young man who would presently get in touch with him. When Thomas asked the young man's name, she said that she could not disclose it, but he would contact the Manns, needing to see both Thomas and Katia together, and no one else. He would give Agnes's name when he got in touch.

It was probably another of Agnes's ways of trying to be interesting, he presumed, so he thought nothing of it, not even saying anything about it to Katia.

A week later, when Thomas was napping, Monika called his

name. When he dressed and went downstairs, he found Katia at the door of his study.

"There is a boy here. He says he knows Agnes Meyer. He says that we agreed to see him."

The boy, who must have been in his late teens, was wearing a yarmulke. He seemed unusually self-possessed as he stood in the hallway. When Katia invited him into the main room, he followed her and then pointed to Monika.

"I need to see Mr. and Mrs. Mann alone."

For a second, Thomas thought that he must be selling something, but that thought was quickly dispelled by the boy's gravity.

When Monika left the room, Katia asked him if he wanted water or tea or coffee but he shook his head.

"It is policy not to accept refreshment."

The young man was so proper and serious that Thomas wondered now if he had not come for some religious reason. He spoke German like a native.

"My job is to visit prominent people so that they know what is happening to us in Europe."

"I have made some speeches on the topic," Thomas said. "And broadcasts."

"We have read your speeches."

"Is there something wrong?" Katia asked. "Is there something we don't know?"

"Yes, there is. That is why I have come to speak to you. It is now fully apparent to us that there is an agenda, agreed at the highest level, to organize the complete destruction of the Jews in Europe."

"In the concentration camps?" Thomas asked.

"That is what the camps are for. They are not for work, or for imprisonment. They are for annihilation. Murder on an industrial scale. They are using gas. It is quick and efficient and silent. The plan is that every single person of Jewish heritage in Europe will be murdered. They want the children as much as the adults. The plan is to have no Jews in Europe."

There was an air of sudden unreality in the room once these words were spoken. The large, high, comfortable space, walled in by plate glass, partitions cladded in varnished wood, the furniture chosen to match the design, seemed to muffle the meaning of the words.

"You know what a difficult position the president is in?" Thomas asked. "There is strong opposition to the taking in of refugees."

As soon as he said this, he knew how heartless and foolish it had sounded.

"I have no interest in the president or his position," the young man said. "It is too late anyway for refugees. People are dead."

"What do you want from us?" Thomas asked. He tried to make his tone soft, concerned, kind.

"We want you to have known, when the future comes. We want you not to be able to say that you did not know."

"Who else are you seeing in Los Angeles?" Thomas asked.

"That is none of your business, sir."

His tone, Thomas thought, had become openly rude.

He seemed too young to be bearing news of such import.

"Were you raised in the faith?" the young man gently asked Katia.

"No. I did not even know we were Jewish when I was a small girl."

"Do you wish you had been raised in the faith?"

"Yes, sometimes. But my father did not want us to live apart from those around us."

"They are making no distinctions between those who did not go to the synagogue and those who did."

"I know that."

"In the future, if there is any future, there will be no Jews in

Europe. You will walk through the cities on the Sabbath and see only ghosts."

"We will not go back," Katia said.

The boy indicated to Katia that she should accompany him to the garden so that he could take leave of them.

The next morning, Thomas put in a call to the president's office, making it clear that, while he did not need to speak to Roosevelt personally, he did wish to speak to someone at a very senior level on a matter of some importance.

When a return call came, he relayed to the official what their young visitor had told them about the camps.

"I wish to know if the information I received is correct."

The official told him he would call him back.

The following day, he received a call from Adolf Berle, assistant secretary of state, who spoke first in a friendly way about Thomas's and Katia's applications for American citizenship. He then responded to a question about the president's health without saying anything too informative. As he started to inquire after his family, Thomas cut him short. He asked Berle if he could address the question of the camps.

"Things are worse than we imagined," Berle said. "Much worse. The scenario you outlined to my colleague during your call is one that we now know to be the case."

"How many people know this?"

"It is known. Soon it will be widely known."

Thomas's broadcasts to Germany were arranged by the BBC. At the beginning, he was asked to write out a speech and have it recorded by a German-speaking announcer in London, but now he himself recorded a speech in Los Angeles; the record was sent to New York and transferred by telephone to another record in London and then played before the microphone.

"It feels like magic," he told Katia, "but it is not. It is the result of those lovely English words—'organization,' 'determination.'"

He tried to imagine someone in Germany isolated and afraid. Somewhere in a dark house or a dark apartment, listening with the volume down low so the neighbors could not hear. While he could address Americans in his faltering English, now he could speak a public German. Using the language of reason, of humanism, he could appeal to a common sense of decency.

"A German writer," he said, "speaks to you whose work and person have been outlawed by your rulers. Therefore I am glad to take the opportunity which the English radio service has offered me to report to you from time to time about all that I see here in America, the great and free country in which I have found a homestead."

There were occasions when he could not keep his anger in check at the obedience of ordinary Germans, which grew, he thought, more unpardonable from day to day.

"Since what my fellow countrymen," he stated, "are inflicting upon humanity is so atrocious, so unforgettable, then I cannot conceive how they will be able to live in the future among brother peoples of the earth as equal among equals."

He wondered if anyone listening remembered the tone that he had taken during the previous war and asked themselves if he could possibly be the same man, as he insisted now that Germany was a nation like any other, with ordinary advantages and ordinary faults, unexceptional.

"That is the way it should be," he said. "Germany is not, by its nature, special. It is surrounded by its enemies now only because it made those enemies. And its barbaric acts against the Jewish population have placed it beyond redemption. To be rescued, it will have to be defeated."

If he could change his views so radically, this should be a way of encouraging some of his compatriots to rethink their politics too. If he could come to his senses, then so could others.

In the recording studio, he tried to keep his tone measured and calm. He hoped that the occasional trembling in his voice might be enough to let listeners know the depth of his feeling.

When, later in the year, Erika returned, there was a letter waiting for her from the FBI, which wished to interview her, wanting to know the names of anyone in America who had been involved in the anti-fascist movement in Germany before 1933.

Katia said that Erika must have left the two men who came to interview her well shaken, as she had observed them from the veranda as they departed from the interview. They looked rather happy that it was over, Katia said.

Erika, for some days, veered from being in a rage, wanting to write articles about her ordeal, or give lectures or interviews about it, to becoming irritable at the least thing.

"The questions they asked! How ill-informed they are! And how persistent and lacking in even the smallest delicacy."

From the last phrase, Thomas divined that they had asked her about her relations with women.

He was almost relieved when a letter came on FBI notepaper asking him to make himself available for an interview that would best take place at his own domicile. His presence on their list of interviewees might lessen Erika's feeling that she was being singled out.

"If they ask me any questions about you," he said to Erika, "I shall say that I am your poor innocent father and no one ever tells me anything."

"They will accuse you of communism," she said.

"Brecht will be overjoyed."

When the appointment was made, and the two men, one fresh-faced and eager-looking and the other older and dour, came to the house, he decided to see them in his study. The main room seemed too preposterously Californian for an interview with the FBI about anti-fascism. The atmosphere in his study might encourage them to be respectful.

As soon as all three were seated, the older one took him through his rights in a deadpan voice. Thomas explained that they would have to speak slowly and forgive him his struggle with the language that was not his native one.

"We can understand you perfectly," the older man said.

"And I can understand you too."

They made clear then that they were here to find out about Bertolt Brecht and his associates and Thomas realized that he would be in a difficult position no matter what he said. Brecht had certainly been hard to avoid in the circle of German exiles on the west coast, but his contempt for Thomas and his work was also widely known. Although his visitors promised complete confidentiality, he suspected that news of this encounter would leak out. He thought of contacting Brecht before the end of the day to let him know that this meeting had occurred, or doing so through Heinrich, who was in regular contact with Brecht.

"Do you know if Mr. Brecht is a Communist?" the older man asked.

"I do not know about people's political sympathies unless they let me know about them and Mr. Brecht has never discussed such things with me."

He found the rage he felt at the questions caused his English to become more confident and accurate.

"You know the First Lady?"

"And the president indeed."

"Can you state that they are not Communists?"

"It would be surprising, would it not?"

"So, can you state that Bertolt Brecht is not a Communist?"

"It would be surprising."

"Why would it be surprising?" the younger one asked.

"If he were a Communist, he would surely have gone to the Soviet Union, where Communists are welcome rather than come to the United States where they are not welcome. I think that speaks for itself."

"Have you read his writings?"

Thomas hesitated for a moment. He did not want to disparage Brecht's work to these two men. It would open too many other questions.

"In Munich his work was performed sometimes, but he was not very popular in Bavaria."

"We understand that this Mr. Brecht is a regular visitor to this house."

"He has never been to this house. He may see my brother, but he is not part of our world."

"Yes, we know that he is close to your brother. Do you and your brother have the same political views?"

"No two people have the same political views."

"In the United States, some people are Democrats, others Republicans."

"Yes, but they will not have the same view on every single matter."

"Is your brother a Communist?"

"No."

"Your daughter?"

"Which one?"

"Erika."

"She is not a Communist."

"I am asking you again if you are familiar with Mr. Brecht's work."

"I am not."

"Why not?"

"I am a novelist. He is a playwright and a poet."

"Do novelists not read plays and poems?"

"His plays and poems are not quite to my taste."

"Why not?"

"They are not for me. Many others admire them greatly. There is no particular reason. In the same way that some people like movies, and others like baseball."

He saw them look at each other, and knew that they thought he was patronizing them.

"We would ask you to take this matter very seriously," the younger one said.

He nodded and smiled. If this were happening in any country in Europe now, he would have reason to be afraid. All he had to do here, however, was play a game with these two men, make sure to tell them nothing that was patently untrue, and not insult their intelligence, but also say nothing that might damage Brecht or open up the question of their hostility to each other.

"How many times in the past year have you met Mr. Brecht?"

"I see him sometimes at gatherings of the German cultural community, but we have no lengthy conversations."

"Why not?"

"I am a private man. My attention is focused on my work and my family. As anyone will tell you, I am not social."

"Can you tell us the content of even the shortest conversation between you and Mr. Brecht?"

"It might strike you as peculiar, but we do not even talk about literature, let alone politics. We might talk about the weather. I genuinely mean that. Our conversations are casual and polite. We are Germans. It is not in our nature to be garrulous. We are writers. It is in our nature to be guarded."

"You are being guarded now?"

"Anyone being interviewed by the FBI is guarded."

The interrogation continued for another hour, mentioning Thomas's relationship with the Roosevelts and the Meyers as though it caused suspicion, circling around the number of times Thomas had met Brecht and his opinion of Brecht as a playwright.

The last questions were, he thought, the strangest of all.

"If I use the phrase 'the working class,' what does that mean to you?" the younger one asked.

"I lived in Munich in 1918 when there was a Soviet revolution in the city. It was the time before inflation. We lived very well in the city at that time. We feared this revolution, just as we later feared fascism. The revolution came to nothing but it was done in the name of the working class."

"Where is that working class now?"

"With the Nazis."

"Would Mr. Brecht agree with you?"

"You will have to ask him."

"We are asking you."

"I think he may have views on that question that are more subtle than mine."

One evening at a gathering of Germans in Santa Monica, most of them composers or musicians, Thomas noticed the composer Arnold Schoenberg, whom he had met briefly some time before. They now had a short and friendly conversation.

Thomas began to attend social events where he thought Schoenberg might be. Of all the German-speaking artists, he thought, Schoenberg was the most important.

In his invention of the twelve-tone system, Schoenberg had established the theory of atonality in classical composition most clearly. German music had been fundamentally altered by him.

Thomas did not want to become close to him, or discuss his work with him. Instead, he wanted to observe him, get an impression of him. From the beginning, from the very first encounter, he almost knew what he was doing.

For his novel, he was imagining a composer living in Germany in the 1920s, a man who had signed a pact with some dark force so that his great ambition could be realized. He saw the shape of the book he would write about this composer. His narrator would be called Zeitblom; he would be a German humanist and friend of a famous composer. Zeitblom, in the novel, would be the one watching, noticing and sifting. The other protagonist, the genius composer, would be a dark, unknowable figure, haunted. He would bring destruction with him, including, eventually, the destruction of himself. Knowing him would wither the souls of those around him.

Thomas smiled at the thought that the sweet Californian skies, the beautiful soft mornings when he could breakfast in the garden, the abundance, the blameless beauty, had not conspired to alter his mind. Rather, the gray skies, the rainy springs, the long winters, the raked light on the Isar River, or the recalcitrant weather of Lübeck, had forged a sensibility so solid that it could not be transformed or even affected by this extended spell in paradise. Thus, his novel would show no sign that he had ever been away from Germany.

Thomas and Katia followed the news each day, reading the morning papers and listening to the radio at lunchtime and in the evening; he noticed that their mood could be swiftly transformed by a setback or a victory. When the Axis forces were briefly successful on the Eastern Front, they were despondent, but when news came of successful Allied bombings in the Ruhr, on Berlin and Hamburg, they started to imagine that the war would soon be over.

Also, the letters and phone calls that came from the children could depress them or put them in good humor. Elisabeth followed the war, especially on the Italian front, with close attention. And the phone calls from Monika, who had gone to New York, were almost funny, filled with her misadventures and her disagreements with landlords and taxi drivers. It was a relief sometimes that she did not mention the war.

"She is fighting her own little war," Katia said.

Since Michael did not try to keep in touch, Katia started to call Gret, who allowed Frido to come on the line to speak to his grandfather. Golo was in London working with the German-language division of the American Broadcasting Service. His letters were as meticulously composed as Erika's were untidy, with her spidery handwriting down the margins. Klaus wrote less often than the others. Sometimes it seemed that his letters were written very late at night, with many sentences deleted by the army censor.

In her phone calls, Agnes Meyer told Thomas to be careful with every word he said, even in private. There were some in Washington who were now planning the complete destruction of Germany, ensuring that all its industries would be put beyond use forever, and that its people would be ruled by the Allied victors. Soon, she said, he would be needed to speak out against this.

In December 1944, Nelly took an overdose of pills. Heinrich discovered her unconscious. She died in the ambulance on the way to hospital. When he found her, Heinrich said, she was peaceful and beautiful.

The German writers still living in Los Angeles came to her funeral, including Brecht and Döblin. There was a brief service, with Heinrich wiping his tears away. When he set about walking away alone, Thomas indicated to Katia, who followed him and brought him back to Pacific Palisades in their car. He lay on the sofa after lunch, and then they took him home.

After her death, Heinrich spoke about Nelly incessantly; he described her kindheartedness, how she cared for him as no one else ever did.

"In America, she could not manage," he said. "She could not manage America."

He got comfort, he told them, from touching and smelling her clothes and did not give anything away that had belonged to her. In the mornings, he worked, and then, he said, he spent the rest of the day thinking about her. Everything after her death, he said, was different.

He told Thomas and Katia that he had received a letter from a friend who wrote that, in this terrible time for the world, she wished only for a well-ventilated tomb, a soft coffin with a bed lamp above for reading and, most emphatically, no memories. He felt the same, he said. Except the part about the memories. He would like to have his memories.

Thomas was due to give a lecture at the end of May 1945, to be entitled "Germany and the Germans," as part of his role at the Library of Congress. While he did not expect the president or the First Lady to be in attendance, he presumed that they would read the lecture, as it was to be printed in advance. He wrote with Roosevelt in mind, knowing from Agnes Meyer that the president was still more preoccupied in defeating Japan and had not applied his mind in any detail to the future of Europe.

Germany would have to be defeated, Thomas thought, and forced to recognize its own crimes. Everyone who held office would have to be put on trial. The country itself was already in ruins.

"The Nazis have ensured," he wrote, "that the body of the Reich will not be rescued alive; it can only fall apart, piece by piece. There are not two Germanies, a bad one and a good one, but only one, in which the best qualities have been corrupted with diabolical cunning into evil. The evil Germany is the good one in misfortune and guilt, the good Germany perverted and overthrown."

Even when he took a walk with Katia by the ocean, he was in silent dialogue with Roosevelt, thinking about what he would say to him were they to meet in Washington. Thus, in April, when news came of Roosevelt's death, he was despondent. No one else, he believed, would be able to steer the Allies towards maintaining a balanced approach to Germany. Without Roosevelt, Stalin and Churchill would do their worst. He did not credit Truman with any of Roosevelt's gifts.

For a while, he wondered if his lecture in Washington should not be a panegyric for the dead president, but Agnes Meyer warned him that this would serve only to make enemies in the Truman camp.

What he wished to say was, he thought, perhaps too complex to matter in this time of simple polarities. He was insisting that all Germans were to blame; he wished to argue that German culture and the German language contained the seeds of the Nazis, but they also contained the seeds of a new democracy that could be brought into being now, a fully German democracy. For his example, he went to Martin Luther as an incarnation of the German spirit, an exponent of freedom who was also a set of opposites in which each element contained its own undoing. Luther was rational, but his speech could be intemperate. He was a reformer, but his response to the Peasants' Revolt of 1524 was insane. He had in him all the fury and foolishness that inspired the Nazis, but he also contained a willingness to change, to see reason, to want the sort of progress that might inspire a new Germany.

Luther contained extremes, he wrote, but also healing dualities; the German people were made in his image. Anyone who believed otherwise knew nothing of the country and its history.

He sighed as he read over the lecture. What influence he had in Washington depended on the idea that Roosevelt approved of him, saw him as a rational man who would be at his most useful now that disputes about good and evil should be replaced by more pragmatic discussions. Once Roosevelt was gone, the kind of argument Thomas wished to make, invoking the past in all its intricacies, attempting to make subtle statements about the present, would be seen as obscure, irrelevant by those who had replaced him.

Thomas resolved that he would go to Washington and put himself through the motions of speaking as though it might matter, but he knew that he would not be alone in seeing the event as an empty spectacle.

The moment the news came that Hitler was dead and that Germany had finally surrendered, Thomas called Heinrich with the intention of inviting him to supper and having him spend the night. These days, on the phone, Heinrich seemed exhausted, his voice weak. This time, however, he wanted an argument.

"Now we'll see the English and the Americans for what they are," he said.

"Maybe we'll see the Germans too," Thomas said. "There will be trials."

"They will make the country into one big America. The thought of the troops giving candy to children makes me sick."

"If I had a choice . . ." Thomas began and then stopped.

"Between?" Heinrich asked. "A choice between?"

"Between having my country liberated by the Americans or the Russians—"

"You would take the candy," Heinrich interrupted.

When Thomas told Katia that Heinrich did not wish to join them, she said that she would go and see him in the next few days.

"We have champagne," she said, "but I thought it could wait until some of the children are here. I often dreamed that I would like to celebrate Hitler's downfall by having an ordinary evening. We could have one of the evenings that Hitler never wanted us to have."

"Ordinary?" Thomas asked. "After all that's happened?"

"Just one night," Katia said. "We will pretend. In the meantime, I have the Riesling from the Domaine Weinbach that we like so much. It is being chilled as we speak."

Chapter 15
Los Angeles, 1945

The structure of the novel was now clear in his mind. It would be narrated by the self-effacing German humanist Serenus Zeitblom, a friend from childhood of the composer Adrian Leverkühn. Allowing Zeitblom to tell the story meant, Thomas believed, that the narrative could, at times, be personal and emotional as well as biased. While Zeitblom was sincere and trustworthy, his vision was limited, his powers of analysis circumscribed.

Zeitblom, writing in a doomed Germany, would begin the later chapters with an account of the actual progress of the war. He was Thomas's double, milder than the author, but living through the same years, the years of Hitler, hearing the same news. Both author and fictional narrator were alert to a time in the future, a time when Germany would be destroyed and ready to be remade, when a book like the one being composed might have a place in the world. While Zeitblom feared a German defeat, he feared a German victory even more.

He opposed the triumph of German arms, because what gave rise to Hitler repelled every element in his own decent spirit. If fascism survived, the work of his friend the composer would be buried, a ban would rest upon this new music for perhaps a hundred years; the music would miss its own age and only in a later one receive the honor that was its due.

Each day, in the time leading up to Hitler's downfall, as Thomas noted the news, he felt Zeitblom's presence. He imagined Zeitblom slowly realizing, as he did, that Hitler's reign was coming to an end. He had Zeitblom register, in his narrative, "our shattered, battered cities falling like ripe plums."

As he wrote, he had dream readers, of whom his own narrator was one. They were the secret Germans, the ones in internal exile, or they were the Germans of the future, in a country emerging from the ashes of the conflagration. In the books he had written since 1936, when his work was banned in Germany, he had been unsure if anyone at all would read them in the language in which he wrote them. They were written for an audience he could not imagine. Now, as he worked for readers who lived in the shadows or might emerge into daylight in the future, he could use a tone that was hurt and hushed, and create an atmosphere as someone might light a vaulted space with candles.

When the war ended, both Klaus and Erika were in Germany, Klaus in uniform working for *Stars and Stripes*, the army magazine, writing about the German cities in the aftermath of surrender, Erika reporting on a defeated Germany for the BBC. Golo was also in Germany, charged with setting up a radio station in Frankfurt. From Munich, Klaus wrote to his parents to say that the city had been transformed into a gigantic cemetery. Only with difficulty, he said, could he find his way through once-familiar streets. Large swathes of the city had been razed to the ground or reduced to rubble. He had dreamed of approaching the old family house on Poschingerstrasse, throwing out whatever Nazi official was living there and moving back into his old room. But there was not even a door in place on which to knock. The house was a shell. It had been used as a sort of brothel during the war, he learned, designed to produce Aryan babies.

Erika was one of the few allowed to see the Nuremberg prisoners in their cells. When the identity of their visitor was later disclosed to the captive Nazis, a few of them, she heard, regretted that they had not been able to have a serious talk with her. "I would have explained everything to her," Goering had cried out. "The Mann case was handled all wrong. I would have handled it differently." Erika, on informing her father of this, added that he had missed his chance to live in a castle and have his wife wear diamonds, with Wagner's music blaring all around.

Klaus, using his army pass, went to Prague to see if he could find Mimi and Goschi. After a long search, he located them, and wrote a detailed letter to his uncle about their condition. Heinrich came to see Thomas and Katia to show them the letter. Goschi, Klaus wrote, had nearly starved during the war, but she had not been detained. Her mother, on the other hand, had spent several years in Terezín and was lucky to survive. Klaus could hardly recognize the beautiful Mimi, he wrote. She had suffered a stroke. Most of her hair and many of her teeth had fallen out. She could barely speak and her hearing was affected too. That she was still alive appeared miraculous. She and her daughter were completely destitute.

Klaus wrote to his mother asking her to send them food packages, clothing and money, but not to write in German, as it was not a popular language in Prague.

Thomas knew that Heinrich still had constant worries about money. It struck him that his brother might return to Germany, especially if the eastern part of the country were to be under Russian control. He thought of offering him money for the fare. Now, having been shown the letter from Klaus, he watched his brother walk away, with shoulders hunched in grief. Heinrich blamed himself for what had happened to Mimi.

Thomas noticed how heated the tone of Klaus's letters became. His account of meetings with Franz Lehár and Richard Strauss, neither of whom suffered from any guilt about having lived comfortably in Germany as the war went on, made Klaus seem almost unhinged. When he had asked Strauss if he had ever considered leaving, Strauss had asked why he would have left a country that had eighty opera houses. Klaus relayed this to his parents in capital letters with many exclamation marks.

Klaus did an interview with an unrepentant Winifred Wagner for the army magazine. She spoke about Hitler's Austrian charm, his generosity and his marvelous sense of humour. Klaus wrote home to say that he had believed the views quoted in his article would cause outrage but that no one appeared to have even noticed.

He sent clippings from his *Stars and Stripes* pieces: "I felt a stranger in my former fatherland. There is an abyss separating me from those who used to be my countrymen. Wherever I went in Germany, the melancholy tune and nostalgic leitmotivs followed me: You can't go home again."

Klaus was able to find out what had happened to his friends: many had been tortured, others had been murdered. He saw how some people who had collaborated with the regime slowly began to acquire positions of influence. He wrote to his parents to emphasize that the German people did not understand that their present calamity was the direct, inevitable consequence of what they, as a collective body, had done to the world.

"When all this is over, I don't know how Klaus is going to live," Katia said. "Nobody needs a German who cannot stop telling the truth."

In the weeks after the war Thomas thought of Ernst Bertram. Bertram was somewhere in Germany now. If he did not feel shame, then he must at least know how to display the suitable outward signs of it. Since he would, as a Nazi supporter, be summarily removed from his academic position, his knowledge of Nietzsche and his world would be of no further use. It would be hard for him to defend himself, he who had gloated when the Nazis burned books by famous writers.

Hitler would still have risen and all the murder and mayhem would still have happened without Bertram, but, Thomas believed, his support and the support of some of his friends offered intellectual ballast for the movement. Fascism became less about greed or hatred or power once Bertram could call down the support of various dead philosophers and use fancy phrases about Germany, its heritage, its culture, its destiny.

In the years when windows were broken, synagogues burned, when Jewish people were dragged from their houses, when there was no mistaking what was to occur, Thomas wondered how this learned man managed to avert his eyes or assuage his conscience. And what strategies did he use to ingratiate himself with the authorities who were imprisoning other homosexuals? Did he ever imagine how it would all end: the cities in rubble, people starving, committees set up to make sure that no one like Ernst Bertram would ever be allowed to speak again?

When, some months later, Michael and Gret announced that they were to visit Pacific Palisades for a month with their two boys, Katia said how much she was looking forward to their visit as it would lighten the atmosphere in the house, which had been darkened by Thomas's dedicated work on his novel, the news from a defeated Germany and the calls, growing increasingly shrill, for Thomas Mann and his family to return to their homeland and take part in its reconstruction now that fascism had been defeated.

As soon as Michael and his family arrived, Thomas began to find ways to amuse Frido. Several times, in the first few days, he left his study to seek out the boy during the hours he normally devoted to work. He even encouraged Frido to visit him as he wrote, stopping his writing to lift him in the air, performing the same magic tricks for him that had delighted his own children when their mother was away, and drawing pictures for him.

Michael made withering remarks about the book his father was writing. What did he know about the mind of a composer? For the sake of peace, Thomas tolerated his son's musings on the nature of music that were directed at him with an undertone of resentment. Michael seemed to object to the fact that his father was appropriating the very discipline that Michael had been studying all his life. Thomas tried to distract him by scowling menacingly at Frido, who squealed with laughter, having to be warned by his mother that he must conduct himself properly at the table.

"How can he conduct himself if his grandfather is behaving like a clown?" Michael asked.

Since his grandson had no friends who spoke German, the language had come to him from his parents. He used a mixture of baby language and adult speech, never failing to amuse Thomas.

His own mind, he thought, was heavy with German as he struggled with the stilted tones of his narrator and the parodies of German styles. Hearing the innocent and confident gabble of his grandson charmed him. It did not remind him of his own childhood, when children had not been encouraged to speak at any length, nor indeed of his own time as a father of young children when his brood were more interested in interrupting one another than speaking to him. This stream of words that came from Frido was new and refreshing. When he woke in the morning, he smiled at the thought that he could hear this child talk and find ways to entertain him throughout the day until it was time for Frido to go to bed.

"When Erika is here," Michael said, "she will make you stay in your study all day."

As they waited for Erika to arrive, Katia heard from her own brother Klaus Pringsheim, who had come to America from Japan with his son, and wished to visit while Erika and Michael were there.

Katia busied herself preparing for the visitors, rehanging some pictures, moving boxes that had lain under the beds since the house was built. She had lived for more than forty years away from her family. Her parents had died in Switzerland during the war, her father unreconciled to his fate as exile. Her brothers were scattered. The family house in Munich had been demolished to make way for a Nazi Party building. The prospect of a visit by Klaus made her behave as if, in her mind, she had never let her early life in Munich be consigned to the past.

Thomas regretted coming out to the front of the house when he heard Klaus's car. Klaus had lost his beauty, he saw, but he had retained his sardonic air. Thomas watched as Klaus took in the shiny, pristine property, the carefully managed gardens, the exquisite view, putting his arms out in mock appreciation and then shrugging to suggest that, for someone like him, it was all pretense, nothing much.

"So the bird has found her gilded cage," he said, as he embraced his sister.

Klaus's son stood beside him, taller than his father. As he looked around him, he remained serene, detached. He bowed formally as he was introduced, before shaking hands.

Klaus addressed himself only to his sister, but as Erika forcefully joined the conversation, he included her. He did not even glance at Thomas.

Soon, at the table, he mocked Thomas's daily routines. But Thomas still stayed in his study all morning, strolled and napped in the afternoon and read in the evening, avoiding Klaus Pringsheim as much as he could. After a few days, at lunch, Klaus mentioned that he had been told what Thomas was working on.

"A novel about a composer? Yes, I have known a good number of them, and of course I studied under Mahler. You know, he was a much less haunted figure than his music might suggest. He was possessed by ambition and frightened by his wife, but there were no demons really."

Thomas saw no reason to reply. When he looked at Katia, he noticed that she was gazing admiringly at her twin brother.

The following day, Klaus raised the subject of *Death in Venice*.

"My grandmother loved it and could not stop admiring it until my mother ordered her to cease and desist praising it inordinately. My father was convinced that once the book had appeared, people were leering at him when he went to the opera. I made many friends because of the book, pederasts all. I didn't have to pay for my own champagne for about a year."

Thomas observed Erika stiffen in her seat.

"It is much admired, that story," Erika said. "All my father's work is much admired."

The earnestness of Erika's tone, the simplicity, seemed to catch Klaus Pringsheim unawares. He listened patiently to Erika's account of the Nuremberg trials and how the English prosecutor had believed that he was quoting from Goethe when the quotes were, in fact, from her father's novel about Goethe. Klaus did not speak again for the rest of the meal.

"I am told that you read each chapter aloud when it is completed," Klaus said over dinner the next day. "I would love to be part of the audience for that."

He appeared chastened and looked as though he meant what he was saying. But then he turned to his sister.

"Now that my looks have gone, in order to impress people I must be able to talk about my brother-in-law's home habits."

When Thomas caught Erika's eye, he felt that she was as inclined as he was to throw a glass of wine at Klaus.

"Perhaps we could talk about Japan," Katia said. "I believe the emperor thinks he is God. Did he ever attend one of your concerts?"

• • •

On Friday of that week it was arranged that Thomas would read from his novel. Thomas would read two chapters, the first about the arrival of a boy called Little Echo to brighten the life of his uncle, the solitary composer, and the second about the death of the same little boy.

As the time approached, he dreaded the reading. It would be easy to read the factual opening, and not difficult to read the descriptions of the small boy and how welcome he was with all his charm and beauty. Katia, he felt, would know instantly that he had used Frido for this creation. He almost wished that he had chosen something more obscure, whose origins would not be recognized by his listeners.

They all gathered around, including Golo who had recently arrived, as though for a happy family occasion. As he had worked on these scenes, he had been aware how dark and personal they were. He had given his German composer the very thing that he himself loved: a young, innocent boy. But since Leverkühn, his composer, could only damage those who came close to him, the boy was destined for death. This would be the most human part of the book as he registered the pain of that loss. It would show the cost Leverkühn had paid for his overarching ambition. The pact he had made with the devil would move from the realms of folktale and fantasy into a space that was sharply real.

He began, glancing at Katia a few times; she was smiling in approval. When he came to the death of the boy, he read slowly, not looking up at any one of his listeners. He wondered if he had not included too much detail of each phase of the illness in all its shivering, frightful drama. The boy was in pain, calling out "Echo will be good, Echo will be good." The boy's sweet face changed beyond recognition, horribly, and when the gnashing of the teeth started, Little Echo looked as though he were possessed.

Thomas, once the little boy was dead, had done what he needed to do. He put the pages aside. No one in the room spoke. Eventually, Golo switched on a lamp close to him and stretched, making a low, groaning sound. Klaus Pringsheim had his hands clasped and his eyes fixed on the floor. His son sat palely beside him. Erika stared into the distance. Katia sat silently.

Eventually, Erika moved to turn on the main light. Thomas stood up. He pretended to be studying the pages he had been reading from; he knew that Katia was approaching him.

"Is that why you befriended the boy?" she asked.

"Frido?"

"Yes, who else?"

"I love Frido."

"Enough to use him in a book?" she asked and walked quietly across the room to join her brother and his son.

Chapter 16
Los Angeles, 1948

Elisabeth cast her quizzical eye on him.

"My daughters don't like being laughed at, either of them."

"I thought it was just Angelica," Katia said.

"It is also Dominica," Elisabeth said. "So please don't upset them."

Since Dominica was barely four years old, Thomas thought it strange that his granddaughter was being discussed as though she were an adult.

Elisabeth, with her two serious daughters, had come to stay, her husband, Borgese, having gone to Italy on some mission that was deemed too delicate to be described. During the first lunch, Thomas, on finding that Angelica did not want ice in her water, had said that every good little girl of his acquaintance generally longed for ice.

"Little girls who don't like ice are often not very nice," he said in English.

Angelica, who was eight, became instantly upset and turned to her mother to express her unhappiness. Elisabeth suggested that she go to the kitchen and ask that her lunch be served to her in the garden at a place of her choosing.

"I will come in a while and make sure you are all right."

She glanced stonily at her father.

"It was a joke," Thomas said.

"She does not like to be referred to as a little girl," Elisabeth said. "Or as not very nice."

"How clever of her," Erika said. "I never liked that either."

"I am sure I never called you a little girl," Thomas said.

"Or not very nice," Katia added.

Later, Thomas and Katia, in hushed voices in his study, asked what had happened to Elisabeth in her decade away from them. Thomas's relationship with his two grandsons was based entirely on jokes and banter, on thinking of new names to call them or playing tricks on them, and he could not imagine why his granddaughters would not also enjoy such lighthearted attention. They must have inherited their humorlessness and sensitivity from a long line of dreary Borgeses.

Angelica arrived at lunch the next day pale-faced and aggrieved, like some princess whose dignity had been threatened. Thomas noticed that Erika moved into the place beside her.

"What are you reading at the moment?" Erika asked her.

"In our family, it is difficult," the child answered, "since we speak Italian to our father and German to our mother and my sister and I speak English to each other. So we have such a range of books to choose from. But at the moment I am reading Lewis Carroll. He is having quite an influence on me."

On their walk, Thomas and Katia agreed that in their childhoods such a tone would have been greeted with derision by both parents and siblings.

"Do you think," Katia asked, "that this is how other American children behave? Or is it something that has been specially created in Chicago by Elisabeth and Borgese?"

The following morning, in the living room, Erika had a map of Europe on the floor and she was showing Angelica all the places where she had been, with Angelica asking considered questions.

In the corner, Dominica was playing with dolls, while Elisabeth sat reading.

"Aunt Erika is going to take us to the pier at Marina del Rey," Angelica said to them in a German that Thomas thought bore traces of an Italian accent.

"Both of you?" Katia asked.

"Yes, for ice cream and hot dogs."

"But mind, no mustard on the ice cream," Thomas said and then realized that the remark might be seen to mock their outing, suggesting that they did not really know how to eat their food. He retreated.

"They make excellent hot dogs in Santa Monica," he said.

"So we have heard," Angelica said, looking up from the map.

Over lunch, in the absence of Erika and the two girls, Thomas was surprised by Elisabeth's vehemence against Germany.

"I will have nothing to do with that country," she said. "I have no interest in what it does or doesn't do. I don't want to set foot in it or think about it."

Thomas wondered if Elisabeth regretted marrying Borgese and tried to find a question that might elicit some clue about this.

"Do you blame Germany for destroying your youth?" he asked.

"I don't blame my parents and I don't blame my former country. I don't blame anyone."

"Blame your parents for what?" he asked.

"One, that I have no proper education. Two, that love always came to me as a kind of reward."

"A reward for what?" Katia asked.

"For being quiet, for being charming, for being a good little girl."

"You were not charming to your younger brother," Katia said.

"What a nuisance Michael has always been!" Elisabeth said.

She began to laugh.

"Have you had many affairs since your marriage?" Thomas asked.

He heard Katia holding her breath. He himself was almost shocked that he had dared ask the question.

"One or two," Elisabeth replied and laughed again.

"Did you have an affair with Hermann Broch?" he asked.

"We fumbled once, maybe twice. I wouldn't call it an affair. But that was before my marriage. He was very funny when I knew him."

"And he was known for being very rude," Thomas said.

"Not to me," she replied.

She had become, Thomas thought, formidable and edgy. He wished she would stay longer.

He had not noticed a moleskin-covered notebook beside her on the table until she opened it.

"I have some questions for both of you written out," she said.

"I'm sure you do," Katia replied.

"First question. Why is Erika here?"

"She has nowhere else to go," Katia said. "Nowhere. Before, she could lecture. But now no one wants to hear about Germany and the war."

"What about her husband?"

"Auden? He was never really her husband. She hasn't seen him for years."

"Why is she not with Bruno Walter? I thought she might marry him once his wife died."

"He has other plans," Katia said.

"What is she doing here?"

"She is going to work as her father's secretary. And, as much as I will let her, she is going to help run the household and make all the decisions."

"Why don't you encourage her to find a life of her own?"

"Your father needs her."

"She intends to stay here with you forever?"

"It seems so," Katia said.

"And where is Monika?"

"She is in New York," Katia said. "Have you not heard from her? I get a letter a day sometimes."

Thomas looked at her, surprised. He had not been told this before.

"She says her dream would be to find a place where there are no books," Katia said. "So she is not eager to visit us just now. But I'm sure that will change. It always does."

Elisabeth ran her finger down her list of questions.

"Why did you marry him?" she asked her mother, pointing casually at her father.

Katia did not even hesitate. She spoke as though she had prepared her reply.

"Of all the possibilities, present, past and future, your father was the least preposterous," she said.

"Was that the only reason?"

"Well, there was another, but these are sensitive and private matters."

"I won't ask again."

Katia sipped her coffee and appeared to be gathering her thoughts.

"My father was a philanderer. He could not stop himself. He wanted any woman he saw. I have not had that problem with your father."

"Would you like me to leave the room so you can say more?" Thomas asked, smiling.

"No, my love. I have nothing to add."

"Why do you still see Alma Mahler?" Elisabeth asked.

"Ah, that is an interesting one," Katia said. "She is atrocious. And since Werfel's death, she has become more so. She drinks and she speaks her mind. I have nothing good to say about her."

"And yet you see her?"

"I do. She has something of old Vienna about her. I don't mean the old cultured Vienna and all that. I mean a sort of joy that they took from life then. I loved it when I saw it and it is gone. It will not come back. Perhaps Alma is the last."

"Finally, Klaus wrote to me to say that you have been sharp with him."

"He doesn't know where to go," Katia said.

"You don't want him here?"

"We cannot finance him indefinitely," Katia said.

"But you can Erika?"

"Erika will work for her father. Can you imagine Klaus doing that?"

"So that's the criterion?"

"Stop!" Katia said. "I don't know what to do about Klaus. Can we leave it at that?"

"I don't want to upset you," Elisabeth said.

"Can we leave it at that?" her mother repeated.

When Klaus returned to Pacific Palisades, he was, at the beginning, so thin and haggard, so withdrawn, so broken, that even Erika judged it unwise to have an argument with him. When Thomas asked her if he was taking morphine, she shrugged as if to say that much was obvious. Perhaps, Thomas thought, something in Klaus's personal life had further unmoored him. But Klaus had a way of letting private wounds drift by while worrying instead about his literary reputation or getting into a state of fury over public events. He was obsessed by Gustaf Gründgens, Erika's first husband, who had become Goering's favorite actor during the war. Gründgens, having been released from captivity by the Russians, had quickly gone back on the stage in triumph. His appearance on his first opening night after the war garnered a standing ovation. When Klaus attended, Gründgens was greeted with cheers by a packed house.

Several times, Thomas heard his son recount the scene for anyone who would listen. While his German compatriots, he said, would not offer open support for the doomed Nazi leaders and their slogans, they could display their real lack of repentance by lauding an actor who had been a favorite of the Nazi leaders.

"What cannot be done in daylight," Klaus said, "can be done in the dark."

Klaus was indignant at the very idea that he himself might return to live in Germany.

"I left in 1933 not for something I did but for something they did, and my unwillingness to go back to live there is not because of who I am but because of who they are."

He would have made an excellent speechwriter, Thomas thought, or a culture minister.

Two months earlier, Klaus, who could not drive, had written to Katia to say that he wished to live in Los Angeles, perhaps in a cottage close to his parents' house. He asked his mother to look out for such quarters and inquire about the price. Also, he added, he would like to employ a young driver who must be able to cook and also have a pleasant appearance. He would like to stay for six months, he said, and take meals sometimes with his parents.

Katia was indignant. Thomas could not tell what she was most offended by, whether it was Klaus's sure, casual view that his parents would pay his rent, or the mention of the young good-looking driver, or the idea that he would merely stay six months. Katia replied to Klaus, letting him know that he would not be supported in this way and that his proposal was quite outrageous. It was, Thomas thought, the first time she had written to him so sternly.

Now, as Klaus stayed with them, they could hear him moving around in the night and were aware, as he veered from being sleepy and silent to talking nonstop at the table, that he was consuming a variety of drugs. Most days, he did not bother to shave and, despite his mother's insistence that there was plenty in his wardrobe, he did not often change his clothes.

Klaus was now in his early forties. He had a different idea every day for a book he might write or an article a magazine might commission. One moment it was a biography of Baudelaire and the next a novel to be published under a pseudonym about homosexual life in prewar New York, and then it was an article about his own experience of Germany after the war and then a long piece about train travel in America. He did not ever join them for breakfast and sometimes had to be woken when lunch was ready. He avoided the sunlight in the garden.

"If you could only get up early in the morning," Katia said, "you would write a book that the whole world would read."

When Thomas saw Klaus shaved, with his hair tidied, wearing a freshly pressed suit and a white shirt and new shoes, his suitcase beside him as he waited for a car to take him to Union Station, he could see from Katia's guilty look that she had given him money to go back to New York.

Thomas was alone for a time with his wife and daughter. As Erika busied herself with his papers, making suggestions on each day's work and keeping his correspondence up to date, Katia became distant from him. There was a spot in the garden where she took a deck chair and a book, or she got involved helping the gardener.

Since Erika dealt with the mail and controlled his diary, sometimes at the table all of the conversation was between the two of them, Katia sitting silently. There was seldom open conflict between the two women. However, one day when Golo was present, Erika was displeased that the salad had not been properly dressed and then insisted that the vegetables had once more been overcooked.

"It is as if we are back in Munich with that awful food," she said.

"What awful food?" Katia asked.

"Oh, thick gravy masking any other taste and overcooked everything. Stodgy! Inedible! Bavaria!"

"You were grateful for it at the time."

"I knew nothing else."

"I suppose that is correct. And you knew no manners either and you still don't," her mother said. "I often wonder where we got you."

"From a night of passion, I am sure," Erika said.

"Like one of yours with Bruno Walter!"

Katia turned pale once she had spoken and looked at Golo. Thomas saw Golo indicating to his mother that she should say nothing more. Thomas's own aim was to finish his meal as quickly as he could and retreat to his study. He was not surprised when Katia did not knock on his door later asking him if he was ready for their daily walk. She had gone for a drive with Golo.

Klaus came back from New York looking even more washed-out and disheveled than before. Thomas was aware that Katia and Erika had decided to postpone telling him what had caused Klaus's return.

For the first few days, Klaus remained in his room, his meals delivered to him on a tray.

"I have made him promise not to roam the house at night," Katia said. "We all need our sleep."

"What is wrong with him?" Thomas asked.

"Erika knows better than I do. He went to some stupid party in New York and there was a police raid, but not before he had taken some concoction. Don't ask me what it is called but it causes highs and then lows. He is on an extended version of the lows."

When Klaus started to join them for supper in the evening, he was voluble and excitable, sometimes unable to finish his sentences, but unwilling to let anyone else speak. He grew animated on the subject of Monika, whom he had seen in New York.

"She has been evicted from several hotels for hoarding food in her room and for not paying her bills," he said. "Here we are living in luxury whereas Monika, who suffered more than any of us, walks the streets like a tramp. Something should be done for her. I told her that she needed to keep in touch with us all."

As he looked from one to the other at the table, he moved from sounding like a madman to becoming almost calm.

Soon someone began to call Klaus incessantly from San Francisco.

"It's Harold," Katia said.

"I don't care if it is Winston Churchill," Thomas replied.

Harold, it seemed, was a lover of Klaus's from New York who had come west and, to coincide with Klaus's arrival, had managed to lose his job in San Francisco. He was on his way to Los Angeles. The phone calls were a due warning.

At meals, there was talk of Harold being drunk, or Harold having enticed some third person, a young man of low reputation, into a hotel room in downtown Los Angeles with himself and Klaus. And then Harold was arrested and Klaus had to provide bail.

As Erika and her mother discussed this, Thomas noticed that each of his children appeared to relish the problems or flaws the others had. Klaus sounded sensible once he could talk about Monika. Elisabeth was content that Michael acted petulantly and she almost purred when Erika behaved badly, as did Golo. Erika was now united with her mother in worry about Klaus and Harold. Klaus's failure to come home each night made the two women, who had been avoiding each other, join forces. At first, they bemoaned how badly Klaus was conducting himself. Then they worried about how it would all end. Finally, they started to propose solutions to the crisis, including the possibility of Erika and Klaus collaborating on a screenplay of *The Magic Mountain*.

When Thomas heard this, he took Katia aside.

"We should let them have their fantasies, but we must not harbor them ourselves."

"Erika is optimistic about the idea."

"Let her be optimistic."

This was, he knew, the nearest he had come to criticizing Erika to Katia.

When Harold was released from one jail, he was incarcerated in another for a different offense. Erika had to drive Klaus to visit him.

"He sounds like a most interesting person," Thomas said to Katia, "this Harold. I think I prefer him to all my other children-in-law, including Bruno Walter and dear Gret and that noisy Italian whom Elisabeth married and even the librarian in Princeton whom Golo briefly favored."

"Klaus tells me that he is very good-looking," Katia replied.

They laughed in a way that they had not laughed in a while.

"All we need now is Monika," Thomas said.

"I have sent her the money to go to Italy," Katia said. "That's where she wants to go."

"To work?"

"Don't ask. When she gets safely there, I'll keep you informed. And I've been thinking about Klaus. He should really have his own apartment. He told me that he has found somewhere and the price is reasonable. And he also wants to buy a car and take driving lessons. All the things I told him we would not pay for, I agreed to. The minute I see him, my heart goes out to him. I suppose he knows that. I have become the sort of mother I despise."

At the beginning, having been freed from prison, Harold joined Klaus in his new quarters, but soon, having caused further havoc, he disappeared, leaving Klaus alone. When Katia and Erika once more expressed their sympathy for Klaus, Thomas was puzzled.

"This is what he wanted. An apartment close by and a car. The only thing missing is the chauffeur he demanded. He is alone. Surely it is every writer's dream to be alone?"

The phone rang at one o'clock in the morning; he heard Katia answering. She came at once to his room.

"Klaus has cut his wrists. He's in Santa Monica Hospital. The doctors say he's not in any immediate danger. I'll drive to the hospital. Erika is still asleep. Let her sleep until morning."

Not long after Katia had left, Erika knocked on his door.

"The car is missing," she said. "Where is my mother?"

Erika then insisted on following Katia to the hospital in her own car.

Thomas went to his study. For a second, he thought he should call Golo, or maybe Elisabeth. It would give him some comfort to tell someone else about this, not be left alone in the house waiting for news. But it would be easier to wait, stay here alone, and try to pretend that Klaus was asleep upstairs, or still in New York.

If Klaus resembled anyone in the family, he thought, it was his aunt Lula. Lula had the same darting imagination and inability to be content. The ordinary day did not interest her, but rather, in the beginning, a day in the future when marriage would solve her problems. Once married, she looked forward to a time when children would make her happy. When her daughters were born, she would plan for a bigger apartment, or a complete redecoration of the main rooms, or a holiday. As a child, he remembered, Lula would skip the middle part of a novel so she could live in the excitement of the end.

So, too, Klaus wanted publication more than he wanted the dull process of writing. The excitement of injecting himself proved irresistible to Klaus as it had to Lula. And when the thrill could not be maintained, there were not many other choices.

Thomas waited in his study, letting thoughts about his son come in and out of his mind, hoping that he would hear the sound of cars in the drive and Katia and Erika would be home.

He thought of calling the hospital, but knew that someone would surely phone him if there was any news.

By the time they appeared, Thomas was in his bedroom. When he went downstairs, they told him that the cuts in Klaus's wrists had not been deep, and that he would survive.

Someone in the hospital contacted a local newspaper about Klaus's attempt to kill himself. This, in turn, was taken up by national and international press so that the phone rang regularly with old friends and curious acquaintances seeking news of Klaus's welfare.

When Golo came to stay, his mother and sister chided him for lifting the receiver each time the phone rang and placing it back in its cradle. Even as news came of Klaus's improved state, Golo did not raise his head from whatever book he was reading. When Thomas tried, however, to deplore Klaus's attempt at suicide with Golo so the two of them could form an alliance in the house, Golo responded coldly.

"My mother is worried," he said.

Thomas went back to his study. Erika soon knocked on the door and told him that Klaus, who was to be released from hospital that day, had expressed a wish to go swimming before being taken home.

"He switched on the gas, knowing that the neighbors, whose kitchen window is right beside his, would smell it, especially since he had left the kitchen window open. And then, when they banged on the door, he grazed his wrists with a blunt knife. And all that fuss for nothing!"

Klaus moved into a hotel in Santa Monica so that he could spend more time with a resurfaced Harold, whom Katia had banned from ever coming to Pacific Palisades. Thomas learned that Christopher Isherwood was in the same hotel.

"Could that be the same Christopher Isherwood who once found you a husband?" he asked.

Erika nodded.

"What a cheeky little fellow he was! I often thought a stretch in uniform might do him good. Can we take it that the liberation of the world from tyranny has been achieved without his assistance?"

"He did not fight in the war," Erika said.

"Could we ban him as well as Harold?"

Alma Mahler called.

"I know how worried you must be. When suicide is in a family, it is like beauty or blue eyes. It never goes away. Both of your sisters! Did anyone in the earlier generation also do away with themselves?"

Thomas told her that they did not.

"But, of course, no one spoke about it then. How did your father die?"

Thomas assured her that the senator had died of natural causes. He tried to think how he might change the subject.

"My stepfather and my stepsister and her husband took poison when they heard that the Red Army were coming into Vienna," Alma said.

Thomas knew that some of her family had been Nazis, but thought that she might have learned not to refer to them.

Now that she was a widow and the war had ended, Alma began to travel, first to New York and then to Europe. When in Los Angeles, she kept in touch with even the most minor figures among the exiles. If someone had published a new poem or written a string quartet or been involved in an accident or a feud, she spread the news or came to visit.

Since she had tended to respond with enthusiasm to his work,

Thomas could not fathom why she sought to cause trouble when his novel *Doctor Faustus* was published. He had told her about the book as he worked on it, feeling that she, perhaps more than any of the exiles, might understand the pressures on German composers in the years after her husband's death. While she was often silly and had ridiculous opinions, she knew a great deal about music. She loved the idea of forbidden chords and sounds that could entice the devil into the room. And she was fascinated by late Beethoven. Sometimes, when there was a piano available, if he mentioned some composition, she could play the melody from memory.

He had made no secret of the book, even giving readings of chapters as they were completed to guests who came to the house. But he had not raised the subject of the novel with Arnold Schoenberg because he found him too learned and distant, too intimidating. He felt that Schoenberg would make it plain to him that Thomas did not know enough about music to write such a book.

Thomas presumed, since the émigré world was so insular, that someone would have passed the news on to Schoenberg that he was writing a book about a modern composer. When the book was published, however, it was obvious that no one had.

In retrospect, it was, he knew, unwise to have sent a copy of the novel to Schoenberg with an inscription that said: "For Arnold Schoenberg, the real one, with best wishes." The phrase "the real one" could be taken as a compliment suggesting that while Mann's character was fictional, Schoenberg himself was not fictional, he was real. But it could also be taken to mean that Schoenberg was the real one and Mann had created a version of him in his composer who had made a pact with the devil.

By the time the book came out, Schoenberg's sight had deteriorated enough for him not to be able to read it. Instead, he pondered on the inscription and on what he heard about the book.

At first, it was unclear to Thomas how Schoenberg had started to believe that people in Los Angeles would think that he himself had syphilis, as the fictional composer did. All he knew was that Schoenberg, while wandering in the aisles of Brentwood Country Mart, met one of the German émigrés and informed her out of the blue that he did not have any venereal diseases.

When the woman expressed surprise at the idea that this was even a possibility, Schoenberg explained why he felt he needed thus to reassure her. It was that book by that Thomas Mann, he said. The woman drove straight to Pacific Palisades and told Katia what the composer had said.

It occurred to Thomas that Alma Mahler might be the person to calm Schoenberg down, let him know that the novel was an intricate creation and reassure him that no reader could ever believe that he himself had syphilis just because the composer was based on him.

Alma agreed with him that Schoenberg had behaved absurdly in the Mart; she said that she would speak to him and perhaps the Manns could come to supper with him and his wife where they could all raise a glass to the publication of a marvelous novel.

What she did not tell Thomas was that she had already called at the Schoenbergs' several times since the appearance of *Doctor Faustus* and had given the composer and his wife an alarming account of the book's contents. All this was relayed to him by a friend of the Schoenbergs.

It was simple, she had told Schoenberg: Thomas Mann's composer had invented the twelve-tone system, and so had Schoenberg; Mann's composer had syphilis and was in league with the Devil, thus people might think that he also shared these features with Schoenberg.

Thomas worried that if Schoenberg went to a lawyer, he himself would be forced by the Knopfs to unravel all the strands of the book, outlining what was true and what was made up. He shivered at how hard it would be to show from what strange depths this book had come.

Doctor Faustus, despite its recondite content, was a bestseller in America. Any lawyer that the Schoenbergs approached would take this into account. If the composer were to sue, he would, Thomas believed, demand for himself a share in the royalties, or he could even want both royalties and damages. Because of the dense amount of textual argument that would ensue, the costs of defending a case like this would be ruinous.

In the early mornings, as he lay in bed, Thomas could picture a scene in which he would be ordered to hand over all the income from the book to Arnold Schoenberg.

The row between Thomas and Schoenberg made Alma, when she came to see them, even more excited than usual.

"I don't think you understand Arnold Schoenberg, do you? His work with atonality is not a trick or just technical. It comes to him as something spiritual."

She stopped for a moment as Thomas looked puzzled.

"Schoenberg is a deeply religious man. He became a Lutheran in all good faith, as he has returned to his Jewish roots with absolute humility and seriousness. He is not immodest enough to see his music as devotional, but he sees it as a bulwark against materialism. So when he witnesses his technique used as a prop in a novel, adopted by a man, however fictional, who has associations with the Devil and whose creative urge is spurred on by syphilis, then he is not pleased."

"Yes," Thomas said, "it is a grubby business writing novels. Composers can think about God and the ineffable. We have to imagine the buttons on a coat."

"And give venereal diseases to German composers," Alma added.

•   •   •

Sometimes at night, when Katia had gone to bed and Erika was not in the house, Thomas played Schoenberg's *Transfigured Night* on the phonograph and he regretted that he had hurt the composer with his novel. The piece was tense and restrained, but layers of carefully modulated emotion broke through. He knew it was written before Schoenberg invented his twelve-tone system but he saw that it was pointing towards a style that would, in the future, grow more distilled. He wished he could have spoken to Schoenberg about this and hoped that he might be able to do so if they could be reconciled.

To the composer, he must seem venal. He needed material for his novel as a ship might need ballast. His was not an art that could ever manage to be pure. As he listened to the strings moving faster, and the tone of pleading rising and falling, he wished he were a different sort of writer, less concerned with the details of the world and more with larger, more eternal questions. It was too late now; his work was done, or most of it.

How curious it was that across this American city lived the man who, when he was young, composed this lush music! Schoenberg, Thomas imagined, was still awake in the untransfigured Californian night. Some of those early yearnings must still be with him, and he must feel sorrow that such tender expression was no longer possible. Some of the same emotions that the music evoked had, Thomas hoped, been captured in his novel, but words were not notes and sentences not chords.

Erika was now his driver as well as his editor, his enforcer. She took the phone calls, banked the checks and replied to invitations. She dealt with the Knopfs in New York, making clear to Blanche Knopf that everything to do with publishing, including the smallest matter, must come through her.

And Erika enjoyed infuriating Agnes Meyer by refusing to let her speak directly to her father.

One afternoon when the phone rang, Thomas had nearly reached it when Erika lifted the receiver.

"No, you cannot," he heard her say. "My father is in his study. He is deep in his work."

Thomas whispered, asking who it was, as Erika, putting her hand over the mouthpiece, informed him that it was his friend, the woman from Washington, D.C. When he indicated that he wished to speak to her, Erika shook her head.

"I can give him a message," she told Mrs. Meyer, "but I cannot interrupt him."

As he stood close, he could hear Agnes haranguing Erika, who, having said her farewells, soon put the receiver down.

"I am electric light," she said, "and Agnes Meyer is a bat. I turn on and she flies off."

When the FBI contacted the house seeking to conduct some further interviews with Erika, she insisted that it was Mrs. Meyer who had encouraged them.

"They have left me alone for two years. Why are they back? That wretched Agnes is waging her own war against peace-loving people."

"Peace-loving people?" Katia asked. "Would that be you?"

Thomas expected Erika to be in the same sort of fury against the FBI as she was against many others, but instead she shook her head in worry, as though genuinely frightened.

"I have been really stupid about this citizenship business," she said. "I was too busy in the war to follow through on my application. They can have me deported at any time."

If she had to leave America, Thomas thought, Erika would have nowhere to go. She had a British passport, but she knew no one in England. There would be no room for her outspokenness in the new Germany, east or west. And Klaus had moved to France, where he was languishing in Cannes. Thomas understood that, while Erika was willing to write to her brother and support him, she did not wish to find herself in the same predicament as he was. She did not want to be alone and stateless, someone who had served her purpose in the struggle against fascism and had no further use.

The FBI came to the house twice; the second interview lasted, Thomas noted, almost a full day, with a break for lunch. That evening, at dinner, Erika explained what had transpired.

"Sex, sex, sex. That is all. I wish I'd had the sex they think I've had. And when I said it to them: 'Have you never had any sex?' one of them answered: 'Not outside the state of matrimony, ma'am.' And he is lucky I did not drag him by his protruding ears out of this house and leave him in a state of matrimony in the street outside!"

The FBI had insisted, once more, that Erika had enjoyed relations with her brother Klaus that were less than healthy, and, more dangerously, they had insinuated that they had indisputable evidence that Erika's marriage to Auden had taken place only so she could get British citizenship, and the marriage had never been consummated and never would be because of her predilections and his.

Their visitors seemed not to know about his daughter's long love affair with Bruno Walter, but this was hardly the moment to mention it, Thomas thought.

"They have us all mixed up. They think you wrote Klaus's books and they think we are all Communists."

"I hope they don't think I am a Communist," Katia said.

"They don't even know that you exist!" Erika said.

She made it sound like an accusation.

Once the row with Schoenberg had begun to die down, Thomas hoped that he and Katia could enjoy their declining years in

Pacific Palisades in peace. Many of the émigrés had gone back to Germany, but the Manns had no plans to do so. Thomas was slowly being made aware, however, that his efforts not to become involved with Germany were causing bitterness in his homeland.

"No one objected when I left in 1933," he said, "but now they think I have a duty to return. And what is strange is that I get abusive letters from people I have never met, but I don't hear at all from anyone I knew."

"They need scapegoats," Erika replied. "And you are an easy target. No column or editorial feels complete unless there is an attack on you."

"And I think the American press is confusing me with you and your brother. They think I am some sort of left-wing agitator. Apparently, I am on a list."

The two hundredth anniversary of Goethe's birth was to come that summer, and Thomas, in an essay, tried to connect Goethe's thinking with the needs of the contemporary world. He could, he thought, preach, using Goethe's example, that in public as much as private the world should recoil from single ways of seeing things, and begin to think in myriad ways. Goethe's paradigm could be nourishing to a world threatened by a savage clash of ideologies. The writer's mind was protean, his imagination was open to change. Humor and irony were essential tools for him.

Both Erika and Golo, who read the first draft of the essay, thought that he was being too idealistic, not suspicious enough, that he was making Goethe out to be a spokesman for the United Nations, but Thomas persevered, letting Erika get actively involved only when the essay needed to be radically cut so that it could become a lecture. It would be delivered first in Chicago and then in Washington, D.C. Then he would take his first trans-atlantic flight to London and deliver the lecture at Oxford. From there, he would go to Stockholm via Göteborg and deliver the lecture once more.

When an invitation came to visit Germany, Erika advised him to turn it down.

"You do not want to travel there now," she said. "It is too early. It is best to refuse all invitations to Germany."

"I would like to honor Goethe in his homeland during his bicentenary," Thomas said. "But it is not simple. I know it is not simple."

"His homeland is in the mind of his readers," Erika said. "You can hardly say it is Germany. Is Buchenwald his homeland? You would hardly like to go there in honor of Goethe!"

Thomas and Katia decided, however, after much discussion, that, if they were going to Stockholm, they would go to Germany and Switzerland as well, maybe visit Zürich first and then Frankfurt, where Goethe was born. Thomas had been offered the Goethe Prize from the city of Frankfurt. If he accepted, he could then think of going to other cities, perhaps even Munich. The thought of seeing their ruined house caused Katia to go silent. Thomas did not even want to discuss with his wife or daughter the prospect of traveling into East Germany.

The question was how to let Erika know that they had determined, despite her wishes, to go back to Germany, if just for a short visit.

Erika did not let a day go by without further denouncing Germany. Her attacks grew more even intense than Elisabeth's when a Munich weekly newspaper called her an agent of Stalin. This was reprinted by other newspapers in West Germany. If it had been twenty years earlier, Erika would have known the editors of these papers personally and would have easily cleared her name. Now she knew no one. What surprised her was that not one newspaper supported her, or wrote that there was no evidence at all to uphold the assertion that she was an agent of Stalin.

When Katia broke the news to her over dinner that they really did intend to include Germany in their visit to Europe, she shrugged.

"You two can go where you like. I will go as far as Switzerland with you. If you lose your suitcase, or your glasses, or forget the name of the hotel, or need to be guided safely past greasy town councillors, I will not be with you."

It was as well, Thomas thought, that Erika glanced dartingly around the room and did not look at her mother as she said this. Katia, he could see, was on the point of expressing satisfaction at the thought that they might spend time under a protection other than that of their daughter.

"I would be grateful," he said, directing his gaze at Erika, "if you did not tell Heinrich that we are going to Germany. He is in regular touch with the authorities in the East, some of whom are old friends of his. I do not want an argument with him."

"But he will find out and he will want to know what you plan to say in Germany," Erika said.

"About what?"

"What do you think? About the division of your own country!"

"It is not our country now," Katia said. "Not anymore."

"Then why are you going back there?" Erika asked.

Thomas liked the preparations for setting out, explaining to the postman that they would be gone some months, watching the suitcases lining up in the hallway. And once on the train, he enjoyed waiting for night, when the staff would come to make up their beds in the compartment for the stretch of the trip that would take them as far as Chicago.

In Chicago, he remembered not to make any jokes in front of Angelica, and hoped that Borgese would not talk too much about the minutiae of postwar Italian politics.

Katia, clearly, had spoken to Erika and Elisabeth and asked them to be civil to each other. In the sitting room, as they took tea, she monitored progress. Erika spoke of the journey and the beauty of the landscape.

"My mother slept as soon as we set out," Erika said, "and then she read some book in English."

"It's rather trashy," Katia said. "But your father read it too. It's called *The City and the Pillar* and it is about a young man."

"I enjoyed it," Thomas said.

"Your Goethe audience will need something more exalted," Erika said.

"The Magician comes in many guises," Elisabeth said.

Even though Katia had asked Erika not to mention the possibility of Germany being included on their tour, she saw that her daughter could not resist.

"Germany!" Erika said. "Imagine!"

"Are you going back to Munich?" Elisabeth asked.

"We do not know," Thomas replied. "Nothing has been decided."

"If you go there, could you ask them to give us our house back?" Elisabeth asked. "The war has been over for four years. It is the least they can do."

"I have lived for so long now with the idea that we have lost everything," Katia said, "that I don't want to think about getting things back. Most people lost a great deal more than we did."

"What happened to the manuscripts of my father's books and all the letters?" Elisabeth asked.

"They are lost," Katia said. "We gave them to Heins our lawyer for safekeeping. His house was ransacked or it was bombed or they were stolen. They might turn up, but I have given up thinking about them."

"With Germany quite rightly on its knees," Erika said, looking pointedly at Elisabeth, "our property is perhaps the last thing we should all be thinking about."

Chapter 17
Stockholm, 1949

The war was over; Thomas had not experienced it. He did not know what its aftermath meant. He would have to get used to that. He was ready to settle down in the Grand Hôtel in Stockholm, with Katia and Erika in rooms near his, and prepare to be fêted by the Swedes. His Goethe lecture would be given also in Uppsala and then in Copenhagen and Lund. Afterwards they would go to Switzerland and hear the German language spoken in the street for the first time in more than a decade.

On his first day in Stockholm, he agreed to take a tour with Edgar von Uexküll, whom he had known since the 1920s, and who had been arrested for his involvement in the plot against Hitler a year before the war ended. Although they spoke freely, there was a gap between them caused by what they each had done during the war.

Thomas could feel an edge of disquiet coming from his friend, a worried look that appeared most when Thomas voiced a belief that was definite. Uexküll had been opinionated and loquacious and convivial when he knew him, a man who enjoyed argument and spirited conversation. Now he had some banal views that he must have gleaned from the newspapers.

Thomas found it difficult to imagine what it must have been like when that coup against Hitler failed, how afraid Uexküll must have been. Even though his connections deep within the regime had saved him, it must have been close.

Having taken a tour of the city, Thomas parted from Uexküll and went to meet Katia in a café.

"I am too old for this travel," Katia said. "I woke at three and got dressed and took a walk. The staff must think I am mad."

As he and Katia entered the hotel, Erika was waiting for them in the lobby. The expression on her face was dark. She did not even greet them but approached them quickly and then walked away from them again, beckoning them to follow. At first, when she spoke, Thomas was not sure he had heard her properly, but when he asked her to repeat what she had said she shook her head.

"I cannot talk about it here. But he is dead. Klaus is dead. He took an overdose."

They moved slowly, without speaking, from the lobby to Katia's room.

"I happened to be lying on the bed," Erika said. "I could have been on a walk."

"The phone call was for you?" Katia asked.

"I don't know who it was for. It was put through to my room."

"Are you certain? Were they certain?" Katia asked.

"Yes. They wanted to know what arrangements to make."

As Thomas listened, he wondered if it were possible that she had misunderstood.

"Arrangements?" he asked.

"The funeral," Erika said.

"We have just heard the news," Katia said. "Do they really want us to decide about the funeral?"

"They want to know what to do," Erika said.

Katia kept fiddling with the rings on her fingers. When she had difficulty pulling one of them off completely, her hands began to shake.

"Why do you need to take that ring off?" Thomas asked.

"What ring?" she asked.

Thomas glanced at Erika. This was the news they had dreaded, but now that it had come, it seemed untrue.

"Did they give you a number to call?" Thomas asked.

"Yes," Erika said, "I have it here."

"Can we phone them back and make sure that it is Klaus, that he has been identified?"

Katia spoke as though she had not been listening.

"I don't want to see his coffin lowered into the ground," she said. "I don't want to witness it."

"I asked them over and over if they were sure," Erika said.

"And they asked you about arrangements?"

"I can go alone," Erika said. "And then I can make arrangements when I arrive."

"You cannot go alone," Katia replied.

When Thomas sought to comfort Katia, she turned away.

"Klaus has been leaving us for a long time," she said. "We have already said our farewells to him. Or I thought we had. Now I cannot believe this has happened."

"Michael's orchestra is close by," Erika said. "I think he is in Nice."

"Call him," Katia said. "And get word to Golo, and we will try to find a way to contact Monika. I will phone Elisabeth. For a second just now, I wondered which of us would get in touch with Klaus, but he is the one who is dead. It is hard to think that we won't ever see him again. Even now, his voice, for me, is alive. He is alive."

She stopped for a moment.

"He is still alive for me. I am too old for this. I will never believe it."

"We are only a few hours away from Cannes," Erika said. "We can easily change our plans."

She looked at Thomas, indicating that he should say something.

"His mother must decide," Thomas said.

"But what do you think?" Erika asked.

"I think he should not have done this to Katia, or to you."

Neither of them responded and he could sense their disapproval of what he had just said. In the silence that followed, he tried to bring the conversation back to practical matters. He realized that no one had mentioned Heinrich.

"One of us should call Heinrich?"

"I don't want to call anybody," Katia said, "and I don't want to talk about arrangements and I don't want to hear what Klaus should or shouldn't have done."

For the next hour, they waited in the room. Erika lit cigarette after cigarette, going to the balcony when the air was too full of smoke. Katia ordered tea, but then ignored the tray when it came. When the phone rang, it was Golo. Katia signaled to Erika that she should speak to him.

"They think it was an overdose, but how can they say? He always took sleeping pills. Yes, yesterday. He died yesterday. They have been trying to find us. Yes, he left a note with my mother's name and my name and, no, nothing else. He was rushed by ambulance to the hospital, but it was too late. I always knew one day it was going to be too late. We are all shocked but none of us should be surprised—"

"Erika, don't say that!" Katia interrupted.

"The Magician is due to speak in two or three days," Erika said to Golo, ignoring her. "I don't know if we are going or not."

Thomas could hear a very loud "What?" from Golo.

Erika handed the receiver to her mother. Katia listened for a while.

"Don't tell me how I feel, Golo!" she said eventually. "No one must tell me how I feel."

She handed the receiver back to Erika, who gestured to Thomas, asking if he wanted to talk to Golo. Thomas shook his head.

"I will call you soon when we know more," Erika said.

• • •

Thomas knew that they were waiting for him to speak. All he had to do was ask Erika to let the organizers in Sweden and Denmark know that he was leaving for France as soon as they could find a flight. And, in the coming days, she could cancel his trip to Germany. They would go to Cannes and see where Klaus died and then follow the coffin to the place of burial. And then they would go to somewhere quiet in Switzerland or return to California.

He caught Katia's eye. It was obvious that she was not going to say anything.

All Thomas could think about was how Klaus might have been rescued one more time.

When they met later, Erika urged him to make a decision about what to do. He was hoping that Katia would make her wishes clear. He had no idea how to talk to her and no idea what she wanted. It was odd, he thought, being with someone for almost half a century and not being able to read their mind.

Over dinner, Erika told them that she had checked at the desk and there were flights to Paris in the morning. Katia, who had not touched her food, sipped from her water glass and pretended that she had not heard.

In the lobby, Katia said: "I don't want to be disturbed until the morning."

"What about the funeral arrangements?" Erika asked.

"Will funeral arrangements bring him back?" Katia asked.

Erika called Thomas's room early in the morning to say that her mother was already in the dining room having breakfast. When he joined them, he saw that Katia was wearing her best clothes.

"Has anything been arranged?" he asked.

"Nothing," Erika said. "We are waiting for you."

A porter brought a note for Erika; she left the table. Thomas and Katia did not speak when she was away. When she returned, she sat down on the chair between them.

"That was Michael. He will go to Cannes."

"In time for the funeral?" Thomas asked.

"We have not fixed a date for the funeral," she replied.

Later, when he did not find Erika in her room, he went down to the lobby. As he sat in one of the old armchairs watching the guests, he remembered the hotel lobby in Saltsjöbaden years before, harassing the manager about their luggage, their desperation to get out of Sweden before they were trapped by the war. He had already made sure, by then, that Erika and Klaus were protected. And once he returned to Princeton, he had set about rescuing the other children one by one. Well, he had failed to rescue Klaus. He would give anything to put back time, to be on that journey home to America. He longed to be anywhere in the past, to be able to stop what had just happened, to have insisted that Klaus travel to Sweden and accompany them to Germany. If his mother had implored him, surely he would have eventually accepted.

Just then, he saw Katia come out of the elevator and cross the lobby towards the small café. She walked slowly, like someone in pain. She moved towards him, but she did not see him. It struck him that he was perhaps the last person in the world she wished now to see.

When Carla killed herself, he had his mother to console. When Lula died, he had his own family to be with. Now, despite the presence of Katia and Erika, he was alone. There was no one he could turn to. Katia and Erika were alone too. None of them wanted to talk to one another, and neither he nor Katia wanted to make the arrangements for Klaus's funeral, nor did they want Erika to take on that task.

Back in his room, Thomas looked at the sheaf of papers he had on his desk. He reread the last sentence he had written. It seemed natural for him to see what might be added. He began to work.

Erika did not knock. She was in the middle of the room before he realized that she was there. She gasped when she saw him working.

"I have arranged for him to be buried in three days' time," she said. "The funeral will be on Friday."

"Have you informed your mother?"

"I told her, but she did not acknowledge that she had heard."

He still had time, he knew, to ask Erika to organize flights for them.

"What do you think we should do?" he asked.

"My mother is in no condition to travel."

He wanted to tell Erika that he did not believe her, that this was the sort of thing she had started to say about her mother so that she could exercise more and more control.

"I will speak to her."

It would be late morning in Chicago. When Erika left him, he called Elisabeth, knowing that her mother had already broken the news of Klaus's death to her.

He told Elisabeth that they were not going to Cannes.

"Was that Erika's decision?"

"No."

"Does my mother not want to go?"

"I am not sure."

"So, you decided?"

"I decided nothing."

"Someone decided."

When the call was over, he wished he had told Elisabeth that he could not face seeing the coffin and following it through the streets of Cannes, knowing that Klaus lay lifeless inside. But, more than that, he could not face the prospect of Katia making that journey, walking away from the cemetery with Klaus buried in the ground, when none of them could offer her any comfort. He knew it was wrong not to go. If he had stayed talking for longer, Elisabeth would have emphatically told him so. He almost wished that she had. He wished something else had been decided, and then he found himself wishing that none of it had happened at all, that no message had come that Klaus was dead.

By evening, Erika told him that she had spoken to Monika and also, once again, to Michael.

"What did Monika say?"

"You do not need to know. She is in Naples and is coming to Zürich to meet us. She takes the view that we cannot do without her."

"And Michael?"

"He will be at the funeral."

"I am sorry for prevaricating so much," he said.

"Do you want to cancel the lectures? I can explain what has happened."

"No, I will go ahead. If I don't give the lectures, I don't know what else I might do."

"Go home, maybe?"

"That is one possibility."

"Shall I speak to the organizers?"

"No, I will go ahead as agreed."

That night, as he was preparing for bed, Katia came to his room and stood in the doorway.

"Someone connected Heinrich to my room," she said. "He just got a message to call but he didn't know why, and so I told him."

"I am sorry. I should have spoken to him."

"He told me that he has come to see death as soft. The dead are at peace, he said. He stayed on the line for a while and we didn't say much more. We didn't need to. And then we said goodbye. I could hear him crying as he put down the receiver."

• • •

A week later, in Copenhagen, Thomas received a letter from Michael. It was delivered to his room. He was relieved that it had not been handed to him in the dining room. He did not want Katia and Erika to see it.

"My dear Father," Michael wrote, "I was there when they lowered Klaus's coffin into the ground and I played a largo for his generous soul as they covered him with earth. The beauty of the place where he is buried made his death unbearable. Nothing was comforting, not the blue sky, not the glittering sea, not the music. Nothing.

"You may never have noticed this, but Klaus, even though he was so much older than me, did not try to be a surrogate father to me, but, instead, always succeeded in being my older brother, a brother who listened to me and looked out for me when no one else did. He lived much of the time unnoticed in his own house. I remember how brusquely his views were dismissed by you at the table and I remember his hurt at seeing that you did not think his views were important.

"I am sure the world is grateful to you for the undivided attention you have given to your books, but we, your children, do not feel any gratitude to you, or indeed to our mother, who sat by your side. It is hard to credit that you both stayed in your luxury hotel while my brother was being buried. I told no one in Cannes that you were in Europe. They would not have believed me.

"You are a great man. Your humanity is widely appreciated and applauded. I am sure you are enjoying loud praise in Scandinavia. It hardly bothers you, most likely, that these feelings of adulation are not shared by any of your children. As I walked away from my brother's grave, I wished you to know how deeply sad I felt for him."

Thomas placed the letter under a book on his bedside table.

Later, he would read it once more and then he would destroy it. If Katia and Erika found out that it had been sent and asked him about it, he would say that he had not received it.

At the airport in Zürich, they were met by Michael, who gave his father a gruff smile and then hugged his mother and sister. As they were making their way to a car, they saw that Monika had been standing in the shadows all the time. Ignoring Erika and her mother, she went to her father and embraced him tearfully.

"This is not the time for tears, Monika," her mother said.

"When is the time for tears?" Monika asked. "And who decides?"

"I decide," Erika said.

In the hotel that evening, Erika and Michael had assembled for him a selection of German press cuttings on his impending visit to the country and his possible visit to the Eastern Zone. Most of them were vitriolic. Thomas was particularly puzzled by the ones that criticized him for not remaining in Germany, as others had done, in its time of difficulty.

"I would not be alive if I had stayed in Germany," he said.

Soon they were joined by Katia, whose expression was stoical and resigned, and then by a tearful Monika.

"Now, Monika," Katia said, "I told you I want no crying."

Katia announced that everyone should be on their best behavior because Georges Motschan was about to arrive. Thomas had met Motschan briefly before the war when he had come, on the instructions of his wealthy father, to offer Katia's parents help if they should seek refuge to Switzerland. Once her parents left Germany, he had become a regular correspondent of Katia, always making clear that he would be ready to look after the Manns if they should decide to live in Switzerland.

"He is a most civilized person," Katia said. "My parents adored him."

When Georges arrived, the atmosphere changed. The waiters became even more attentive and the hotel manager presented himself at the table to make sure that all the guests were comfortable.

Georges Motschan was tall and well-dressed, in his early thirties. Thomas wondered if it would be accurate to describe him as polished, like some elegant piece of silver that had elaborate carvings and filigrees. But when Georges spoke, he no longer seemed rarefied or highly wrought; the voice was deep and authoritative and manly. It was evident from his bearing that Georges was rich, but he exuded something else that Thomas had almost forgotten about. Edgar von Uexküll had elements of it, but in him it was broken, whereas in Motschan it shone. Motschan, it was plain to Thomas, had lived with books and paintings and music as natural things, in the same way as he had been cared for by servants and had his meals cooked for him by others. He was discriminating, with a mild whiff of arrogance. Even the way he took in the table and sipped his tea, Thomas observed, arose from generations of slow Swiss comfort. Thomas nearly laughed out loud when he noticed how much in awe Monika appeared to be of this young man. And then he glanced at Katia and Erika: they were gazing at Georges Motschan.

When Georges saw the press cuttings on the table, he looked through them and shrugged.

"We must pay no attention," he said. "The malice of the Germans is not to be appeased."

He then made clear he had not come on a social visit, but to offer his services.

"The problem you will have in Germany and in the Eastern Zone is how to arrive and depart. You cannot wait in train stations. In the East, you cannot be seen in a state car. My Buick, which serves its purpose on Swiss roads at least, might be the best way to travel, and I am also making myself available as your driver. I am even ready to wear a uniform should that be necessary."

"I think you look quite well as you are," Katia said.

Thomas saw that she was openly flirting with this young man.

It was arranged that he would drive Thomas and Katia to Vulpera in the Eglantine, where they could rest, and then he would collect them and drive them to Frankfurt, Munich and, if they should decide, Weimar. Erika would go to Amsterdam, Monika would return to Italy and Michael continue his tour with his orchestra.

When Motschan drove up to the Schweizer Hof in Vulpera, Thomas was almost tempted to ask him if he would not stay with them at least for a day. He would like to discuss the visit to Germany.

"I don't know what kind of reception I will get. I don't even know why I am going."

"What you must realize is that you cannot win," Motschan said. "If you remain in California, they will hate you. But if you return, they will hate you for having been in California in the first place. If you only visit cities in the West, they will call you an American stooge. But if you visit the East, they will call you a fellow traveler. And everyone will want you to visit some shrine, some prison, some site where an atrocity happened. No one will be pleased except you, and you will be pleased only because, within a short time, you will be able to return to California. The war is over, but it casts a long shadow and there are many resentments, and, during your visit, the resentment will be directed at you."

Once in the hotel, Georges discreetly called for the manager. Thomas noticed him handing a large banknote to the head porter. Having introduced the manager to the Manns and, having had a quiet word with him, Georges prepared to depart.

"Your name is not on the books here. Your rooms are in my

name. It is important that no one can find you. Someone will come looking for you, probably a reporter. He will not find you in this hotel."

As they traveled up in the elevator, Thomas would not have been surprised if Katia had insisted that she was tired and would have supper alone. Instead, however, as they approached her door, she stopped and said that it would be nice for them to have dinner, just the two of them.

It struck him as he took in the valley from the balcony in his room that Klaus would be interested in this, his father's first journey back to Germany. It would have been good at the end of each evening to have had a drink in the hotel with Katia and Klaus, with Klaus commenting on the speeches and the officials and the tone of the crowd. This new Germany, coming in two zones, was an experiment and would make a subject for the sort of book that Klaus could have written.

In ways, he thought, he was too old for all this change. He wanted to be in his study, and already he was thinking about a novel he might write and hoping that he would live long enough to complete it. He had seen enough Germanies, he thought, for a single lifetime. This new one would have to make progress without his presence, or the presence of his son.

Over dinner, Katia reminded him that Georges had been born in Russia and spoke Russian as well as he did German, French and English.

"The family is worth a fortune."

"I never knew where the money came from."

"First it was fur," she said. "That is why they were in Russia. Now they have, as Georges explained to my mother once, money that makes money. And like a lot of Swiss, his father did well in the war."

● ● ●

A week later, Thomas and Katia took the sleeper from Zürich to Frankfurt while Motschan traveled by car with their luggage.

There had been threatening letters sent to German newspapers and so the Swiss police accompanied them to their carriage, making them highly conspicuous. In Frankfurt, as they were taken briskly with a police escort to the city's official guesthouse at Kronberg, they saw the rubble heaped up in gaps between buildings. Entire streets seemed to be missing. The sky itself was a deadened, murky gray as though it too had been bombed and cleared of all its color. The block they drove by had been razed to the ground; there were just puddles and dried mud where commercial buildings had been. And even the lone figures trying to walk on the unpaved surfaces looked abandoned and forlorn.

Thomas gripped Katia's hand when they came to a crossing where they could see buildings that were half-ruined. Somehow, this sight was more direct and graphic than the scene of total destruction. What had survived, even though the windows were blown out and the roofs fallen in, gave them a sense of what had once been here. He studied a building whose whole front wall had been blown away leaving each floor visible as though for some elaborately layered theater performance. He could see the radiators still attached to the wall on the first floor, like a parody of their prewar purpose.

When Motschan appeared, it was agreed that all the journalists who had gathered would be told that Thomas would give no interviews until the next day.

That evening, at the large reception, he moved around in a sort of dream. People asked if he remembered them from readings and dinners and conferences long ago. All he did was smile and make sure that Katia was close to him. A few times, he inquired from Motschan if Ernst Bertram, whom he had contacted, had come. Until now, he had harbored no interest in meeting Bertram again, but in this mêlée, with so much confusion, with men and women reaching to touch him or grab his attention, he would like to have seen Bertram coming towards him.

In the morning, when he spoke to the press, every question centered on the possibility that he would visit the Eastern Zone, which was under Soviet control. No one was satisfied when he said that he had not made up his mind. When it was agreed that there would be one final question, a voice from the back of the group asked him if he was intending to return to his fatherland for good, now that it was free.

"I am an American citizen," he said, "and will be going home to the States. But I hope this will not be my last visit here."

That evening, in the Paulskirche, as he received the Goethe Prize, he noted the delegation from East Germany in the front row. At the end of his speech there was a standing ovation. If he was not welcome here, he thought, then the authorities had worked out a perfect way to disguise it.

When, after a dinner, they eventually arrived back at the guesthouse, Motschan informed him that a friend of his was also staying there and wished to speak to him before he retired. For a moment, Thomas presumed that the friend was Bertram. On hearing the name, Katia said that she would prefer not to have to meet anyone else that evening. She went to her room.

Thomas was preparing what he might say to Bertram, how he might begin, but when Motschan led him into a small reception room that was almost an office, he did not at first recognize the man who was waiting for him and introduced himself in an American accent. He had a crew cut and a square jaw.

"It is years since we met," he said. "I am Alan Bird. We met in Washington at a dinner given by Eugene and Agnes Meyer. I think it was quite a heated affair. In my world, quite legendary. I work for the State Department."

Thomas remembered his name, and he remembered being suspicious of him even then.

Bird indicated to Thomas that he should sit down; he made a sign to Motschan that he should close the door behind him as he left. Thomas was intrigued by his air of pure intent. Bird was, he thought, like a hungry hound. He resolved to speak as little as possible.

"My mission," Bird said, "is simple. I represent the U.S. government and I am here to tell you that we do not wish you to travel to the Eastern Zone."

Thomas nodded and smiled.

Bird opened the door quickly, checking there was no one on the other side before closing it. When he turned back to Thomas, he moved from English into fluent German, with some minor mistakes in pronunciation but otherwise faultless. He began to speak as though from a script.

"Relations between us and the Soviets are deteriorating. Events like this evening and your visit to Munich are helpful for us. One step over the border, however, will be a propaganda coup for them. It will be reported all over the world."

Thomas nodded again.

"Can I take it that this is understood?" Bird asked.

Thomas did not reply.

"I saw the delegation from the East there this evening," Bird went on. "A grim bunch they were. From our side, the best thing would be a press conference in the morning saying that you will not go into the East until it is free, with free elections, a free press, freedom of movement and no political prisoners."

Thomas still said nothing.

"I need your assent," Bird said.

"I am an American citizen," Thomas said. "I believe in many freedoms, including my own freedom to visit my own country."

"The Eastern Zone is not your country."

Thomas folded his arms and smiled.

"While an American citizen, I remain a German writer, faithful to the German language, which is my true home."

"There are many words in that language the people cannot say in the East."

"If I visit, I will say what I please. There are no restrictions."

"Don't be naïve. Everything that happens if you cross that border will be restricted."

"Are you attempting to restrict me?"

"I am talking sense to you. I represent a country that rescued you and your family from fascism."

"Goethe was born here in Frankfurt, but he lived his life in Weimar. I have no interest in whether Weimar is east or west."

"Weimar is Buchenwald. That is what Weimar is."

"And is Munich Dachau? Is every German town and city so tainted? Can I not reclaim the word 'Weimar,' give it back to the language as belonging to Goethe?"

"Buchenwald is not empty. It is where the Communists now have their prisoners, thousands of them. Will you pass the camp by with your gaze averted? Is that what Goethe would have done?"

"What do you know about Goethe?"

"I know that he would not want to be associated with Buchenwald."

Thomas did not reply.

"We don't want you to go," Bird continued. "If you do go, you will find America a cold place on your return."

"Are you threatening me?" Thomas asked.

They stared at each other with open hostility.

"I will be in Munich for your speech," Bird said as he turned to leave. "Maybe you will have come to your senses by the time I see you there."

"You are keeping a watch on me, then?"

"After Einstein, you are the most important German alive. It would be negligent of us not to know what you are doing."

Georges Motschan drove them with princely authority from Frankfurt to Munich. His voice was powerful enough to be heard clearly in the back seat.

"I did not like the cut of those men from the Eastern Bloc last night. I would not enjoy having them as prison guards."

"Your accent reminds me of Davos," Katia said. "You make me almost miss the sanatorium."

"Of course, as we know from *The Magic Mountain*," Georges replied, "those clinics were little factories for killing people at great expense. How wise you both were to leave!"

What was strange, Thomas thought, was that, despite the constant flattery directed at his work, it was Katia whom Georges was interested in; it was she he sought to impress. He had adjusted his mirror in the car so that he could see her face as she spoke.

Georges, Thomas thought, had a way of endearing himself to others without being in the least obsequious. His good manners were perfectly pitched. He seemed to know how much he should speak and what subjects he should range over and what tone to take. Being with him reminded Thomas of those early days in Munich when he had been in the company of cocky young artists, knowing that he himself was a timid provincial. Georges Motschan, with all his carefully modulated tact, made him feel not only provincial but also old and out of touch.

He comforted himself in the back of the car by dreaming about what Georges would look like in some well-appointed bedroom when he was naked, with light from snow, blue and white, coming in through the window.

In the morning, when Georges had asked Thomas and

Katia if, on arrival in Munich, they wished to visit the house on Poschingerstrasse, they both had immediately answered no. When, smiling, he asked them further if there was anything at all they wished to see in Munich, they both also said there was not.

"We want to go to the hotel," Katia said, "stay there, attend the event and the dinner and then leave in the morning."

In the city center, there were craters in the roads so they had to proceed very slowly. They passed through ghostly streets. No building had been left undamaged, some were in total ruins, one or two standing alone, but with gaping holes and windows smashed and doorways boarded up.

Thomas pointed to a half-ruined building, with rusty girders poking out through gravel heaps in front of it. He claimed to recognize it, believing that they were driving along Schellingstrasse. Katia insisted that it could not be Schellingstrasse.

"I walked here every day. I know all these streets."

But as the car edged forward, they saw a sign that said Türkenstrasse on a half-demolished corner building with coiling water pipes spilling out of it like guts.

"I should know that building," Katia said, "but I thought it was on some other corner. I am confused now."

Thomas was aware that they were nearing Arcisstrasse. He knew the names of each street that led to it, but he could not clearly identify any of them. It was only when they passed the Alte Pinakothek that he was confident that he had got his bearings. When they came to the corner of Arcisstrasse, he saw the Nazi building that had replaced Katia's parents' house.

"That is where our house was," Katia said. "I would not willingly have come here, but I am glad I have seen it."

Thomas thought of nights at the opera, the glamour, the opulence. Where were all those people now? Where did they live, the ones who had survived the war? Munich would be built again, and, as Georges drove, they saw signs of reconstruction. He did not know how long it would take. All he knew was that he would not live to witness it. This was the city Klaus had seen at the end of the war. Thomas was close to tears when he realized how much joy Klaus would have got from a Munich that was coming back to life.

When he thought about going to East Germany, Heinrich's image came into his mind. He knew that the Communist leaders were still interested in having his brother return to Germany and live permanently in the East. Just as Germany was divided, so too, it appeared, were the Mann brothers. Thomas had paid homage to power in America and benefited from the country's largesse. He would naturally be presumed to be loyal to the West. Heinrich, whose left-wing credentials were impeccable, had not become famous in America and felt no pressure to do the country any favors.

Thomas determined that he would not be told by the Americans where not to go in Germany. He noted that Alan Bird wanted him to give a press conference to announce that he would not enter the East. Even if he refused to do that and kept quiet about his decision, the Americans would certainly leak it. Word would then spread that Thomas Mann had been bossed around by his Yankee masters.

If he did decline the invitation to go into the East, he knew that he would be despised by his fellow German writers, including his own brother. He would be denounced as an American stooge as Georges had warned. He now had to choose between being vilified as a writer who had exchanged his honor for influence in Washington and comfort in California or being seen by the Americans as deeply ungrateful and disloyal. It came to him clearly that he would be more content to be ungrateful and disloyal. He would travel into the Eastern Zone if he pleased.

That next morning, once more, the press conference focused on his proposed visit to the East. He noticed Alan Bird sitting in a relaxed pose alone in one of the back rows, his elbows resting on the chairs on each side of him. Thomas smiled at him and bowed. Should he go to Weimar, he told the journalists, it would be to emphasize the essential unity of Germany. Since the German language was not separated into zones, then he saw no reason why he should not visit every part of Germany.

By the end of the press conference, when a precise question about his intentions was directed at him, he let it be known that he had, in fact, decided what to do. He would be traveling to Weimar. He looked at Alan Bird and bowed before he was accompanied out of the room by Georges Motschan, who had been standing in the wings as his protector.

Katia and he sat down to lunch, remarking on what had also come to their attention in Frankfurt, the sumptuous menu. Even in the Savoy in London, where they had stayed, the menu had been restricted because of postwar rationing. This did not seem to be happening in Germany. He thought it strange that the streets were so empty and yet the supply of food had been restored. Perhaps it was only in hotels.

"We will be forced," he whispered to Georges as they entered the banqueting hall that evening, "to shake fleshy hands that not long ago were sticky with blood."

While in Frankfurt the aura of ease and good cheer had been merely distasteful, here, because it was his own city, it unsettled him deeply. In his dreams, he had expected a Germany to arise in which a dinner like this would be attended by a new generation nervously ready to re-create democracy. But everyone in the banqueting hall looked to him middle aged and overfed as well as jolly and at home. The more wine and beer consumed, the louder the voices grew and the more feverish the laughter. Soup was served, followed by some kind of fish, then there were several meat courses, including platters of pork and roast beef. He watched as the men around him, the figures who held power in Munich now, took advantage of each course, the man opposite him calling hungrily for more gravy to be poured over his beef.

He could, in his mind, hear Klaus back in the hotel talking fervently about the book he would write called *The New Germany* in which he would do justice to the atmosphere in this hall. Katia, to his right, was being entertained by Georges Motschan. Neither of them appeared to be paying attention to anyone else. Since the man on his left, some kind of high official, did not say anything of any interest when they first spoke, Thomas saw no reason why he should engage him further. He simply sat in his place, picking at his food, as more and more platters came.

He thought of the Munich he had known, the city of young artists and writers and impassioned debates in cafés at night, the city of Katia's parents that was so open to high eccentricity as much as to high culture. In that old world, everyone was famous, the poet who published in a stray magazine was famous for his verse, as the artist who had made some woodcuts was pointed out in the street. Munich was a city in which there was a rumor about everyone; it was a metropolis that became even more socially engaged and sexually careless when inflation rose and even money ceased to be solid.

Money, he thought, was solid here in this hall. As dessert was served, with waiters carrying huge vats of cream to cover pies and tarts, he suddenly realized where he was. Rather than the Munich of delicate souls and exalted social textures, this was the coarseness of the Bavarian village come into the city. The guests were so comfortable here that, after a while, no one paid him too much attention, the guest of honor. He studied their mouths opening in raw laughter, the swagger in their gestures, the uncouth, thickset way they dealt with one another. They and their kind would prevail, he thought. He could talk about Goethe all he pleased, but this was the future.

He saw no reason why he should make his departure formal. He indicated to Motschan that he and Katia would slip out. As they stood up to go, however, he saw Alan Bird, flanked by two other men in American-style suits, moving as though to waylay them.

"I don't want to see that man again," he said to Motschan.

"Double back now," Motschan whispered. "Walk quickly towards that door that leads to the bathroom. There is a side exit there. Do not stop."

As the Americans approached, Thomas turned away from them. He tried to look like a man going to the bathroom. Once he was out of the hall, Katia and Motschan followed, and Motschan led them into the open air.

"It will be easier if we walk to the hotel. They are too conscious of bad publicity to harass you any further."

It was arranged in the morning that their luggage be taken without ceremony to the Buick, which would then drive around to the back and collect them there. They would spend the night in Bayreuth and then go into the Eastern Zone.

In Bayreuth, at the Goldener Anker, the manager, once Motschan had demanded that he treat his guests with all due deference, started to grovel, coming to their table again and again to inquire if they wanted anything more. In the morning, Thomas hoped that they could leave before this fellow reappeared, but he was waiting at the bottom of the stairs for them, accompanied them to the breakfast room and then stood in the lobby as their luggage was taken down.

"I have one request," he said. "It would mean so much to us if you signed the Golden Guest Book. It would be such a privilege."

He had the book on a stand in the lobby.

"We don't often display it," he said. "But this is a very special day for us."

The manager held the page open and gave Thomas a pen. When he had signed his name and put in the date, he flicked through the previous pages to find that they were blank.

"We have left sixteen pages empty," the manager said, "one for each year of your exile."

Thomas turned back more pages until he came to the names of people who had previously signed the book, each person with his own page. He saw pages signed by Himmler, and Göring, and also Goebbels.

"Distinguished company," he said to the manager, who, with his hands joined, succeeded in looking both pleased and concerned at the same time.

In the car, Georges was indignant.

"They should be made to burn that book. It is one of their skills. They know how to burn books."

"Please get me out of this country as soon as you possibly can," Thomas said.

Motschan explained that he had been given instructions about which border crossing he should take.

"If I have been given these instructions, so has the press," he said. "But there is another way to cross where we will not be noticed."

"Do you think we should come and live in Switzerland?" Thomas asked Motschan.

"Why do you imagine I am looking after you both with such care?" Motschan asked, laughing. "This is a sample of what Switzerland would do for you if you should return. I represent the nation, but we don't use that word. I represent the Swiss spirit, but we don't talk about that either. Maybe I can say that I represent a literary canton of Switzerland and we would be honored to have you both among us."

At the border, they were stopped by a group of young Russian soldiers who seemed to be alarmed at the appearance of the Buick. While some of them stood blocking the path of the car, a few went running to a nearby shed. A large and older Russian soldier peered out of the shed and then came towards the car. Motschan got out. Thomas pulled down the window so they could hear their friend speaking Russian.

He did so with a supreme confidence. The Russian officer was apparently demanding that Georges turn back and take a border crossing farther to the north. Motschan was shaking his head and pointing straight ahead, indicating that he intended to drive across the border towards Weimar using this crossing.

"This is what Russia must have been like when they had serfs," Thomas said when a few of the younger soldiers, mere boys, began to examine them unceremoniously through the other window.

"This is why they shot all the aristocrats," Katia replied as Motschan made a terse sign to the soldiers that they should step out of the way. When one of the soldiers approached him and spoke aggressively, Georges poked him in the chest with his finger. And then he returned to the car and started the engine.

After they had traveled some distance, they were stopped by soldiers again, but this time to let them know that five minutes ahead there would be an official welcome, and from there they would be accompanied by a cavalcade to their destination.

It occurred to Thomas that if they had decided not to travel to Europe at all, Klaus might not have attempted suicide. Perhaps it was the very prospect of them coming close to him that made him desperate. Thomas was sure that Katia had already thought of this, and perhaps Erika too, and maybe even the others. He could not understand why it had taken him so long to see it.

He heard cheering and then he saw that people, including children, had lined the streets and were waving at the car.

In Weimar, an entire floor of the hotel had been reserved for them; they were guarded by uniformed police and a few burly men in suits. At the first lunch, he found himself seated beside a General Tiulpanov, who was the commander of East Berlin. The general was fluent in German. Into his face, Thomas saw, a thousand years of Russian history had been poured. It was clever of the general, he thought, to confine the conversation to Russian and German literature, talking to him about Pushkin and Goethe.

The further back they went, Thomas believed, the safer they would be.

He wanted to ask the general if he knew about Goethe's presence here, and how strange it was that the poet had been inspired by the very landscape on which the Buchenwald concentration camp was created.

But the general's mind was elsewhere for the moment. As he smiled suddenly, looking around the room, he exuded an astonishing charm, like a man who wished only joy to his fellow mortals. When he stood up, the room became hushed. The general closed his eyes and began to recite:

> "For the doctrines we are teaching
> Do not censure us unduly:
> Seek the answers deep within you
> If you'd understand them truly."

When he stopped, Thomas, without standing, raised his voice and took over:

> "There you'll find the ancient message:
> Man, that self-contented wonder,
> Seeks his own self-preservation
> Whether here on earth or yonder."

They took turns, each of them, until Goethe's poem had ended. There was rapturous applause. Even the waiters, Thomas saw, joined in the ovation.

That night, when he had spoken of Goethe and human freedom, he was unsure what the cheering and ovation signified. For a few moments, he wondered if it meant that the audience was happy that someone from outside had come into the Eastern Zone, thus lessening their sense of a looming isolation. Or, he wondered, were they under instructions to cheer? Then he was taken up by the force of the applause, the smiling faces, the loud words of praise.

Later, in the hotel, he saw that Katia and Motschan had not shared his elation.

"That general," Motschan said, "will rule the world, or he will be recalled and shot."

The next day, as Georges and Katia followed his official car in Motschan's Buick, with the crowds cheering once more along the route, Thomas almost took pleasure in picturing the wryness of his companions' response to all this warmth. And he supposed that Georges and Katia thought he was a fool for waving so enthusiastically at those who lined the streets and for accepting the offer of an official car for this leg of the journey.

He knew, as they knew, that Weimar was Buchenwald now and that the general, so friendly and cultured, was, as Alan Bird had told him, holding prisoners in the very camp where the Nazis had murdered so many. And they knew that Goethe had dreamed of many things, but he had never imagined Buchenwald. No poems about love, or nature, or man would ever serve to rescue this place from the curse that had descended on it.

Chapter 18
Los Angeles, 1950

In the offices of the FBI, there were files on him and his brother and on Erika and Klaus. Those files, replete with suspicions and rumors and innuendoes, would be the record of their time in America. Perhaps there was one on Golo too, if reading too many books could be viewed as anti-American. And maybe even Monika, if shouting loudly outside a writer's study might be considered a possible federal offense.

In Europe, he believed, as well as files, they had memories. They remembered the stance Heinrich had taken during the First World War, and during the Munich Revolution, and his speeches and articles that sought to prevent the rise of Hitler, and the work he did for left-wing causes in exile.

During his short time in East Germany, Thomas had noted things that he might recount to Heinrich on his return, the feeling, for example, that the crowds waving flags on the streets might have been there under duress. But Heinrich did not want to hear about his brother's trip to Germany. If Thomas so much as mentioned it, Heinrich changed the subject.

The East Germans awarded Heinrich the German National Prize for Art and Literature, and invited him once more to live in East Berlin. He would be given a secretary, a driver and a comfortable apartment along with a generous stipend. His books were already selling well in the new state.

In America, Heinrich's books were out of print. If he were known at all, it was as the author of the novel that had been filmed as *The Blue Angel*, and also as the brother of Thomas Mann. In his new apartment, there was an eating nook instead of a dining room. Heinrich referred to this regularly as a sign of how bad things were. Despite his left-wing opinions, he was ever the son of the senator in Lübeck.

Heinrich decided that he would accept the invitation to East Germany and leave California for good, pointing out to Thomas that he would not have much baggage, as many of the things they owned had been pawned by Nelly and he had not bothered to retrieve them.

In those late winter days, as he planned his departure, Heinrich spoke of the possibility of writing a play about Frederick the Great, but then worried that, since he was in his late seventies, it might be too much. Some of the old excitement returned, however, as he reread the writers whom he had most enjoyed— Flaubert, Stendhal, Goethe, Fontane. When he spoke to Thomas about scenes in books by these writers, he sounded as enthusiastic as when they were both young and in Palestrina.

"Can you ask those Communists to have Effi Briest and Emma Bovary there for me when I arrive in Berlin?" he asked Thomas. "I will need good company."

Mimi had died in Prague after the war. She never recovered from her incarceration in Terezín. Sometimes, Heinrich went over his years of happiness with her and how he believed, in coming to America, he had let her down. Katia understood how to relieve the gloom that would enter Heinrich's spirit at the thought of poor Mimi by asking him something about Nelly. Just hearing Nelly's name could make him more animated.

Heinrich could also become animated at the mention of his brother Viktor, who had died the year before. Viktor's wife had been a low-grade Nazi and Viktor had followed the party line. Heinrich could not contain his contempt.

"It proves something I have known all my life," he said. "Where there is brightness, there is also an idiot. When you have two writers like us, and two splendid sisters, both filled with life, you will always have a little runt and he will always marry a Nazi."

As usual, Heinrich was beautifully dressed when he came to see Thomas and Katia. He moved more slowly than before and often became silent, bowing his head as though he had fallen asleep, and then making some wry or astute comment.

"I have a feeling," he said, "that anyone who goes back to Germany won't be as welcome as we imagine. It will be a hard place for all of us. They think we were sunbathing as the bombs rained on them. They will like us more when we are dead."

He opened his eyes and looked at Thomas and smiled.

Despite his poverty and his need for support, Heinrich had never lost his ability to be arrogant, insisting on the importance of his own work and the value of the causes he had espoused. He spoke as though his own opinions were beyond dispute. He appeared to enjoy quoting from letters he had received from Klaus Mann over the years, remarking how much he missed his nephew and what a stalwart figure he had been in the battle for democracy. No matter how kindly Thomas tried to interpret this, it sounded to him like a rebuke.

In his house in Santa Monica, on the night before he died, Heinrich had been listening to a Puccini opera. The brain hemorrhage he suffered in his sleep meant that he did not wake again.

Heinrich was laid to rest beside Nelly in the cemetery in Santa Monica, a small crowd of family and friends in attendance. A string quartet played the slow movement from Debussy's quartet in G minor.

As they walked away from the grave, Thomas, the music still

in his mind, was aware that he was now the last; the other four had gone. With Heinrich dead, he would have only ghosts against whom to measure himself.

For years now, he understood, he had been living in some strange opposition to Klaus and Heinrich. Klaus had been unsettled, not knowing where to live; Thomas, on the other hand, remained in Pacific Palisades. While Heinrich lived in poverty, Thomas continued to make money. While the other two had strong opinions, Thomas wavered politically. They were fiery, he was circumspect. But now that they were gone, he had no one to argue with, except Erika. And he found her so irascible that it was hardly worth disagreeing with her.

When he took his afternoon walk with Katia by the beach in Santa Monica, he continued to be aware of the young men in swimming trunks. However, instead of feigning tiredness so he could stop and study one of them, he stopped because he was genuinely tired. Still, he carried the images of them home with him and nurtured them as night fell. He was fascinated when Katia discovered among Heinrich's papers many sheets with drawings by Heinrich of fat, naked women, just like those Thomas had found more than half a century earlier in Palestrina when he had stealthily examined the papers on his brother's desk.

It was easier to concentrate on essays than on a novel or stories, writing a few paragraphs a day and reading to refresh his memory. But he knew that soon he would have to find a subject for a novel that would intrigue him enough to make him want to get up in the morning.

After his visit to Weimar, he began to receive petitions from citizens of East Germany asking him to intercede with the authorities on their behalf. Usually, he forwarded these letters to the writer Johannes R. Becher, who was close to power in East

Germany, whom he had known in the 1920s. He wondered what Heinrich would have done were he alive and in the pay of the East German government. He liked to think that his brother's uncompromising stance would have continued in East Germany.

When an anti-Communist magazine, in an article called "The Moral Eclipse of Thomas Mann," referred to him as "America's Fellow Traveler No. 1," his attention was drawn to it by Agnes Meyer.

"All of us who are associated with you are being asked to defend you," she said.

"I am not a fellow traveler. I do not support communism."

"Saying that is not enough. This is not a time for prevarication in America. There is a new war and it is against communism."

"I am against communism."

"Is that why you went to East Germany and were fêted there?"

When Thomas was named as a Communist by a hotel in Beverly Hills that did not want to host an event at which he might speak, he could not blame Heinrich or Klaus for tarnishing his reputation as an imperturbable man of reason. Nor could he blame Brecht, who was living in East Berlin. It was beneath his dignity, he thought, to write to the newspapers to announce that he was not a Communist. What was even more disturbing was the realization that not only his moral authority but his status as a great man had dissolved in America.

This left him free. If Klaus and Heinrich had been alive, they would have attacked the infantilism that had become widespread in American life. Now he himself could do so, becoming braver as the attacks on him grew more strident, attending a birthday dinner for W. E. B. Du Bois, for example, and later joining the appeal in support of the Rosenbergs. He could also send birthday greetings if he wanted to Johannes R. Becher and be denounced for his action in the House of Representatives, being told that ingrates were seldom invited back to dine.

Katia insisted that she always knew, from the shrill sound of the ringing tone, when the caller was Agnes Meyer. If she believed it was Mrs. Meyer on the line, she then demanded that Erika answer the phone. Erika began by imitating her father's voice, letting Agnes complain at length about some political stance that Thomas had adopted or failed to adopt, and then, with a laugh, telling her that she was, in fact, speaking to Erika Mann, a person whom Mrs. Meyer openly despised.

The last time this had occurred, Agnes had said to her: "Why don't you go back to Germany?"

That evening, Erika had performed a most scurrilous monologue in the voice of Agnes Meyer, mixing her political views and her sexual dreams, emphasizing how much she wanted to be held firmly in the arms of the Magician and pleasured with his wand.

But the idea of going back to Germany had to be treated seriously. When the FBI came again to interview Erika, she lost patience with her interrogators.

"Yes, I told them I am lesbian. Of course I am lesbian! What did they think I am? And Queen Victoria was lesbian, I informed them, and Eleanor Roosevelt was one too, and so was Mae West, and so was Doris Day. They listened calmly until I said Doris Day and one of them said, 'Hey, ma'am, I think Miss Day is a normal American woman,' and I laughed so much that the one who thinks Doris Day is normal had to go and get me water. While he was away, his colleague told me that they would not be recommending me for American citizenship, and if I left the country, I might not get back in."

A year before, Thomas might have been careful not to feed her rage, but for the first time in his life he had nothing to lose. He was old and had no one to impress and no one to compete with. When he wrote a letter to a friend who had returned to live in Germany, he stated that he had no desire to rest his bones in this soulless soil of America to which he owed nothing and which knew nothing of him, and he did not mind when this letter was shown to a German newspaper. It was the truth. He smiled at the idea that it had taken him seven and a half decades on earth before he could freely speak the truth.

But the truth now was that he was no longer welcome in America and there was no cause that America espoused that he supported. Speaking out against America's paranoid way of turning inwards could, he thought, make him feel morally worthy, but it was a pose as much as any of the others he had taken on in his life. He wondered if speaking out had ever made Klaus or Heinrich wake in the night feeling like a fraud, someone who would soon be found out, as he did?

He had managed to explore this idea of the duplicitous most fruitfully, he felt, in a story called "Felix Krull," written forty years earlier. As he sought a theme now, his mind went back to the figure of Krull from his story, who was a crook, a confidence man, someone with an extravagant, licentious disposition.

If he were to be offered a chance to say a final word about the human spirit, he would like to do so comically, he thought; he would dramatize the idea that humans could not ever be trusted, that they could reverse their own story as the wind changed, that their lives were a continuous, enervating and amusing effort to appear plausible. And in that lay, he felt, the pure genius of humanity, and all the pathos.

It was decided that he and Katia and Erika would leave America and settle once more in Switzerland.

There was a time, he was aware, when this decision would have been front-page news in America, with reporters flocking to the house so that he could pontificate about his reasons. There might even have been appeals for him to stay, or articles outlining his contribution to the war effort. Once, he realized, he had possessed gravity. His prominence lasted a decade and then it wore off.

The candelabra that had come from Lübeck to Munich to Switzerland to Princeton to California would now be put into a crate once more and shipped back to Switzerland, Katia having written to Georges Motschan to let him know that they were in search of a house near Zürich, preferably with a view of a lake.

Erika was relieved at the news of their determination to leave, and did not even respond when Katia suggested that her failure to satisfy the FBI might be responsible for this latest upheaval.

"We are doing this for you," Katia said. "But I don't see any gratitude."

"Oh, stay here, then," Erika replied, "but the FBI will come for you next. Asking you questions about your marriage, like they asked me."

"I did not marry Auden," Katia said.

Katia looked at Thomas, unafraid, it seemed, at where this conversation might lead.

"It will be marvelous to have you with us in Switzerland," he said to Erika.

Since Golo decided that he wanted to leave America too, only Elisabeth and Michael would be left in that country. When Katia wrote to Elisabeth to let her know of their plans, Elisabeth replied saying that she would make one last visit with her daughters to Pacific Palisades.

At the end of dinner on her first evening, Elisabeth told them that Borgese was in Italy because he was dying. Soon they would travel to be with him. He did not want to die in America.

"And what will you do?" Katia asked her when the girls had gone to bed.

"I will start my life," she said. "That is what Borgese says. But I don't know how I will live."

"Will you stay in Chicago?" Thomas asked.

"I might stay in Italy. The girls are Americans, but they are Italians too."

"And what will you do there?" Katia asked again.

"I really can't imagine life without Borgese. I am in shock. We all are. The diagnosis is very clear. He has been brave. I am not sure that I will be brave when I have to raise the girls without him."

Katia moved to embrace her. Even Erika had tears in her eyes.

"What about our phone calls?" Thomas asked.

"I could never get through the week without them," she replied, smiling. "They will have to continue. Who else will tell you about my sister Erika and her doings?"

She looked at Erika, daring her to comment.

The house and the garden seemed more beautiful once he knew he would lose them. When he and Katia saw Elisabeth and her daughters off at Union Station, it struck him that every detail in the station, from the signage, to the goods on display in the shops, to the open, relaxed manners of the staff, to the waves of heat that hit them when they went back towards the car, was going to become a past that could not be retrieved.

A few times, he was inclined to suggest to Erika and Golo that they should go back to Europe alone and have their lives, that he and Katia would remain here to the end under a blue sky, as their pomegranate tree came into bloom and then bore fruit.

He moved from room to room until his own private staircase was a ghost stair and his own study the room where a ghost had worked. And *Doctor Faustus* became a text that would forever haunt this house, no matter who lived here. And the aftersound of the music played in the light-filled drawing room would grow closer to pure silence each year, until time ended.

It did not matter that he would remember these rooms, the lawn, the single high palm tree at the back of the house, the American hydrangea at the driveway entrance. He would not witness them again. The high heat of summer or the dramatic sunsets or

the luminous mornings would be seen in the future by others, but
not by him. He had lost Lübeck and Munich. And now he would
lose this, Pacific Palisades. He had come here only because the
Nazis drove him out of Germany, but the atmosphere was not
tainted by that, as it was not tainted by the lapse in American hospitality that now caused him to depart.

Switzerland, to Thomas, survived on a myth of high Protestant
morality even though it kept money safe for scoundrels. Just as its
banks were open to the opulent, its borders were usually closed
to those in need. The country had mountains and lakes, some cities and a large number of storybook villages, but that was hardly
enough for seriousness. Its citizens, Thomas believed, spent most
of their time keeping themselves clean. They did this with such
zeal that their rage for hygiene spread to their lakes and mountains, their railway carriages and hotel rooms, their chocolate and
their cheese, and indeed their banknotes.

He admitted to Katia that he got nothing but pleasure contemplating Switzerland. This new country of their exile would,
he insisted, become a perfect place to write a novel about a man
who could not be trusted and who, after each escapade, lived to
see another day, like Switzerland itself. Just as he could only have
written *Doctor Faustus* in America, a country that did not have
the Faustian bargain as one of its myths of foundation, now he
would create Felix Krull in Switzerland, a country that preached
sermons, with many references to Calvin and Zwingli, precisely
against swindlers and con men like Krull.

When they arrived in the lobby of the Dolder Grand Hotel
outside Zürich, having left Golo to travel to Munich, Georges
Motschan was waiting for them once more. He had the staff
assembled, with the manager stepping forward to greet Thomas,
Katia and Erika.

As they were being served tea in the English manner, Thomas saw his wife and daughter whispering with Motschan until Erika began to giggle.

"So he has left? He isn't here?"

"I have asked," Motschan said. "I called a week ago and I inquired again today."

"He has fled," Katia said.

"What are you talking about?" Thomas asked.

"Franzl Westermeier," Erika said. She had become serious.

"He isn't here anymore," Motschan said.

Thomas wished all three would stop observing him. He did not know what to say. He could hardly tell them that he had been thinking about Franzl for the past two years and had managed to intercept the irregular letters that came from him. He knew that Franzl was in Geneva. He had written to him to say that, since he was returning to the hotel where they had met, he was thinking of Franzl even more than usual.

"He was very kind," Thomas said. "We will miss him on this trip."

He tried then to change the subject. But in the days that followed, the image of Franzl stayed in his mind.

He had caught sight of Franzl first when the waiter was crossing the lobby with a tray. As he passed him, he acknowledged Thomas with easy charm. Later, he asked for his autograph when Thomas was having tea in the afternoon. He was well-built with brown, wavy hair, soft, blue eyes and impeccably white teeth. When he had signed his name, Thomas let his hand linger for a few seconds on the hand of the waiter, who seemed pleased by this.

The next day when Thomas encountered the waiter in the lobby, he stopped him and asked his name. He introduced himself as Franzl Westermeier and said that he was from Tegernsee, near Munich.

"I knew you were Bavarian," Thomas said and asked him if he intended to stay in Switzerland. The waiter had a sweetness in his smile combined with a directness in his gaze. He became serious as he told Thomas that he would like to move to South America, but before that he planned to get a job in Geneva. When Erika appeared and pulled at his sleeve, Thomas bowed to the waiter, who continued on his way.

"You cannot flirt with a waiter in the lobby of a hotel with the whole world watching," she said.

"I barely spoke to him," he replied.

"I am sure I am not alone in thinking otherwise."

Later, when Katia came to his room, she asked him if something had happened.

He told her that it was nothing really, just that he had noticed a waiter who reminded him of old Bavaria.

"Yes, I saw him too. Georges remarked that you did not look well when we arrived. But now you look much better."

That evening, as they had dinner with Motschan, there was no sign of Franzl. He tried to imagine what the waiter might do on his evening off, what clothes he would wear, what company he would keep.

On their next encounter, he knew that he detained the waiter for too long, having quickly waylaid him as he was crossing the lobby. Erika was not there to see, nor Katia either, but some other members of the staff, who had been told by Motschan to look after the famous writer, were bound to have observed it. That same afternoon, he was hurt, on entering the lift and finding Franzl there, that Franzl nodded brusquely and then ignored him.

He wondered if it would make sense to call room service in the hope that Franzl would be the one to attend on him. When he rang for tea, however, another waiter appeared. He tried to be polite to him, but it was hard not to feel unlucky that it had not been Franzl.

Each morning, he woke with an erection.

There was a shaded place at the very end of the hotel garden with a single table and a few chairs. Katia and he had often had their lunch served there. The day before their departure, she suggested that he eat there alone, insisting that she had an appointment with a dressmaker, and Erika one with a dentist.

As he sat at the table, the silence was interrupted only by the sharp chirping of birds. It occurred to Thomas that this would be a good moment to be found slumped over. He smiled when it struck him that, in his best suit and tie and his newest shoes, he was perfectly dressed for this, and would look distinguished if he had to be taken away by stretcher.

He closed his eyes for a moment, but opened them when he heard someone approaching. When he saw that it was Franzl, who wore his most beaming smile and carried a menu, he realized what Katia and Erika had done. Motschan must have intervened. He wondered who he had paid and hoped that the waiter who stood in front of him had benefited from Motschan's munificence.

"I have missed you," he said.

He kept his voice quiet, and hoped that the tenderness was apparent.

"I would like to keep in touch with you," he added.

"That would make me happy," the waiter said. "I hope it would not be an imposition."

"Meeting you has been the best part of my stay here."

"You have been a most welcome guest."

For a moment, they locked eyes tenderly.

"I am sure you are hungry," Franzl said, blushing. "We have excellent pasta today. It is made here in the hotel by an Italian chef. And there is a white wine, a special Riesling from the Domaine Weinbach. Your wife told me you like it. And perhaps some cold soup to start?"

"I will have whatever you recommend," Thomas said.

For the next two hours, the waiter came and went, staying for a while each time, talking about his parents and shivering at the mention of the winter in the Bavarian Alps.

"I miss the skiing," he said. "But I don't miss the cold. It can be cold here, but not like home."

Thomas told him about California.

"I would love to see the sea," Franzl said. "And walk on a beach. Maybe someday I will see California."

Thomas, in that moment, felt a sudden dart of sadness that he was soon to leave the hotel.

"Is there anything more you want, sir?"

Thomas glanced up at him. While the question sounded as if it had been asked in all innocence, Franzl surely must have some inkling of what he was feeling. He hesitated, not because he thought for a moment that they could repair to his room together, but because he knew that this would be all he would get, this short, fabricated intimacy.

He was an old man being served. For days, he would go over what Franzl's body had looked like when he turned, imagining the sleek, white skin of the muscled back, the fleshy buttocks, the strong, smooth legs.

"No, I do not need anything more, but I am grateful to you for all your attention," he said, making his tone elaborately formal.

"You must remember that I am at your service," Franzl said, echoing Thomas's tone.

He bowed and walked out of their secluded place as Thomas watched him in the dappled afternoon light. He would wait here for a while, he thought, knowing that the scene in which he had just taken part was something that might not, in his lifetime, come again.

Now, two years later, he spent more energy going over that encounter than working on his novel about the trickster Felix

Krull. He still savored every moment of it, thinking back over each
thing that had been said, trying to reconstruct the connection that
arose between them for that short time. It was almost magical,
he thought, that a man of his age could have longings that were
so intense. He flicked through the pages of his diary again and
read an entry from that previous visit. "At lunch the enchanter was
nearby at times. Gave him 5 francs because yesterday he served
so nicely. Indescribable the charm of the smile in his eyes when
saying thank you. Too heavy neck. K.'s friendliness to him for my
sake."

   He would have little cause in the future, he believed, for such
diary entries. His mornings would be spent, as they had been for
more than half a century, working on his novel, with Franzl many
miles away, the memory of him already starting to crumble, even
if the act of conjuring up his way of walking across the lobby of
the hotel, his grace, his smile, still gave Thomas pleasure.

As soon as he saw the house that Motschan had found for them at
Kilchberg, south of Zürich, he knew that it would be his last one.
If they secured it, his wanderings would come to an end. He had
been worried for some time about where Katia might live after
his death. Now the problem was solved. The house was above the
road, with views over a lake to the mountains.

   In the new house, the routine was as always. He regretted the
unpleasant thoughts he had harbored about Switzerland because
he took pleasure in the sense of order and civility in the village,
and in the way the light changed on the lake and how the gathering twilight seemed to swim gently towards them from the mountains.

   He had grown to love his protagonist Felix Krull, in the same
way as he had once loved Adrian Leverkühn, as he also had loved
Tony Buddenbrook and young Hanno. While readers might guess

that Hanno was a self-portrait and see the elements in common between the author and the composer in *Doctor Faustus*, no one would guess how close he felt to Felix Krull. The elaborate tricks Krull played on the world were not just taken from novels about tricksters but were ways for Thomas to harness his own experiences and self-inventions, turn them into a joke. Krull was the dodger, the one who got away with things, the one at the edge of the action picking the pockets of those who were inattentive.

When he was buying the house in Kilchberg, as he and Katia walked from the car to the office of the lawyer in Zürich, he had been aware of his own status. Anyone who noticed him would have seen a man in his seventies, impeccably dressed, moving in a way that was purposeful and dignified. He had with him a money order that equaled the price of the house. He was the father of six children, married to a woman who had proved herself formidable in the detailed negotiations with the owners over fixtures that were being left and the garage arrangements; he was the author of many books written in an elaborate style, unafraid of long sentences and many asides, at ease in evoking the famous names in the German pantheon. By any standards, he was a great man. His own father would even have been intimidated by him.

No one, however, would have been intimidated by the sight of him as he was confronted with his own aging face alone in the lavatory at the lawyer's office. They would have been puzzled by the semi-mocking glances he gave himself in the mirror, the brief, sly, knowing smirk that came on his face as if he were happy that, once more, like his own Felix Krull, he had not been found out.

As he went through his days in the melancholy knowledge that living in a house involved a much-reduced chance of casual meetings with handsome waiters, he brought his experiences back to life by making Felix Krull, in one of the many episodes of his picaresque career, a waiter in a grand hotel, proud of his appearance and his uniform, a young man who missed no opportunity to greet the entering guests with every sign of delight, pushing in the ladies' chairs, handing them menus and filling their glasses. He could even allow his handsome hero to have a tryst with a visiting Scottish lord who was subject to his allure much as Thomas had been to Franzl's.

Just as Arnold Schoenberg believed he would die on the thirteenth day of the month, which he did, Thomas believed that he would die at the age of seventy-five. When he did not, he saw what came after as a sort of gift, like being offered the chance to live halfway outside time. In his study, when he turned to look for a book, he could easily be in Poschingerstrasse or in Princeton or in Pacific Palisades.

On afternoons when a lull in the wind darkened the lake water and freshened the blue-gray light on the mountains, he wondered if he might have really died in California and if this was not just an interlude after death when he would, as part of a bargain, see Europe one more time, and have one more house, before he faded and had no more dreams.

He never thought that he would live to be eighty. Heinrich had died shortly before his seventy-ninth birthday; Viktor was fifty-nine when he died, his father fifty-one, his mother seventy-one. But the years slipped by. Erika, for the twelve months before his eightieth birthday, was in a state of excitement over how the celebrations would be conducted.

There were other writers, he knew, who would disdain public celebrations of a birthday, leaving such things to movie stars, but since he had been brutally hounded out of Germany and politely ushered out of America, he welcomed the prospect of being publicly honored in his last place of exile.

On the day, he enjoyed receiving messages of congratulations, including one from the Kilchberg Post Office, which had to handle the mountains of post. If his American publisher Alfred Knopf wanted to fly across the Atlantic for the birthday, that seemed reasonable to him. He was happy too that Bruno Walter, just a year younger than he was, wished to conduct *Eine Kleine Nachtmusik* at the Schauspielhaus in Zürich in his honor. When he read an encomium from François Mauriac that said: "His life illustrated his work," he thought of Felix Krull and smiled at how little Mauriac knew.

Since he received greetings from the president of France and the president of the Swiss Confederation, he expected the same from the government of West Germany, but Adenauer left it to a junior minister.

He was on display, he thought, as he had been for much of his life, more as an ambassador for himself than as a person.

In the days after the celebrations, however, when his surviving children were staying at Kilchberg, including Monika, whose skin had become nut-brown in Capri, they were so busy being themselves that they sometimes failed to notice him. One night, it was only when he announced that he had to go to bed early that they paid attention and demanded that he stay with them for longer.

Although Erika had been warned by her mother not to insult her two younger sisters and to let them finish if they began speaking, she could not stop herself telling Monika that incessant swimming and sunbathing could only lead to further foolishness and insisting to Elisabeth that keeping her American-born daughters in Fiesole, as she had done since Borgese's death, would make them natives of nowhere. She should take them back to America.

"They have to be from somewhere," she said.

"Unlike us?" Elisabeth asked.

"At least we know we are Germans," she said, "although it does us no good."

Golo and Michael spoke quietly to each other about books and music, as they had always done. When Thomas joined them, he observed that no matter what he said, both of his sons were only too eager to contradict him.

His four grandchildren found common ground. He loved how they spoke English to one another in brave American accents and then moved instantly into German as soon as one of the adults asked them something. Frido, now in his teens, was as charming and beguiling as he had been as a baby.

On some of those evenings, all they needed, Thomas thought, was Klaus to arrive, Klaus disheveled, drained from some round of literary parties, needing sleep and then feeling an urge to start an argument about what was happening in Europe, the Iron Curtain and the Cold War replacing fascism to keep him fired up.

Thomas knew he was dying. When the pains in his legs developed, he went first to the village doctor so that he could be prescribed painkillers. As the doctor was writing the prescription, Thomas asked him if it could be anything more serious than an arthritis that came with old age. He saw the doctor glance up at him and hesitate. The look was dark and ominous and it stayed with him.

Since the pains persisted, Motschan arranged for Thomas to see better-known doctors. While no one told him that his complaint was life-threatening, their reassuring manner did not convince him. Once Katia and Erika joined forces in trying to get him to refuse any further invitations that involved travel, Thomas knew that something had to be wrong.

The birthday celebrations and the time afterwards with the family were overshadowed by an event that had taken place in Lübeck a month earlier. This had affected him in ways that, even as the birthday gatherings went on, he could not fully understand. He felt shaken by it, his journey to Lübeck to receive the Freedom of the City.

When he received the invitation, he had imagined that accepting might be a private reckoning with the city and with his father's legacy. Even now, after all the years, he still let his mind linger over his father's last will and testament and the implication that Heinrich and Thomas had disappointed the senator and would proceed, in the future, to disappoint their mother. Two world wars had been waged since the will had been made, but the injustice still bothered him. He looked at the shelves where he kept the books he had published, in the original German and in translation, and he wondered how much of the effort put into them came from an impulse to impress his father.

He wanted to see the city, although it had been disfigured by the bombing. And he had intimated to Katia that he would prefer it if Erika did not accompany them, that perhaps his daughter could do battles on his behalf from home with more effect.

Erika let him know that the mayor of Lübeck had suggested that he and Katia stay first at the Kurhof in Travemünde, with a car at their disposal. Thomas smiled at the mention of Travemünde. It would be May, before the season started. But the weather would be warm enough to walk on the beach.

He could not remember the name of the woman who was his mother's companion all those years ago, but he recalled the badly tuned piano in the hotel and the orchestra that played in the evening. What came to him then, as he conjured up these things, was a change in the air, as though he were waking on one of those very mornings, the days ahead appearing infinitely long, each moment to be relished and lived in without any worry or hesitation, a dampness in the room and even a coldness in the early morning sunlight, and the sea breathing in and out just a short walk away.

"The Magician has fallen asleep," Erika said.

"Tell them I want to go to Travemünde," he said.

On the journey between Zürich and Lübeck they made stops so that he could exercise, but the getting on and off the trains and into cars and then into hotel rooms had exhausted him more than he wanted Katia to know.

The mayor was almost embarrassed that more had not been done to restore the churches and civic buildings that had been bombed. As Thomas and Katia walked towards Mengstrasse, he saw that weeds were growing over wasteland where there had been houses. In that moment, he had a sudden sense of what the bombing must have been like, the terror in this place. And then, with total clarity, he remembered an argument with Klaus about the bombing of Lübeck. If Klaus were alive, he might have come with them and witnessed the center of the city still in ruins.

At the ceremony he looked into the crowd as though figures from the past all had come to be here with him—his father, his grandmother, his aunt, his mother, Heinrich, his sisters, Viktor, Willri Timpe and Armin Martens, the mathematics teacher Herr Immerthal.

In his speech, he spoke about coming full circle, mentioning the city's disapproval of his first novel, asking how his teachers at the Katharineum might feel if they saw him now. They would have wondered how the dim-witted boy could have learned so much. As he spoke, the audience seemed remote from him, as he must seem from them. He was in pain but he did everything he could not to show it. When the sustained applause came, he was finding it hard to stay on his feet.

Later, back in the hotel in Travemünde, he was almost disappointed, depressed. He had wanted to feel more than he felt. He had not come full circle at all, he saw, but had merely stumbled along. He was the piece of crooked timber they had been told about in school. What a fool he had been to think that this offer of the Freedom of the City would give him anything more than a reason to regret not having stayed at home, not having been content to imagine Lübeck from the comfort of Kilchberg!

His father was dead. There was no purpose now in trying to find him to tell him that one more honor had come his son's way. No one had asked him if he wanted to visit the family graves and he was relieved about that. But someone had told him that the bombs had gone deep into the bowels of Lübeck, deep enough to smash open the grave of the composer Buxtehude, who had been organist at the Marienkirche for forty years.

Afterwards, as they calculated the damage, Thomas was told, nothing of the composer's grave remained. He had asked several times if this had happened to many graves in the old city to be informed of course, yes, parts of the city had been incinerated.

The day after the ceremony was Sunday. He woke early and, on finding that the car and driver were waiting outside, left a note for Katia to say that he had gone into Lübeck for a stroll. The morning was warm, but he was glad he was wearing his heavier suit since he thought he might go to the first service at the Dom in Lübeck and it would not do to be casually dressed.

When he arrived, the organ had just begun. The church had been restored, he saw, or perhaps had not suffered as badly as the Marienkirche in the bombing. As he stood at the edge of a pew, an elderly woman made space for him, smiling at him solemnly and graciously in a way that women from Lübeck did from as long back as he could remember. This was the smile, he thought, that his mother could never fully learn. She smiled too broadly, and women in Lübeck noticed and disapproved.

From the sheet provided, he saw that all the music was by Buxtehude, both the organ music and the choral music. For a second, he remembered that shop in New York where he bought records, lamenting that only Buxtehude's organ music was available and none of the music for voices.

The pastor, a young bald man wearing a ruff, stood on a high podium during a break in the service. In his sermon, to the apparent satisfaction of all, he reminded them that they would soon be dust. Thomas wished Katia were with him so they could talk later about the sort of Sunday lunch the congregation could look forward to, closer to their hearts, perhaps, than the prospect of becoming dust. When the pastor had finished, a young woman, accompanied by a small string ensemble, sang an aria from a Buxtehude cantata. Her voice was thin and she seemed nervous at the beginning, but as the melody itself grew stronger so did her singing until the notes seemed to linger and echo in the higher reaches of the old vaulted building.

He asked the driver to wait for him while he had hot chocolate and a marzipan tart in one of the nearby cafés.

It was strange, he thought, what he remembered. Willri Timpe. Herr Immerthal. And then how many other names escaped him, no matter what he did. He knew that he had not played any record by Buxtehude since Princeton, nor heard anyone mention his name.

He was pleased he had taken a corner table since the café was filling up, and he was happy too that no one among the Sunday morning crowd recognized him. A story came to him, it must have been told by his mother often when they were children. It was never referred to again, certainly not in Munich. It was a story about Buxtehude's daughter. Each year, the story went, when young organists came, including Handel himself, to learn the secrets of his trade from Buxtehude, Buxtehude promised each one that he would tell him enough to make him the greatest composer in the world, if he agreed to marry his youngest daughter Anna Margareta.

But even though his daughter was beautiful and accomplished, all the visitors refused, since all of them had romantic commitments at home, and therefore they left without learning the secret.

And then, as a suitor was finally found for his daughter, a suitor who had no interest in music, Buxtehude was afraid that he would die and the secret would be lost to the world. Little did he know that a very young composer in Arnstadt had heard about him and had decided to walk all the way to Lübeck to see if he could discover the secret.

Thomas paid his bill and walked towards his grandmother's house. He could see his two sisters now, waiting for the rest of the story, both of them in their night attire, and he could see Heinrich sitting apart from them. And always in a story their mother would sigh and say that she had work to do and would continue the story tomorrow. And they would appeal to her, beg her to finish the story. And she always would.

The young composer's name was Johann Sebastian Bach, she said, and he walked to Lübeck through wind and rain. Often, he could find no boardinghouse and had to sleep in haystacks or in fields. Often, he was hungry. Very often, he was cold. But he was always sure of his purpose. If he could get to Lübeck, he would meet a man who would help him to become a great composer.

Buxtehude was almost in despair. Some days he really believed that his sacred knowledge would be buried with him. On other days, in his heart, he knew that someone would come and he dreamed that he would recognize the man immediately and he would take him to the church and he would share his secrets with him.

"How would he recognize the man?" Carla asked.

"The man would have a light in his eyes, or something special in his voice," her mother said.

"How could he be sure?" Heinrich asked.

"Wait! He is still on his journey and worried," she went on.

"Every day, the walk seems longer. He has told the man he works for that he will be away only a short time. He does not realize how far Lübeck is. But he does not turn back. He walks on and on, asking all the time how far Lübeck is. But it is so far that some people he meets have never even heard of Lübeck and they advise him to turn back. But he is determined not to, and eventually when he reaches Lüneberg, he is told that he is not far from Lübeck. And the fame of Buxtehude has spread to there. But, because of all his time on the road, poor Bach, normally so handsome, looks like a tramp. He knows that Buxtehude will never receive a man as badly dressed as he is. But he is lucky. A woman in Lüneberg, when she learns of Bach's plight, offers to lend him the clothes. She has seen the light in him.

"And so Bach arrives in Lübeck. And when he asks for Buxtehude, he is told that he will be in the Marienkirche practicing the organ. And as soon as Bach steps into the church, Buxtehude senses that he is no longer alone. He stops playing and looks down from the gallery and sees Bach and behind him he sees the light, the light Bach has carried with him all the way, something glowing in his spirit. And he knows that this is the man to whom he can tell the secret."

"But what is the secret?" Thomas asked.

"If I tell you, will you promise to go to bed?"

"Yes."

"It is called Beauty," his mother said. "The secret is called Beauty. He told him not to be afraid to put Beauty into his music. And then for weeks and weeks and weeks, Buxtehude showed him how to do that."

"Did Bach ever give the woman back the clothes?" Thomas asked.

"Yes, he did. On his way home. And on her piano, he played music for her that she thought came from heaven."

Some windows, Thomas saw, in the old family house, the house of *Buddenbrooks*, were boarded up. The mayor had promised that the whole building would soon be restored. Lübeck, it appeared, was proud of it now, the house that had given life to a book. Thomas, as he stood in front of it, wished he could ask one of the others—Heinrich, Lula, Carla, Viktor—if they too remembered that story about Buxtehude and Bach. It had not come into his mind for years.

Maybe there were other stories that he would remember, long-forgotten ones that he had heard in the company of the others who had also lived in this house, and who now had moved out of time towards a realm whose boundaries were still unclear to him.

He glanced at the house again and walked through the city towards the car that would take him back to Travemünde, where Katia would be waiting for him.

Acknowledgments

This novel has been inspired by the writing of Thomas Mann and his family. A number of other books have also been helpful. They include: *Thomas Mann: Eros and Literature*, Anthony Heilbut; *Thomas Mann: A Biography*, Ronald Hayman; *Thomas Mann: Life as a Work of Art*, Hermann Kurzke; *Thomas Mann: A Life*, Donald Prater; *Thomas Mann: The Making of an Artist, 1875–1911*, Richard Winston; *The Brothers Mann*, Nigel Hamilton; *Thomas Mann and His Family*, Marcel Reich-Ranicki; *In the Shadow of the Magic Mountain: The Erika and Klaus Mann Story*, Andrea Weiss; *Cursed Legacy: The Tragic Life of Klaus Mann*, Frederic Spotts; *House of Exile: The Lives and Times of Heinrich Mann and Nelly Kroeger-Mann*, Evelyn Juers; *Thomas Mann's War: Literature, Politics, and the World Republic of Letters*, Tobias Boes; *Arnold Schoenberg: The Composer as Jew*, Alexander L. Ringer; *The Doctor Faustus Dossier: Arnold Schoenberg, Thomas Mann, and Their Contemporaries, 1930–1951*, ed. E. Randol Schoenberg; *Hitler's Exiles: Personal Stories of the Flight from Nazi Germany to America*, ed. Mark M. Anderson; *Franklin D. Roosevelt: A Political Life*, Robert Dallek; *Malevolent Muse: The Life of Alma Mahler*, Oliver Hilmes; *Alma Mahler: Muse to Genius*, Karen Monson; *Passionate Spirit: The Life of Alma Mahler*, Cate Haste; *Dreamers: When the Writers Took Power, Germany 1918*, Volker Weidermann; *Munich 1919: Diary of a Revolution*, Victor Klemperer; *Exiled in Paradise*, Anthony Heilbut; *The Second Generation*, Esther McCoy; *Bluebeard's Chamber: Guilt and Confession in Thomas Mann*, Michael Maar; *Bruno Walter: A World Elsewhere*, Erik Ryding and

Rebecca Pechefsky; *The Bitter Taste of Victory: Life, Love, and Art in the Ruins of the Reich*, Lara Feigel; *The Sun and Her Stars: Salka Viertel and Hitler's Exiles in the Golden Age of Hollywood*, Donna Rifkind; *Seven Palms: The Thomas Mann House in Pacific Palisades*, Francis Nenik; *Down a Path of Wonder: Memoirs of Stravinsky, Schoenberg and Other Cultural Figures*, Robert Craft; *Adorno in America*, David Jenemann; *Dieterich Buxtehude: Organist in Lübeck*, Kerala J. Snyder; *German Autumn*, Stig Dagerman. *Thomas Mann's Doctor Faustus: The Sources and Structure of the Novel*, Gunilla Bergsten; *Weimar in Exile: The Antifascist Emigration in Europe and America*, Jean-Michel Palmier; *A Hero of Our Time: The Story of Varian Fry*, Sheila Isenberg.

I am grateful to Mary Mount at Penguin UK, Nan Graham at Scribner in New York, and my agent Peter Straus, for their scrupulous attention to my book, and to Holger Pils for the generous sharing of his deep knowledge of Thomas Mann's life and work. And also, as usual, to Angela Rohan, as well as to Catriona Crowe, Hedi El Kholti and Ed Mulhall, and Piero Salabè from Hanser Verlag in Germany.

About the Author

Colm Tóibín's novel *The Master*, about the American expatriate writer Henry James, was named one of the ten best books of the year by the *New York Times Book Review*, the *Washington Post*, the *Boston Globe*, the *San Francisco Chronicle*, *Entertainment Weekly* and many other periodicals. It won the Los Angeles Times Book Prize and was shortlisted for the Booker Prize. Tóibín is the author of ten novels, including the bestselling *Brooklyn*, winner of the Costa Book Award, two collections of short stories and many works of criticism. Tóibín is the Irene and Sidney B. Silverman Professor of the Humanities at Columbia University.